COMPELLING DANGER—
AND ALLURING PASSION . . .

It was him!

The gunfighter.

Mr. Smith, he called himself. At least, that was the name he had signed in the register at Dashers Hotel.

He was everything Kate had said. He was unconscionably good-looking. Merrie couldn't imagine what he would look like if he ever smiled, for his face seemed carved of rock, smooth and square, his mouth wickedly alluring, ruthless. But it was his extraordinary eyes that were compelling, lethal in a much more fundamental way. Under the shade of his black Stetson, she could not tell their color, but the jewel-like gleam and the lush sweep of his lashes were stunning.

Added to this, his very forthright inspection — the lazy browse of his eyes over every inch of her — made Merrie burn. His shaded eyes delved into her own, and she found that she ceased to breathe for one hot, pulsing minute . . .

JOVE WILDFLOWER ROMANCE

*A breathtaking line of searing romance novels . . .
where destiny meets desire in the
untamed fury of the American West.*

Don't miss these Jove Wildflower Romances — coming soon . . .

GAMBLER'S DESIRE
by Maryann O'Brien
July 1995

and

ABILENE GAMBLE
by Margaret Conlan
August 1995

Texas Kiss

Alexandra Blackstone

JOVE BOOKS, NEW YORK

If you purchased this book without a cover, you should be aware that this book is stolen property. It was reported as "unsold and destroyed" to the publisher, and neither the author nor the publisher has received any payment for this "stripped book."

TEXAS KISS

A Jove Book / published by arrangement with
the author

PRINTING HISTORY
Jove edition / June 1995

All rights reserved.
Copyright © 1995 by Adrienne Schwartz.
This book may not be reproduced in whole
or in part, by mimeograph or any other means,
without permission. For information address:
The Berkley Publishing Group, 200 Madison Avenue,
New York, NY 10016.

ISBN: 0-515-11638-6

A JOVE BOOK®
Jove Books are published by The Berkley Publishing Group,
200 Madison Avenue, New York, NY 10016.
JOVE and the "J" design are trademarks
belonging to Jove Publications, Inc.

PRINTED IN THE UNITED STATES OF AMERICA

10 9 8 7 6 5 4 3 2 1

Farraway and Hargraves
Attorneys at Law
16 Front Street
Dodge City
Kansas

Silver Spur Ranch
Hollow Creek Canyon, Texas

Dear Mr. Sinclair,

In lieu of your recent illness, Mr. Hargraves and I concur with your decision to appoint your heir, Miss Meredith Amber Sinclair, as custodian to the Corona Vault and its contents. According to your stipulations [I refer to Legal Document 412, dated February 13, 1853, paragraph (c) IV: (amended May 11, 1878)] matching keys to the vault shall be retrieved only in person by you or your appointed heir.

As that heir, the aforementioned Meredith Amber Sinclair, must be presented by you to Mr. Hargraves and/or myself before witnesses, we suggest a meeting at your earliest convenience to that end. I would require several weeks notice of your impending arrival in Dodge City so that the relevant documents can be duly amended and suitable witnesses sworn for the purpose.

We trust that your remarkable recovery continues and assure you of our continued devotion to your very best interests.

Your humble servant,
Jessop Humbert Farraway,
Attorney at Law

ONE

"IMPOSSIBLE," MERRIE SAID out loud, "it can't be."

She quickly glanced about, as if the dusty, false-fronted buildings could corroborate what she had just seen. But the main street stood mute and empty. There was no one around except for herself and the vanishing figure of a woman down at the tail end of town. Merrie blinked. The glare was blinding.

Surely that was Liza scurrying along the planked sidewalk, keeping to the squat noonday shadows like a prowling thief?

For a moment, she hesitated, then she followed the woman down a narrow side street off the main road.

A cloud of dust whirled up. Merrie rubbed her eyes and tilted her Stetson back on her head. When she looked again, the woman was disappearing behind the bright canary-yellow door of the most notorious house in Hollow Creek.

Merrie gasped!

Number 1A, End Lane, was well known to everyone past the age of milk teeth, although strictly speaking, young ladies like Meredith Amber Sinclair were supposed to *pretend* that they didn't know anything about number 1A, or what went on there. It was simply an annex of the flashy whorehouse next door; an exclusive hideaway for those discerning gentlemen who preferred privacy to the more public rowdiness of the house, and had the money to indulge themselves.

But Liza at number 1A? "Impossible!" said Merrie again. Her snobbish, high-strung stepmother would never stoop to such a risky venture. For another second, she stood there in the middle of the road, hovering between indecision and intrigue.

What if . . . , Merrie wondered, what if I crept up to those open windows down there on the ground floor? Would I be able to see anything?

No, I mustn't, she admonished herself, quite disgusted that she had, even for a moment, contemplated spying on her stepmother. Because she disliked Liza so intensely, it was all too easy to think uncharitable thoughts about her. "I can't," she repeated, this time aloud to emphasize her decision. "I just can't."

"Why not?" a voice asked. A deep, masculine voice, whose dark cadence seemed, for an instant, to vibrate somewhere deep inside her, in a place that had nothing to do with sound.

She spun about, red to the ears with mortification at being caught talking out loud to herself. She stopped dead in her tracks.

It was him!

The gunfighter.

He sat on a horse, as dark and dangerous-looking as himself.

She knew him instantly, even though she had never set eyes on him before. The gunfighter.

Mr. Smith, he called himself. At least that was the name he had signed in the register at Dashers Hotel.

The whole town had been abuzz with the news of his arrival a few days before. Merrie's friend Kate had ridden out to the Silver Spur Ranch to tell her all about him. No one knew why he had ridden into town. No one was stupid enough to ask him.

He was everything Kate had said. He was unconscionably good-looking. Merrie couldn't imagine what he would look like if he ever smiled, for his face seemed carved of rock, smooth and square, his mouth wickedly alluring, ruthless. But it was his extraordinary eyes that were compelling, lethal in a much more fundamental way. Under the shade of his black Stetson, she could not tell their color, but the jewel-like gleam and the lush sweep of his lashes were stunning.

Added to this, his very forthright inspection—the lazy browse of his eyes over every inch of her—made Merrie burn.

It was more than strange, but she found her mouth tingling as she watched him examining her. Alarmingly, she felt the peculiar sensation drift down her body in the wake of his

TEXAS KISS

perusal. His shaded eyes delved into her own, and she found that she ceased to breathe for one hot, pulsing minute.

She was suddenly self-conscious, hardly a sentiment that she was familiar with. As the daughter of a man like Ash Sinclair, Merrie had never encountered such blatant discourtesy from any of her young men friends, or yet from any acquaintances. Matt was always unfailingly polite. He would never allow his eyes to roam where they shouldn't, *and he was her fiancé*. She was suddenly irritated by the gunfighter's daring.

"What?" she heard herself say.

"What do you mean, *what?*"

"I don't follow." Merrie frowned.

He gave her a look that clearly questioned her faculties. "Lady, I'd like to know *why* you can't get out of the road," he said, each word conscientiously pronounced like a pastor's Sunday lesson.

His sarcasm unraveled what remained of her own good manners. Nothing he said made sense, anyway.

"Your *likes and dislikes* are none of my concern. Would you please let me pass," she said.

The lane was extremely narrow, and further constricted by a ditch that had opened up along the one side. One of them would have to let the other pass. They each seemed equally determined not to be the one.

The gunfighter's eyes narrowed slightly.

"There's nothing stopping you, lady. Be my guest—step right up."

"Are you going to let me pass or not?" she dared him, unwilling to be bullied. Besides, the steps leading up to the raised walkway were several yards down the road.

"Let you pass? Hell, would I be crazy enough to stop you?" The look he sent her was candidly scornful.

He nudged his horse, and with an abrupt surge, the spirited stallion gained the bleached wood walkway. It creaked ominously, but that didn't deter the gunfighter.

Merrie gasped at his flamboyance. "I don't believe it."

"Then, we're even, lady, 'cause I don't believe this whole

conversation," he said. He maneuvered his horse across the planks with reckless ability, the fringes of his fawn-colored jacket fluttering wildly in his wake.

She watched him spur the animal back down to the road farther along. Then she turned away. Just before she rounded the corner of Main Street, however, she glanced back down at number 1A, and froze.

The gunfighter was in the process of opening the canary-yellow door. Without looking back, he entered, closing the door behind himself. There was no doubt about it; his movements were just as stealthy as her stepmother's had been.

Merrie was stunned. Stunned and furious.

What was going on here? Had her stepmother planned a tryst with the handsome gunslinger?

The yellow door winked at her, taunting her with its furtive secrets.

She hated herself in that moment, almost as much as she disliked Liza, but she was damned whatever she did. If she looked, she was no better than a Peeping Tom, but if she didn't . . . how would she know if her suspicions were correct?

Her mind made up, she hurried down End Lane again, telling herself that her reasons were altruistic, but an ugly little voice told her that she was a snoop—nothing better than a snoop.

Outside the door, she hesitated, then she went around the side, to where the windows were low to the ground and open. Merrie could see the pale lemon curtains fluttering in the light breeze.

A low, throaty sound floated out through one of the windows, accompanied by a rhythmic thumping. A woman cried out softly, a strange primal sound it was, completely unnerving, for it straddled a range of emotions from pain to ecstasy and made Merrie hot and uncomfortable.

She dared a peek. She drew back, her heart thudding wildly, her throat dry, and then she dared another quick look into the room behind.

The interior was dim; the gauzy curtains teased her sight. But she was able to catch a glimpse of two naked forms writhing together upon a rumpled bed. The man was undulating between the woman's open thighs. The woman was arched against him, her head thrown back against the pillows, shuddering beneath her lover's rapid strokes.

Merrie jerked with shock.

It only took a second for her to verify that the woman was Elizabeth Sinclair, her stepmother!

It was difficult to see, for the room was full of deep shadows, by contrast to the brilliant Texas noon. And yet she was certain the man was the very same one she had been arguing with but moments before. His head was nestled on the far side of Liza, but his thick dark hair and the sinuous flexing of his muscular body was evocative of the reckless Mr. Smith as he sat atop his huge stallion.

Merrie was outraged! She felt betrayed and dirty all at once, nauseated that she had demeaned herself by spying on her stepmother. Mostly, she ached for her father.

And then Liza looked up, her gaze fixing on the window! Had she seen her, realized who it was?

Merrie stifled an anguished cry and raced away.

She ran blindly up the deserted lane and down Main Street, only stopping when the stitch in her side pulled abruptly on her senses. Very slowly she straightened up, her chest heaving from her exertion. For a long while, she simply stood there in the shadow of the buildings, vaguely aware that the drowsing town was stirring around her; siesta was over. She could hear the clink of glasses from Dashers, the faint rumble of the water under the elevated railroad bridge.

The everyday normalcy of it all was shocking. Surely the sky should have darkened.

Merrie simply couldn't believe what she had witnessed. It was incredible! Disdainful and difficult, Liza had always been, but never unfaithful, surely? And with Ash so ill . . . How could Liza do such a thing to her wonderful father? Merrie mourned.

Even more alarming was the bewildering problem of what to do about it. What a dilemma, to find herself in such a situation.

It was bad enough that her father was so terribly ill, but Merrie was constrained, not only by her natural reluctance to interfere in her father's second marriage, but by the difficult relationship between Liza and herself.

They barely tolerated each other. All of Hollow Creek knew that they disliked each other, even though they maintained a polite facade in public.

Merrie did it for Ash's sake. She adored her strong-willed father and would do nothing to hurt him. Why Liza kept up the pretense in public, Merrie didn't know.

Up until this day, she had thought it was because Liza loved Ash very much. Now she knew that wasn't so. But what she was to do about it, she didn't know.

Two

A DOOR BANGED down the street a way, jolting Merrie from her tangled thoughts and recalling her reason for coming to town. She shook herself into action and set off toward the telegraph office.

On the first Monday of each month since Ash fell ill, his doctor telegraphed an appraisal of her father's progress. Today, just as always, the telegraph from Loring Strafford's Clinic was waiting for her. This time it was wonderful news.

"He's coming home," she told the balding man behind the ticket window. Her eyes glistened.

Jem Tech, a sharp-nosed old codger and an infamous gossip, nodded sagely and promptly recited the contents of her telegraph out aloud for her. "Yesserie, coming in on the ten-forty, Tuesday next. And you an' me is the first to know," he added.

Knowing Jem's penchant for gossip, she had warned him about letting the town know her business before she did.

"Tuesday," Merrie echoed.

"Reckon that will give you time enough to hitch a wagon," Jem said.

"Just over a week," Merrie said, staring at the telegraph in her hands as if she thought the words might just disappear off the paper. She didn't feel too steady on her feet. The day had held one shock after another. But this was something of a miracle.

"Always said he'd pull through, if any a body could," said Jem. "Nothing can hinder Ash Sinclair if he has a mind to do something, not even the Grim Reaper."

The smile on Merrie's face was pure sunshine. It was true. Her father was the most stubborn man in the world, and the most enduring. He had founded the town of Hollow Creek some years before Merrie was born. It had not been easy, but he had fought for its prosperity. Perched on the lip of the Palo Duro Canyon, the town now served as local center and railhead for the surrounding ranches; it thrived.

Merrie knew that the same fighting spirit, that vital appetite for life, had enabled Ashton Sinclair to survive his near fatal illness. She knew that now, but for almost a year it had not looked as if Ash would pull through at all.

As she made her way back down Main Street, Merrie was in high spirits. Very much like her father, she thought proudly, she had endured also. When Ash had suddenly fallen ill last July, it had been the most natural thing in the world for her to step into his shoes and run the Spur Ranch with the same fire and gumption that embodied her father's personality. But it had been tough. The opposition to her, a female, taking the helm of so wealthy an enterprise had been obstructive, even petty, and very wearying.

No, it has not been easy, she thought, waving to one of the townsfolk, and I hope Ash is proud of what we've managed to do out at the Spur. I'm certain he will like the profits . . . the biggest since he began here thirty years ago, she told herself with a profound sense of accomplishment.

Hollow Creek was bustling. She was stopped frequently by folks asking after Ash. Carts rolled down the street, off-loading their wares outside Linnett's, the general store. A couple of cowboys raced by only to dismount in a great cloud of brown dust. They tied their horses to the hitching post outside The Holler, the largest saloon on Main Street. Merrie recognized one of them as belonging to the Lazy D, her fiancé's ranch. They doffed their hats to a young lady who preened prettily for them, swishing her dainty skirts and fluttering her eyelashes.

Merrie laughed. It was her friend Kate Brown.

"You're shameless," she said, catching up with Kate.

Far from being abashed, Kate jiggled her curls with saucy nonchalance. "Why, because I enjoy the attention? Unlike you, Merrie, I'm very partial to men."

"Good grief, whatever makes you think I'm not?"

"Well, just look at you," Kate said, wrinkling her nose, "and whatever did you fall into?" She scanned her friend from the top of her dust-caked blond hair down her very long legs, shamelessly displayed in men's work pants. Really, only Merrie Sinclair would get away with such unconventionality.

"Sonna needed help with the hogs," Merrie said, grinning. She swiped at the knees of her work pants, raising a cloud of dust.

"You're a mess. Just look at your lovely hair, stuck at the top of your head like a horse's tail, all dusty and sweaty."

"Thanks, I like the way you look, too," Merrie chortled.

Kate snorted and then caught sight of the telegraph in Merrie's hand. "You have news?"

"Wonderful news. Ash is coming home next week."

"Hooray! We're going to have a shindig," Kate said, whirling her skirts.

"Guess we may, at that," said Merrie, quickening her pace a little. Kate hurried to keep up, her pace far more ladylike than Merrie's no-nonsense stride.

"I don't suppose *he'd* come," Kate said dubiously.

"Who?"

Kate's eyes did a quick check about as if she expected eavesdroppers to jump right out at them. "That gunfighter I told you about, that Mr. Smith."

Merrie colored at the reminder of her morning's escapades, but Kate was oblivious to everything but her anticipation. She had wanted to meet the mysterious Mr. Smith since first setting eyes on him.

"Of course he might not be a gunslinger at all," she said enthusiastically. "That's only Jem Tech's opinion. It would be right hospitable to invite him," Kate continued, "and just you wait until you see those blue eyes of his . . . fair sizzle a girl— Oh, watch out."

Kate jumped back just as a man came barreling out of The Holler Saloon and knocked into Merrie.

Merrie stumbled, but the man clasped her and she managed to straighten up. She pushed her broad-brimmed hat off her face and frowned at him. He was one of the men from the Lazy D she had seen earlier. She thought his name might be Jacko.

"Uh . . ." the cowboy mumbled, his face as red as his bandanna.

"You all right, Merrie?" Kate asked.

Sheriff Hagan came through the swinging door just then but stopped short when he saw the girls. Very tall and thick-chested, Tom Hagan was an imposing figure of a man.

Known throughout the county as a uncompromising lawman, Sheriff Hagan kept a tight rein on things in Hollow Creek. Cowboys who tended to be rowdy at times, bragging about their exploits or simply letting go, were sure to run afoul of the sheriff and his disciplining arm.

Merrie thought he might be in the process of exercising that arm right now. She couldn't approve of the sheriff's methods, though, because Jacko looked like an innocuous enough fellow.

The sheriff touched the brim of his hat. "Mornin', ladies," he said.

His handsome face was flushed. With excitement? wondered Merrie distastefully. The man seemed to enjoy hitting the cowboy, hitting him hard enough to send him spinning through the doorway.

"Jacko, tell the ladies you're sorry, then beat it," said the sheriff.

Jacko mumbled something, picked up his hat, and scooted off back into the saloon.

"Any news about your father, Miss Sinclair?" Hagan asked.

The words were polite enough, and yet . . .

There was something behind the bitterness of his eyes, the pinprick pupils that seemed to disappear at times, that made her feel . . . well . . . unsafe.

"He's doing much better, thanks," Merrie answered and hurried on her way.

Kate blushed prettily. "She's in a rush," she said by way of apology.

"I'll say," Hagan said, tipping his hat up on his head and watching the long-legged girl cross the street. The work pants she wore did little to disguise her coltlike shape. That horse's tail under her hat bounced like the tail on a spirited filly, too.

"She has a shindig to arrange," Kate added before hurrying off after her friend.

"Does she . . . ?" said the sheriff softly, bending down. He picked up the paper Merrie had dropped. "And what is it we're celebrating?"

He read it. It was a telegram. He glanced at it and then pursed his lips thoughtfully.

THE LIVERY STABLE was dark.

Old Bob, the owner, was fast asleep. His chair, tilted back against the barn door, wobbled dangerously in time to his loud snores.

Merrie found Sonnet in his usual stall. The huge palomino whinnied softly in greeting and gobbled up the carrot Merrie treated him to. She soon had him saddled and was just leading him out of the stall when the man came into the barn.

It was difficult to make out his features, for they were shadowed by his hat. But there was nothing ambiguous about his frame; *it was the gunfighter!*

Merrie was certain it was him. His shoulders were very wide, and the cut of his fringed jacket seemed to emphasize this. His guns, Merrie noticed, were slung low on his lean hips. He was very tall, taller than she had first guessed. His gait was smooth and lanky, as if he had calculated the exact amount of movement necessary to keep him mobile and expended just that, and no more.

He nodded politely when he saw her standing there staring at him in the gloomy light, and made to pass her by. When he realized that she was still staring at him, he came to a stop. Thin sunbeams, vibrating with dust motes, played across the wedge of light between them.

Merrie gasped. That strange hot feeling swamped her again, and she immediate thought of Kate's description: *. . . just you wait until you see those blue eyes of his . . . fair sizzle a girl,* Kate had said.

For a crazy instant, she even understood why cold-mannered Liza had succumbed to temptation. This was a man who swept away reserves and took what he wanted without the flicker of an eye. The tempestuous scene she had witnessed at number 1A flashed across her mind, and she winced. With that thought came the immediate and unequivocal revulsion she felt for a man who would steal another man's wife.

"You're disgusting," she said in her iciest, most derisive voice.

The man stiffened. "Can't say I'm partial to you, either," he said. His voice was like deep, quiet water sliding through a subterranean tunnel.

It has the power to roll over me and engulf me, Merrie thought wildly. She had to get away from him.

It was all very well feeling the insult done to her father, but it was quite another to voice her sentiments out loud when she had no idea just how uncivilized the man was.

He was dangerous—a man with a gun and, most likely, a reputation as a fast draw. Certainly he didn't respect either her status as a woman or her standing in the community at large. Her encounter with him earlier that day had clearly demonstrated that. God only knew what he was capable of.

As she came alongside him, trying to pass by, his hand snaked out and grasped her wrist.

"Someone drop you on your head when you were a kid? You're the most ornery person I've ever met." They were so close, his words brushed against her face.

"We've never *met*. I would never acquaint myself with a . . . with someone like you," she said proudly.

His scorching gaze blazed furiously, and she shied back against Sonnet's reassuring flank. The horse moved skittishly, as if he, too, felt the fire of the man's anger.

"You had better explain yourself, lady, and fast," he said. "I don't take insults lightly."

"I explain myself to no one," she parried angrily and wrenched her arm free of his light hold. Taking advantage of the moment, she sprang up on Sonnet's back and kicked the horse forward. Then, with a charge of relief, she ducked low under the lintel of the barn and was on the street.

THREE

"Whiskey, mister?" the barman asked.

Kyle Delancy glanced lazily down the length of the bar and gave a small nod in the direction of the shadowy corner. The soft chink of his spurs marked his leisurely progress to his seat. A sudden silence wafted through the saloon like a plume of smoke from a gun.

Two dozen eyes watched him with unabashed interest. Strangers always provoked inquisitive speculation, but a loner with two guns slung low on his hips was fodder indeed. Not that he minded much. Kyle Delancy was used to the gawking, the inevitable challenge, the attempt to strong-arm him. He had been in scores of towns like Hollow Creek and likely would be in scores more. Trouble was his business. He was good at it; he found it, solved it, and got well paid for doing so—very well paid, because he was, quite simply, the best in the business.

"You're Smith, staying at Dashers?" the barman said, setting the whiskey shot down and pouring.

Kyle tipped the brown-gold liquid down his throat and wiped his mouth with the back of his hand. His fiery blue eyes slid over the barman without even a flicker of acknowledgment.

In the ensuing silence, the barman poured a second shot. "Not that it's much to me, but if you are, there's a telegraph arrived for you," he continued and made to move away. He was more curious about the gunslinger than sense allowed, but then Virgil Tech had as much appetite for gossip as his older brother, Jem.

Kyle slipped a few coins on the counter. "You got any of that French brandy? Don't care for this," he said, pushing the shot glass away.

Virgil Tech scooped the money into his palm and went off to get the French brandy. You couldn't tell it from his face, but Virgil was about as pleased as a possum eating persimmons. Virgil hadn't displayed an expression on his deadpan face since his twelfth birthday. It was just his way.

Kyle ran his eyes over the gawkers reflected in the mirrored wall behind the bar. They still stared at him through the smoke that blanketed the saloon, though one or two groups had gone back to their poker or their chatter. No trouble there, far as he could tell. At least not yet. It was late already. The place wasn't all that full anymore, which was just how he liked it. Nothing like a good liquoring-up to loosen tongues. Information was what Kyle Delancy was after. He would start with the barman.

The unpainted furniture and gray walls of the saloon were etched behind the languid smoke that curled and hovered about the long, narrow room. There was a piano in the corner, but it looked almost unable to stand on its legs, and no one attempted to play it. The low clink of glasses, a cough, a maudlin laugh, punctuated the hum of conversation. Now and then a cowboy scraped back his chair and headed unsteadily for the swinging doors. Virgil's wasn't The Holler. Virgil's was a more humble place, but Kyle hoped to gather as much information from Virgil as he had from the people he had met at The Holler the night before.

The barman considered his unspoken offer of a brandy with a frank look that weighed the dangers to a nicety, then decided to chance it. After all, it wasn't every day a gentleman asked for good brandy in his saloon. And his assessment of the man in front of him was exactly that.

Mr. Smith was a gentleman. Of course, that didn't preclude that he was also a gunslinger and downright deadly, but there was a refinement and lucidity about the man. It was evident in his taste, first and foremost, and in his clothes and manners as well. From his doe-soft jacket to his snug-fitted black pants, Mr. Smith's distinction was evident. Not a speck of dirt marred the polish of his Spanish leather riding boots, and the conchas that ringed his black Stetson were some of the finest hand-engraved silver discs Virgil had ever seen.

"Name's Virgil, Virgil Tech," he said. "So what you after, Mr. Smith? Or should I say who? Telegraph made no sense to me, though you don't look interested in it either."

If he thought to get a rise out of the man, he was sorely mistaken.

"Where's it from?" Kyle asked, as if there were nothing untoward in strangers reading his private correspondence.

"Dodge City. Mighty fine place, so I'm told, but I never went there myself. You from there, Mr. Smith?"

Kyle ignored the question. "What did it say?"

"Didn't make no sense," Virgil said. He looked at the ceiling, clasped his hands together as if he were reciting poetry, and said slowly, "'Ready; set; go.'" He looked at Kyle expectantly, but the stranger was not giving out information.

"Sure?" Kyle asked smoothly.

"My brother, Jem, never get's a word wrong. Been working the telegraph since it come here."

"Probably knows more than anyone else in Hollow Creek, too," Kyle said.

"Doubt that," said Virgil.

"How's that?"

"'Cause I know more about Hollow Creek than even Ash Sinclair, and he founded this town."

Kyle smiled inside; he had him pegged just right. Here, with his poker face and his thin fingers, was the town gossip. Kyle settled down to hear, in boring detail, the doings of Hollow Creek. "Can't be much to tell. Town's not much on excitement," he said provocatively.

The barman's shinny pate got slightly pink, a sure sign of deep affront. "One of the most important towns in this here part of Texas; one of the first on the cattle run. Why, sir, I'd have you know, we have the most head of cattle per acre in these parts, and our ranchers are about the most successful cattlemen in the business. Why d'you think the railroad came here? Well, that was Ash and his brother Grenville's doing. Brought good business to this town."

"That so?" Kyle said, tipping his hat up a trifle in mock surprise.

"It is. You should see this place on county fair day. Or during roundup. Fair hums, it does. Get's so as a body can't hardly find a place to grab a meal, and we got some mighty fine kitchens, too."

"Must say, dinner at Ma Tuminy's was damn good. Thought it was a fluke."

"Pride ourselves in our victuals . . . ," Virgil said.

"This brandy—not bad, either."

". . . and our women. Why, we're famous for our lovely ladies. Far and wide they come to Dashers—"

"Unmannerly," Kyle commented, deliberately misunderstanding which ladies the man was referring to.

"Pardon?"

"Unmannerly. Females looking like cowpokes and smelling just as bad. Far be it for me to criticize your fair town, Virgil, but you mentioned it."

Virgil Tech squinted across at the tall, dark stranger who had registered under the name of Smith at Dashers two days ago. Hell be damned if the man wasn't criticizing the manners of Hollow Creek's fallen doves. What'd he think? They would be like drawing room ladies?

Maybe, like his name, he wasn't what he seemed. Not for a moment had anyone in Hollow Creek believed that Smith was his real name. It could be he didn't approve of loose women. "You a preaching man, Mr. Smith?" Virgil said suspiciously. "You against the ah . . . pleasures of the flesh?"

Kyle shook his head. "No objections at all."

Virgil raised his brows in question. "You baffle me, Mr. Smith, sir," he said. "There can be few more accommodating ah . . . lovelies than what Dashers has to offer."

"Don't doubt it, Virgil, but the one I object to wore working pants and a liberal dousing of pig's swill. Her talk wasn't parlor prattle, either."

Enlightenment dawned on Virgil. He gave a congested wheeze of a laugh. "Oh heck, you're talking about Merrie Sinclair. Meredith, Ash Sinclair's daughter. She fair lore unto herself, that one. Been running her daddy's spread since he took ill last year. Done a fine job, too, though there's still some grumbling about it not being a proper thing for a girl to take on. Joined the Cattlemen's Consortium, too. Not very popular with that bunch. They definitely don't take to females being part of their group. Have a run-in with her, did you?"

"You have a problem with that bottle, Virgil?" Kyle pushed his glass forward.

"Uh, no . . . n-no, Mr. Smith, sir," Virgil said, and uncorked the brandy hastily.

Kyle took it from him and poured very slowly into his glass. The gleaming liquor glided slowly down the long goose neck of the bottle. It glazed the tumbler's sides first and then seeped up, up to the brim. Kyle held it up to the light. The rich, heavy color reminded him of the gleam of sun-gold hair that he had glimpsed under Miss Meredith Sinclair's jaunty Stetson.

He hunched over his glass and pulled down his hat. "Tell me about this Sinclair who founded Hollow Creek," he said. But he listened with only half an ear as the barman prattled on about heroic military action and influence in Washington after the war, about a gold hoard richer than a pirate's trove, cattle and railroads. And all the while Kyle thought about his two encounters with Merrie Sinclair earlier that day.

The lady was more than a little shapely. Hell, he had never seen so much shape on a female—her legs started somewhere under her ears. In her work pants it had been easy to see the neatness of her waist and the saucy curve of her backside. Should be against the law for women to walk about like that, he thought irritably.

Her vest hadn't hidden any of the lush swell of her breasts. They were full and high, he had noticed, and very womanly indeed. She was tall for a woman, all legs and curves, and while he could not tell what she looked like under the layers of dust, there had been nothing wrong with her profile. No sir, nothing at all. It was the inside that was the problem, not the outside. The girl was crazy.

First she hogged the lane and stubbornly refused to get out of the way, and then she accosted him in the livery. Just like that! Hell, she had to be crazy; there was no other explanation for such outlandish behavior.

Still, he couldn't help but be intrigued. After all, she was part of the reason he had come to Hollow Creek.

Watching out for her safety was going to be one hell of an interesting task. There were few women he could think of as ornery and spirited as the long-legged Merrie Sinclair.

It was the last thing he should have been thinking of, but as he sat there listening to Virgil Tech regale him with the virtues of Hollow Creek, he contemplated his job with a new sense of challenge. It would be intriguing to discover more about Merrie Sinclair. He was, he told himself, curious to see what lay under that clinging coating of dust.

FOUR

JUST OUTSIDE THE town limits, Merrie realized that she was not using her head. The way to get rid of the gunslinger was to pay him off. After all, he was a man for hire, wasn't he? Well, she would simply pay him to leave town.

It occurred to her that she did not know just what he was doing in Hollow Creek. Whatever it was, whoever had hired him, she would simply double the fee and send him on his way.

Could she do such an outrageous thing?

Determined not to allow her stepmother's infidelity to harm Ash, especially since his homecoming was imminent, she needed to act decisively. The meddlesome folk of Hollow Creek would revel in such juicy escapades; they would be waiting, ready with the sordid story, when Ash's train came in.

The thought of what would happen if Ash found out made her sick with worry. Perhaps consideration for her father's health might dissuade folks from telling him what his high-and-mighty wife had been up to while he lay ill in an Eastern hospital.

Liza's callous disregard for her husband sent another wave of determination through Merrie.

She turned Sonnet back toward the town. She would find a lad and send a note home telling them that she intended to spend the night with Kate.

The sun was still high, the air like smelted lead. The water of the High Hollow lay green and placid under the late afternoon sky, as if it, too, were hesitating, tired out by the heat. Small birds warbled in the dusty brush along the track. Out along the ridge, a spiraling plume of smoke announced the arrival of the five-fifteen train.

* * *

It was very late but the rabble-rousers were still at it. Merrie could hear them in the streets below. Their raucous antics, punctuated by the tinny pounding of the piano player, seemed to run endlessly through her aching head. She could also hear the occasional coarse laugh from Dashers' customers, the fluttering giggle of their whores, as they made merry through the night.

She sat near the open window so that she could watch the street. The gunslinger had not come in yet.

It had been easy to find his room. It was the only one unoccupied. Dashers had an outside staircase, so no one had seen her but a drunk on his way down. He had been too soused to recognize her, and in any case, she had kept her hat low over her eyes when she finally slipped into the hallway.

The room was well situated; top floor with windows looking east across the valley to the water, and a fine view of Main Street. Merrie was surprised by the luxury of the room. Garish it was, all plush velvet and embellished gilt-wood furniture, and the amenities were modern and lavish. It appeared that Mr. Smith was a man of considerable means—and late habits.

After hours of waiting, she had washed her filthy face and hands in his commodious porcelain basin and even eaten the remains of a meal left behind. It seemed Mr. Smith did not like dessert, for he had left two plump raspberry tarts sitting on his tray and a creamy rice pudding in a covered dish. Merrie had eaten them with gusto. Then she had settled into a chair and watched the pale evening lights dwindle and the sky turn to gray, then black.

She had not wanted to light the lamp. Even though she was a self-assured young lady and mostly did what she wanted to do, without thought to convention, she felt it wouldn't have been prudent to bring attention to herself. Not in a place like Dashers, anyway, and not in a room belonging to a man—certainly not a man like this gunslinger. So she had sat for hours in the dark, and it was wearing her thin. Not that she was afraid of him; she wasn't, she assured herself, but she wanted to be done with the nasty business.

When he finally came in, it was with such unnerving silence that it took a few moments for her to realize that he was there, knees slightly bent, his gun pointing directly at her. No light came from the landing. He must have seen to that. She sat perfectly still, her heart pounding loudly, her ears straining for the sound of his gun trigger. She could not even hear him breathe.

"I only want to talk," she said when she could force the words past her clenched teeth.

He paused a moment, then eased out of his stance and jolted his gun back into the holster on his hip. He leaned back against the doorjamb, arms loose at his sides.

"So talk," he said. His voice was slow and smooth.

It seemed to wrap about her like heavy silk. She didn't like what he could do with his voice.

"Could we have some light?"

"By all means," he said, but he didn't move.

Merrie rose from her chair. She was vastly annoyed to find that her legs felt wobbly.

"I have a proposition, mister," she said as the lamp flame sprang up reassuringly. "How would you like to earn double what you've been promised?"

Kyle's brow rode high. "I'm listening, aren't I?"

"Leave town. Leave Hollow Creek and don't come back. I'm prepared to make it worth your while."

"Why?"

"I'm sure you can work it out. Oh, and there's another part to this bargain," she said, picking up her fawn-colored Stetson. "You're to leave Liza Sinclair alone. Don't see her, don't communicate with her. I'll make it more than worth your while."

Silence.

Merrie saw the man's eyes narrow, his mouth thin with distaste. It put her hackles up. Liza was beautiful, that much was true, but she was cold, a really unlikable personality. Did this man covet her for her beauty alone, or was it that she belonged to someone else? Merrie knew there were men like that, men who only wanted what someone else already had. She shied way from such thoughts, because they were disquieting.

"As soon as I'm satisfied that you have fulfilled your part of the bargain, I'll send you a bonus. A fat bonus," she prompted.

"I don't think so," said the gunslinger slowly.

"Do you doubt that I can pay you, mister? I assure you I'm good for it."

Kyle came away from the door. Funny, he thought to himself as he crossed to the chair by the window, how fate worked. It was almost as if his thoughts had conjured her. He had no idea what she was blabbing about and didn't much care, either.

He was intrigued. . . . He gave what he hoped was a thoughtful grunt and eased himself into the chair, propping his boots on the bottom rail of the bed and tipping his hat forward over his eyes. That way he could study her without being obvious about it. She was all legs—long, shapely legs that sent his blood galloping through his veins. He could imagine them wrapped around his body.

He didn't notice the dust-caked work pants, the drab brown waistcoat, or the streaks of dirt in her untidy hair. He saw instead her wide-set eyes and pert nose, the blushing smoothness of her high cheeks, and the fullness of her peachy mouth. She was golden, sun-swept gold like the desert, and her eyes were dark, emerald-green. And while she was not a classic beauty, she was stunning. Her height, her almost sinfully curved body, and her coloring all melded together to form a lush, provocative woman.

Contrary to his nature, he found himself intrigued by Merrie Sinclair. Normally, he would have turned her out of his room, for he disliked women who made overt advances. Kyle Delancy was a very careful man and did not indulge in frivolous relationships, nor did he ever play at seduction. Certainly never with unsophisticated cowpokes! But to his surprise, he found himself teasing her, encouraging her obvious interest in him.

TEXAS KISS

She'd come to his room! He did not set himself up as a judge, but he was surprised about that. From what he had gathered from various sources, Merrie Sinclair was not the type to visit men in their rooms. But then, there was her eccentric behavior this morning to consider. What the hell was she up to?

She was prattling on about the Sinclair name.

"My word is as good as my bond. Just name your price, I'll meet it."

"Kind of doubt that," he said softly, finding that his interest melded into a misty fascination with her leggy body.

In her agitation, her long-legged movements, the glint of temper in her eyes, tantalized his already awakened senses. He only half followed her conversation. What would she taste like? he found himself wondering. His blood simmered.

"Mister, I've told you. Whatever it is, I'll manage. Just so long as you're gone by noon tomorrow. Leave me a name and where you want the money sent. It will be there."

"You don't know my price," he said, rising.

"Then name it."

He came to where she stood. There was no more than a hair's breath between them. Merrie looked up in alarm, her vivid eyes locked with his. She was suddenly aware of herself in that strange way she'd been earlier in the day. Her mouth felt full and tingly. Her pulse grew loud, heavy in her ears, and she stumbled back.

The gunfighter caught her arm and steadied her.

She stared at him, glanced down at the hard, sun-browned fingers that gripped her arm and then back at his mesmerizing face, as if she couldn't believe that he held her. His eyes were very, very blue. She jerked away and backed toward the door.

"How much money do you want?" she managed. Her voice sounded scratchy to her.

"Do you think money is the only legal tender hereabout?" he asked.

She looked at him, perplexed.

Kyle saw the utter bewilderment on Merrie's lovely face and swore softly to himself. This kid was as innocent as the day she was born. He doubted that she had been kissed properly yet. *What in hell was she doing in his bedroom?*

"I-I can't pay you in land, if that's what you want. My Uncle Grenville left me land, but I don't inherit legally until I marry. If you're prepared to wait two years, when I plan to marry I can have the lawyer draw up papers."

"I don't want land," he growled.

"I have this," she said, unfastening the small gold locket she wore around her neck. It had been her mother's, and she was loath to part with it. However, under the circumstances . . .

"Bring it here," he said.

She walked over and dropped the glittering thing into his outstretched palm.

He didn't even look at it, but put it into his pocket.

"I don't think so." His eyes never left her. "Something else."

"W-what?" she asked.

All he could see were emerald eyes, soft velvet lips.

Kyle wanted to laugh and would have if he hadn't been suffering with his libido, fighting for control. She was ripe, ripe and sweet as a peach, a sun-drenched, honey-filled female with legs more seductive and elegant than should be allowed by law. And he was a fool to allow his chivalrous conscience to interfere. But he knew he could not take advantage of this green-behind-the-ears innocent. He had principles, strict principles.

It was what differentiated men from animals. He had seen what the animals could do to people. None knew better. He was a very careful man on that score. After all, family history had taught him the lesson in harsh terms—he was not likely to forget family history.

He would allow his conscience to speak, but he would give himself a little taste, a keepsake from Merrie Sinclair to take with him when he went.

"You're in a whorehouse, for Christ sake," he told her, "and you can think of no other way to pay a man?"

Realization dawned. Merrie's face grew rosy, her eyes

TEXAS KISS 27

flashed with temper. But before she could express her outrage, Kyle bent his dark head and kissed her open mouth.

His heat stunned her. His arms locked about her, bringing her flat against his chest. She felt her breasts rubbing against him, tightening, the peaks hardening to sensitive points. Surely she should die of embarrassment. She did not. Instead, she was dizzy with the luscious sensation of his mouth covering her own, his rock-hard body pressing against hers.

Merrie felt his tongue glide into her mouth, stroking, tasting, mastering her will. At the same moment, one of his hands drifted up over her thrusting breast. It was an intimate invasion, a trespass too fundamental and erotic for her innocent temperament not to be shocked. Like a wild bird caught in a snare, she began to struggle frantically.

Kyle knew he had crossed the boundary he had set up himself. The moment he felt her straining against him, he let her go. He watched her through the slits of his eyes, as she raced for the door in panic.

"Seems there's some not for sale, Legs. At least not for the price you have in mind. Let me know if you change your mind, though. I'll be around for a while."

Merrie brought her hand across her trembling mouth as if she could wipe his touch off that way. She was horrified that she had allowed her stepmother's lover to kiss her! A swift flood of guilt and shame overwhelmed her. "You are disgusting, mister. You should be run out of town."

"You fixing to try it?"

"I just might, at that. I want you gone from Hollow Creek, and I do have some influence in this town."

Kyle laughed softly. "Legs," he said, taking a step toward her. "You don't scare me. Let's call the good citizens up here now and let them decide, should we?"

Merrie flushed furiously. "My name's not *Legs*."

"Mine's not *Mister*, it's Kyle. Kyle Delancy."

"I don't know why you're busy introducing yourself to me. We're not likely to see each other again. You've forced me to it. I'll just be certain that your lover never sets eyes on you again. If you don't have character enough to leave another man's wife alone, I'll make sure she leaves you alone. Good evening, Mr. Delancy. It was certainly not a pleasure."

Merrie drew her Stetson down over her head and peered around the opening door. A couple weaving their way down the passage almost collided with the door. The man swore.

Kyle yanked Merrie back and shut the door firmly.

"Not that way, Legs," he said irritably. "Not if you care for your lofty Sinclair reputation."

He hauled her across the room to the window.

Merrie looked dubiously at the dark drop onto the balcony below. She shook her head.

Kyle grinned. His teeth gleamed white against his dark tan. Merrie found herself staring again. Good Lord, but he was devastating when he smiled. His bluer-than-blue eyes fair ignited with deep, dark fires.

"I'll hand you down. You'll only have a short fall and then you can make your way around the outside stair."

Merrie looked down again and shook her head vehemently.

"Scared? I would have thought a girl who could run her daddy's cattle business would be tough enough for a little jump in the dark. And by the way, you're a liar as well as a yellow coward."

"You're one to talk," she said furiously and climbed onto the sill. "You're judging me? You're a gunslinger, an adulterer, and you have the audacity to ju— Oh, help!" she cried as her grip on the windowsill slipped.

Kyle grabbed her arm, and then the other one, just above the elbow. His hands rock-steady, he then lowered her out of the window, so that she was suspended above the balcony one story below.

He didn't want her to look down and panic. "Look at me, Legs," he told her, his voice a seductive whisper.

Very slowly he brought her up, lifting her by her arms alone until she was face-to-face with him. She felt his breath wash over her mouth, felt him brush her lips with his own. "Next time you tell me you had no pleasure in our meeting, remember this, Legs," he said and tasted her mouth again. Soft and sinuous, his lips caressed her, beguiled her into thinking that the world naturally catapulted through space like a drunkard lurching down Main Street. And while she still reeled from his kiss, he hung down over the sill and let go. She dropped like a stone onto the balcony just a yard below and lay sprawled for a moment, her breath quite stolen away, but otherwise unhurt.

A soft laugh made her look up.

"Give me back my locket, you thief," she hissed at him.

"Think I'll keep it for saving your reputation," he said, and tipping his hat politely, he eased back inside. His voice wafted down through the night, seductive and cool. "Always a pleasure to assist an acquaintance," he said. And the window came down with a thump.

"Oh . . . you . . . Damn and bebother," Merrie hissed, picking herself up and dusting herself off. She shot one last look up at the window, just in time to see the light doused.

To her chagrin, there was nothing further she could do but go home. She had failed so far, but she refused to give in.

Tomorrow she would endeavor to rid Hollow Creek of the gunslinger. She would find a way. There must be some statute in her late Uncle Grenville's law books about lechers. She would find it and run him out of town.

FIVE

"IT WON'T WORK, Liza," Merrie said, jamming her Stetson down on her head, "so you can stop trying to distract me." She had come home as soon as it was light. She was worn out and edgy, having spent an uncomfortable night curled up next to Sonnet in Old Bob's Livery Stable. Still, she was determined to have it out with Liza.

Merrie had waited for her to come down to breakfast, and then confronted her. It had not been easy to talk about what she had witnessed at number 1A, End Street, but she had done it.

Liza gave a tittering laugh. "Your hat at breakfast is what is distracting, my dear Merrie. Actually, *your* hat at any time is distracting."

The day promised to be hot; Merrie would need the protection of her broad-brimmed hat. Her stepmother, however, disapproved of her wearing her working hat in the house, especially in the breakfast room.

It was Liza Sinclair's favorite room, and she had decorated it in a rather busy floral of lavender sprays against a fuchsia-and-bottle-green background. There were lacy sheers over the long, narrow French doors, as well as frilled chintz drapes. The bench cushions matched the fussy print, and the same lavender flowers were hand-painted on the cream spindle-leg furniture. Ash hated the room, as did Merrie. Neither ever ate breakfast there. But it was a sunny, feminine room, a perfect foil for Elizabeth Baxter Sinclair's soft pink dimity morning dress.

As always, Liza was immaculately turned out. Her red hair, stylishly coiffured, gleamed upon her head. She sipped her breakfast tea daintily. She was doll-like in face and figure; petite and emotionless. It was difficult to think that blood actually traveled in her veins.

Nevertheless she was beautiful. Her pale face was a breathtaking oval, her lashes, dark and thick, lay bashfully against the tender blush of her cheeks, hiding brown velvet eyes.

Not that she didn't spend a goodly amount of time before her mirror every day. For Liza, grooming was an art that she had perfected. From the intricacies of her chignon down to her delicately slippered feet, from her highly buffed fingernails to her artfully cinched waistline, Liza Sinclair was flawless.

"I mean to have this out here and now, Liza," Merrie said. "I want answers. Yes or no. Are you going to stop seeing your lover, or do I have to take further actions?"

Liza played with her teacup a moment then smiled at her stepdaughter. The smile did nothing more than change the shape of her mouth. There was not an ounce of warmth in it.

"Are you blackmailing me?"

"If I need to, yes. Are you going to give him up?"

"I don't think you're in a position to blackmail me."

"Take my word for it. I'm perfectly capable of doing you a great deal of harm."

"That remains to be seen."

"I don't think so. I've seen all I need to. You're an adulterer."

"And you, Miss High and Mighty, are far from the virtuous little cowhand you pretend to be."

She very slowly and deliberately put aside her napkin and, taking up the silver teapot, poured fresh tea into her china cup. She sipped, watching Merrie all the while, set her cup down, and dabbed her mouth with the linen.

"You're grabbing at straws, Liza."

"I assure you, I'm not. You see, I know you were not at Kate's last night."

Merrie raised her brows. She had sent home a note yesterday, telling Sonna, the Spur's housekeeper, that she was staying in town overnight with the Browns. What, she wondered, was Liza scheming now?

Liza took a sip of tea and slowly set her cup back down with elaborate delicacy. She smiled at Merrie.

"Kate came out here yesterday afternoon looking for you.

TEXAS KISS 33

She was excited that Ash was coming home, and wanted to help arrange the shindig, she said."

"At least she was pleased about Ash; that's more than you can say for yourself."

"That is not the point of my story."

"What is?" Merrie said. She sounded cavalier, but her heart was sinking.

Liza's eyes flashed with delight. She twitched her napkin aside. "What is?" she mimicked. "Let me tell you, then. When it grew late and you were obviously not coming back, I persuaded Kate to remain here *overnight*. Imagine my surprise when the boy arrived with your message."

Merrie colored furiously. Of all the luck, to be caught in a lie by this Jezebel. "I think you made that up," she said.

"She's in the yellow bedroom. Take a look."

"That doesn't change the fact that you're a . . . I will not let you cheat on my father."

Liza gave a throaty laugh. "You're such a child. At least up until last night you were. I wonder, Meredith, are you still? Never mind. Time will tell."

"Don't concern yourself with my business, Liza. Just get rid of your gunslinging boyfriend before Ash comes home."

"My what?"

"Don't pretend, Liza, I saw you. I told you that. Your Mr. Smith, or whatever his name really is, had better be out of town by Wednesday."

Liza looked startled for a minute then smiled broadly. "My, my, but you've really learned to poke and pry, haven't you? A real busybody to match your frumpy appearance."

"You're as disgusting as he is. You condemn me, but it's you who is the faithless tramp consorting with gunslingers, and who knows what other riffraff."

Liza's cherry-red mouth lifted at the corners. "At least he's got what it takes, little Miss *Honeybunches*," she said, deliberately using Ash's pet name for Merrie. "Unlike your precious father, whose only manly attribute is the purse he dangles."

"Stop it," Merrie said in a desperate voice.

"Why? It's the truth. Everybody knows it. Ash hasn't been in my bed for years. He wouldn't know what to do once he got there either."

"You're sickening."

"Now, now, let's be careful, shall we, or I might take it into my head to confess my true feelings for you."

"What you think of me makes no difference. But you wronged my father. I will not stand for it."

"Your absence last night didn't wrong him? Want to tell me where you were, Meredith? And who you were with?"

"My conscience is clear, Liza. Can you say the same?"

"*Honeybunches,* let me tell you the facts of life. It won't matter a thing if you were sewing altar cloths in a hermit's den. When the town hears about your little ah . . . absence from the Spur last night, you'll become Merrie *Strumpet* Sinclair."

"No doubt you will make certain that the whole town does hear about it."

Liza rose from her chair with effortless grace and fluffed out her pretty skirts.

"Now," she said as she drifting past her stepdaughter in a cloud of honeysuckle scent, "you understand."

When she was all the way across the entrance hall, she paused, and turned her beautiful face toward Merrie, and said coldly, "Try to interfere in my business, Meredith, and you will be unable to show your face in Hollow Creek again."

"No one will listen to you."

"At least one person will. Your father. I shall make certain that he hears."

"He won't believe you, either," Merrie said.

"I wonder what it will do to him to discover that he has a whore for a daughter?"

"You don't scare me, Liza. It's you who is the whore," Merrie said, but her heart ached. What a corner she had managed to get herself into.

"You folks from Dodge City sure is peculiar. This here telegraph don't make no sense, Mr. Smith. 'Phoenix returning, stop. Watchers all the way, two on—two off, stop. Notify me at all checkpoints, end,' " Jem Tech said, scratching his balding pate.

"How much, old man?" Kyle said.

"You sure you want to pay money to send it?" Jem said incredulously. There was no telling to what extravagant lengths some folks would go.

Outside the ticket office window, Kyle leaned further down to avoid the wood awning scraping the top of his hat. He ducked a little more, until his hard blue eyes squeezed down on the man framed on the other side of the ticket window. Hollow Creek's station office, a gray planked building, seemed almost toylike in size. There was just enough space inside for the operator and the narrow shelf for his cashbox and telegraph machine. Beyond the side wall, a sod-roofed lean-to rested furtively on two notched poles and provided shelter for passengers.

Jem Tech eased his braces up over the shoulders of his collarless shirt several times, his pointed nose twitching nervously.

"Bring the reply to me direct this time, old man," Kyle said, ignoring the question.

Jem gulped. "Sure thing, Mr. Smith."

"Name's Delancy. Don't take detours with the reply."

"Don't rightly know what you mean by that, Mr. Smith, sir."

Kyle grunted. "The name's Delancy."

"B-but the book at Dashers says Smith."

"Didn't know books could talk, old man," Kyle said, straightening up. "Just see you bring the telegraph direct to me this time."

Jem's thoughts percolated a moment. Then he pointed to the gunslinger and hooted. "Didn't know as books could talk, he says. Didn't know as books could talk. Just wait till I tell the boys that one, just you wait."

Kyle was on his way back to town before old Jem finished hitting his knee and cackling. He followed the crenelated shadow cast by the false-fronted buildings on Main Street, the inky demarcation vivid against the dun-colored street. Fine brown dust blew into his eyes, and he tilted the angle of his Stetson a little more.

The morning was hot and promised to get hotter. High and pale, the dome of the sky was like a metal lid over the gasping earth. Even so, there were people on the streets. They naturally gravitated away as Kyle made his way down to the livery, the soft chink, chink of his spurs marking his passage.

Kyle didn't even notice anymore. He was used to folks shying away, trepidation and curiosity etched upon their faces. He'd spent many a day alone in friendless towns like Hollow Creek. But, as he didn't need the acknowledgment of others to know who he was, it made little difference to him.

He was used to relying on no one. His early years, spent in the squalor of a New Orleans slum, had taught him to trust only in himself.

For certain big jobs, like this one, it was necessary to hire reliable men, and he did. Nevertheless, everything they did was overseen and checked by him.

But his usual easy concentration seemed lacking today. He knew exactly why, too. It was the Sinclair woman. How ironic their meeting was! He supposed her wealth fostered the idiosyncratic behavior—her accosting him like she did yesterday, for no reason that he could make out.

Crazy.

And then, of all things, she had come to his room. His thoughts flew to their meeting last night. How incredible she had felt when he held her briefly.

What a luscious peach she was. Her mouth had tasted sweet, sweet and fresh as golden summer. She had provoked a strange combination of irritation and agitation in him.

He shifted in his saddle, nosing his horse toward the outskirts of town. Setting an easy pace, he allowed his mind to trickle through recollections of their far from ordinary encounters.

As naive as she was, Merrie Sinclair possessed as sharp and worldly an attitude as any man he knew. She wanted something

TEXAS KISS 37

and went after it, ignoring convention, and even practicality. She'd wanted him out of town. He wondered why. He had not paid too much attention to what she'd been saying at the time; now, however, he remembered something of it. She'd called him an adulterer . . .

Wait up, thought Kyle suddenly, *an adulterer?*

Where in hell had that come from? he wondered.

Suddenly he was annoyed. Who could tell with women? They didn't make logical sense. Certainly not Merrie Sinclair. He would do well to put her out of his mind, he thought, but he couldn't quite rid himself of her tantalizing presence. His exasperation grew. He was hot enough without torturing himself any further.

Slipping his canteen off the saddle horn, he pulled out the stopper. He tipped it to his mouth, soaked his bandanna, then he adjusted his dark Stetson and wiped his face and neck with the cool cloth.

The land sweltered. It was the end of summer. There was not a splinter of shade along the road. Here and there markers indicated the direction of a ranch or stony path that led to the creek. At times he caught a glimpse of the lazy green water and the blur of low-growing bushes, struggling for life. The road wound on in dusty silence, although once or twice he halted, listening because he thought he detected the following clop of a horse, there at the edge of sound.

But there was nothing.

Nobody was out in the noonday heat, not even an insect. It must have been the crack of stones splitting, or a trick of the heat itself, which seemed to evaporate the very blood of a man and leave his husk for kindling. Kyle narrowed his eyes against the glaring white of it.

Some twelve miles from town, the road turned sharply north between the ridges of burnt umber hills. From a distance, it looked like a solid wall of unbroken rock, but there was a rift, a narrow way, almost entirely hidden in the folded rock face. This opened onto a wide valley on the canyon floor.

From Virgil Tech he had learned that Ashton Sinclair and his brother Greenville had many years ago discovered the secret canyon pass. They had established their famed Silver Spur Ranch just below its mouth.

Nowadays the pass was easy to find. The road marked the way. Kyle followed a narrow cleft, deeply shadowed, savoring the relative cool of the rocky path that threaded through the gap and then dropped into the canyon below. The horse's hooves echoed in the crags above, and now and then a few rocks loosened by wind and sun tumbled down onto the path with a hollow sound like goblin's laughter.

The path tipped down at the end, and he saw a lush and fertile valley hidden below. To his right, the Hollow Creek gushed noisily from a channel halfway up the rock face. In a leaping froth of green and white, it joined the great Red River wending its way through the canyon. As far as the eye could see, fat brown cattle grazed in massive herds—there were thousands of them. Way off to the left he could just make out the clutch of trees surrounding the sprawl of ranch buildings.

The Silver Spur lay there, resplendent herald to this rich and prosperous valley. *She lived there.* His little touched-in-the-head visitor of the night before.

Kyle swore. His way lay miles beyond the Silver Spur, at least for now. He had work to do. Someone was trying to extort a ransom in gold from Ashton Sinclair, and Kyle had been hired to discover exactly who that someone was.

There were several suspects, and Matt Cheston was at the top of Kyle's list. He was on his way to the Lazy D for a good look around.

From all the evidence that he had gathered so far, it seemed that Cheston certainly liked the high life. He was also in debt to the tune of some thirty-five thousand dollars. Not a very savory character, as Kyle had discovered yesterday; Cheston was having an adulterous affair with his client's wife.

If that was not sordid enough, the man was engaged to be married to Merrie Sinclair. The thought left a foul taste in Kyle's mouth.

It seemed that Cheston could not wait to legally inherit

through Meredith, and decided to try and get his hands on the legendary Sinclair gold by extortion. Was he simply a greedy fool?

Kyle didn't think so.

Ash Sinclair had not cared for his daughter's suitor, and had put a proverbial spoke in the works. Two weeks before he had been taken ill, he asked Cheston to wait until Meredith's twentieth birthday to wed. For Merrie there was no problem. Cheston, however, may have become impatient—either that or his creditors may have. He wanted to marry right away.

A brief, unpleasant image of Cheston's corrupt hands sliding down Merrie's long, long legs brought a scowl to Kyle's face.

That marriage was unlikely to take place, he told himself, and immediately he scowled even harder. What the hell did he care? an inner voice mocked. Why did his stubborn mind keep circling around Merrie Sinclair?

He was persecuting himself, he thought, and again he shifted uncomfortably in his saddle. He had a job to do, and it would not get done while he was stirring thoughts of Merrie Sinclair around in his head.

He was still chiding himself about it when the bullet hit him square in the back.

The second one got him in the shoulder. His horse shied and threw him; he landed hard on his back and rolled down into the road.

Kyle didn't even feel the fall. He was dropping down, down into a pit so black, so agonizing, that the only thing that filled his despairing and irrational mind was that he would die out here in this valley, alone and under a false name. As the echo of the repeater rifle died in the crags above him, he wondered if the grave marker would read Smith.

Six

Merrie's head jerked up at the sound of the double discharge. The blasts repeated eerily along valley walls, disturbing the herds milling across the valley floor.

The longhorns bunched and swayed their lowered heads, adding their fretful notes to the fading sounds. Cowboys on the fringes of the herd automatically moved to control the jittery steers and prevent them from stampeding.

High up at the pass, Merrie saw a dark horse paw the air, then spin away down the road. The tail of her eyes caught another movement on the crags above the road where it issued from the pass. There was a man up there, Merrie was certain. He was moving furtively, keeping to the shaded hollows of the crags.

"That was a Winchester '73, Miss Merrie," said the Spur's foreman, Buck Peterson. "A repeater."

"It sounded like one," Merrie said, nudging Sonnet through the discordant sea of cows and calves. She shaded her eyes against the glare. "I'm not sure, Buck, but I think there's a man up there on Wolf Fang Pass. I think he shot at someone."

Buck squinted up to where Merrie pointed. He was a man as weathered as the rocks on Wolf Fang Pass itself. He was old now and did not move well anymore. He suffered from debilitating rheumatism. There was nothing wrong with his eyesight, however.

He could still see a rattlesnake at seven hundred paces. There was almost no difference between the leather brown color of his eyes and his skin. Nor was there a patch of ground in the valley that was unknown to him. He knew its secrets and its hidey-holes. It did not take more than a minute for him to make out the gunman peering down from the needle-shaped rocks at the top of the pass.

The man was bent over, watching the road near the mouth of the pass as if looking for something or someone. He was careful to keep himself in the shadows, and Buck couldn't see any of his features, but he was there all right.

"Uhup, 'bout halfway up the pass, I reckon. And there's his target. See, up next to the road, a dark bundle lying there? He got his man okay, but he ain't sure yet. Must be the way the man fell, but the gunman can't see if he's dead."

"Tell Spiker to go after that runaway horse, and then cover me. I'm going to take a look." Merrie kicked Sonnet into motion.

The old foreman put out his skinny hand to stay her horse.

"You take care, Miss Merrie. Mr. Ash'll skin me if you get hurt," Buck said gruffly.

It didn't take Merrie long to reach the fallen man. He had rolled a good way down off the beaten road and lay facedown in the short-cropped valley grass. All the way from the road to where he lay the ground was smeared with his blood. He was not dead, at least not yet. He had been shot in the back, twice. The wounds were bleeding profusely, welling up with each ragged wheeze of breath.

Merrie knew him immediately. Even before she had seen his face, she knew who it was.

The gunslinger!

Mr. Smith, or whatever he called himself. No one could have mistaken that long frame of his, or his thick black hair that now lay blood-splattered across his shoulders. His one arm, flung out as if to soften his fall, somehow evoked a vulnerability that was incongruous with the man she remembered from the day before.

She knelt beside him and gingerly inspected the dreadful wounds. The bleeding had to be stopped quickly. She had the awful feeling that there would not be time enough to save him.

The thought momentarily shocked her. Briefly, she hesitated. She threw a wrathful look up at the heavens, as if in silent protest.

Why him? Why me? Why should I be faced with this dilemma? It just wasn't fair. And yet all the while she rebelled against the notion of aiding the fallen man, she knew that she would. Enemy or no, simple humanity demanded it.

TEXAS KISS 43

Buck and one of the hands came up just then.

"He's alive," she said, amazed that she could still speak with her throat so tight.

Buck examined the man. "Better get him help, right quick, too."

"There's no time to go back for a buckboard," Merrie said.

"Jamie, here, can hoist him up over my saddle. Take him down as smooth as can be. You'd best roust Doc."

Merrie looked quickly back up to the pass, then down into the hazy valley, as if trying to decide. "Take him to the bunkhouse. Maybe Sonna can fix him. Here, let me get his guns off, then we can try lifting him."

Between them they managed to lift the unconscious Mr. Smith onto Buck's horse, draping him stomach-down over the saddle. It was a bloody and gruesome task. Even unconscious as he was, the man groaned agonizingly when they lifted him.

"Hey, I seen this man at The Holler," Jamie said, as he strapped the unconscious man onto Buck's saddle. "He's that Mr. Smith out of Dodge City. I knew him for a gunfighter moment I seen him."

"Looks like the opposition got him, whoever that might be. Doubt he'll be gunslinging anymore," Buck said.

"I wonder who he was after. Asked a lot of questions down at The Holler," Jamie said.

"Thing that worries me is that he was on his way here," Buck said. The creases on his forehead deepened, and his sharp eyes lit on Merrie. "There's no one out this-a-way but the Hobbs up Little Creek draw and Cheston up north way."

"And us," Jamie said.

"You know anything about him, Miss Merrie?" Buck asked slowly.

Merrie's flush was damning, she knew.

But then she realized that someone else had wanted to get rid of the arrogant Mr. Smith, even if their method was a more permanent one than what she'd had in mind. Obviously she was not alone in her dislike of the man.

Mr. Smith probably attracted trouble of this kind wherever

he went. Could it be that his visit to Hollow Creek was for reasons other than mere dalliance with her stepmother?

"Not much," she said truthfully.

"There, guess that will hold him until we get down to the bunkhouse," Jamie said.

Buck squinted up at the crags overhead. "I think our high-stepping gunman has gone, but I'm not sure it's safe along the road."

"Don't worry about me," Merrie said. "I'll be back with Doc Farley before sundown."

"I'll send Spiker up after you. Better have your wits about you, Miss Merrie."

"Here, keep his guns away from him. He's a gunslinger, and you never know what he might do if he even regains consciousness," warned Merrie. She tossed him the heavy gunbelt with its two matching Smith and Wesson six-shooters. The butts were smooth and well handled, evidence of their frequent use.

Buck caught them and whistled. "Fine," he murmured, his eyes jerking from the guns and hand-tooled belt to the man strapped to his saddle. "Very fine. This here's no two-bit gunfighter."

"It didn't stop him from getting shot up like one, though, did it?" Merrie asked, and mounting Sonnet, she headed toward the pass. Sonna would probably be able to save him, but Merrie knew Doc should be there, just in case.

All the long and dusty way to Hollow Creek, she was tormented with images of the tall, lanky gunslinger and her beautiful stepmother together. And here she was giving them the opportunity. It made her culpable in the deceit against her father. All she could do was rail against herself for being a fool and handing Liza to her boyfriend on a plate.

It seemed a spiteful fate that would force her into such a bind.

But there was more, though she was loath to admit it. He evoked an awareness inside her, a white-hot quiver of dubious emotion. She didn't like it at all!

Disgusting lecher . . . , she muttered to herself. No doubt

some poor, thwarted husband had shot him in desperate revenge. Surely it was no less than he deserved.

IT WAS QUITE late. There was no moon. The night was dark, quiet, almost eerily so. The hayloft was lit by a single half-shuttered lamp, and their whispers rustled in the rafters like pigeons in a coop. Quick and urgent, their movements, magnified on the wooden walls, leapt and jerked in erotic parody of their play.

There had been no time for preliminaries. Liza was braced against several bales of straw, her nightgown hitched about her waist, her booted feet well apart. The squirming action of her hips caused the rough straw to cut and scratch her naked thighs and bottom, but somehow it seemed only to fire her lust.

Still she managed to assert her control.

Her lover gasped and strained between her legs, grunting his agreement to her whispered suggestions. He seemed incapable of coherent speech. Even after he looped his belt back into place and tucked in his shirttail, his low murmurs were vague.

Liza had to repeat herself several times before she was satisfied that he knew what she wanted him to do. He pulled his collar up and shoved his hat down on his head after snatching one last kiss from her. Then he waved good-bye.

There was a bright feral gleam in her eyes as she watched him descend into the barn where his chestnut stood. The animal whinnied softly as his master led him forward.

Straining her ears, Liza heard him open the barn door and close it before leading his horse away into the night. Then she turned toward the far side of the loft, beyond the reach of the lamplight, to where the roof angled down sharply to meet the floor of the loft and gloomy shadows lurked.

"You can come out now," she crooned. "He's gone."

A large man rose from the row of empty barrels. Bending almost double, he came within the circle of light cast by the lamp. His eyes were hot with anticipation and lust.

Liza tittered at his obvious arousal. "You like watching, don't you? Let's see how much."

"Your boyfriend didn't do the job right, Liza," the man growled, unbuttoning his pants.

Liza hitched her eyebrows suggestively and ran one white hand over her breasts, but she didn't for a moment take her greedy eyes from the man's groin. Nothing ignited her lust more than her manipulation of these strong and handsome men, especially this one. "Which job are you referring to? Finishing off the gunslinger, or finishing me?"

"Both," the man said. Hooking his boot behind her knees, he sent her tumbling to the floor. "But I aim to fix that, right now."

She cried out at his forceful penetration, and he quickly covered her mouth with one of his huge hands. He was not gentle, but she didn't mind in the least.

"I think," she managed after a little while, "that having the gunslinger alive is rather a boon."

"Why?" the man panted heatedly in her ear.

"My stupid stepdaughter thinks the gunslinger is my lover. So he manages to deflect attention away from Cheston, and that's not a bad idea for right now."

"I don't like it."

Liza laughed. "Oh, yes, you do, by the feel of you . . . I would say quite a lot."

She ran her fingers along his spine in smooth spirals to slow him. Like all men, Liza thought irritably, he was too hasty.

The man grunted. "Maybe, but when the time comes . . ."

"Don't worry, I know what needs to be done," she said.

"I'll just bet you do," he said, as she surged against him.

IT WAS EITHER very late or very early. Merrie's eyes shot open; she was wide awake.

What had wakened her?

Immediately she knew. Someone was moving about, and she just knew who it was, too.

Her stepmother!

Merrie was boiling mad.

When she had returned to the Spur with Doc Farley, Merrie discovered that Liza had installed the wounded gunslinger in the spare bedroom of the main house—a convenient three doors down from her own and not in the bunkhouse at all. Buck was no match for Liza and did what he was told.

In a way, Merrie was furious with herself. There was no one but herself to blame for putting the two lovers so cozily together under the same roof.

A conscious gunslinger he was, too.

Sonna had worked wonders with him. Doc Farley had pronounced the entire operation a great success. He had decided to stay around a few days to be sure that the gunfighter did not take a fever.

Just to be certain, he had repaired to the patient's room with a bottle of Ash Sinclair's finest whiskey (of which he was inordinately fond), and he and the gunslinger had proceeded to make short shrift of the night—not to mention Ash Sinclair's whiskey.

Even now, Merrie could hear Doc Farley's drunken snores from down the hall. He was staying in Ash's bedroom.

She had hoped that Liza would at least wait for Doc Farley to leave the Silver Spur before throwing herself into her boyfriend's arms. But it seemed she was unable to wait.

Well, thought Merrie grimly, I'll not stand for it. She flung the bedclothes off and got out of bed. Her toes curled at they hit the cool floor. She pulled on an old duster jacket over her nightgown and went into the hallway.

It was dark and empty except for a narrow band of light spilling out from under the door of the spare bedroom, way down the far end of the passage.

A quick look into Liza's room set Merrie's mouth into a grim line. The overscented chamber was empty; the floral bedspread lay neatly over the ornate half-tester bed. Obviously Liza had not gone to bed yet, at least not here.

Merrie flung her tousled hair out of her eyes, straightened her shoulders for battle, and advanced down the hall. Before she reached the spare room, however, the door opened, slamming back against the wall.

The gunslinger stood in the doorway. He was naked, but for

the bandages that swathed his chest and back, and he was very, very angry. Braced against the door frame for support, he scowled right into Merrie's shocked eyes.

"Which son of a bitch took my guns," he growled, just as she turned her head away from his startling nudity. Nonetheless, she had seen him quite clearly.

His tall, elegant frame was all sinewy muscle, and he was tanned to a deep bronze except for the area generally covered by his pants. The thing was that he was no longer covered there!

A brushfire erupted somewhere in her belly, and she felt more nervous than a mustang about to be broken. She did not like the feeling at all.

"You deaf? Who took my guns?" the gunslinger shouted. His voice was hoarse, as if he had trouble getting the sounds past his throat, but there was no mistaking the anger there.

"Damn and bebothered, but you're not *wearing anything*," she managed at last.

"Dead right, and I'm not wearing my guns either. You go get them quick, or there's going to be hell to pay, lady," he said.

Merrie darted a quick look into his room. There was no sign of her stepmother. That surprised her.

"Nobody has taken your guns, Mr. Smith; they're perfectly fine. You are not. Get back to bed and cover yourself before you do yourself another injury."

The man staggered forward to grab hold of her. His long fingers bit forcefully into the tender flesh of her arm. It hurt. She could feel the extraordinary heat radiating from him. He was burning up. His face mere inches from her, she could see the fever-glaze over his eyes, the cracked dryness about his angry mouth. He was in pain, considerable pain, by all indications, and Merrie didn't know how he managed to stand up at all.

"You get me my guns, Legs. Now, understand or—" he croaked, then his legs folded and he sagged against her. If the wall had not been there to stop her, she would have fallen, too. The impetus of his fall shoved her back, his dead weight against her, his heavy head laid against her shoulder. She could hear the rasp of his labored breathing; the furnace-like heat of his body seemed to scald her.

Merrie clung to him. If she let go, he would fall onto the floor. Pinned against the wall by his weight, she didn't think she could move.

If she hadn't been so worried, she would have laughed at her predicament. Here she was in the pitch black of night, a naked man in her arms, unable to move. But she suddenly became aware of a sticky wetness all down his back that put all frivolous thoughts out of her head in a hurry. Merrie realized that the wounds must have opened. He was bleeding again!

"Somebody, Doc, Liza . . . help!" she called out, but Doc Farley's snores went on unabated, and her stepmother never appeared. Sonna, she knew, would never hear her, for the housekeeper lived in a small house some distance from the main house.

Merrie was frantic. What was she going to do? She was just contemplating the chances of letting him fall so that she could wake Doc Farley, when the man moaned. "Just you and me . . . Legs . . . just what I wanted," he mumbled in her ear.

"I'm going to try and get you to bed. Do you think you could help?" she said, annoyed that he could be joking when her heart was hammering in fear.

The gunslinger's throaty laugh was warm against her ear. "Always knew . . . you . . . my kind . . . girl," he croaked.

Gingerly she tested her balance, moving inch by inch along the wall, half-dragging, half-supporting the man.

It was difficult, but she managed to haul him finally onto his bed, where she fell with him in a tangled heap, panting, trying to still her racing pulse. She could feel the hard planes of his body intimately. It was disturbing. There was a hot, tight feeling just below her stomach, and her heart seemed determined to leap out of her chest.

She had to get away from him.

Eventually she tried to maneuver his steely arm off her

abdomen, easing her hips out from under one of his legs, but the gunslinger's grip on her tightened.

"Don't leave, darlin'."

"Mr. Smith, I'm going to get Doc Farley," Merrie said, and then she froze as one of his hands deliberately grasped her buttocks. She gave a yelp and shoved him off her.

"You filthy— Oh, good Lord," she gasped as he slid off the edge of the bed and crashed onto the floor with a horrible thud. She scrambled off after him.

Merrie fell to her knees beside him. His eyes were closed, he lay rigid, not breathing. He was deathly white, and beneath him, a dark red stain spread across the yellow rug.

Merrie ran a trembling hand over his burning forehead. Surely he was dying. She was mortified that she had injured a wounded man. How could she have been so unthinking, so impetuous?

"Oh, God . . . I'm sorry . . . Don't die, Mr. Smith, please," she said on a sob.

And then, to her immense relief, she heard him take the softest whisper of a breath, then another and another. She saw the flicker of his lashes, watched as he lifted a hand and beckoned her closer.

"Name's Delancy . . ."

"Don't talk."

"Right . . . No . . . time for words . . . only actions." He grabbed a shank of her hair.

She eased his fingers open and freed herself. "Let me get Doc Farley. You've hurt yourself again."

The man shook his head in negation. "Not true . . . You hurt me. Now you can . . . kiss me good-bye . . . Least you can do," he said, pointing to his mouth.

One of his hands curled about her neck and coaxed her mouth down to within an inch of his, but before Merrie could react, she felt his hand slide clumsily to the floor, and his head rolled to the side. Mr. Smith, or Delancy as he preferred to be called, had blacked out. Either that or he was dead!

SEVEN

STEAM ROSE WITH noxious fumes through the rotting floorboards. It always stank of steam and lye. The laundry was below them. He hated the stink. It made him retch. His throat burned and he hurt. He hurt all over, but mostly he hurt in his heart.

It was the same nightmare he always had. The agony never lessened, though, the blind rage that sizzled his soul.

He saw the man's coin falling into his mother's palm. The chink of the money as it fell . . . he knew he could hear it, and yet it never made a real sound. Just as his sister, lying naked on the couch, made no sounds at all.

Her small white body, just budding with the first flush of puberty, was fragile against the coarse blanket that covered the couch.

The steam boiled around them, searing his lungs, licking like acid at his gut. The room stank of lye and sex.

Kaiten. Just eleven and ruined.

Her eyes had pleaded with him across the room, but only that first time. After Kyle had been severely beaten for trying to interfere, she used to go quietly with her mother's customers, those who liked little girls rather than their exquisite, vicious mother.

Like a lamb to the slaughter.

Kaiten, I'm sorry you hurt so bad . . .

Then, it seemed the customers had no taste for little girls with swollen bellies and turned their lascivious eyes on Kyle.

Already, at nine years of age, he was extraordinary looking, like a dark angel. His luminous eyes reflected the very heaven itself, yet the bitter truth of his life was too atrocious even for hell.

But Kyle was not willing to be a victim. He would not allow them to touch him. He would run. He would escape.

He knew he would escape, if only he could throw off the lethargy, the cloying humidity that made his very limbs burn as if tied down with iron weights.

Seething fumes swirled about him as he lay plotting . . . always plotting. He would get away, and he would take Kaiten with him. He knew if he didn't, the stifling heat would kill him. He fought to raise his heavy head above the vaporous fumes.

"You best get Liza or Sonna, Merrie. This here's no job for a young girl," said Doc Farley, straightening up. He had sewn the gunslinger's wound up again, packed it with clean cloths. Only the one had opened up, but it was the deeper one, and it had bled the most, too.

The man had drifted in and out of consciousness, but not before Doc Farley had dosed him up with a concoction that Merrie thought might be composed of alcohol, some curative powders, and a touch more alcohol. Both men fairly reeked of the strong spirits.

Merrie held the lamp high for Doc Farley, praying that he was sober enough to know what he was doing. It had been difficult to wake him. He was particularly fond of Ash Sinclair's whiskey and had done his best to reduce his absent host's supply.

Now, however, Doc Farley was clearly sobering up fast. The gunslinger seemed dangerously ill, for his fever raged unabated. His body was slick with sweat, hot to the touch. He lay upon his stomach, sprawled across the bed with his arms and legs dangling over the edges, his face almost entirely concealed by the restless movement of his long, beautiful hair as he tossed from side to side. Now and then he seemed to ramble. His tone, fraught with intense desolation, cut into Merrie's heart, even though she didn't know what he was saying.

At one point he cried out, his words coherent and anguished.

"Not Kaiten, please, no . . . ," he moaned. ". . . Kaiten—" His howl was piercing in the stillness of the room and made

Merrie shudder deep in her soul. She watched her raised hand fall and touch his burning forehead, stroke back the wet strands of his gleaming hair.

Doc Farley's face was grim. The horror of the gunslinger's cry was devastating for them both.

Doc Farley cleared his throat. "We've got to cool this one down. He's in a bad way."

"What do you need?" Merrie asked, pulling back her hand awkwardly.

"Cold water, cloths—lots."

"I'll get them and send Sonna up," Merrie said.

The man groaned then, and putting out his hand, he grabbed Merrie's wrist. "Hey, Legs, you running out on me?" he said, his voice low and cracked. "Thought you had more guts than that."

Merrie colored at the doctor's obvious surprise. All the same, she was absurdly relieved that the man had regained consciousness.

"Delirious . . . ," she mumbled vaguely at Doc Farley's questioning look. She pulled her hand away and heard the gunslinger chuckle.

The incongruity of that sound after his heart-wrenching cry was stunning. Merrie felt as if he had deliberately played them for fools, yet she knew there had been nothing trivial about his raving a moment ago. There had been terrible suffering in his voice.

Disconcerted, Merrie tried to move away. The gunslinger managed to grab a fistful of her nightgown and held her fast. Even ill, he had amazing strength in his arms, but then she remembered just how strong he really was. Last night at Dashers, he had held her suspended two floors above the street, his only grip the top of her arms. And then he had lifted her, *kissed her* . . .

"C'mon, Legs, you said you wanted me in bed, right? Get rid of the old geezer, and I'm yours," he teased, his cracked voice a mere whisper.

The man was the devil himself. He was her stepmother's

lover, and here he was making lewd suggestions to her. Doc Farley's face was purple, but it was nothing compared to Merrie's.

"I think your concoction's making him delirious, Doc," she said, swiping the back of her nightgown out of his grasp. "Either that, or he's just naturally a sewer snipe."

"You two know each other?"

"No," Merrie said rather quickly.

"Certainly do," the man said just as quickly. "We're acquainted. Now, Doc, get me some more of that firewater and leave me and Legs here to get better at it."

Doc Farley laughed. "You're a sick fool, Mr. Smith, but at least you got spirit. Any man that can ask for a drink when he's weak with fever, that's the kind of man I'm not ashamed to sit down with, no siree, Mr. Smith."

"His name's Delancy," Merrie said in disgust.

"That so, mister?" the doctor asked, completely indifferent either way.

"Seems so. But get me something to drink, will you? I'm fair dying of fever."

"Merrie, girl," Doc Farley said, easing himself into the chair next to the bed. "You heard Mr. Smith. Fetch up some of your daddy's whiskey and a bucket of cold water. Since we got to work, we might as well enjoy it."

"I'll not be part of your idiocy. You'll probably kill him before his fever has a chance to. And let it be on your head. I'm tired, and I'm going to bed."

"Aw, Merrie, now, don't be like that," Doc Farley groaned.

"Is this a private party or can anyone join in?" Liza said, suddenly appearing at the door.

Merrie jerked around. Her stepmother stood there, her long red hair a thick tumble of curls about her almost naked shoulders and her slinky nightgown, scarcely covered by a long, frothy shell-pink shawl, showing off her supple body in an enticing, scandalous way. Doc Farley's brows disappeared into his receding hairline.

The gunslinger seemed not even to notice the alluring

picture the redhead made, but Merrie wasn't fooled for a minute. He was probably used to seeing Liza in much less.

She threw her filthiest look at them all and brushed past her stepmother, her chin firmly in the air.

"Good night, dear," Liza said silkily.

It was only after she had calmed down, quieted her racing anger, that Merrie realized that Liza had been wearing riding boots under her pale chiffon nightgown! What is more, they had been damp with dew. She had definitely felt the wetness on her bare feet as she passed her stepmother in the doorway.

How intriguing. Liza had clearly been out of doors, but why? Merrie frowned into the gathering dawn gloom, but when she finally fell asleep, she was not any closer to the answer.

A LOUD COMMOTION woke her. She was not surprised that it was the lecherous Delancy man creating it. There was a whole lot of stomping and cursing, then she heard Sonna's gravelly voice raised in protest.

"Well, just you die then, and when you come on crying 'bout it, don't expect no sympathy from me."

Merrie heard some dark, rumbling answer, then a door slammed closed, hard enough to shake the walls. She dressed in a hurry.

Really, she had to get this dreadful man out of the main house, even if she couldn't have him thrown off Spur property. If his fever had abated, she would overrule Liza's directions and have him taken out to the bunkhouse. His mere presence was like a burr under her saddle.

She was damned if she was going to allow Liza and the gunslinger to be left alone all day long while she was out working.

Down the hall, Sonna was bundling dirty linens and collecting empty buckets. She was muttering and grumbling twenty to the dozen, her ample backside wiggling in agitation. When she finally thumped her way into Ash's room, Merrie hurried by. If Sonna saw her, Merrie would have to stop and listen to a long litany of whatever it was Mr. Delancy had done to displease her. Not that it was surprising. The man could irritate a holy statue, and Sonna was not known for her patience.

Merrie knocked on the spare room door, but she did not wait for permission to enter.

Kyle Delancy was sitting on the bed struggling to get himself dressed. He had managed to pull his pants on, much to her relief, but they were not fastened yet. He had one boot on. His right arm was hooked into his shirt, but this movement was clearly causing him a great deal of pain, and he was panting with the exertion. He looked up sharply at Merrie. His devastating looks sent her pulse soaring, much to her absolute disgust.

"Come to give me a hand, Legs?" he said, chortling very softly at her blush. He didn't much like people barging in on him uninvited, especially when he didn't have his guns handy, but then these were very unusual circumstances. Doc had intimated that he could thank Merrie Sinclair for his life. Her prompt action in bringing him to Sonna had saved him. It wasn't every day a man got saved by a golden, long-legged temptress. And that was what she was, even though she wasn't aware of it yet.

He watched her hover uncertainly at the door of his room, as if she didn't trust him for an instant, and he knew damn well she didn't. He had an urge to play with her, tease her a little . . . She was so serious about everything, and nervous, too.

And she certainly wasn't immune to him. Her flustered, wide-eyed gaze was a dead giveaway. It wasn't vanity that prompted him to believe this. He knew very well his appeal for the opposite sex, and had for a long time. He did not lack for female companionship, but he preferred urbane women who understood his rules and played by them.

And they were simple rules: no marriage, no pregnancy, no wandering.

Exclusivity, along with his fastidious nature, meant he did not dally, nor had he accepted unfaithfulness from any of the women he'd courted over the years. The sophisticated ladies he saw seemed to accept his conditions, for he had no lack of companionship. Problem was, he found that he got bored quite often.

Strange, but this unsophisticated cowhand seemed to spark his interest in an unnerving way. Merrie's very inexperience was appealing. She reminded him of spring or very early summer, her vivid sexuality just awakening.

"You going to stand there and stare all day, or you going to help?"

His drawl, the magnetic lure of his deep voice seemed to entice Merrie into the room. She had thought to deliver her orders from the doorway, but her feet somehow took her inside. The room smelled of whiskey, expensive whiskey, and him! It was as if an invisible fist caught her by her shirtfront and dragged her toward the devilish gunslinger. He sat sardonically, one brow lifted in question, awaiting her, as if he'd expected her all along.

"Mr. Delancy—"

"Kyle."

"Mr. De—"

"What a shame, Legs. I didn't realize you had difficulty hearing. You should have said something." He shouted at her as if she were in the next room, mouthing the words with exaggerated care: *"The name's Kyle."*

But Merrie would not be baited. "I'll call you what I like. For the sake of politeness, I choose Mr. Delancy, for now. If your fever's gone, I want you to move to the bunkhouse immediately."

"Can't help you there, Legs. Need bedrest—Doc said so. Bunkhouse is too noisy, too much activity going on. A man can't get his rest there without inconveniencing others."

"You do not strike me as the type of man who would care about inconveniencing others, Mr. Delancy," Merrie said softly. "But you will hear what I have to say because this ranch is mine to run while my father is away, and you will move yourself to the bunkhouse. Do I make myself clear?"

He allowed a lazy smile to touch his sensual mouth. "I really unnerve you, don't I, Legs? Now, why is that, do you think?"

The flush on Merrie's cheeks deepened. She had to swallow, and her throat felt dry and constricted. Confound the man, but he really did get under her skin. It was his all-knowing smile that drove her to distraction. As if he knew just how to rile her, as if he somehow understood the workings of her mind. It absolutely infuriated her. Worse yet, she was starkly aware that Matt never made her feel this deep-seated trepidation. It was an uncomfortable realization.

"Stop calling me that," she finally said. She was angry with herself because she wanted simply to ignore his pet name for her. He used it deliberately. It was an intimate overture, a rude intrusion, as if familiarity with her body gave him license to speak about it.

"I'll call you what I want, for politeness sake, of course," he said and grinned, throwing her words back at her.

"Just get yourself to the bunkhouse. Better yet, get off the Spur altogether."

He looked appraisingly at her, rubbing his stubby chin in deliberation. "Tell me, Legs, do you often visit men in their bedrooms, or is it just that you can't keep away from me?"

"This is not a visit," she said, her voice brittle with anger. "Believe me, my only wish, as far as you're concerned, is for your absence."

He chuckled as her long-held temper finally snapped. "Ah, Legs, here I was thinking that you came to help. Guess I'll just have to manage by myself."

Slowly, he stood then, his powerful muscles rippling as he grasped the brass bedrail to steady himself. He struggled to stand, his shirt sagging around his narrow waist, his pants gaping provocatively about his hips, a knowing look soliciting her comments.

Merrie could not take her eyes from the fascinating line of dark curling hair that snaked down from his muscular abdomen and vanished in shadowy secret beneath the gaping waistband of his denim pants. Devil take him, he was ungodly handsome!

TEXAS KISS 59

The silky length of his hair was dark and lustrous and echoed the blue-black gleam in his seductive eyes. He was wickedly dark; his aura, married to midnight and mysterious warmth, stirred an aberrant sensation somewhere in the area of her lungs, or was it her belly?

Wherever, whatever, she disliked him all the more because his gorgeous, deceitful exterior hid a rotting, festering interior; he was a repository for iniquity.

Her eyes were as big as saucers, wide and green like clear, cool water under shadowy willows. Merrie Sinclair, thought Kyle with a silent chuckle, looked fascinated and terrified all at once.

Kyle realized that he had better sit down for a moment. The delectable Miss Sinclair was beginning to effect his equilibrium, he thought with a smattering of amusement and healthy dose of reproof.

Maybe he did still have a touch of fever. He certainly felt inordinately weak. And then, maybe he simply needed a woman—it had been some time.

He was too bemused to notice how uncharacteristic it was for him to work at charming a woman. Usually it was the other way around. He was only aware of the fact that the polished beauties who usually vied for his attention seemed suddenly brassy and phony by contrasted to Merrie's winsome charm.

Perhaps he would indulge himself just a little. After all, men died of fever, didn't they? And then, she looked so hungrily at him. The least he could do was oblige.

"Come here, Legs," he said, his voice very soft.

When she didn't move, he winced dramatically and leaned back against the pillows. "My back is bleeding again," he lied.

Merrie sprang forward, as he had known she would. In one swift movement, he caught her deftly with one arm, brought her against his broad chest, and covered her open mouth with his. He kissed her softly, just trailing his tongue over the succulent insides of her mouth, her teeth, in silky sweeps that teased and promised, but did not threaten. Her small protest was haphazard and quickly dismissed. He held her fast in his strong embrace, but he smoothed the tight muscles of her neck in languid strokes, giving her the illusion that she could move away anytime she wanted.

She tasted, as he remembered, like fruit, all lush and newly picked, her untutored tongue trying to imitate his. Her lips were opulent in texture like the exotic liquors he had sampled on special occasions. Her scent filled his mind with erotic images, enhanced by the unforgivable length of her legs splayed over his taut body, the abrasion of her luxuriant breasts pressing against his chest.

Merrie's long, golden body was a dangerous threat to his control, he knew, but he kept on telling himself that he would enjoy just one more minute . . . just one more. She seemed acquiescent, and although her daring surprised him a little, for she was obviously fearful of him, he certainly wasn't going to stop now.

His encircling arms brought her closer. His kiss deepened. His tongue thrust deeply, too, in rampant simulation of an exploding desire that swept into his already fevered blood. Kyle felt as if he had been overtaken by a sudden prairie fire. His arousal was rigid against her vulnerable belly.

He knew she could feel it, for she went very still, her breathing stopped as the tattoo of her heart erupted in a frantic rhythm. And when his hands closed over her bottom and pulled her hard against his urgent erection, she gave a soft whimper of fright and pleasure both, and he felt his own heart jump in his chest.

It would have been so easy. They were lying on a soft bed, after all, and Kyle's experience played heavily against Merrie's naïveté. He could roll her over onto her back with no more than a soft push and have her naked under him in an instant. The surge of lust in his blood was all but overwhelming, searing in its heat, eradicating responsibility, consequence . . .

She was gold and ripe, breathless and out of her depth. And he knew it. Bloody hell! He groaned as his overzealous conscience came catapulting forward.

Merrie Sinclair was off limits.

TEXAS KISS 61

He had a job to do for her father, he told himself. But it was more than that.

Innocence such as hers meant commitment. And Kyle Delancy had no time for that. He fancied his life just as it was, thanks.

"You're very taxing on a man's resolve, Legs," he growled, frustration edging his voice. His lids were heavy, his long, thick lashes drooped languidly over the midnight-blue of his gaze. "Thing is, I don't like poaching in another man's domain," he added with brutal effect when she seemed unwilling to move.

That did it! Merrie pulled away from him, rigid from shock, mortified by her wanton capitulation. Her golden skin was rosy with shame; her mouth, wet and trembling, seemed swollen and tender, as were her sensibilities.

Devil hell, but he was right to rebuke her. What kind of moral fiber did she possess? Apparently none. A sick, overwhelming repugnance for herself, and for the dark gunfighter, roiled up in her stomach like bile.

Very deliberately she rose. She straightened her ponytail, which had half slipped out of its corded tie, turning her back on the gunslinger, who now regarded her in unsmiling silence as she worked the heavy coil of gold back into place.

"I'm leaving for a day or two, and I want you gone from the Silver Spur by the time I return, Mr. Delancy."

He didn't answer her. She reached for the door before she turned to face him, as if she didn't quite trust herself to stand without support. Her legs did not feel steady at all. "Did you hear me?"

Kyle swept his eyes down her length, pausing meaningfully on her swollen breasts, their hard crests evident through the thin cotton of her shirt, before looking up and into her storm-tossed green eyes. Merrie felt her heart hurtle into her throat, because it felt as if he had touched where his eyes rested.

"Somehow, I don't think you mean that, Legs." It was perverse of him to taunt her, he knew, but the words were out before he could stop them.

"I certainly do. As you reminded me, I am engaged to be married." She was not surprised that he knew. Hollow Creek was a town that liberally "shared" information about everyone's business.

"Congratulations, Legs," he said, smiling sardonically again. However, a sudden and unbidden image of the rutting couple in the house on End Lane came to him then. The woman with Matt Cheston had been Liza, but somehow she was transposed into Merrie. Merrie with long legs splayed wide . . . writhing . . . thrash—

Kyle slumped onto the bed. He must be feverish, he thought.

Merrie rushed forward again as the gunslinger fell back, almost hitting his head on the brass rail of the headboard. She pushed him against the pillows with a grunt. "Stupid man," she gasped.

He watched her through slitted blue eyes, lethargic, unable to do much else other than peruse the elegant line of her smooth jaw, her neck, smell the resplendent scent of magnolia that seemed to emanate from her lush, golden body.

Frustration was unknown to him, at least this kind of frustration. He never played where he could not enjoy consummation, if he desired it. His groin pulsed with heat. He was disconcerted and uncomfortable. It made him mean.

There was only one decision to make. He had better scare her off. And do it well. Those vulnerable eyes all aflame with a need she didn't even understand, her ripeness; it was more than even his rigid self-control could handle.

He pulled her down on top of him. It wasn't difficult, because she was not expecting it. She immediately began to struggle, but he caught her against him and ground his hips into hers aggressively. His breath now was harsh as he sought out her tender lips, the fullness of her breasts. . . . He was invading, overwhelming her untutored senses.

"Know what, Legs? I think you want me . . ." His voice was low, harsh. He heard the panic and outrage in her gasp, but his lack of discipline riled him, she riled him . . . He didn't know why, so he pushed on tauntingly. "That's why you keep visiting my bedroom. I think you like the danger, kind of gives you a thrill . . . down here . . ."

One of his hands snaked down between her legs; his long fingers cupped her and squeezed softly.

Merrie cried out and wrenched herself from his arms. She was visibly furious, flushed. "You're despicable, you devil hell," she managed to sputter before she raced out of the room, slamming the door after her with a resounding bang.

Yet she still heard him chuckle. The sound was sexy and low, and the goose bumps on her arms rose even higher.

EIGHT

For a moment Merrie rested her back against the solid door, trying to make sense of her catapulting emotions. The man was intolerable, disgusting—a threat to her family. What was it about the man that he managed to bait her so masterfully? Merrie was rarely rude to other people. She had a high tolerance for stubbornness. She had to, really, having worked with men since she was knee-high to a cob.

Putting up with the masculine prejudices against taking orders, or following directions from females, had taught her a great deal about keeping her temper in check. She had found that a cool, calm demeanor in the heat of difficult situations had won her more praise than giving vent to her temper, even when letting loose would have been satisfying.

Stupidity and bigotry abounded when it came to giving a female her due. Patience and an innate belief in her own abilities helped her handle the day-to-day problems she had encountered in the man's world of cattle ranching. It had not been easy, but she had persevered. The Silver Spur had enjoyed its most successful year to date under her leadership.

Yet this one man seemed able to confound her. It was undeniably true that he unnerved her. She disliked the very idea of Kyle Delancy. A roving gunslinger, ready to sign on with the highest bidder. That was bad enough, but he was her stepmother's lover.

So how was it she had allowed him to kiss her? More than a kiss really, it had been an intimate and dangerous foray into the secret depths of her soul. Until now she had not been aware of the existence of her soul . . . at least metaphorically speaking.

It made her tremble to think about the bewildering, fiery

sensations of being in his arms, the overwhelming surge of madness that had obliterated all sensible thoughts from her head. And what about her principles? What about simple right and wrong?

Kyle Delancy was just wrong from start to finish. It proved, she thought and nodded grimly to herself, that evil such as his corrupted absolutely.

Yes, that must be it, she thought, relieving herself of wrongdoing. After all, everyone knew she was an upstanding, honest person. There was no way Merrie Sinclair would do anything so utterly reprehensible as to dally with her stepmother's lover. His chicanery had expropriated her will . . .

From now on, she vowed, pushing open the kitchen door, she would be prepared. Iniquity such as his would find no purchase in Merrie Sinclair.

"Merrie, you just march yourself right back uppystairs and tell that gunslinger of yours that I don't want none of his mulish orneriness," Sonna announced as Merrie came into the kitchen. The Spur's housekeeper had obviously been waiting for her. "I won't have him die on me, just because he's too stubborn to let me change his dressing. There's no telling what misfortune that could bring down. Could ruin all my preserves . . . sour the milk . . ."

It was the very worst thing to say to Merrie just then, and trust Sonna, she would manage to say it. Merrie turned on her with the speed of a striking snake.

"He's not mine," she shouted and slammed out of the back door. But it was not her day. No sooner had she taken a step into the yard than she saw her fiancé cantering up in a dusty cloud.

Good Lord, not now! She moaned and felt guilty heat flood her cheeks. Matt Cheston grinned down at her from his horse.

"Hi there, Merrie honey," he said, dismounting and looping the reins over the porch rail. He sauntered up to where she stood and bent to kiss her. Merrie jerked away from him as if he had raised his hand to strike her. It had been instinctive, uncalculated on her part, but the instant she realized what she had done, she felt even more wretchedly guilty.

"Hang it all, what's up, honey? You all right? You look kinda flushed."

Merrie groaned inside and felt her already burning cheeks catch fire. She wondered desperately if Matt could smell the gunslinger on her.

"I'm fine, fine. Just rushing, you know, sorry." She reached up on tiptoes to brush a kiss on his cheek, ignoring the puzzled look in his eyes. "I just didn't expect you this early in the day," she finished lamely.

"It's after ten, Merrie. I came 'cause I heard you had news about your dad."

Merrie frowned. She hadn't really had time to ride down the valley to the Lazy D and tell Matt about Ash's return. She suffered another pang of guilt. "I was going to send you a message, Matt. Things have been kind of . . . hectic round here. I'm sorry."

Matt grinned ruefully and put an arm about her shoulders. "I heard all about your excitement. As I rode in, I saw Buck. Now, you want to tell me all about your gunslinger?"

"He's not mine," Merrie snapped. She suddenly felt close to tears. "Sorry, Matt . . ."

"That's three sorries in a row. Hey now, don't be upset. Come along, tell me what's got you all fired up. Ain't seen you this way before, Merrie."

Merrie looked up gratefully. He was so understanding, such a gentleman . . . unlike . . . unlike that devil hell upstairs.

Matt guided Merrie around to the front of the house. French doors fronted the rambling, two-story house on both the upper and lower levels. There was a narrow balcony upstairs and a wide wraparound porch on the ground floor, with wonderful views of the surrounding river valley. The porch was deep and cool in the heat of summer, full of golden mellowness in the fall. There were two swings hanging from its mint-green painted ceiling. Matt led Merrie to one. They sat comfortably against the striped cushions, and he put his arm about Merrie's shoulders.

Matt was a big man, tall and stately, some twelve years her senior. His dark brown hair and dark eyes were decidedly his best features, while his nose and mouth were rather thin, giving his face a forbidding, even harsh, appearance. Altogether, though, he was a handsome man, and Merrie had been enormously flattered when he asked to court her. Everyone had said he was the best catch in town. What is more, Matt had seemed agreeable to waiting the stipulated time Ash had set for them. Merrie was only eighteen, and Ash told her that she had to be twenty to gain the inheritance left by her Uncle Grenville.

"I heard the man was shot up on the pass. Did you see who shot him?"

Merrie shook her head. "Not well enough to identify anyone. But there was someone up in the crags. Of course he'd vanished by the time Spiker climbed up."

"Well, you can hardly expect the gunslinger to tell you more. Even if he knows why he was shot, his type never talks."

"I'm not interested in his sordid life. I want him gone, that's all I want."

Matt looked surprised. "That's not right hospitable of you, honey," he said, swinging gently to and fro. "What's got into you?"

"Nothing. I don't like him, is all," she said petulantly. It was not really acceptable, and she knew it, to abjure the unwritten code of hospitality. Texans prided themselves on it.

Matt laughed and pulled her closer. He tipped up her chin and rested his dark, sparkling eyes on her golden face. "No one is asking you to marry the guy, Merrie honey. But you can't turn out an injured man." He kissed her then, lightly, on the mouth, his warm lips brushing gently over hers.

He kissed her like a gentleman. He did not invade. He did not force her mouth open, steal her breath.

Merrie felt the panic rise steadily in her palpitating heart. Nothing! There was nothing in his kiss that warmed her, touched her . . . like . . . Good Lord, no. Why was she doing this? Why was she making these dreadful comparisons?

Almost desperately, she put her arms about his neck, bringing her body closer to his, trying to evoke some of the stirring sensations she had experienced in Kyle Delancy's arms.

TEXAS KISS 69

"How touching—young love," purred the familiar voice of her stepmother. Liza came through the French doors of the breakfast room, a dainty teacup in her hand.

Merrie jerked out of Matt's arms, embarrassed and disconcerted by her own failure to elicit a response from her fiancé or herself. She was also annoyed at her stepmother's intrusion.

"How tasteless, to display yourselves in such a public place, *children*," Liza said, taking a wicker chair across from them. As always, she was perfectly dressed, meticulously groomed. Her sun-yellow morning dress was flounced with pale green and white ribbons. She looked fresh and young and, Merrie thought with a touch of surprise, extremely angry.

"My apologies, dearest Liza," said Matt with a charming smile. "Sometimes, you know, we forget where we are. I haven't seen Merrie for several weeks."

He left it unsaid that while it might be unsuitable for him to be kissing his fiancé on the front porch, it was highly inappropriate for her to be chastising him as if he were the child she had called him. At thirty, he was closer to her age than to Merrie's.

"I had thought you more temperate than that. After all, you seem in no hurry to wed," Liza said, watching Merrie's reaction over the rim of her teacup.

Matt laughed and pulled Merrie closer. He smiled warmly at her and gave her shoulder a squeeze. "It's what the girl's papa wants, and that's good enough for me. So long as she's my little wife at the end of the wait, that's plenty good enough."

Merrie felt herself cringe. Why did he make it sound as if she were an idiot without a mind of her own? Rising, she smiled at Matt, or tried to. She also attempted to ignore the smoldering discontent that had erupted unbidden in her heart ever since . . . when? She did not want to examine that.

"Thanks for coming round," she said. "I've got to get moving. We're busy herding to the winter pastures."

"How long will you be gone?" Merrie did not notice the look he sent Liza. He made no attempt to rise.

"I doubt we'll be back before Saturday." She was thinking

that a few days away from the odious man upstairs in the yellow bedroom would not be a bad thing.

Matt chuckled. "So you'll camp out. Rough and ready, that's my girl."

"She's certainly outfitted for it," Liza chimed in sweetly.

"Will you be back in time to go meet Ash?" Matt asked.

Merrie threw him a puzzled look. "He's not due in till next week Tuesday," she told him. "I thought I'd mentioned that."

"Nope," Matt said and shrugged. "But it makes no nevermind. Kiss me good-bye then, honey, and you get on your way," he said, reaching up for her, his charming smile directed at Liza. "Naturally, that's with your permission, ma'am," he said.

"By all means, sir, so long as you keep it mannerly," Liza simpered.

"I'm a gentleman, ma'am. I wouldn't think of anything else."

"Just you remember then, you're supposed to be charming."

"Ma'am, with the Sinclair ladies around, it's nearly impossible not to be."

"You Southern gentlemen!" Liza tittered, "I swear, you do take lessons in gallantry."

Liza was the epitome of dulcet girlishness if she thought she was getting the proper attention. Merrie turned away in disgust. Then she caught sight of a movement behind the flimsy curtains billowing gently over the French doors.

The gunslinger stood there watching. She couldn't fathom his expression. His gaze was riveted upon the bantering couple. And then his eyes collided with hers. Dark and secretive, they nevertheless commandeered her will. She felt an unnamed shiver slide down her spine. Without knowing why, she instinctively knew that he did not want the others to know he was there, and for some reason she complied with his unstated demand. With an effort, she pulled her gaze from him.

"I really must go," she murmured, and hurried down the steps of the porch.

NINE

"AT LAST!" MERRIE cried, jumping up and racing to the edge of the platform. The sound of a train whistle cascaded down out of the blue afternoon sky. The train had been two days and seven hours late, and Merrie had almost worn a path alongside the ticket office in sheer aggravation.

Jem Tech wiped his forehead in relief. "Not a moment too soon," he grumbled. Merrie had been driving him, and everybody else, crazy the past few days. He threw Rob, one of the ranch hands, a consoling look as Merrie rapped out a dozen orders—all of which she had delivered several times before.

"Bring the wagon up close, Spiker. Backwards, we need it reversed, flatbed nearest the train. Rob, you got those blankets ready? What about the cushions? I knew we should have brought more. It's not going to be comfortable enough for Ash, I just know it. That's a long trip we have to make."

"Miss Merrie, everything is jus' fine. You know that it is," Rob said, tilting his hat back on his head.

Spiker jumped down from the riding seat and squinted up at the sky. The sun was westering already. "Hope you ain't fixing on riding back to the Spur this afternoon, Miss Merrie. It's late, and I'm sure he'll be plum tuckered out."

"Let's see what Ash wants to do. Oh, why can't they hurry up and get here," she said breathlessly.

"Look there," Rob said, pointing out across the water.

At last they could all see the great plumes of smoke popping up into the sky. With a clatter and din, the train rumbled across the elevated bridge and finally, finally came to a hissing, clanking halt at Hollow Creek's station.

Passengers alighted, and conductors began moving baggage from the carriages. Then a handsome woman of about forty came down the steps. She was impeccably dressed. Not a crease or rumple marred her blue traveling cape or well-made bonnet. Over her arm she carried a small brown bag and a folded travel rug.

Gillian Bishop—Merrie registered whom she must be—the nurse, from the Strafford Clinic. She had accompanied Ash from New York to live with them for a time.

With a rush of pure terror as much as God-given joy, Merrie watched as Ashton Sinclair was finally carried down off the steps of the train by an attendant. It was almost impossible to recognize this emaciated, gray gentleman as the robust, vigorous man who was her father, but she knew him. Green eyes, once so like her own, stared right back at her out of a face ravaged by illness, their light almost extinguished. Her heart cracked with grief for his suffering. He had lost more than a third of his weight, aged ten years or more, and come close to dying. But he had defeated the odds, he had returned.

Merrie felt a surge of gratitude for that. She whispered her thanks to God and wrapped welcoming arms about Ash's frail shoulders.

"Welcome home, Ash," she said, her voice barely audible for the clog of tears in her throat. "Welcome."

"HOLD JUST A minute, Spiker," Merrie called as they cleared Wolf Fang Pass. She urged Sonnet around to the back of the buckboard while Spiker brought it to a halt. Ash Sinclair sat propped up in the bed built into the back.

Merrie felt her throat tighten with threatened tears, but she managed to swallow them down, as she had done since his arrival in Hollow Creek yesterday afternoon. She could not get used to the fact that her strong, rugged father, wasted dreadfully by his illness, had lost the power of speech. Nor could he walk or even sit for very long without exhausting himself. But he was alive. Against all odds, he was alive.

"Thought you might like your first look from up here, Ash," she said. She met his grateful look with a smile. "I moved the last herd up to the fifty last week. As you can see, we decided that the dipping trough was too far out and we moved it in to within several yards of the creek. That way we can sluice off more easily. We also cut a road through from the pastures there directly to the pass. That way we don't have to take the herds all around the bend of the river. It saves a full day."

Merrie watched Ash gaze straight down into the lush, broad valley, to where the whitewashed house with its deep wraparound porch peeped out from behind the ring of trees. This was home. The misty gray-green land stretched out flat and open on either side of the river.

It was all his, as far as the eye could see. Beyond the valley's bend, where sky and land blurred together, the walls of the canyon closed in to a width of only a few miles, and tall mesas in rust and coral stalked to the horizon. There, purple shadows rippled and hawks rose on lazy updrafts.

Ash Sinclair and his brother Grenville had been farsighted and energetic men. They had made a fortune in mining, but both had hankered after the wide open spaces of Texas and had returned from the gold mines of California to wrest this vast cattle ranch and the town of Hollow Creek from the barren land.

It was the kind of place they had only dreamed about as children. They had left Texas penniless and made a miraculous strike that had given them more wealth than they ever imagined possible. They returned with their fortune in gold to the hidden valley they had discovered long ago by accident.

Chased off the trail by a band of Comanche, Grenville and Ash had taken shelter in the crags of a nameless tumble of hills, only to discover the narrow cleft leading down to the canyon floor.

Now Ash was returning to the home he had built, to the empire he had carved; he had not expected ever to see it again, Merrie knew. Her father's eyes glazed, and she had to look away herself, knowing she would be sobbing any minute, the emotions were so profound. She was so very grateful for his life.

"I hope you're pleased with what we've done, Father," she

murmured. The pain in her chest grew as she watched him struggle with his emotions. She rarely called him Father.

He was very weak still. It had taken them the good part of the day just to travel in from Hollow Creek. His condition had forced them to spend the night in town. It had seemed to Merrie that she would never get him home. With a sudden thrill of fear she wondered if Loring Strafford had sent his patient home to die. She looked quickly at Gillian Bishop, as if she held the answer. The competent Miss Bishop was an Englishwoman. She never complained and seemed always cool and in control; her very presence was reassuring, solid.

As they wound down into the valley, some half-dozen cowboys streamed out from under the cross-beamed entry to the ranch and raced toward them. Merrie could see Buck Peterson at the rear of the bunch. The old man moved painfully slowly today. Merrie felt a surge of guilt at having left him in charge in her absence. She knew it would hurt his pride, but she simply couldn't allow it anymore. The man was past his prime; it was too much for him.

As painful as the realization was, one look at Buck when he finally rode up confirmed her decision. He looked dreadful.

Still he greeted his boss with gladness, and soon the whole group of dusty men were riding beside them, laughing and welcoming their boss, their good-natured ribbing about Ash being too darn lazy to ride brought a tiny hint of a smile to her father's face. If anyone was shocked at his appearance, they hid it well, and Merrie was grateful for that.

Buck nudged his horse in line with Merrie's. "'Bout time you showed up, Bossman," he said to Ash, beaming all over his ugly face. "We began to think you'd been ruined by them Easterners and didn't want no part of us no more."

"You sound as if you have something against Easterners, sir," sniffed Gillian Bishop with a disapproving look at the foreman. "It occurs to me to wonder just how many Easterners you have ever met."

Buck's thin mouth dropped to his chin as he gawked up at the prim woman in her spotless traveling suit. Everyone else was covered in dust, but not the remarkable Miss Bishop.

TEXAS KISS 75

"Ah, I, ah, beg your pardon, ma'am," Buck mumbled.

"Granted," said Gillian before he could utter another thing. She pulled her watch out of her pocket and clucked her tongue. Then, turning to Spiker, she said, "I'm certain you can get a bit more spirit out of your team, Mr. Spiker. It is past time to get Mr. Sinclair settled indoors."

Buck dipped his head toward Merrie. "Who's she?" he whispered.

"Ash's nurse." Merrie confided, "and we all obey her."

"Don't blame you. Who'd want to mess with that? Wonder how Liza will get on with her."

Merrie shot him a dark look at the mention of her stepmother. She had thought of little else the past few days. Liza and that shameless gunslinger. How to shield her father from the sordid mess? "He's gone, right?" she asked. It was more confirmation than question. There was no need to stipulate which "he" she meant; they both knew well enough. Buck had been issued specific orders to get rid of the gunslinger.

Buck scrunched his shoulders in negation. "It's like this, Miss Merrie . . ."

She felt like wailing. She thought she had seen the last of Kyle Delancy. "Oh, Buck, no," she said with great disappointment. "I don't believe it."

"Well, it's not what you're thinking Miss Merrie. It was . . . well, there was a small problem. A bunch of rustlers up at the fifty and well . . . with Spiker and Rob gone off with you and five others out on the range and all, I was shorthanded. Mr. Delancy . . ."

"Buck," she cried softly at the foreman's use of his name. There was no disguising the respect, even awe, in his voice.

"I know, I know what you said, Miss Merrie, but I ain't never seen anything like it. If I hadn't been there, I wouldn't've believe it. He had them rustlers tracked and caught, roped and down to the sheriff's before I even got myself into the saddle. He's good, Miss Merrie, hell's fire good. And faster than a spitting snake."

"There was shooting?"

"Uh-huh. But not for long."

"Cold-blooded killer . . ."

"There was no one killed. Not for want of trying, though. One of them trash was a might trigger happy 'afore he seen Mr. Delancy's draw."

Merrie sent him a sideling look, her voice dipped in disgust. "And I'm sure Liza gave him a hero's welcome. No doubt she found all kinds of excuses why he should stay."

The foreman shrugged awkwardly. "Well now, Miss Merrie, you know I don't know nothing about Miss Liza."

They drew nearer the entryway to the ranch. A framed timber arch marked the entrance. The long, wobbly shadow from the westering sun slanted over the husk-colored ground, elongating the image of the large spur-shaped emblem that was centered over the crossbeams.

Kyle Delancy was there, leaning against the supports, his arms crossed over his chest, one booted foot crossed over the other. His stance was casual. Merrie couldn't shake the idea that he was waiting there on purpose.

A stripe of shadow cut him in two, hiding most of his face. But Merrie could see his mouth. It was a sensual mouth, sculptured as if by a craftsman. His dark, shadowed cheeks and chin made his mouth look fuller, deeper in hue than she remembered. He needed a shave.

Suddenly a wild image popped into her head of him standing before the shaving mirror, early in the morning, scraping that stubble from his face with sleek, competent strokes. She envisioned her fingers skimming his jaw to test the closeness of his shave. She imagined the scent of his shaving soap lingering on her where she touched him. His jaw was strong and well defined—masculine. The tips of her fingers tingled expectantly.

For heaven's sake! her shocked mind interposed, get ahold of yourself.

She sucked in her breath, furious with herself and dismayed that his mere presence was so disturbing. She hated him, she assured herself, even as she felt his intense perusal glide over every inch of her. Surely he was a master at the art of seduction that he could damage her armor without seeming to attack. It was unconscionable behavior. She had no doubt that he did it deliberately.

Well, it might work on her flimsy-minded stepmother, but it wouldn't work on her—not ever again. She'd not allow it! The very first thing on the agenda was to have Kyle Delancy brought to her father's study.

Buck Peterson might not be able to get rid of him, but she would! It was way past time. But a quick glance at the sinking sun told her that it would have to wait for tomorrow.

She did not acknowledge the tip of his hat. With her spine absolutely ramrod straight, her eyes fixed in front of her, Merrie followed the buckboard up the wide track that led to the house.

It was a relief to see Liza waiting there, even if only for appearance' sake. Merrie had not been sure she would bother. It was sometimes difficult to know what Liza considered important. Today, though, she was dressed for the occasion, flounced and frilled to the nines in pale chiffon and yards of ecru lace. She brought her kerchief delicately to her nose in a gesture of emotion (Merrie wasn't quite sure which emotion) and then glided down the stairs to where her husband sat propped up in his makeshift bed in the back of the buckboard.

"Oh, Ashton," she whispered. Clearly she was shocked at his condition. Her pale face blanched to a deathly white. "I can't quite believe you're here."

Ash reacted passively, but Merrie saw his fists ball instinctively at his sides, and he drew back rather quickly when Liza bent her head to kiss his cheek.

"I expect your weak condition has temporarily robbed you of manners, Ashton, but you could at least say hello," Liza sniffed.

"I've no doubt he'd have plenty to say—" Merrie said in a fury, but before she could say another word, the nurse interrupted.

She stepped down briskly from the buckboard, shook out her

immaculate skirts, and began removing Ash's blankets. "We'll all have plenty to say soon enough, for Mr. Sinclair will thrive now that he's home. But for now, it's bedtime. He's tired out and so, I might add, am I."

"You, I take it, are the nurse," Liza said, making it sound as if "nurse" were the equivalent of "insect."

The indomitable Miss Bishop terminated Liza's rudeness with flamboyant brevity. "And you're the wife?" she answered in exactly the same tone. Then she swept Liza with a brittle smile. "I'll need hot water and two soft flannels and a large towel. Can't abide small kerchiefs that masquerade as towels, can you? Hot tea, buttered toast, sliced fruit and a small toddy, all on a tray. Think you can manage that in ten minutes? Spiffing, and now you'll show me Mr. Sinclair's bedroom, if you please."

Merrie chuckled at Liza's outraged face as Gillian Bishop took command. The next few days should prove very interesting, Merrie thought. Gillian Bishop obviously had specific idea about how things should be done.

NIGHT HAD FALLEN by the time Merrie made her way through the cool evening, aware that autumn was encroaching fast. She had been busy seeing to the many details that Buck simply couldn't manage anymore: organizing special feed for any ailing calves and cows, seeing to fencing details, ordering supplies for the cowhands who would be setting out to inspect far distant parts of the range.

Up at the house, lamps were lit. There was a steaming basin in the washhouse out back for her to use, clean clothes, and the delicious smell of beef stew in herbs wafting out of the kitchen.

In next to no time, she was deep into her second plate of fragrant stew at Sonna's kitchen table. Ash, she knew, was already settled for the night. Gillian was, too. Merrie had no intention of sharing her welcome-home meal alone with Liza.

She had sent a curt note to the gunslinger instructing him to attend her in her father's office after supper. The thought made her tremble inside and out. She shrugged away the uneasiness, managing to escape Sonna's barrage of chatter, and made her way to the paneled study. It was a warm room cluttered with mementos, dark-chocolate leather furniture, and thick wool rugs over the highly polished oak floors.

As in most of the rooms on the ground floor, recessed French doors opened onto the deep porch that surrounded the house. They were slightly ajar in expectation of the gunslinger's visit, and the curtains moved slightly with the cool night breeze. Two lamps cast soft, golden light over the room.

Merrie settled herself behind the desk and allowed her eye to rove over the satisfying surfaces of the carved brass-and-agate horses that stood along the mantlepiece, on either side of a clumsy-looking clock sitting on a thick marble base. The face of the clock was painted with lurid zodiacal signs. The hour and minute hands were styled respectively after Zeus, rampantly male, and a nude Hera. Ash had won it at his first poker game, so he said, and refused to part with it under any circumstances. It was the only thing both Merrie and Liza agreed upon: it was disgusting. Alongside it were various other bits and pieces Ash had collected: mining picks, a piece of rope entwined with a lock of hair, beaded Comanche armbands.

On the walls there were several watercolor paintings of wild mustangs, and one small oil depicting the wide green valley of Hollow Creek. It had been painted by Merrie's mother, and it hung in the place of honor over the fireplace. Wainscoting in a folded linen pattern ringed the room and gave it a comfortable atmosphere.

Half an hour passed slowly; Merrie's head nodded several times before she jerked herself awake. Finally, the weariness of the road overtook her, and she fell soundly asleep, her head resting on her folded arms on the desk.

She woke with a start. It was late. There was not a sound to be heard. Merrie rubbed her eyes, confused for a moment before she remembered what she had been doing in her father's study.

But the gunslinger had not shown up. Merrie realized that he wasn't coming. Furious, she rose from the chair. For the time being, she was stumped, she knew. It wouldn't do her authority any good if it became generally known that her orders were ignored. She had worked too hard to win the ranch hands' respect to have it all blown away by this refusal to acknowledge her summons.

Delancy had moved out to the bunkhouse. Not in deference to her orders, Merrie knew, but due to the fact that Gillian Bishop now occupied the yellow bedroom.

Refusing to feel the fool, she secured the doors, turned down the lamps, and left. There was nothing for it but go to bed. She would deal with Mr. Delancy in the morning. And this time she would make sure that he was sent packing.

There was not a single light left burning anywhere. Sonna, who usually saw to that kind of thing, must have thought that Merrie had gone to bed. Instead of stumbling about looking for matches and lamps, Merrie felt her way upstairs in the pitch dark. It took her a few stubbed toes and a bunch of colorful adjectives before she located her door.

The room was dark but not completely black. The windows were open, curtains drawn back. A suffused light bathed the room, coming in from the deep starry night outside. The scented air shimmered softly like silver smoke wavering and gliding between the inky shadows.

Merrie sighed, delighted to once again be in her own familiar room. Her comfortable bed beckoned warmly. She pulled the pins from her hair and shook her head, sending the heavy skein tumbling down her back almost to her waist. Then she pulled off her boots, her stockings and skirt. Her simple yoked shirt fell onto the chair, and she loosened the ribbons on her camisole and pantaloons. Then her fingers froze. Her breath hitched in her chest. Her head came up with dizzying speed.

It was the tiniest sound that alerted her. What it was exactly she never knew, but there was no mystery as to who had made it.

Her furious eyes picked him out without any trouble at all. Even though he sat completely engulfed in night shadows, she could see him! It was Kyle Delancy.

Ten

The gunslinger did not move. He lounged amid the icy pastel cushions in her pale-green wicker chair. His long legs rested way out in front of him; his hands were casually crossed on his chest, and his chin rested on his knuckles.

Kyle's demeanor seemed as relaxed as a Sunday picnic, until she saw his eyes. They were riveted upon her, devouring her from across the room, wickedly, heatedly scouring her from top to toe.

"How dare you," she hissed, swiping up the cover from her bed. She held it in front of herself, shaking with fury. "Get out of here, Mr. Delancy. Immediately."

"You invited me up for a meeting. Spiker brought me a message."

"You were supposed to meet me in the study, not here."

"Ah, I got it wrong . . . I assumed you preferred bedrooms, Legs."

"Be damned, you devil . . ." She winced as if the very words were distasteful to her. She took a deep breath. "Why I'm surprised, I don't know. You're an adulterer. Women's bedrooms are the place you like best, I've no doubt."

"Actually, I take care not to involve myself with other men's women," he said softly. Exception—Merrie Sinclair, he thought to himself. He grudgingly admitted that she fascinated him. It irritated the hell out of him, but he was damned if he could summon the resolve to let her alone.

It didn't really make any sense at all.

At Merrie's incredulous look, he added, "It makes for too many difficulties. I like life uncomplicated."

"Well, in that we have a common interest. I hate complications, too. You, Mr. Delancy, are a real complication. So just march yourself right out of here and right off Spur property. I refuse to play hostess to my stepmother's lover."

Kyle frowned. She'd made like accusations before, but as the truth of exactly who her stepmother was dallying with was certain to hurt her, he was reluctant to get into that subject. Instead he smiled at her and patted his knee. "Let me tell you a bedtime story, Legs. And then I'll go."

Merrie tossed her golden head. "I don't bargain with hired gunslingers. Get out or I'll—"

"What? Scream? I don't think you will, 'cause it's not an announcement you want to make right now, is it? Not with your father right down the hall. Wouldn't want the old man thinking I was after his daughter . . . or his wife, perhaps? I could mention that . . ."

Merrie felt the terrible urge to stamp her foot down hard on his toes. He was right. She would love to expose him, but that was the very thing she was trying to avoid, for Ash's sake. "I won't play your childish games. Just leave."

His eyes wafted down the length of her body swathed in her bedspread. A puff of night wind came in through the open window, breathing hints of the autumn to come. Still, the night was warm, softly sensual.

He rose effortlessly and came toward her. "I don't think I'll leave just yet, Legs." His voice was low, like a deep wind instrument, sexy. He caught her by the arm and tugged her toward him. She struggled in his grasp, furiously twisting this way and that. Her covering slipped away in the tussle, and she was torn between screaming with frustration and trying to keep quiet.

Kyle just held her; he exerted no effort. She thrashed about, flailing at him with both fists. He managed to dodge out of the way, his arms were so long.

"You'll tire eventually, you know," he said. And with a sudden jerk he brought her up flat against him, his mouth crushing down on hers.

Merrie squealed as he locked his steely arms about her, imprisoning her hands behind her back and bringing her heaving breasts up against his chest. The feel of her in his arms, even dangerously angry as she was now, was wonderful. She smelled of sunshine and magnolia. He wanted to delve into her warm mouth, ravish the succulent insides. But not yet . . . not yet.

She stopped fighting him; her trembling form sank against him unresisting. His kiss softened; he lifted his mouth, stared into the emerald depth of her wild eyes.

He knew she would bite him if she could. She was furious but stood very still in his arms. His hold was not gentle. Lust almost convulsed him as he felt her satin skin brush against his arm; her full breasts, almost spilling from her camisole, taunted him. It was too much . . . too intense.

"Kiss me, Merrie," he said huskily.

He watched as her eyes widened, her resistance wavered. He felt her tremble once, twice.

She let out a pent-up breath. "You mustn't, Kyle. I'm engaged to be married." Her voice, tight with shame, nevertheless sounded too shaky for her peace of mind.

"He doesn't deserve you."

"And you do, is that it?"

"I know what I do for you," he assured her. "I've felt it in your kiss, in your body's response. You're hungry. You want me, too."

She would deny him, he knew it. He dipped his head once more and captured her mouth. His lips were firmly planted, she could not resist his onslaught. He kissed her neck, swept his tongue around her sensitive ear, making her groan softly. He slid his warm mouth down the valley of her breasts. Her head fell back a little. Encouraged, he pushed the crisp white lace of her camisole aside, and then, his eyes locked on her shocked face, he brought his teeth gently to nibble at the crest of her exposed breast.

Merrie cried softly. Her knees seemed to buckle as he tugged on her nipple. He sucked, softly at first, then more demandingly. His tongue swirled over the stone-hard crest before he took it deeply into his mouth.

Eventually, he brought his mouth back to her velvet lips. This time there was no restraint. His kiss was daring. His tongue thrust into her mouth, mating wildly with hers.

He let go her hands and clasped her to him as if it were impossible to get close enough. He knew she was scared, for he heard her gasp, heard the catch in her pounding heartbeat.

Still he held her captive in his arms. His long legs bracketed her hips; his hands held her bottom possessively, forcing her to feel his aching hardness. Never in his adult life had he felt this demented wildness inside him. Never!

Stop. He heard his own derisive conscience yell at him. Playtime had turned into something quite different. It was no longer amusing.

He squeezed his eyes shut against the crimson glare of lust that had swept uncontrollably through him.

He knew things had gone too far. For a moment he did not know if he could stop himself. His breath rasped in the silence between them as he tried to regain his composure. He had rarely been so quickly aroused as he was now. Christ, he couldn't even kiss the girl without almost . . .

Hell, he was ready to throw her down on the floor, he realized. That unprecedented lack of restraint terrified him. He cast her aside. She stumbled to her knees beside the bed, grabbing the fallen bedspread.

Kyle picked up his hat off the dresser by the door. He turned his head, facing the door still, his body tense, stiff even. He didn't look at her. She could see his sculptured profile, the twitch in his jaw, the flash of his devastating eyes.

"You better keep away from me, Merrie," he said. "You're much too innocent to be playing grown-up games." Gone was the teasing, the casual tone he usually used with her. He was all business, harsh now and cold as winter frost. "I'll go about my business and keep out of your hair. You just make sure you keep out of mine."

"Devil's own! Just get off my property and see that you stay off." She felt hysterical, felt the sob of shame and frustration welling up in her throat and closed her eyes against the burning tears. "And another thing . . . give me my locket . . . my—"

She heard the door closing softly behind him and collapsed onto the bed. There she lay in a tempest of dismay. Her clothes felt tight and hot on her, rubbing her tender skin, chaffing it.

Still she lay, mortified, deeply disgusted with herself, for she had allowed him to touch her again, kiss her again. She had kissed him back. She had loved the feel of his arms about her, caressing her. Loved beyond reason what he did with his mouth . . . Dear God, was it normal to do those things?

"Please . . . please . . . no," she moaned. What was wrong with her? Was she degenerate . . . Was he?

He's Liza's lover, she reminded herself, but a shrill voice taunted her, telling her that she was infatuated with him, no matter that he was her stepmother's lover. The man who could destroy her father.

It was very late before Merrie managed to fall asleep, and then all she dreamed about was the fire of Kyle's touch, scalding her, peeling away her skin with each blazing stroke of his tongue.

Eleven

❦

THE DAY WAS gray, but Merrie was too excited to worry about that. She had not even noticed the gathering gloom on her way to town. Only while she was waiting at the railroad station did she suddenly look up and see fat drops splattering down, here and there.

"Better come inside, Miss Merrie. Train's going to be late," Jem Tech said.

"No thanks, Jem," Merrie said, gazing down across the elevated bridge. She could see nothing out there yet, not even a thin column of smoke. "I have to go down to Linnett's a moment. I'll be back."

Merrie made it to the general store before the rain came pelting down. Even as she whipped through the door, a small crowd followed her inside. Out on Main Street, the sudden showers sent everyone running helter-skelter, coats and jackets held high over their heads.

One very tall shape caught her eye. It was the gunslinger—there was no mistaking him. He ducked in through Dashers' front door with another man, just as the grey sheet of rain cut off her view.

For one startling moment she thought the other man looked like her father, but she knew that was ridiculous. She put it out of her mind entirely. The improvement in Ash's condition over the past few weeks was nothing short of miraculous. He was eating well, taking walks, even talking a little. But he was not up to riding into town just yet. She must have been mistaken.

Ash was back home with Gillian. They were planning a huge party for the following week. More than a party, it would be a grand fete of various entertainments: races and games, dinners, dances, and a huge ox roast. Everyone in Hollow Creek and the vicinity was invited.

In a way she was surprised, and even a little alarmed, to discover that Kyle Delancy hadn't left Hollow Creek yet. What, she wondered, was keeping him here?

Certainly not Liza. Her stepmother hadn't ventured from the ranch since Ash's return. It appeared that she was too busy keeping a wary eye on her husband and Gillian Bishop.

Nor had she seemed greatly perturbed when, one night at dinner, someone had mentioned the gunslinger's name in conjunction with Sheriff Hagan's investigation into the shooting. There were no suspects, no answers. No one expected any—certainly not the gunslinger himself. Consensus was that such men had enemies everywhere. According to Liza, if they got shot at, it was only what they could expect.

Merrie recalled her stepmother's callous opinion with a small shiver. Liza had always been cold, but the last few days, Merrie had sensed a change in Liza—a change for the worse. A finger of apprehension poked her ribs as she made her way to the back of store and the dressmaker's cubicle.

"You want something hot to drink before we begin?" Mrs. Linnett asked, holding out a cup of steaming tea.

The owner's wife, a bespectacled woman with a handsome head of curly brown hair, had been sewing for the ladies of Hollow Creek for twenty-five years. She was an excellent seamstress, a little dour in character, though she was kindness itself.

Merrie took the cup and thanked her. Peggy Linnett had been very fond of Miranda Sinclair, Merrie's mother, and had watched out for Merrie since Miranda's death.

Merrie wasn't very good at choosing fancy clothes. Her experience centered on the shirts and pants she wore for ranch work. These had to be rugged, well-made items for roping and herding, branding and riding the range. Working day and night with longhorns was tough and very physical. She often relied on Peggy to guide her when choosing finer clothes.

TEXAS KISS

"It's ready," Peggy said, pulling aside the curtain over the recess. Merrie's party dress hung there.

"Beautiful, Peggy." Merrie clapped in delight and quickly tried it on.

It really was lovely. A party dress in mint-green voile with forest-green trim and yards of fullness in the skirts, it was a dancing girl's delight. There were five petticoats, all trimmed with lace and pale icy-green satin. The bodice was fitted, the neckline demure but scooped just low enough to hint at the fullness beneath. Peggy had stitched tiny cactus roses in white lace and rich velvet ribbon across the bodice. Fashionable puffed sleeves and a long-tailed velvet ribbon at the waistline provided the finishing touches.

"Yes, it is," Peggy said. Sighing as she circled Merrie, she sent her eyes heavenward in a moment in reflection. "Your mama would have been proud to see you turned out so well."

Merrie smiled. Peggy said that every time she fitted Merrie for a gown. She gave some perfunctory reply. Her memories of Miranda were of a beautiful, not very happy woman who often took to her bed. Her health had been delicate, and she had never adjusted to the rough life of a Texas ranch.

"You look so like her," Peggy said for the hundredth time.

"So everyone says. I can't see it really, never have."

It was true that she looked like Miranda, but as Ash was fond of saying, she was just the opposite in spirit. Where her mother had been timid, Merrie was bold. Miranda had disliked horses and never rode. She had hated the longhorns, shied away from even going outdoors, sometimes for weeks, because the smell of them made her ill.

Merrie was the absolute antithesis. Her pride in the Spur was only equaled by her enthusiasm for the work. She was skilled at roping, branding, and riding.

"You mean Ashton doesn't want you to think you do."

Merrie had heard similar things from Peggy and Sonna before. They made her extremely uncomfortable. Rumor said that when Miranda became ill that last time, Ash had not taken any notice of her until it was too late. She had died with a day of getting the fever. Merrie had been only five at the time; it was impossible for her to know what had really happened. She trusted Ash too deeply to think him capable of such heartlessness.

The memories, as well as the controversy, made her feel very sad and lonely at times. But she kept those kinds of feelings to herself, usually masking them with breezy diversion.

"Ash has nothing to do with it, Peggy. My mother was very sickly. You know I'm not."

"I didn't say your temperament was anything like Miranda's. Ash made certain you were as tough as nails, teaching you men's work."

Merrie laughed. "And it's just as well he did. Otherwise we wouldn't have done so well this year."

Peggy snorted and began unfastening the velvet ribbon and tiny looped buttons. "Well he's home, at last," she said as if that magical fact could solve all misgivings and put things back into their allotted place.

There was no use arguing. "Yes, he is," agreed Merrie.

"Take it off, now, Meredith, carefully, if you please, and I'll wrap it for you."

Merrie whirled one more time in front of the looking glass. She couldn't quite believe it was her, and she didn't want to take off the lovely airy dress. With one last look, she reluctantly eased herself out of the gown and handed it to Peggy.

BY THE TIME she had paid for the purchases at Linnett's, the rain had stopped. Merrie walked gingerly along, trying to avoid the muddy puddles in the road, her arms piled high with packages. She had her own dress and dancing shoes, Liza had asked her to pick up several packages for her, and there was medication in a large blue bottle for Buck Peterson. He was poorly again.

Outside Ma Tuminy's Eating House, she met Jacko, Matt Cheston's ranch hand. He was slouched against the wall, one foot resting against the wall, hat tipped forward, as if he had been waiting for her to come out of Linnett's.

As it turned out, he had been.

"Morning, Miss Sinclair," he said, jumping to attention like a soldier, snatching his hat off his head. "Been waiting for you."

"You have?" Merrie said, suspicion suddenly flaring inside her. She was supposed to meet Matt in town today.

Jacko nodded his sandy head. "Mr. Cheston, he said for me to find you and assist you, as he can't make it."

Merrie frowned. "No explanation?" She was angry and disappointed.

They had arranged the meeting several weeks ago, after Merrie had ordered a wonderful new one-man buggy for her father. As Ash could no longer ride, the buggy would enable him to get about unassisted. She was relying on Matt to keep the gift out at the Lazy D until the night of the party.

She glared at Jacko. The young man colored and shook his head. "C-can I do anything for you, miss?" he stammered.

Merrie felt bad. It wasn't his fault, after all.

"No, I'll manage," she said, giving him a quick smile, then she changed her mind. She shoved the boxes into Jacko's arms. "Actually, you can take those round to the livery on End Street. Give them to Old Bob. He'll keep them for me. Tell him I'll be needing one of his drover horses up at the station in about half an hour, will you?"

Jacko set his hat down on his head with one hand while balancing the packages with the other. "Sure thing, Miss Sinclair," he said. The flush didn't leave his face, nor did he seem to be in a hurry to leave.

"Well?" Merrie asked, sensing he wanted to say something more.

"It's like this, ma'am," he said, shrugging his shoulders. "Mr. Cheston, he wants for you to ride out to the Lazy D tomorrow, if you can. He said to ask."

"And if I can't?"

"Then he said to give you this," the young man said, fishing in his pants pocket and nearly tipping the packages over in his effort.

It was a letter, sealed in a brown wrapper. Merrie took it and unwrapped it. She had a sinking feeling even before she read it what was written there. She knew the ranch hand was staring at her as she read.

Nor was her feeling wrong. Her eyes darted like fire over the untidy block letters. It seemed that Matt had to make a sudden trip out to Denver and wouldn't be able to attend the party. She was seething by the time she finished.

Merrie pursed her lips and took a steadying breath. "You tell Mr. Cheston that he can certainly expect me. I'll be at Kettlespout Rock before noon."

Jacko just nodded. "I'll be on my way then."

"Don't forget to tell Bob about the drover. You may as well tell him I'll be keeping a buggy down at the livery for a week or so," Merrie said.

Jacko nodded. One of the smaller packages slipped off the pile and fell on the ground. Merrie leaned forward to pick it up just as Jacko did, and the two almost banged heads together. Merrie leaned to the side to avoid hitting him and fell herself.

Jacko was so mortified that he had caused a lady like Merrie an injury that he promptly dropped the boxes and packages, then knelt to help her up.

"I'm not hurt," she assured him, dusting herself off. "Really, I'm not." She was all muddied down the one side, and there were small scratches on her hand where she had tried to stop herself from falling.

Jacko, on the other hand, was almost apoplectic with concern. He kept on trying to dust off her clothes and then got red with embarrassment for trying to touch her. "Aw hell! Right sorry, Miss Sinclair, ma'am, excuse my clumsy . . . hell," he kept repeating over and over.

Finally, Merrie just burst out laughing. She placated him as best she could and helped him retrieve the dropped parcels. Her only hope was that her beautiful dress was packed well enough to withstand Jacko's kind ministrations.

The rumpus caused quite a commotion. A number of folks had observed the ungainly tangle of Merrie Sinclair and the ranch hand from the Lazy D on the muddy street. There were

TEXAS KISS

raised eyebrows aplenty, and even a few snickers. But one observer was not amused.

Kyle Delancy turned sharply when he recognized Merrie cavorting about with a rough-looking youth. A blaze of singular emotion skittered through him. He did not recognize it, never having experienced it before, nor did he stop long enough to analyze it, but it was jealousy. The boy had his dirt-stained hands all over Merrie's long, curvy body, and Kyle didn't like it at all, at all.

He made a beeline for them.

He didn't remember seeing the man before, but he sure as hell would make it his business before this day was too much older to find out just who he was.

Kyle heard Merrie laugh and felt the muscle in his jaw twitch with tension. His eyes narrowed. Merrie was scrambling for her parcels and assuring the man that no harm had been done.

No damn harm. Hell!

Some harm was definitely going to be done, and he, Delancy, intended to do it.

He closed in on the two fast, leaned over, and jerked Jacko to his feet. The poor man dropped all his parcels again. Merrie gave a startled cry. She obviously hadn't seen Kyle coming. But he ignored her for the time being.

It was the unfortunate Jacko that he addressed.

"The lady's engaged to be married, and if she doesn't choose to remember it, I suggest you do. It can get a whole lot unhealthy around here if you forget that. Do I make myself clear?"

Jacko nodded vigorously.

"That's reasonable. Now, scram!"

Jacko fled. The packages were strewn all over the place.

Merrie felt like stamping her feet in frustration. Her emerald eyes flashed dangerously at Kyle.

He wanted to shake her. Right here and now. He was that furious. It unnerved him. He couldn't stand violence against women. It nauseated him. The kind of men who hurt women were beneath contempt in his eyes. Yet here he was shaking with the urge to slap her.

"How dare you!" she cried, not caring if the whole of Hollow Creek saw her screaming at the dangerous gunslinger. "What right do you have scaring poor Jacko like that?"

"So that's his name. Good. In my hurry to get rid of him, I forgot to ask. This way if he doesn't care to remember my warning, I'll have a name to give the undertaker."

"You're insane," Merrie said.

"You're engaged, dammit, woman," he ground out. He knew he was being totally illogical, but he didn't care. "Don't you remember that?"

"That's none of your concern, Mr. Delancy. And if I recall, you were the one who told me my fiancé didn't deserve me."

"Just because your fiancé's playing in the gutter doesn't mean you have to jump in with him."

Merrie was shocked. "Liza's viciousness seems to have rubbed off," she said, hurt that he would speak to her so.

He hitched an eyebrow. "You are out of your depth, Legs. You don't know what you're talking about. Now, do you want to tell me why it was necessary to flirt with 'poor Jacko' in broad daylight?"

Merrie blanched. "I don't have any idea what you're talking about."

He glanced skyward in exasperation. "The freckled-faced boy with the packages, Jacko. What were you doing with him?"

Merrie was incredulous. She couldn't help it—she gave way to a cascade of laughter. Apart from the absurdity of the misconception, Merrie was fascinated to discover that the gunslinger appeared to be *jealous*.

"Doing with him?" she parroted, mirth slurring her words.

Kyle's short temper simply snapped. He almost exploded. "What the hell's so funny?" he shouted.

Merrie wiped her eyes. "Not that it is any of your business, but the 'boy,' as you call him, is Matt's *errand boy*. He works out at the Lazy D, and he brought me a message."

Kyle glanced down the road, shrugged at the attention they

were calling to themselves, then smiled at Merrie. "He brought you good news, then?" he said mildly, once he had absorbed his mistake. Smooth as silk, he was.

Merrie smiled. There wasn't a hint of discomfort over his faux pas. He was as self-assured as ever. "You really are too much, Mr. Delancy." She bent down and began picking up packages.

Kyle helped her.

"Not as much as you are, Legs," Kyle said, smiling.

The sun came through the ridges of cloud just then, bathing the wood buildings and the street in thin golden light.

Merrie turned her face up toward it. "I really thought the day was going to be a wash," she said.

"You mean it isn't?" he said, straightening up.

She shook her head mischievously and loaded her packages into his arms.

"Not when I get to see Kyle Delancy playing errand boy for me. Would you kindly drop this lot down at the livery? Bob's expecting them."

She stretched up on tiptoe and dropped the last package on top of the pile. Then she swung about and strode off toward the railroad station, leaving the frowning gunslinger standing in the middle of Main Street looking completely bewildered, his arms laden with pretty pink and lavender boxes.

TWELVE

"READY?" MERRIE ASKED from the door of her father's bedroom. "Everyone's here, Ash, and waiting for you. You ready to face them all?"

Ash beckoned his daughter into the room and wiggled his eyebrows appreciatively. She really did look splendid. Her dress was perfection, the coloring bringing the emerald of her eyes to sparkling vividness. It was neither too girlish nor too sophisticated, and it definitely enhanced her tiny waist and full bustline to best advantage.

People had come from miles around to welcome Ash home and attend the three-day extravaganza that Merrie and Gillian Bishop had worked hard to put together.

Tonight's celebration was a barn dance complete with half a dozen fiddlers, to be followed the next day by horse races, a full military marching band on parade, boating on the slow river, and picnics. There was to be a great ox roast tomorrow night and a formal sit-down dinner for the finale. A troop of circus folks from Europe who were traveling about the country had agreed to entertain them. There were several singers, banjo players, a string quartet from New York (arranged by the indomitable Miss Bishop), and a veritable army of cooks, who had been imported from as far away as California.

Excitement glowed on Merrie's face. She felt her father's fingers tremble as he stroked her cheek, and she saw the fierceness of his pride in her, his love. It made her heart full.

"Watch out for the bees, honeybunches," he managed to say. It was his favorite admonition, reminiscent of her childhood, when Ash would tease her that she had too much honey inside.

Merrie hugged him in delight. Just a few weeks after getting home, Ash was making great progress. He could only articulate slowly and with great difficulty, but he was speaking. He was even working a few hours each day on the books—all, of course, under Gillian's watchful eye.

Gillian, stately in wine velvet, crooked her finger at Jamie and Spiker, both scrubbed and beaming in their Sunday best. They would carry Ash down to the festivities in his bath chair.

Liza met them on the stairs. As always, she looked magnificent. She wore champagne lace edged with elaborate royal-purple embroidery. Her gown, with its daring décolletage, was the latest thing from Paris; it just barely covered the rouge tips of her breasts and showed them to their fullest advantage. Merrie wondered whom she was after tonight.

All of Hollow Creek had turned up, and a good number of the Cattlemen's Consortium with their wives and families. There were even some men there from Ash's early mining days. Bankers and politicians and two Mexican families from across the border were also present. They were very close friends of Ash's, and their daughters had spent a few summers up at the Spur with Merrie.

Ash had made a lot of friends, and as he climbed to prominence, he had made some enemies, too. Merrie had no doubt that some of the smiles she witnessed this night were not altogether honest. A year of taking her father's place had taught her to be wary.

A great shout of welcome rang out as Ash was pushed forward, Merrie and Liza on either side of him. He raised his hands to quiet everyone down. Merrie knew that most wouldn't even know what the effort cost him, but Ash was determined to welcome his friends with his own words.

"Welcome all," he said. His voice, once boisterous, was reedy and hushed. Most people had difficulty hearing what he said, but it didn't deter him.

"My family welcomes you all. I'm glad to be home. Glad I have a home to return to," he added. "Thanks to my daughter's considerable expertise, I'm glad to tell you all that the Spur's a whole lot healthier than I am." Ash swiveled his head to look at his wife. For just a moment there seemed to be a silent communication between them, grave, unreadable. "My wife can attest to that."

The crowd laughed, but Merrie saw that Liza's shoulders stiffened, as if she feared what her husband might add. She looked away.

Ash opened his arms in a wide, sweeping arc and smiled at the gathering. "I heartily welcome you to the Silver Spur Ranch. My house is yours. Enjoy yourselves."

The musicians struck up and began to play, and the dancing started immediately.

Merrie didn't have time to reflect on Ash's strange words, as she was claimed for one dance after another. Although everyone knew that she was engaged to be married, it didn't deter the many young men who now vied for her attention.

As most were from around Hollow Creek, she'd been friends with them for years. Tonight was a celebration, and if Cheston was stupid enough to leave his gorgeous young fiancé to their ministrations, then that was his bad luck.

Besides the eager young swains, there were several others watching Merrie Sinclair. Her stepmother, for one, with undisguised contempt, or was it jealousy? And then there was the infamous gunslinger known as Mr. Smith. Few people saw him secluded out of the way in a dark corner, shrouded in smoky shadows, untouched by the golden pools cast by myriad hanging lanterns.

From this vantage, Kyle could see, but not be seen. This suited his purpose. He watched now, through slitted eyes, the exquisitely transformed Merrie in her frothy feminine attire, swinging in a circle on the arm of her latest partner. Her head was thrown back; her slender ankles, beautifully stockinged in pearly silk, showed under the yards of lacy petticoats. Her breasts, pushing against the thin material of her gown—modest though it was—appeared very voluptuous; her waist, impossibly tiny by contrast to the fitted bodice and the fullness of her skirts.

Who would have thought it? The contrast between Merrie

clad in work pants and Stetson and this glorious, golden angel was stunning. He had thought her lovely before, but this . . . Christ, she was a danger to his health.

Not that he hadn't known it, hadn't learned it a month ago in her bedroom. He had gone to tease her, to play a little, and the tables had been well and truly turned on him. He had scooted back to town, a nice, safe distance, even though that was not ideal for his job.

Still, he had managed; everything was arranged, the traps baited, the plans laid. Tonight he would meet with Ash and go over his part one last time. Then he would set off home. Back to Dodge City. And the jaws of his well-contrived trap would spring shut, and they would have their culprits.

Dodge City. He couldn't wait. He could visit a certain friendly widow who lived on the edge of town. He felt a great deal of relief at the thought. Abstinence was not to his liking at all. His sexual frustration was at an all-time high. He grimaced at that admission, his flashing eyes slicing through the dancers to find the object of his torment.

The music reached a crescendo, and the men spun the women up into the air and caught them, everyone shrieking with laughter.

Kyle saw Merrie's partner lift her effortlessly above his head, her flying skirts swirling about them both in a flurry of icy green—like froth on a wave. He had an unreasonable urge to slam his fists into the man whose hands circled her tiny waist.

He took a quick swallow and set his whiskey glass on a nearby table. He had a meeting at ten, and even though he was two hours early, a walk in the fresh autumn air would do him good, he thought wryly.

It was then she saw him. Their eyes locked. Kyle felt a sudden, very deliberate hitch in his heartbeat. It disgusted and alarmed him. He considered such a phenomenon infantile, moronic, and certainly not suited to his self-image. And yet there was no denying it was there.

What would be the harm in one dance? he asked himself just

before he thought with satisfaction of removing Merrie's dancing partner's sweaty fingers from her curvy body.

"Excuse me, but the lady's engaged to be married—you're trespassing," he said, and smoothly disengaged Merrie from her partner's hold. The man, a shiny-faced youth carrying a dozen more pounds than were good for him, was startled to find himself forcibly moved aside. He began to protest, and then recognition dawned, leaving his mouth in a red gape.

Merrie, however, had no difficulty voicing her objections. "But not to you, Mr. Delancy, as I've mentioned before."

"I thought his name was Smith," the chubby cowboy said, suddenly finding his voice.

Merrie glared at him, then glared at Kyle, but the gunslinger, innocent as a choirboy, merely smiled warmly at her and swirled her into the dance.

For several minutes, Merrie was too focused on trying to keep up with his quicksilver steps and complicated turns and spins. It seemed that Kyle Delancy, also known as Smith and God only knew what other names, was not a simple gunslinger after all. He could dance superbly. And that kind of expertise was not to be found in the wilderness. He made Merrie feel as if she floated across the barn floor like so much dandelion fluff.

Breathless, her heart racing, she let him spin her round and round the dance floor. Not once did he allow his seductive eyes to lift from hers; not once did he allow her to slip or misstep, no matter how fast he spun her about. His touch was firm, warm, unbearably intimate, even though he was the quintessential gentleman, careful never to bring her closer than a body's width, his hand placement perfect.

Merrie could not speak, so strong was the desire to melt against him as she had that night in her room . . .

Oh God, she thought despairingly, he is too ungodly handsome. His eyes, blue as summer's midnight, caressed her, peeled away her resistance, her willpower. It seemed as if her mind emptied then, like a dam with too much water in it, her internal protests spilling over, draining away into the secret, silent earth. She began to tremble, remembering the potency of his hot mouth on her aching breast.

She gasped—mortified that she would recall the very incident that she had spent the last month deliberately forgetting. Actually, she had thought he had finally left Hollow Creek. There had been no word or rumor of him for the past week or more.

That had helped her in the belief that she was finally over her silly infatuation. She had thought that she was immune from him. Now she could see that it wasn't so. She trembled inside like a silly schoolgirl. That made her furious. He was here, brash and uninvited, and meddling in her social life as well.

The music ended.

Merrie closed her eyes briefly. She moved away from him as fast as she could. Kyle did not move away, but stayed his ground, staring at her, his extraordinary blue gaze fixed on her as if searching for something, perhaps unsure of what it was. The look was intense, hot, leaving her more breathless than before.

To her alarm, she quickly realized that they were the focus of much attention, standing there in the middle of the dance floor, eyes locked, just staring at each other.

Merrie heard a woman's snide giggle, and the mutter of talk about them ebb, and she blinked. He was the devil's own son, she thought angrily, convinced that he practiced this kind of seduction all the time.

"I suppose I should be grateful that you did not allow me to fall flat on my face, Mr. Delancy, even though you're as reckless on the dance floor as you appear to be in all other things. I hope you will choose someone else as your next partner. I'm afraid I only venture my life once of an evening."

Kyle smiled at her polite tone. She spoke very softly: almost no one else could hear what she said; only the modulation of her voice carried.

"If you consider that living dangerously, Legs, you really do live a protected life."

"I'm perfectly content with my life the way it is."

"Really," he said. One dark brow lifted in disbelief. "You work like a dog morning and night because your father is too ill to resume his responsibilities here. You cannot hire a replacement for Peterson, who should be assuming more of the work but doesn't because he's as useless as he is faithful. You're a softy, Legs, a real pushover for a sad story. And then, let's not forget the absent fiancé, shall we? He's nowhere to be seen, even on a night like this." He gestured around the decorated barn. "But you're content with your life, right?"

Merrie ground her teeth. It was absolutely true, every word, but that made it all the more intolerable coming from him! Buck was too old to work, too old and too tired. The burden had fallen to her and was difficult.

Worst of all, Matt had been a sore disappointment to her. Since Ash's return, he had only visited once, and then when her father was asleep. He'd made no effort to see Ash, to welcome him home. His excuse for not coming to the celebration was that he was going on a business trip to Denver. Some cowman there had a special sale slated for that week. He was selling some prime Durham bulls that Matt had been after for years. He was sorry to miss Ash's homecoming, he said, but it couldn't be helped. He wouldn't be back until the day after the celebration.

Angry and disillusioned, she had tried to persuade him to delay his trip. They'd had an all-out shouting match over it. Matt had refused, telling her that she was oversensitive. She could hardly expect the Denver man to change the day of his sale just because she was having a shindig.

She had left in a fury, without saying good-bye. And somehow this blue-eyed devil was insightful enough to discern her unhappiness.

Her cheeks felt hot with embarrassment; she lowered her thick lashes to hide from his penetrating look. "It really is none of your business, Mr. Delancy."

"Funny thing, but I keep telling myself that, then I keep ignoring it. It's not out of character: I'm stubborn."

"You could have fooled me," Merrie said, a hint of a smile creasing her lips.

Kyle's eyes darkened perceptibly. He knew it was a mistake; he knew he was a few short hours from leaving Hollow Creek and the delicious Miss Meredith Amber Sinclair, with her golden innocence, her outrageous body, and her susceptible green eyes, for good.

She spelled commitment, and that far he was not prepared to go. All the same, he could not quite walk away. Logically, he knew it was a mistake, but deep down he only knew a keen hunger, a remorseless need to kiss her, hold her one last time. One last time, he assured himself, never hurt.

He even went so far as to tell himself he would do it as a chivalrous gesture, a service to her so that she would realize when she kissed him that she could not love, should not love, Cheston. He was absolutely wrong for her, but then he knew Ash Sinclair would probably be telling her that soon enough, anyway.

"I have something of yours," he told her.

Her eyes widened. He realized that she was terrified that he would whisk her golden locket out, here and now, and return it to her in full view of their very attentive audience. And then wouldn't the gossips have something to speculate about?

He shook his dark head. "Not here," he said, bowing formally as if taking leave of her. "Meet me outside your father's study in half an hour."

"Why don't you just leave it under the doormat there, in front of the French doors?"

"No, I think it's best that I give it to you in person," he told her.

Merrie looked at him suspiciously. He was quite able to make a scene if he wanted to, and the look he gave her said he wanted to.

She nodded curtly and moved away. She was determined not to do his bidding. He did terrible things to her insides, made her jittery as a hen in a fox's den. No, she definitely wouldn't go near the study in half an hour, or any other time.

"Oooh! Merrie Sinclair, I don't think I'll ever forgive you," said Kate Brown, suddenly looming up behind her.

Merrie grinned at her. "What did I do now? Come with me, Kate, I simple must splash my face; it's burning hot."

"Told you he'd sizzle you with those blue eyes. Really, everyone's talking. He never did dance with anyone else, Merrie, and I'm not sure that's fair. After all, I saw him first."

"I take it you're referring to Mr. Delancy?"

"It thought he was Smith?"

"By all means, let him be Smith. And you can have him; he's certainly not mine."

"How wonderful," Kate sighed, batting her lashes in anticipation. "Um . . . I don't suppose you know where he is? I can't see him anywhere."

She stood with Merrie at the open door. There were many people milling about the entrance and along the path leading to a cluster of blue and yellow tents. These tents served as dining halls and kitchens, and they were full of the clatter of dishes, glassware, and chatter. On either side of the path stood tall firebrands that wavered in the crisp autumn air, seeding the paths with licking plumes of orange light.

There was no sign of Kyle Delancy anywhere.

Suddenly Merrie had a perfect idea. The very devil was inside her. She thought to teach the arrogant Mr. Delancy a lesson he sorely deserved. And it would teach her silly friend to be more discerning, also.

"I've every idea where he is, and what is more, you shall have your very wish and meet him there. How fortunate that our dresses are so similar." Taking her astonished friend by the hand, she pulled her along the path, hurried past the tents, and made a beeline for the main house.

"Where are we going, Merrie?" Kate asked breathlessly.

"We're going to get you my shawl. It's the very thing to disguise your hair . . . ah . . . perfect for these cool autumn nights."

"But I'm not cold," Kate said.

"Yes, you are," Merrie told her. "You've no idea how cold

you are. I don't believe *Mr. Smith* would take that as a positive sign of your emotions."

"Oh," said Kate tripping along with considerable speed, "then by all means let us get the shawl."

Merrie thought her friend's haste was about the most unseemly thing she had ever seen.

Thirteen

There was a sickle moon out. The sky was deep velvet, and the slender cup of silver shone with audacious clarity. Along the muddy banks of the river, frogs croaked and crickets chirped their last summer songs. Autumn was yet to brush its gaudy colors across the landscape, but misty heralds wafted over the lazy water, a reminder that the seasons were about to turn.

Down along the Red River was a half-mile stretch of nut and fruit trees. Some were indigenous, and some had been planted, cultivated into a pretty arbor with pathways and picnic spots and even a small jetty. Ash Sinclair had created it as a gift to his first wife, Miranda.

Merrie remembered hazy summer days spent with Miranda, picking fruit, dangling their bare feet in the smooth green water, fishing off the jetty. She didn't know if it was the actual memory of these days or Ash's telling her about them that made the place special for her, but it was.

This evening, though, Merrie realized that she wasn't the only one walking its length. Suddenly she was reluctant to show herself, annoyed that her father's guests had trespassed here when there was so much else for them up at the main house. The river and the wooden jetty were a good two miles from the house.

She had come out here to escape Kyle Delancy, knowing full well that he would be furious with her for tricking him. He was sure to be astonished when Kate arrived outside the study. Merrie could just see her batting her eyes up into his surprised face.

Yet, there was another, more important reason she needed time alone. She had finally admitted that she simply couldn't trust herself to be with the gunslinger. His mere presence was a threat to her resolve, and she truly did not know how much resistance she had left. He seemed able to expropriate her will with just one of his piercing blue glances. It was not a comfortable admission. She berated herself as shallow for succumbing to so obvious a rake as Kyle Delancy.

Now, however, all thoughts of a respite vanished as she saw two shadowy shapes making their way along the waterside. The very tall one was obviously a man; the other, short and petite, a woman. They stopped every now and then, talking, gesticulating. The earnest hum of their voices carried in the still night air, although Merrie could not hear what they were saying. Still, it was apparent that they were arguing about something.

At one point the woman raised her voice in protest. The man quickly looked about. He did not see Merrie, for she was keeping very still, her shimmering dress hidden under the folds of a voluminous cloak and hood that she had worn to stave off the mists that sometimes rose from the water on nights like this. She retreated into the break of nut and mulberry trees, watching, fascinated now, as the two drew nearer, their argumentative voices growing louder, clearer.

As the woman came closer, Merrie saw immediately that it was Liza. She, too, wore a dark cloak, the heavy cowl draped over her perfectly styled hair. What on earth was her stepmother up to now? Was she with the gunslinger right under Ash's nose?

Merrie's eyes went almost hesitantly to the man, tall and foreboding alongside her diminutive stepmother. Merrie gave a start. It certainly wasn't who she thought it would be; *it wasn't Kyle Delancy*.

The man was shrouded in a thick poncho. He seemed older, too, for he stooped slightly.

But who was it?

In the dark, with his hat pulled down over his face, it was impossible to tell. Also, he was wearing a bandanna around the lower half of his face, shielding himself from the night air.

Something told her, though, that he was not a savory

character. Just what it was that made her think so, she did not know. She felt a thrill of pure ice ride up her spine.

Just then the thin moon sailed into a rack of clouds. The night grew darker. Thankful for the lowering light, Merrie drew carefully back as the two passed right by her.

"I don't like it," the man was saying. "Let me do things the way we planned. Don't worry about the nurse. She won't be a problem, I'm telling you." His proximity to the water and his bandanna distorted his voice, making it sound hollow, odd.

"No, no, no. The French doors. I'm telling you it's the best way. That way you don't have to be concerned about complications and interference," came Liza's insistent reply.

The man grunted, but before he could answer, Merrie gasped. Something slithery had run over her foot. She only just stopped herself from screaming out aloud.

"What was that?" Liza hissed, stopping only a yard away from where Merrie stood shielded by the trees.

"Someone's in the trees. Stay here," the man said.

To her horror, Merrie realized that he was coming back toward her hiding place. A frantic hammering began in her tight chest; she felt her pulse dip and race like wild and frantic horses.

With a swallow of apprehension, she remembered a heavy wood bench that sat under the thickest and oldest of the wild plum trees. When she was a child, it had been a favorite hiding place. Not even knowing if the bench were still there, she inched her way back into the arbor.

Very carefully lifting her skirts and cloak as high as she could, Merrie moved swiftly and silently down the path. Heavy footsteps warned her that the man was close behind. Her eyes searched desperately for the bench. It really was the only cover around. There was nothing to shield her from him, nothing to prevent him from spotting her, unless she could find the—

Aha! There was the plum tree. It leaned slightly to one side, its tired old branches curving protectively over a decrepit old bench. Unless one actually knew it was there, the bench was difficult to make out under the netted twigs and branches.

Merrie scrambled under the rickety slats, scooting yards of skirt in after her, and held her breath. Not much of a hiding place! she lamented. She had to trust in the darkness and pray that the man did not bend over!

The footsteps came closer, closer . . .

She dared not move.

Closer . . .

Not a finger. The muscles of her neck and legs rigid, her arms locked underneath her, eyes straining, she waited.

The footsteps came up . . .

She even held her breath.

. . . and then receded.

After a moment, the footsteps returned, slower now, the tempo relaxed, less weighted.

She heard the man call out that it was nothing, heard her stepmother say something in a relieved voice, and then there was silence.

Long after she was certain that they had gone, Merrie remained where she was, her head full of perplexing questions. Only when she could not stand the musty smell of the rotting wood any longer did she eventually crawl out. She tried to dust herself off, but she was absolutely filthy. Her dress, she saw with dismay, was in a dreadful state, even though most of it had been protected by her heavy cloak. Sonna would be furious.

What, she wondered, heading back toward the house and praying that no one saw her, was the chance of getting a hip bath taken up to her room? The bathhouse was out of the question with so many guests staying over. She would have to smile very sweetly at Juggs and hope he wasn't too drunk to haul the buckets up for her.

THE MOON SLID behind a bank of thin clouds, drenching them with misty silver. Night deepened.

"You're sure there was no one there?" Liza asked a second time.

Her companion grunted impatiently. "I said so, didn't I?"

TEXAS KISS 111

The pale gold lace of her gown peeped through the folds of her dark cape as they hastened back along the path. The ground was damp, and she knew that her dancing slippers would be ruined. Usually, out in the West, ladies wore boots laced up to the middle of their calves, but Liza preferred the dainty slippers worn by Easterners when they attended dances, and she was determined to wear them. They had cost a fortune, and she wondered if Sonna would be able to salvage them.

There had been no time to run upstairs and change into her boots when the signal came. A red light flashing twice every three minutes meant she was urgently needed. She had been in the middle of a dance with the president of the Cattlemen's Consortium and had made a hurried excuse before rushing down to the river.

The signal had been altogether unexpected. With their plans so ripe, she had experienced a moment's apprehension.

"You could be wrong," Liza snapped, glancing back at the covey of trees. "Just like you are about tonight. With so many people about, now's the best time to make our move."

"Shut it," her companion said. He began coughing. The sounds were muffled against the bandanna tied about the lower half of his face. There was no mistaking the fact that it was a nasty cough. It came from his chest, rasping and low. Eventually he stopped, bending over slightly, his shoulders heaving with the effort to control the spasms.

Liza clicked her tongue in disgust. "As I said, I hate delays like this—it puts me on edge."

"Can't be helped. Send a message and tell our boy to wait a few days."

"I don't like it, I say."

"Shut it, Liza," the man said gruffly. "I'm sick of your whining. Just send the message to Cheston." The man started coughing again. This time he staggered a little, wheezing fearfully before managing to catch his breath again.

"You don't know what it's like living with that half man and his brat forever watching me. And now there's that English angel of mercy fussing over him day and night. I tell you I can't take much more."

"You'll manage."

Liza spun toward him. Her beautiful face was cold with scorn. "That's easy for you to say. Maybe you don't have what it takes anymore, either? Maybe we should go on ahead. Matt will do exactly as I say."

The man caught her arm, twisted it deftly behind her back, and hoisted her up so that only the very tip of her toes were touching the ground. She screamed softly, but he whipped his hand over her mouth. His enormous strength was evident as he held her there suspended for a long moment. Bending down to her ear, he ran his tongue along the convoluted shell, licking and teasing the sensitive hollows before whispering, "And maybe you need me to hurt you a little, just as a reminder, huh?"

Liza groaned.

The man gave one jerk on her arm and released her.

She backed off a step or two, rubbing the ache from her arm. Fear and excitement were etched upon her face.

The man saw it and laughed.

"No, I really don't have to worry about you doing anything stupid, Liza. You like me too much. Or should I say, you like what I can do for you." He began to laugh again, but another fit of coughing took him then.

"Oh, for God's sake. We had better delay it a few days until you get rid of that cough. You'll ruin everything."

"Just see you have everything ready on your end. A few days ain't going to make a difference."

"Oh no? And what about that gunslinger? I tell you he's up to something, and I don't like it that you haven't been able to figure out what."

"How many times must I tell you? He's what he says he is, a land agent's snoop. I'll see to him when we get back."

"He's threatened Matt with foreclosure. By the time we get back, it may be too late."

"Now you're all cut up about Matt? Since when? It's not

going to make any difference, not to Cheston anyway," he snorted in disgust.

"What do you mean?"

"Use your head, Liza. Cheston's not coming back from Dodge City. I ain't fixing on cutting three ways, when two's better."

"But we need him. If something goes wrong and my stepdaughter inherits, we need an available bridegroom."

"Do I look stupid? Stop fretting. First we get our hands on that gold—then we get rid of Cheston."

Liza smiled slowly. Her velvet eyes reflected the slender moon sailing out from behind the rack of clouds. "Then I must make certain I take advantage of whatever time is left to Matt. He has a number of . . . ah . . . talents I will be sorry to lose."

FOURTEEN

"Just leave that bucket next to the tub," Merrie said. "Thanks. You can get back to the festivities now."

"No trouble, Miss Merrie. No trouble at all. Everything's just about done for the night," the handyman said. He emptied one of the buckets into the wooden tub and set the other down beside it.

"Oh? No poker games still going?" Merrie knew his weakness for cards and gambling.

The man grinned sheepishly. "Nope. Most got cleaned out."

Merrie shook her head as she shut the door.

It took her no time at all to get out of her party clothes. She always insisted on the fastenings of her dresses being where she could get at them, and refused to wear the requisite stays and girdles so favored by those who followed the dictates of the day. She was very slender from her exacting regime. Apart from the day-to-day running of the ranch, Merrie rose early and often stayed out with the herd until sundown. She had learned early on that working right alongside the men garnered more respect and obedience than if she merely dictated from her father's office.

The water was blissfully hot, and she silently thanked Juggs for his efforts as she soaped away the cobwebs and dirt. She couldn't help but think about the creepy crawlies that might have found a home in her hair, along with the twigs and crumbled leaves. She gave her scalp a thorough scrubbing.

It was not quite so easy to rid herself of the memory of the night's adventure. She puzzled over what she had heard, trying to make sense of it, trying to dismiss the growing unease that had come over her.

The "nurse" mentioned was obviously Gillian Bishop. *Don't worry about the nurse,* the man had told Liza.

How strange. Why Liza should be troubled about Gillian, she couldn't imagine. But one thing was certain, her stepmother was plotting!

Merrie could not go to Ash with the problem. Meddling in her father's marriage was out of the question; she had never run to him with the mean things Liza did, and she never would. But she was custodian of Ash's well-being. Liza had made it patently clear that her duty to Ash ended on the day he took ill. Still, it was up to Ash to deal with his wife on that score, and so far as Merrie knew, he had chosen not to do so.

Merrie submerged herself, rinsing off the soap. Her hair was thick, and she ducked a number of times before she was satisfied that all the soap was out. Then she rose and poured the last bucket over her head, gasping slightly, for it had cooled while she had wallowed in the tub, fretting over Liza and the mysterious man in the bandanna.

It was the barest sound that made her look up in alarm. She blinked the water from her eyes and stared agape at the man lounging against the headboard of her bed, his booted feet impudently resting on the quilted bed cover.

"Kyle!" she managed, and sat down in a hurry, splashing the water all about the floor.

"Amazing. I thought you didn't know my first name."

"Get out," Merrie cried, clasping her knees. "Just get out."

"You took the words out of my mouth. Get out, Legs." The order, imperious as it was, was tempered by the modulation of his voice. Smooth and deep as a wind instrument, it sent a shaft of excitement right through her belly.

She fought for the outrage she knew she was entitled to, but the fluttering in her stomach made it difficult. "How dare you . . . just remove yourself from my bed . . . my room."

His eyebrows rode up his forehead, his expression clearly challenging. "We have unfinished business, you and I, Legs. You'd better get out that bath."

"What?" she gasped, appalled, as he produced his six-shooter and nudged the barrel up into the air a few times.

"Out," he ordered.

"You wouldn't," she breathed.

"Shoot you? Never. I'm not known as a merciful person. But a few shots in the air would bring a couple of curious folks in here right quick—including your daddy. The door's not locked."

"Why," she shivered in the cooling water, "why would you do that?"

He threw her a dark look, a speculative, troublesome look. "I have my reasons. Now . . . if you would . . ." He got up, his movements smooth, predatory. He grabbed a towel and stood there holding it for her as if they were at a formal affair and he were merely helping her with her wrap.

Only he was not a polite, affable companion for an evening's revelry. He was a seducer, an adulterer.

"Merrie," he said very, very softly.

It was as if he touched her. She shuddered again.

"Turn your back," she said. Her lips were turning blue with the quickly cooling water.

"Not on your life," he said, his voice even lower, almost a whisper.

She gazed up at him. It was her undoing. His eyes were hot, blazing into hers, setting fire to her bones, melting them.

She was freezing and burning all at once.

She stood. Rising from the tub, her lithe young body proud and straight, she was determined not to show him what he did to her. She was determined to ignore the wildfire raging through her trembling legs.

The water sluiced off her long-legged, golden body. Kyle responded immediately to those scandalous legs, the luxurious breasts, the tapered waist. The lacy curls between her legs, darker, richer than the hair on her head, enticed his burning gaze. She was a summer sylph, sun-kissed and splendid, and he wanted her badly.

He cursed his lack of resolve. He had known what coming

here to her bedroom could cost him, but he had come anyway. Oh yes, he had come. He had convinced himself, with clever arguments, that no one ever made a fool of him and got away with it. He had assured himself he would wake her up, give her a dressing down, and leave right after he had kissed her as he had intended earlier. Kiss her—no more than that. Leave her and this blasted little town with its little infidelities and ugly squabbles.

But he got to her room only to find her in the tub! Naked—she was gloriously naked. He felt then the sharp clatter of his heart and knew he would do far more than just kiss her—a lot more.

Now he watched himself reach out for her, lift her against him, wet and chill, and dangerously, magnificently female, and he cursed himself again.

But it did no good, because he had no intention of listening to his own practical conscience.

He claimed her mouth, hungrily, insistently. His tongue drove unhesitatingly into the sweet depth of it. Every skill he had honed since he had first learned about passion, he brought to bear against Merrie Sinclair.

He held her close, his hands anchoring her head and hips, allowing her almost no movement at all. She was locked inside his arms, her heart beating wildly against his chest, her breath ragged with undeniable excitement.

Merrie bucked recklessly at the feel of his vivid threat.

"Please," she cried, throwing her head back from his devouring lips.

He lifted her into his arms and carried her to the bed. "Please what?" he asked as he dropped her.

"Please get out. I . . . you . . . I can't believe this. You have no right to be here . . . to do this." She scrambled across the bed, grabbing the patchwork quilt, covering herself as she jumped off the far end.

"Your eyes say you're a liar; your body does, too," he told her. Then he unbuckled his gunbelt and threw it down on the night table. His lanky movements took him across the room in

TEXAS KISS 119

a few strides. He reached the door, locked it, and pocketed the key. He didn't even look at her while he unbuttoned his ruby-colored waistcoat and shucked it off with his long black jacket in one smooth movement. She heard his boots hit the floor and wondered who else might have heard them.

Oh God, this couldn't be happening to her. She *shouldn't* let this happen, but she was mesmerized by the beauty of his body. He was strong, immensely virile. The dark, curious hair on his body, so unlike her own, fascinated her. The breadth of his shoulders by contrast to his flat, narrow waist was daunting. But not nearly as daunting as his long-fingered hands at the buttons of his pants, and what they portended.

He unfastened the last button, stepped out of his pants, and she squeezed her eyes shut defiantly, only to find them opening of their own traitorous accord. She was fighting herself, fighting him. It wasn't fair. Why should she be in such a predicament?

"Why don't you go down the hall? Liza would welcome you . . ." She felt the panic in her voice and cringed.

His head came sharply up; his eyes blazed hot and blue.

"I don't understand why you're doing this to me." Merrie watched him come toward her. "I hate you . . . She is willing . . . Please, Kyle," she whispered as he claimed her mouth again.

His kiss was absolutely magical: soft, insistent, incredibly tender. The tempo of his thrusting tongue increased as the kiss lengthened. He stole her breath and her will. She did not want him, she tried to convince herself. She protested his invasion, his relentless onslaught, until he lifted her again and sank onto her bed, holding her tightly against his thundering heart.

"I want *you* willing . . . no one else," he told her softly.

"I don't believe you." Merrie forced herself to reason through the tidal surge of pleasure at being in his strong arms. She knew this was madness. "I mustn't believe you."

As she struggled to get away, he twisted quickly, pinning her under his strong legs. He wrenched her arms above her head, jerking her body up against him, and gazed down at her.

"Don't fight me, Merrie. Don't fight yourself. Let it happen. It will be good, I promise you."

"You arrogant bastard . . ."

His brow rose. The beautiful tilt of his smile, triumphant, ruthless, shone all over her. She felt it warm her chilled body, as if it were the very rays of the sun. How did he do it? He was breathtakingly handsome, a fiendish seducer, and she knew of no buffer between her desperate denial and the raging need to yield to him.

"You got that right, darlin'," he said, "I never did know my daddy's name. Through and through, that's exactly what I am. Maybe next time you go provoking a man, you'll be sure to find out if he's likely to turn on you."

"My God, is that why you're doing this? Because of a silly prank?"

He stared at her a moment and shook his head. The dark silk of his long hair brushed against her naked breasts, hardening the peachy nipples instantly, bringing his intense gaze to them before he raised his eyes once more and gazed into hers.

"No. I'm doing this because I want you. *Because you want me.*"

She began to shake her head, to deny it. It was true, she thought, wretchedly true. *She did want him.* She didn't want to . . . She wished she were indifferent to him. Something powerful seemed to explode inside her, and the ache of her lonely heart told her to yield to him.

"I can read you, Merrie. Your eyes say you're starving."

"Starving," she echoed on a wisp of sound.

She had lost her fight against him, against herself, and she knew it—he knew it. There was a moment of surrender, and then all thoughts beyond the immediate vanished. His gaze burned blue, validating his mastery over her emotions. She closed her eyes against that dangerous admission and allowed herself only to feel.

He lowered his mouth to her aching breasts, one and then the other; he sucked the nipples deeply into his mouth.

She cried out. Hot pleasure streaked from the crests to somewhere below her belly.

He nibbled, soothing the torment he had created there, only to repeat the process again, and then again.

Mindlessly, she threw her head from side to side, gripping the bed covers. She felt the inexorable surge of her hips at the marble hardness of his sex, and she could not stop herself.

She felt her legs give way to his manipulation, the nudge of his hard length settle between her thighs. He no longer held her hands prisoner, and still she did not throw him off but lay vibrant in his embrace, relishing the magic of his touch.

And he touched her everywhere. His fingers, deft and exquisitely adept at their art, slid into her, stretching, opening, infusing blissful sensations that both tormented and ravaged her body. She writhed, surging up against the turbulent rhythm of his fingers. She was swept into the cataclysmic rapture that his skills demanded. Without breath, without restraint, she climaxed fiercely, jerking up into his hard body, crying out his name, astonished, blissfully trembling as tiny ripples of pleasure coursed through her very soul. Her arms closed over his back, crushing him, holding him against the hammering of her heart.

Never had she dreamed of such intimacy, of such savage sensations, and while she reeled still, he invaded her body further. She cried out softly as he penetrated her, gasping as the broad head of his erection began to push forward. His strong hands gripped her bottom; he held her securely, kissing her mouth, her neck, the delicate pulse in the hollow of her throat.

"That's it, darlin' ride with me . . . hold tight," he said, his voice husky. "Hold tight," he breathed into her mouth, and drove through her maidenhead.

He lay quite still then, swallowing her cry, soothing away her shock with tender kisses. "All right, it's all right," he assured her, kissing her eyelids, the hectic color on her cheeks. His mouth found hers again, stoking her passion with the ravishing mastery of his kiss.

He flexed his hips, feeling her velvet heat envelope him in a dreamlike vice. He had never felt such triumph before. She was gossamer and fire all at once. He felt scorched by her heat, and it took all of his willpower to restrain himself from letting go.

He stroked gently, easing in and out of her glorious tightness, and felt her timid response grow with each surge of his hips. When she began responding, he rotated his hips, eliciting a soft moan of pleasure from her. He brought the wonderful length of her legs up high about his hips, hooking one of his arms under each knee and clasping her open thighs with his hands. He delved deeper as she opened more fully to his strokes. The tempo increased. He heard his harsh breath, the sexy purr in her throat answering each demanding lash of his body.

Pleasure, like a huge wave erupting from the ocean depths, rushed his senses, effervescing, swelling until it almost overwhelmed him. He felt himself lengthen, then impossibly lengthen again. He thought no more, but surrendered to the wildness, the urgent, thrusting need, that carried him over the edge. He surged into her, shuddering as he climaxed almost savagely, endlessly, his head thrown back, grimacing to prevent himself from bellowing out his pleasure.

He withdrew carefully, knowing that she would still be tender. He fell back against the pillows, shielding his eyes with his arm, trying to gather his wits and calm his thunderous pulse.

Christ, he thought, now he'd done it. Now he'd put a noose about his neck as surely as if he'd committed murder.

Fool. Bastard, his practical voice assured him. He turned his head slowly. She was staring at him, emerald eyes aglow with passion—anger, too.

He couldn't blame her. He refused to blame himself. Christ, she was magnificent.

He closed his eyes—shutting out her condemnation, her perplexed silence.

She deserved better from him than silence. And yet . . .

He knew, with certainty, exactly what girls like Meredith Sinclair expected. But he wasn't going to give her what she wanted. He was a bastard, he knew it, but he was not prepared to marry her.

Not her or anyone else.

He was heading home, back to Dodge City, and she could just marry. . . . Hell no, she wouldn't be marrying Cheston, that was for sure.

Maybe there was no need to worry. Maybe there would be no consequences to bother about. Wryly, he doubted that she would consider him as husband material anyway.

Merrie Sinclair was a capable rancher; she could take care of herself—find her own husband, if necessary. Actually he had met very few women quite as competent as Merrie—hell, there weren't too many men who could run a spread like the Spur with such success. He turned back toward her.

"You okay?"

She stared up at him, silent, puzzled, unsure of herself, him, the night.

"I know it's a little late, Merrie, but what kind of time is it for you? Monthly, I mean, you understand?"

Merrie's eyes widened as the meaning of his words dawned. She felt a thrill of pure rage fill her. Very deliberately she picked up the nearest piece of clothing from the floor and pulled it on. It was Kyle's shirt. It overwhelmed her for a moment—his presence, his shirt, the blatant intimacy they had shared, the wonder, the ecstasy . . .

He managed to douse it all instantly with the implication of his question.

Merrie hardened her trembling heart, lifted her proud chin, and stared directly into his devastating blue eyes.

"Why concern yourself?"

He had the grace to duck his head for a moment, she noticed, but then he shrugged.

"Tell me or not, it's your choice."

"Oh, *now* I have a choice?"

He got up and began dressing. Merrie turned away from his powerful body, the slightly erect bulge of his sex, evidence that he was capable of continuing the seduction, if he so chose.

"You always had a choice. I would never have forced you."

"But you knew exactly what to do to make me want you."

He shrugged again, sat to pull on his boots, and then leaned back against the chair, crossing his one foot high over his knee and contemplated her for a while.

"Do you want to tell me?" he said eventually.

Merrie fisted her hands. The need to hit him almost made her ill, cramping her stomach, constricting her throat.

"Why would you want to know?"

He sighed, exasperated with her obstinate childishness. "So that I can decide what is to be done, if there are any consequences from our lovemaking."

Merrie gasped. There was no reticence in his manner or choice of words. Kyle Delancy did not stumble about the bedrooms of his mistresses, regretful or shamed by his selfish pursuits. Oh no, he simply took what he wanted, saw to any "consequences"—although how exactly, Merrie did not have the faintest idea—and then went on his way.

Until tonight, Merrie had not really known what it was that men and women did in the marriage bed, only that it was where a woman submitted to her husband. Running a ranch with the constant cycle of breeding animals, she had realized that it couldn't be too different from what she had seen in the paddock and the pasture, but as that had appeared strange and rather messy, she had preferred not to think about it at all.

What she had shared with Kyle, however, had shocked her, deep down inside. She felt as fragile as thin glass, as vulnerable as a bud on a frosty morning.

All the same she had pride, a lifetime full of pride to mask the stabbing pain she felt from Kyle's callousness.

"I wouldn't tell you what you wanted to know if my very life depended on it."

Kyle arched a brow and stood. "Suit yourself," he said. He lifted his gunbelt and buckled it on. He flung his waistcoat and jacket over one shoulder and went to the door. He stood there a moment, hesitating, playing with something in his trouser pocket. Merrie thought it was the key.

She watched him, her breath hitched, waiting.

He turned.

Stared.

His eyes raked her sitting there in his large shirt, her arms locked about her bent knees, her golden hair, dry now and curling at the edges floating over her like a magical cape. She stared back at him, furious, hurt, wide emerald eyes locked with his.

He came back to the bed and ran one finger under her proud chin. She glared back at him.

"When you're not so angry, maybe you'll change your mind. I was going to leave in the morning, but I'll wait at Dashers for a few days, in case you do."

Merrie jerked away from him.

"In your dreams, mister. I wouldn't come to you—"

"I know, if your life depended on it," he finished for her.

He turned then and left, closing the door very quietly behind him.

FIFTEEN

IN PLACES THE canyon walls drew together to a distance of only three feet. Trapped in the narrow way, the new morning sunlight percloated, making the layers of terra-cotta and umber glow.

As she rode down into the canyon, Merrie watched red-tail hawks resting with almost impudent lethargy on invisible ridges of warm air. The high cap of the sky was hard and blue. To her left, the sleek glide of the Hollow could be heard chortling over rocky outcrops or spilling over stone. Mostly, though, a measureless and mesmerizing silence lay over the deep chasm. Sonnet's hooves echoed loudly between the mesas and the crags.

Merrie took solace from the vastness, the rich earthy tones, the familiar scent of grama grass, the cottonwoods and mesquite. She loved it all; the very solitude was a balm.

All the same she could not shake the memory of the gunfighter. He had stolen away so much more than just her virginity. She felt keenly a sense of . . . not loss, exactly, but depletion. Somehow the person that she had been, up until then, was no more. Like laughter cut off in the middle, or empty packages, she felt incomplete, and very unlike her usual unconstrained self.

It was hard to give coherence to her troubled thoughts, because she didn't know what it was that bothered her so. There seemed to be an empty place inside her, as if she hadn't eaten for a while and had lost the urge to.

Disturbing as that was, it was nothing compared to her dismay when she began measuring her emotional entanglement with Kyle against the placid friendship she had enjoyed with Matt Cheston over the past year and a half.

Friendship alone, Merrie now knew, wasn't enough—could never be enough!

She could not marry Matt. How could she ever have been willing to? His almost colorless attention was a far cry from the sweeping whirlwind of emotions that Kyle Delancy evoked.

No, there could be no marriage.

Nor, under the circumstances, could she ask it of Matt's pride.

A fearful loneliness swamped her then, for she realized that she would always hunger for the kind of fire she had found in Kyle Delancy's arms. Found so briefly and lost, she thought, painfully.

In the long, restless hours of the night, she had come to her decision about Matt. She had sent a rider out with a note early this morning, asking Matt to meet her at Kettlespout Rock. That was why she was riding now, down through the galleries of junipers as the shadows of the mesas shortened. The white-hot disc of the sun rose high above her.

It would take her several hours to reach the pedestal rock, and some hard riding to get back before dark. Merrie was determined, however, not to put off the unpleasant task for a moment longer than necessary.

At Whitesnake Draw, the Hollow joined the broad waters of the Red River once again and marked the northernmost boundary of the Spur. The canyon walls drew apart, and here wild turkeys and deer still foraged amid the buffalo grass and the blue grama grass with its seed tassels that looked like musical notes.

Matt was waiting at Kettlespout for her. She spotted him at once, hunkered down next to a small campfire, drinking coffee from a battered tin cup. He rose, grinning in his good-natured way. She dismounted and made her way across the stony cobbles of lavender, gray, and yellow shale, leaving Sonnet free to graze alongside Matt's chestnut.

"Hi there, honey," Matt said. He put his arms out at his sides and leaned back a little, his expression sheepish. "Am I forgiven yet?"

Merrie felt hot guilt at his words. If anyone should ask for forgiveness, it should be her. She had no idea how she would tell him, or even *what* she would tell him.

"I hated missing your party, honey, but it couldn't be helped," Matt said, not waiting for her reply. "They're in demand, those critters. You know how long I've been waiting to buy some real good Durham bulls, and this guy was selling at a real good price."

"I'm sure," Merrie said vaguely.

"Aw, c'mon, honey, don't be like that. Kiss me, and forget it, will you? It was just a shindig, after all, not our wedding."

"There's not going to be a wedding," Merrie said unhappily. She felt her shame even more acutely in the broad light of day. Never had she thought herself capable of such deceit, but somehow she couldn't find the words to tell him what had happened.

Matt looked at her in astonishment for a moment. "Well, now that's just plain in the face stupid. You got to get your priorities fixed, Merrie, honey."

She nodded her head. "That's just what I did. I thought very carefully. I'm sorry. I don't want to hurt you, Matt, but I can't marry you. I realized that it wouldn't work."

Matt grinned boyishly. He took off his hat and ruffled his fingers through his dark brown hair as if trying to find just the right tone to take with her. A thick gold ring glinted on the little finger of his right hand.

"You got nothing to worry about, honey. You know we're not set to marry for a couple of years yet. I'm sure when you think about it, you'll see how unimportant a little shindig is between us."

He sounded so reasonable. He was always sensible; nothing ever really troubled him, Merrie thought with a prickle of resentment. He might not always agree with her, but he always remained placid and logical in his arguments. Whenever they disagreed about anything, Merrie was the one who got really angry and shouted, while Matt simply dug in his heels and stuck to his guns with his affable smile in place. It had driven Merrie crazy on more than one occasion.

"It has nothing to do with Ash's homecoming."

"Fact is, you're madder than a old wet hen, all 'cause I missed that shindig. Why don't you just come right out and say so and have done? It'll make you feel right better, honey."

"Matt," Merrie cried, "it has nothing to do with the shindig."

Alerted by her obvious discomfort, Matt's expression became a little thoughtful. He studied her for a moment in silence and then burst out laughing.

"Hey there, and I thought it was serious," he choked out. "You been messed with, haven't you, honey? That good-looking gunslinger been courting you, has he?"

Merrie was shocked. His amusement was crushing. Just how Matt had discovered it, she did not know. At that moment she didn't much care, either. The fact that he could make light of what had been an anguished decision for her was a real blow.

"You obviously aren't going into a decline over it, Matt. At least I won't have to be too concerned about disappointing you." She was proud that her voice remained steady. The last thing she wanted was for her raw wounds to show.

Matt wiped the back of his neck with his kerchief. The sun burned mercilessly above and cast a fat shadow of the Kettlespout over the toes of his boots.

"Honey, you don't need to feel bad," he said, grinning at her magnanimously. "You're young, naive. You shouldn't blow things out of proportion. Most little ladies like to feel flattered by the attentions paid to them by gentlemen. It don't bother me none, and it shouldn't bother you."

When she gaped at him wordlessly, he continued. "You're right pretty, Merrie, honey. It's bound to happen from time to time. But that don't mean we can't get married."

Anger pricked her tongue. He hadn't understood her, not at all. "Maybe you just want the brutal truth spoken out loud?" Merrie asked.

He shrugged and a noncommittal grin flashed across his face. Merrie wanted to scream.

It seemed he was being deliberately obtuse. She felt bruised, as if she were tumbling chaotically head over heels through nowhere, while he fed her platitudes. Wasn't he even just the slightest bit disappointed in her, jealous even? After all, they had been courting for more than a year.

It occurred to her to wonder just how Matt Cheston really felt about her.

"There's nothing you can't tell me, honey. I don't shock easily. If it'll make you feel better, just tell me all about it."

At boiling point now, she spun on her heels. "Kyle Delancy did not pay me gentlemanly attention, nor did he flatter me, believe me. I will not marry you, and it has nothing to do my naïveté and everything to do with the fact that I don't *want* to marry you."

"You're overreacting."

Merrie thought she would hit him. He was almost laughing. She stared at him, incredulous that he could be so insensitive, slighting her delicate confession with inappropriate amusement.

She could have been a child stealing apples from his orchard and been subject to a more severe rebuke.

It was humiliating.

"The gifts you gave me, I'll have Juggs take them to the Lazy D tomorrow," she said, drawing in a controlled breath.

"Don't talk silly, Merrie. What would I do with the darn things? In any case, you're just sore. I'll come visit Friday, and we'll talk about it. Just watch, you'll think differently by then," he told her.

"I won't. It's over, Matt."

He laughed again. "Women!" he said, as if reminding himself of a forgotten fact. "Don't never try understanding them."

He hitched the collar of his chamois-colored jacket and set his matching hat a little closer on his head. The brilliant heat seemed to flatten him a little.

"I'll give you plenty of time to get over your pique, my little

June bug. Don't you worry none, and if it will make you feel better, we won't mention Delancy again."

Merrie shot him a scathing look. There wasn't really anything else to say. What on earth, she wondered, had she ever seen in him? He was fatuous, inane. She couldn't help but compare him to the gunslinger. He was as bland as porridge and just as tasteless.

Sonnet had strayed down into the thin cottonwoods sheltering along the lee of the pedestal rock, looking for tender shoots to nibble at. She caught up his rein and mounted swiftly.

Drained and fatigued, she turned back in the saddle. There was more than simply her restless night to thank for that. A sober, more brittle world seemed determined to intrude upon her. But strangely enough, she was also aware of a fierce exhilaration, a flame licking inside her that spoke of delight.

She wondered how to reconcile that with her bruised feelings. It didn't make sense at all.

"Good-bye, Matt," she said.

She didn't wait for his reply, but urged Sonnet to a brisk canter. She didn't look back. Not even when she heard him shout to send greetings to Liza and Ash.

Sixteen

"Oh, Sonna, it's you," Merrie said in relief. "You gave me a start."

The chubby housekeeper stood in the doorway of the tack room, arms folded over her ample bosom, and glared at Merrie in silence.

The tack room smelled of leather soap and linseed oil. Harnesses, bridles, and saddles hung on hooks along the walls. In dim cobwebby corners were old broken buckles, brass loops, and halters awaiting attention.

"Well?" Merrie said, when Sonna continued frowning at her.

"Would you like to explain yourself, young miss?"

Merrie felt her cheeks redden. "I don't know what you mean," she said.

Sonna waddled in, pulled up one of the three-legged stools and sat down gingerly, as if she didn't quite trust it to support her weight. Sonna always had had a well-developed sense of survival.

"Would you like to tell me what is going on with you? And don't you tell me nothing."

"There is nothing."

Sonna sighed. "Nothing? For days now, you've hardly shown your face. You ruined your father's homecoming. Bad enough you shunned your friends and relatives. They all gone home now, and you still got a long face. And all you can say is *nothing*?"

"I . . . It's . . . I was tired out, is all." Merrie hung up the harness she had been polishing and took down another.

"Really? Since when have I known you? You can't fool me. You're hiding away, and I want to know why."

"Who runs this outfit, anyway?" Merrie said, suddenly annoyed. "Just leave me alone, will you, Sonna?"

"That I won't. You're not eating. You grab something on the run and don't show your face until dark. Now, I think you're in trouble, Merrie, and I aim to fix it. So first you tell me what happened, then I can see what needs to be done."

Merrie felt her heart leap into her throat. She ached to throw her herself into Sonna's sturdy arms and howl like a baby. She knew she couldn't do that.

Apart from the fact that it would terrify the old woman, she had sworn never to mention *his* name ever again. Besides, as wonderful as it sounded, Sonna couldn't do anything to help her.

Nobody could.

She had been a fool. A thrice-cursed fool. She had allowed herself to be seduced by a devastatingly handsome rogue, a heartless, blue-eyed adulterer. She would never be quite the same again.

But she knew it was even worse than that! Deep shame twisted about her heart. Her stepmother's lover! And she had condemned Liza for her weakness!

She hated Kyle for what he had done to her. She hated herself even more, because she had known exactly what he was. Still, she had allowed him to make love to her. Love! She almost laughed. What they had shared had nothing to do with love . . .

Merrie bit down hard, grinding her teeth against the ache inside.

"It's that stepmother of yours again, isn't it?" said Sonna, her gravelly voice sharp with annoyance.

Merrie shook her head.

"I'm fine, Sonna, really. I just got a dose of the wintertime blues. It's a little early, but I guess I've been working too hard."

Sonna snorted in disbelief. "It's hardly fall yet. You think I'm stupid, young miss? Now, you listen to me. Ash wanted to see you, but I delayed him. Told him you were putting up the new sheds, you right pushed for time."

"Sonna, you didn't have to lie." Actually Merrie was relieved. The very last thing she felt like doing was facing her father. He would know in a minute that something was up.

"Right, I don't, but I did. He's in a rare temper, he is."

Merrie's brows rose in question.

"He and Liza had a bang-up row this morning," Sonna continued. "Ash called her into his study, and he really let her have it. Not a minute too soon, far as I'm concerned. But he's plumb tuckered out from the row, and he don't need any further aggravation from you."

"I must go and see if he's all right," Merrie said, throwing down the polishing rag.

Sonna grabbed her. "Lordie, you take a look at yourself, Merrie, and tell me how you're aiming to help your daddy with that woebegone face of yours."

Merrie nodded and sank back onto her stool. "You're right. One look at me and he'll realize how . . ." She looked up sharply at Sonna and found the housekeeper's button eyes fixed on her with as knowing a look as she had ever seen. She took a breath, and then slowly exhaled. She knew she couldn't allow herself to cry, and she badly wanted to.

Sonna saw her struggle, Merrie knew, but the woman who had always been there for her, helped her into her first party dress, been around to discuss the tooth fairy, and the trials of being a stepdaughter, that woman came to her aid now, just as she always had.

"Tired. You're tired out, right? Okay, so you don't want to talk to me. Go speak to that fancy fiancé of yours, but talk to someone. Get it out of your system."

"Fancy fiancé, no more," Merrie said softly. "I broke off our engagement yesterday."

Her aggravation over Matt's indifference had dissolved into a despondent ache in the region of her heart. It reminded her sharply of the childish insecurity she had felt when Ash first told her that she was getting a new mother. And that had been before she had really known what Liza was like. That kind of feeling, she knew, had more to do with hurt pride than anything else. Her fiancé had hardly thrown himself over a cliff over their breakup.

"Well now, that's the best news I've heard in a month of Sundays." Sonna nodded her head.

"You never did like him much, did you?" Merrie said thoughtfully.

"Merrie, you've been through some tough times, but if you ever thought that man could help you through difficulties, you were in for a big disappointment. His backbone's made of mush. Ash isn't crazy about him either, so you won't get any grief from him."

"Really? He never said anything." She was surprised and a little relieved.

"Why d'you think he wanted you to wait two years?"

"Oh, come on, Sonna. That had nothing to do with it. Everyone knows that my Uncle Grenville put that provision in his will. He wanted me to be certain that I wouldn't marry before I was twenty years old."

Sonna laughed. "You never believed that, did you? Why, Ash is just longing for grandchildren. Your late uncle did as well. They wanted to be assured of the family's future. Your marriage, young miss, is just that—the future."

Astounded for a moment, Merrie allowed that information to sink in. She thought about all the other times Ash had done things to protect her from the harsher realities of daily life.

She sighed with irritation. "I don't understand why Ash can't deal with me honestly. He's always doing things 'for my own good.' He always has. Why didn't he just refuse us permission to wed?"

"'Cause you were more excited than a barrel of monkeys, that's why. The county's most eligible bachelor! Lordie, but we never heard the end of it. And your daddy, he never denied you anything. He just hoped your good sense would prevail if he gave you enough time to think about it."

Sonna stood up, her knees creaking. She shook her finger at Merrie. "But don't you go showing him your long face, y'hear?"

Merrie nodded. "Thanks, Sonna. I love you, too," she said and dipped the cloth into the oily mixture she was using to polish up the leather.

"Course you do. Who else would put up with you? Now, I want to see you at suppertime and no fussing."

"I can't . . . Liza—"

Sonna nodded knowingly. "I know just what you need, young miss. A nice quiet time away from all the nonsense, and Liza most of all. Now, you take yourself down to my cottage, and I'll see to it that Juggs brings you a nice tub. I'll be along in a couple of hours with a good hot meal. You can take the spare bedroom. I'll not disturb you until noon tomorrow. Now, how does that sound?"

Merrie's face became animated. "Oh, Sonna, what a good idea," she said and smiled, delighted with the thought of escaping the main house, Liza, and her own bedroom most of all. It had been almost unbearable the past few nights to lie in her bed alone with her guilt, her remorse . . . her vivid memories . . .

She was inundated with memories of him, his touch, his scent . . . the passionate blue depth of his eyes.

Sonna laughed. "You remember how it used to rile Liza? She hated it that you preferred my cottage to the main house."

Sonna's little bungalow had once been a defunct milking shed some two hundred yards from the main house. Ash had renovated it for her when he brought Liza to the Spur and it became obvious that the two women hated each other on sight. Sonna had refused to live in the main house. For Merrie, the best treat of all had been when she was allowed to sleep over at Sonna's.

"I'll bring your nightgown and a couple of books and we'll light a fire. It will be like old times."

Merrie smiled fondly at Sonna, feeling a small tickle of pleasant anticipation. She rubbed the supple leather in her hand but stopped as a thought occurred to her.

"Sonna, do you know what Ash wanted?"

"No, but whatever it is, it'll wait. That Miss Bishop dosed up your daddy with that *Eastern medicine* of hers." She might well have been speaking about poison. "Not that I hold with it, I don't. But he fair needed something. He was sheet-white after his set-to with Liza. Miss Bishop, she had me call Juggs and Spiker to carry Ash to bed with orders that no one come near him for the rest of the day."

"You sure he's all right? Maybe I'll speak to Gillian."

"It can wait until tomorrow, Merrie. He's stronger than you think, is Ash. Now, you take yourself off to my cottage. I'll tell them up at the house that you've gone off to bed early."

Merrie looked at her thoughtfully. "Do you think he told Liza to leave, Sonna, or is that wishful thinking on my part?"

Sonna shrugged. "Would be no more than she deserves. You know I don't hold with her. But Ash, he's like all men. They see a pretty outside and they want to own it. They make fools of themselves, but by the time they find out what the inside is like, it's too late."

"You could say that say about women, too," Merrie said quietly. "They are just as weak when it comes to a handsome outside, and just as eager to make fools of themselves."

Sonna's button eyes sharpened, and she pursed her fleshy lips. But Merrie was oblivious of the old woman's perceptive look. In her own self-sufficient manner, she was thinking of practical ways to shrug off her blues. A night in Sonna's pleasant cottage was just the place to start.

IT WAS WAY past the middle of the night when Merrie suddenly came awake. A piercing scream hung in the dewy night air, thin and far away. Merrie flung herself out of bed and almost stumbled into Sonna. The old woman was pale with fright.

"Did you hear it?"

"What was that?" said Merrie at the same time.

The scream came again and then again. It was obviously a woman's voice, a woman distraught, terrified.

"The main house," said Merrie, fear making her voice hoarse.

Merrie and Sonna glanced at each other and made for the

front door. Out on the path leading to house, they met up with sleepy-eyed cowboys strapping on guns, pulling on shirts, hobbling into boots as they ran.

There were several lights burning in the main house. Even before they reached the porch, the front door burst open and Gillian Bishop tumbled out. She was barefoot and obviously hysterical. Long, brown hair streamed around her face, a dreadful gash had been opened across her temple, and blood was pouring from her mouth. Her nightclothes were streaked with blood; one sleeve had been torn almost completely off. On a woman who was always controlled and in command, her disheveled state was all the more alarming.

She almost fell down the broad steps in her haste, then stumbled into Merrie's outstretched arms, sobbing, snatching words incoherently from unfinished sentences.

"They've taken . . . Ash, masks, wearing masks . . . dreadful men . . . horrible, bitter voices . . . Oh God, Ash . . ."

Merrie's heart seemed to stop. She was trying to shush the raving woman and make sense out of what she was saying. She saw some of the cowboys rush into the house, others, aghast, came crowding around them. She looked up, bewildered, stunned as Spiker came tearing through the door again.

"He's gone, Miss Merrie, gone. Bed's empty, room is wrecked. Looks like they were trying to tear it apart, yours, too. There's nothing left whole in either of the rooms."

Jamie appeared behind him. "Study's pretty tore up, too, and the porch doors are wide open," he said.

Instantly, Merrie recalled the argument she had overheard. Liza had told the shadowy man, *The French doors,* and he had said, *Don't worry about the nurse. . . .*

Merrie eased Gillian and herself down onto the bottom step with Sonna's help. "Where's Liza?" Merrie asked, her voice like ice. "Didn't she hear anything? Gillian?"

The weeping woman shook her head.

Spiker shrugged uncomfortably. "I'll go look," he said and went back into the house.

Buck came up just then, his face wreathed in worried lines.

"Juggs says there are several horses missing. What's going on here?"

"We were just about to find out," Merrie said, turning to the sobbing woman in her arms. "Gillian, you must try and tell me what happened. Slowly, now. Ash is gone. If we hope to catch up with whoever has taken him, we need your help."

Merrie felt the Englishwoman nod her head. "They came to Ash's room. It was very dark . . . late. They were dragging him out by his legs . . . horrible . . . They had a hood over his face, his chest, down to his arms. They'd tied a thick rope about him; he couldn't move."

"Who, Gillian, who was it? Did you see?" Merrie prompted when Gillian began crying once again.

She shook her head and looked up at Merrie. "I came in, you see, because I heard scuffling. There were two of them. Masked. They both wore black masks and long ponchos."

"Was one of them big, paunchy?" Merrie asked.

"They were both big. One of them saw me at the door and hit me . . . He hit me in the mouth, and then it all went black," she said, her torn mouth trembling again.

Merrie looked up into a sea of furious faces. Cowboys generally were a breed of men who abhorred violence against defenseless women, and Gillian Bishop had quickly become a favorite around the Spur. As a practicing nurse, she had been called upon to patch and remedy all manner of ailments, feigned and real, and had done so with efficiency, and a lighthearted touch of friendliness. The men were clearly outraged that she had been beaten.

Spiker shoved his stout fingers through his hair and caught Merrie's eye. "Liza's gone," he confirmed. "Her room's been neatly cleaned out, too. But here's the strange part—nothing's broken."

"Jamie, you ride into town and get Sheriff Hagan," Buck said.

But Spiker pushed through the crowd of men and shoved a piece of paper into Merrie's hand.

"Don't think that's a good idea. Found it on her bureau, Miss Merrie," he said.

Merrie unfolded the paper and read out loud: "'We have him. If you want to see him alive, don't follow. We'll be in touch.'" It was not signed. It didn't have to be. She knew beyond doubt that her stepmother had arranged for Ash to be abducted, but why? Why? *We'll be in touch.* They would barter Ash's life for money, obviously. If he lived through the trauma . . .

A grimness settled upon her. Like a chill and poisonous mist, it oozed through her heart and her soul. She felt a fury like none she had ever known.

All these people were looking at her as if she could magically come up with the answers. What was she going to do? What?

"It's a good thing that gunfighter's still in town," Sonna said, in the ensuing quiet. "You're going to have to hire him, Merrie, and get him to track these man-thieving cretins."

Merrie's head shot up. "I thought he'd left days ago," she found herself saying, her surprise was so huge.

"No. He's still at Dashers. Must have been paid a tidy sum 'cause he's been drinking it away for days now," said Buck. "Never seen a man consume so much whiskey."

"Yeah, you'd better get him sobered up before you set him on his way," Spiker agreed.

"You and Jamie can go bring him out here, Spiker," Buck said.

"No," Merrie said. "Definitely, no."

Buck shrugged. "He's the only one who can do it. I've seen some gunfighters in my time, but I ain't never seen anything like him."

"No. I won't have him anywhere near this," Merrie said vehemently.

"Maybe you fixing on sending Sheriff Hagan out alone?" Spiker said, shaking his head sorrowfully. "You know, Miss Merrie, he never goes nowhere without a posse. I plain don't trust him."

"Neither do I. Never have," said Jamie. Several of the others concurred.

"You best get that Mr. Smith. If he plays his life like he plays poker, he's a sure straight shooter—even drunk," Juggs said, admiration clear in his voice.

"I won't have his name mentioned," Merrie said, furious with them all.

Buck scratched his head, perplexed.

"But I—"

"Sonna, take Gillian in," Merrie said, carefully peeling the Englishwoman's fingers from her arm. Gillian was in such deep shock that she didn't protest, but dutifully went off with Sonna.

Merrie stood then and contemplated the stubborn wall of men. They were all staring right back at her. Waiting for the word . . . What in God's sweet heaven was she to do now?

Buck saw her torment, the weight of her decision. He knew her through and through. He'd been around since she was born. Next to Ash, she was the best rancher in the business. As far as Buck was concerned, that was the only measure of a man, or woman. Merrie had done a mighty fine job of running the Spur, even against some formidable obstacles. He couldn't have been more proud of her than if she'd been a boy. But right now she was out of her depth.

The old foreman shared a few discreet words with the cowhands. They began slipping off into the darkness, one by one, until only he and Merrie were left on the whitewashed porch.

"We're running out of time, Buck, and I don't know what to do," she said, as soon as the last man vanished down the path.

Buck looked at her. Yellow lamplight from the hall spilled out of the doorway and rippled down the steps of the porch onto her. Just then she looked very young, and very lost.

But there was something more, something Buck didn't understand. He spoke softly, as was his way. There was no disguising his concern, not only for Ash, but for his young mistress, too. He felt badly about her misgivings, but somehow

TEXAS KISS

he must make her see beyond her dislike of the man. There was too much at stake.

"You're going to have to go to that gunslinger, you know," he said softly. "Miss Merrie, you don't have a choice. Ash's life depends on it."

"I know," she whispered, "but not . . . *him*."

Buck heard her distress. He had never known Merrie to waver the way she was now. When something had to be done, she did it. She had more heart and courage than twenty men.

Obviously, there was something between the gunfighter and Merrie. She had vehemently objected to his staying about the ranch, he remembered. But whatever it was, he had to convince her to see the necessity of hiring him on.

"You want Ash back alive?" he eventually asked her.

Stricken, she jerked her eyes to him.

"Then you've got to hire the man," he told her. "Take my word, you ain't never seen anything as lethal. The way he tracked those rustlers and— He can follow a ghost into Hell."

"I don't doubt that," she said grimly. "He's related to the devil, himself."

"What better than a devil, when you're chasing after the devil's brood?"

Merrie gave a little smile. "You're right," she said.

SEVENTEEN

Stop, Kaiten. You got to stop! he pleaded. His heart was crumbling away.

He couldn't stand it any longer, and yet he knew what it would mean when the screaming stopped. He couldn't stand that either.

But she didn't stop. Not for a grotesquely long time.

She screamed with all the fury and despair of her wretched young life.

It wasn't a human noise. He heard it still, that scream. It made him old inside. He was only nine, but it made him old.

Stop, he whispered. It hurt his ears. Through the whiskey haze he watched again as she pitched and heaved on the ragged pallet. He could see vestiges of the shed they had called home. Stinking, rotting fish and rust—he imagined he could smell their dockside hovel. Their pathetic refuge from their vicious mother.

Not that she had tried to find them; she hadn't.

His mouth was so very dry, he felt his tongue crack. His eyes burned fiercely. *Stop.* He brought his hands up to cover his ears.

"You say something, Mr. Smith?" Virgil Tech asked.

Kyle felt himself jerk just the way his sister's bloated body had jerked that far-off, nightmarish day in New Orleans.

He tried to focus, to shed the horrible memories and their clawing persistence. In his current condition, it wasn't easy.

Good reason not to get drunk, he lectured himself, not for the first time, and promptly told himself he had good reason to drink.

Her name was Merrie Sinclair.

Damn good reason.

Concentrating hard, he reached unsteady fingers toward his glass.

"Mr. Smith, sir?"

The barman's image slowly swam into view. His poker face, his hair smoothed to glossy perfection on either side of his center part looked blurred about the edges. The bottles behind him on the shelves stood in shadowy ranks, their images doubled and confused by Kyle's vision and the reflecting glass behind.

"Do you want Maisey to help you back to Dashers, Mr. Smith, sir?"

"D'you know, Virgil, you can't bury folk in the ground in New Orleans?" Kyle managed at last. He croaked, and his words sounded as if he were trying to swallow them.

Virgil took up his cloth and began polishing the glass in his hand again.

"No sir, Mr. Smith," he said, "can't rightly say that I do."

"Water table too high. Bodies would float right out of the ground," Kyle said.

"That so? Where they put them?"

"Above ground. Marble, they use marble. Smooth, cool. Some fancy tombs, some plain, but all marble."

"Whew, that must cost a bundle," Virgil said.

"More than I had." He rose unsteadily on his lanky legs and clutched the counter a moment.

He left the barman staring after him. He knew how drunk he was, and so he walked very carefully. Not since Etienne DeLace's funeral had he ever got this drunk. Christ, he missed Etienne!

A wavy image of his adoptive father swam into his head as he weaved between the tables and early poker players. They watched him in wary silence, untrusting, some belligerent. None were stupid enough to test him.

Mariette DeLace still lived in the same house on Bienville Street in the French Quarter. To him, a little boy of nine, it had seemed the grandest palace imaginable. The pink stucco house was frosted with wrought-iron and faced a cobbled courtyard where a fountain spouted into a smooth, silver pond. It had been more than a palace, though, for it had saved his sanity, offered him succor from a harsh and immeasurably cruel world. And Etienne and Mariette had given him something even more precious: love.

He visited Mariette whenever he could. It wasn't simply his gratitude, profound as that was, but that he truly felt renewed by the bounty of her unselfish, unequivocal love.

Although eighteen years had passed since Mariette and Etienne had taken him in, he still believed their coming into his life had been a miracle, not simply coincidence.

Since the War Between the States had robbed the DeLaces of their own son, they had visited the cemetery of St. Louis once a week. It was there they had found Kyle, collapsed beside his sister's body, at the gates of the cemetery. What kind of grotesque journey he had made to bring her there, no one would ever know.

But that was as far as he had managed to get. Penniless and lost to unavailing grief, he had come to the end of his road, only to find a miracle.

He grinned, recalling Mariette's adage: *coincidence is for the fool, miracles are for the marvelous.*

The frowsy blond coming down Dashers' stairs smiled back at him suggestively.

He stumbled, clutched the banister, and righted himself before eventually making it to the top landing. It took him several minutes to unlock his door and several more to locate the bed, but eventually he fell back with a sigh of pleasure into the comfortable plushness of the red velvet eiderdown.

It was a pleasure that was short-lived.

Dashers' whores were entertaining their customers, and there was nothing reserved about them. Through the thin walls, he could hear quite clearly the lusty moans, saucy laughter, and the protesting groan of abused furniture.

He swore and closed his eyes, but he knew he wouldn't find any sleep.

He still hadn't had enough to drink.

The aggravating noise was bad enough, but it was nothing compared to the persistent memory of Merrie Sinclair that had haunted him for the past few days.

The fact annoyed him intensely.

Hell, was he crazy? He had to get out of Hollow Creek and away from her. This waiting was driving him insane.

He cursed himself for getting involved with her in the first place. Whatever she had, and he certainly couldn't define it, Merrie Sinclair had demolished his resolve. He disliked that intensely. Still, he had no intention of relinquishing responsibility. His convictions were etched upon soul; he would not forswear them, not now, not ever.

But it didn't mean that he had to abide this little town, this gaudy whorehouse while he waited, surely? Every day there was a danger of running into Merrie, and every day he waited to see her. He told himself he just wanted the whole thing over and done with, but the truth was he wanted to see her.

That was why he got drunk. But he didn't seem able to get drunk enough.

Maybe he would head out tomorrow. He could always come back and check up on her in a few weeks. He doubted she was pregnant anyway.

What he would do if she was remained a nebulous uncertainty. Surely she wouldn't marry him, even if he did ask her. Beyond this, he refused to think about it. He was in no hurry to get himself leg-shackled.

His job was almost finished. At least he damn well hoped so. Everything he had worked toward and planned for was coming to a head. He could sense it. It was imperative that he be in Dodge City for the finale, and he didn't feel like wasting any more time hanging about here.

As soon as it was daylight, he would head back to Dodge City.

It would help to get his mind back on his work.

The women there were uncomplicated and sophisticated, and lots of fun. They could certainly help his out-of-control lust, if he so chose, and could restore balance to his life again.

Maybe, he thought, once he got back, he would also be able to douse this reckless, hungry wanting . . . ?

EIGHTEEN

THE DOOR POPPED open with such force that Merrie nearly fell into the room. Kyle pulled her inside the minute he saw who it was and closed the door quickly. He scowled at her, then spun his gun back into the holster with a smooth twist of his wrist.

"Well, I must be dreaming," he drawled sarcastically.

Merrie grimaced, recalling her scornful words to him the night they made love. She took a breath.

"It's not what you're thinking," she assured him. Her voice was cold, aloof. She held herself tall and very straight to keep her hurt from showing.

"Oh, and what am I thinking?"

She threw him a furious look. She hated being here. Just seeing him made her furious with herself all over again. Surely she could get someone else to help her find her father. But then she remembered Buck's words about the man's tracking abilities.

"Ash is gone. Abducted. I want to hire you to find him."

She saw the lightning-quick change in the man and couldn't quite believe her eyes. One minute he was a cynical, fairly inebriated man, unsteady on his feet, the next he was all efficiency, sharp-eyed and fully awake.

"When?"

"About four, maybe five hours ago."

"Anybody see who did it?"

"Gillian Bishop, his nurse."

"I know who she is," he said irritably. "How many were there?"

"Two men, big, they wore masks. They beat her senseless."

"How'd they get in? Liza?"

Merrie couldn't have been more astonished.

"How did you know?" She felt a sudden thrill of fear slide down her back.

Kyle saw it. He reached into the pack at the foot of his bed and pulled out a clean shirt. "No, Legs. I'm not in cahoots with her; I just know her type." He sighed impatiently when he saw the look she sent him.

"I'll just bet you do," she said softly and swallowed down hard.

He grunted but said nothing.

Merrie groaned inside. She needed him. It irked her right down to her bones, but there was no other choice. Hagan wouldn't go out after her father's kidnappers without a posse at his back. She needed a lone gunman, someone who could stay hidden and strike quickly when the opportunity presented itself.

It was then she noticed unmistakable signs of his impending departure. He had been in the process of packing. A few moments more, and he might have been gone. A neat pile of clothes lay on the bed, waiting to be packed away. His saddle lay ready near the door. On the dresser there was a small tin of boot polish and a buffing brush, an oil rag next to its pouch, for cleaning his guns she supposed, and the golden trinket she had given him that long-ago night when she had first tried to bribe him into leaving Hollow Creek.

She was surprised he had kept it.

Her eyes snapped back to him, and she saw that he had been watching her, a clear challenge in his expression.

"I want—" she began, but he shook his head very slowly, interrupting her. Then he sauntered over to the bureau, scooped the necklace off the top, and slipped it into his pants pocket, his eyes never leaving her face.

A thin trickle of ice swept down her spine. It was intriguing. Bewildering. It was deliberate, there was no doubt about it, and she could not say why it disturbed her so, but it did. He seemed unwilling to give the necklace back. She wanted that locket, but realized that now was not the time to be arguing over it.

She watched Kyle slide the bone buttons into the holes of his shirt, his graceful fingers moving easily, competently.

"Tell me everything you know, from the beginning," he said.

Merrie told him briefly what had happened out at the Spur.

"Can you help? I'll pay you whatever you decide is fair. A business arrangement," she finished.

Kyle's brow hitched. He closed in on her, intimidating, tall; he seemed to steal her breath without laying a finger on her. She refused to move away and stood her ground. She was tall, but even so she had to tilt her head back to hold his gaze.

His blue eyes washed over her, into her. She felt the trembling begin somewhere deep inside, building, swelling, until she had to look away, fearful of crying out his name.

She hated him when he did this to her. She hated his seducing, fervent scrutiny. She despised her own weakness.

He seemed satisfied with her tacit defeat. Still he seemed to sense that she did not want him to touch her, and he refrained from doing so.

"There are conditions." he said.

"What conditions?"

"I make the rules, Legs. It's the only way I work. My way, my say, no arguments. Deal?"

Merrie shook her head. "I must know all the rules before I will agree to that."

Kyle grinned. "The rules are, there are no rules."

Merrie sent him a troubled glance. "At least tell me this: can you find him? Buck Peterson says he's never seen anyone track better than you."

"I'll find him," he said, without preamble, completely confident in his abilities.

"There's one thing more," she said, turning away from him.

He didn't query her. She knew he was looking at her, his scorching blue gaze peeling away her self-confidence, but she was determined in her course. She had faced far more belligerent men this past year and survived the ordeal, even if the threat posed by the Cattlemen's Consortium did not endanger her equilibrium in the way this man did. She knew how perilous it was for her to be near him, but she had to accompany him. She had to find her father.

"I want you to take me and Gillian Bishop along with you," she said.

Kyle laughed—a sound like deep water chuckling over rocks. The sounds traveled over her back like cool fingers.

"I travel fast and light—I work by myself."

"And when you catch up with Ash, you'll know just how to doctor him. He's a very sick man," she said, letting the idea hang in the air.

She felt his gaze flare into white-hot contemplation. When she finally turned back to him, his narrow eyes fairly crackled with antipathy.

"You got a deal. But I'll take only one of you. You choose. The nurse, or you."

She was horrified. She barely managed to survive Kyle Delancy in the civilized setting of home and hearth. How would she be able to resist him out there in the wild, alone, unfettered by any societal restraints? She couldn't do it. She wouldn't do it.

"Wait, I . . . I can't go with you. Not alone."

He shrugged. "Suit yourself," he said indifferently. "Get the nurse and bring her here."

Merrie opened her mouth to protest, but she saw it would be senseless. Kyle Delancy was not someone you argued with. What's more, he knew she would never let Gillian go in her place. There really never was any choice.

"You have a deal. I'll go, Mr. Delancy."

"I thought you might."

"I don't care what you think. I just want you to find my father. Starting right now. He's not well. He won't survive too long out there with that gang of thugs."

"Let's get this straight. You don't give the orders, I do." He pulled a pencil stub and paper out of the bureau drawer and jotted several things down. When he'd finished, he handed it to her. "Get everything that's on here and meet me at the livery, at noon."

TEXAS KISS 155

He moved about the room, packing up his remaining possessions and strapping his bedroll. Then he hooked his gear over his shoulder and headed for the door, his long strides purposeful.

"Bring that pack of mine down to the livery."

"Anything else, master?" she said, annoyed at his authoritative tone.

"As a matter of fact, Legs, yes. I think after you've slept with a man, it's customary to call him by his first name. Try it, will you?"

Merrie's hard held fury exploded. It was too much. *He was too much.* Her beloved father was missing, viciously abducted by his own wife, and Kyle was being flippant.

"*Mr. Delancy,* I want to be clear. This is a business arrangement. Strictly a business arrangement. Touch me, and I'll shoot you."

"Thanks for the warning, Legs. But I guess I'll take my chances. You don't seem all that threatening to me."

"I'd advise you to take me seriously. I know how to protect myself."

Kyle looked at her speculatively a moment and nodded. "Duly noted. My advice to you, Legs, is this: learn to relax. We've some stiff riding ahead. With that attitude of yours, you might just snap in two.

She turned away from him all the same, reluctant to let him see how mortified she was.

"Don't be late. Noon at the livery," he said, opening the door.

"Where are you going? I suppose it's not outside the accepted *rules* to ask?"

"It's daybreak. I want to see what the ground looks like. They took a fair number of horses, according to you. They'll probably try to run them here and there to confuse their real direction. But there's only one way out through Wolf Fang Pass, and once I have them lined up, I can tell which horses are carrying the real thing and which are decoys."

It was comforting to hear that Kyle had a direction, a plan.

Somehow it made the sick, helpless feeling in Merrie's stomach ease a little. She felt her legs give a bit and decided to sit down.

She saw Kyle react. He closed the door and came toward her. She shied back into the chair, knowing that if he touched her, she would give vent to the burning tears ravaging her insides. She closed her eyes tight and heard him curse softly.

"You haven't had much sleep, have you?"

She shook her head.

"Get some rest while you can," he told her. "We'll be riding hard. And Merrie, think about this. They didn't kill Ash. They want him alive for some reason. It's probably in their best interest to keep him alive until they get him to wherever it is they're taking him. So don't give up," he said and retreated back across the room.

Merrie's eyes came open. She stared at the tall, dark man beside the door. His long, virile body was tense—a panther on the verge of springing after its prey. He was impatient to get going, she could tell.

He was ruthless; he took what he wanted, on his terms, as he so fondly reminded her. Yet, he had tried to relieve her anxiety. How strange, she thought. It was the last thing she expected of him.

"Lock the door when I'm gone," he told her and left.

SHE DID SLEEP. Curled up on Kyle's bed. Even the disturbing scent of him couldn't prevent her from falling asleep almost instantly. She had been unable to get a good night's rest for close to a week now, and with the upset of Ash's abduction, sheer exhaustion had finally won out over her agitation.

When she woke with a start, it was already late in the morning and she had to scramble. Linnett's General Store on Main Street was her first stop. There she got flour, ground corn, bacon, nuts, and molasses. She packed in several tins of beans, coffee, dried beef jerky, and the first of the autumn apples. Feed for the horses and a thick bedroll for herself were next. Added to this she got several items for herself (as she had brought nothing along) and completed Kyle's request for ammunition, iodine, a new kettle, and rope.

Peggy Linnett was in a rather morose mood as she packed up the goods, tying them into neat, portable bundles for Merrie. To Merrie's relief, Peggy did not speculate on what the purchases might mean. In fact, they could just as easily have been bought for a sojourn out on the range. Kyle had insisted that Merrie not communicate with anyone about her impending journey, and certainly she wasn't to mention the fact that Ash was missing. So it was with a sigh of relief that she managed to leave Linnett's store and head down to the blacksmith, where Sonnet was getting re-shoed.

The saddlebags and packages were heavy, and so she left them at Linnett's to be picked up on her way.

She almost jumped out of her skin as she rounded the corner of Main Street and felt a hand on her shoulder.

"Well, if it isn't Miss Sinclair, I do declare," said the familiar voice of Kate Brown.

Merrie spun about. "Oh, Kate, it's you."

"Yes, it is, and I don't know that I ever want to speak to you again," Kate said, tapping her foot on the wood sidewalk.

Merrie felt a fleeting pang of guilt. She had tricked Kate the night of the party, even though her prank had been aimed primarily at Kyle. And then she recalled what that little hoax had led to. Kyle had stormed into her bedroom, stormed her resistance, and made passionate, unforgettable love to her. Her life had been turned upside down. The emotions played across her face, coloring it first with softness and then with rosy guilt. She looked back at her friend in momentary silence.

Kate couldn't miss the meaning of her friend's scarlet face, even if she didn't know the details.

"Oh, Merrie," she said, her eyes growing as big as saucers. "What have you gone and done? You're engaged to be married!" She was clearly shocked.

The very last thing Merrie wanted now was to have to give Kate a lengthy explanation of her breakup with Matt, let alone her involvement with Kyle.

"Really, it was all a joke. I didn't mean to embarrass you, Kate. I just thought it might be amusing for you to turn up—"

"Why would you think it?"

"Because you so badly wanted to meet him."

"Well, it wasn't funny. Mr. Smith was very angry when he saw it was me, not you. What are you up to, Merrie? I don't believe you, anyway. You're red in the face and that means you're guilty. Now, what are you up to?"

"Nothing . . . I must be on my way, Kate. I'm . . . late," Merrie said.

"Not so fast. I want an answer. You're greedy, Merrie. I see it all now."

"Whatever are you talking about, Kate?"

"You want them both. The gunslinger and Matt Cheston. That's bigamy really. If the sheriff was in town, I'd have you arrested."

Merrie was startled. She had known Kate all her life, and although Kate had a tendency to be flighty, she'd never been nasty. But there was no mistaking the decidedly spiteful look on her face just then. Fact was, loneliness did strange things to people.

"What do you mean?" Merrie asked, her disappointment hard to conceal.

"I've just come from there. My cat's missing again, but Tom Hagan is gone for a few days," Kate said.

Merrie forced herself to laugh. "That's not what I mean. Really, Kate, bigamy is only if I marry them both. Likely as not, I won't marry anyone. In fact," Merrie said, suddenly thinking of a way to get rid of Kate, "you should consider Matt yourself. I don't think he and I are well suited anymore."

Kate blinked in astonishment. "You really mean that?" she asked, her head cocked to the side, her expression serious.

Merrie nodded.

"We haven't been getting along very well lately," she said in a confidential voice. "In fact, we've decided not to marry."

Kate's face brightened considerably. "How sad," she said.

Merrie nodded.

"Is he sad, do you think? Would he appreciate a visit from a friend to cheer him up?"

Merrie nodded again. "What a good idea. And now I really must go," she said. To her relief, Kate didn't delay her any further, and she hurried off down the street.

When she looked back, her frivolous friend was nowhere in sight.

NINETEEN

"Keep your goddamn horse away from those tracks," Kyle said, his temper flaring. "Bringing damn amateurs out on the trail—must be crazy," he muttered to himself. Dismounting, he hunkered down to inspect the ground.

Merrie wanted to scream at him. She certainly was not an amateur, having ridden the range for several years now. This past year had taught her even more endurance. There had been long days in the saddle and rough, drafty outdoor camps. But she didn't quite trust her emotions right now to tell the arrogant man what she thought of his opinions, so she kept quiet.

In any case, her prime concern was for Ash. No matter what Kyle had said, her father's condition was still very weak. The stroke he had suffered had been massive. It was a miracle that he had survived, and now this . . .

Added to her aggravation, though, was the complication of just being with Kyle. He disturbed her—deep down in her soul, he disturbed her.

She detested the kind of man he was—an adulterous lecher. He hadn't even denied his liaison with her contemptuous stepmother, even when he acknowledged that she was involved in this treachery against Ash.

But she was not impervious to his allure. No, she definitely was not. Even while she reprimanded herself about her weakness, she had to admit it, though it ate at her pride. Bad enough that he had seduced her, he had also discarded her. Yet she seemed unable to resist hovering near his flame, like a fated moth.

It was humiliating. If she had been able to expunge him from her life, never setting eyes on him again, then perhaps she could have conquered her vulnerability. As it was, she was forced to seek his assistance, obliged to him for her safety, and for her father's.

It was driving her crazy!

She had no more wish to spend time with him than he with her.

Since leaving Hollow Creek, she had watched his mood darken. The trail he had followed was a difficult one, made worse by a sudden windstorm that had blown buff-colored sand over everything. Where he had picked up tracks, they had been deliberately confused. Some veered off left and right; others went south, and several went north. Merrie didn't see how he could tell which ones he was following. She only knew it was hot and uncomfortable, and Kyle's short-tempered rudeness was infuriating her beyond endurance.

Added to that, whatever he saw on the ground was disconcerting him. Hunkering down on bent knees and fingering a handful of sand, Kyle had gazed absently off into the blue until she thought he had fallen asleep there. But eventually they had ridden off, backtracking a couple of times, now coming in close to the Red River, now turning away. Merrie was beginning to have second thoughts about her companion's abilities.

Then, just as the sun sank into a ruddy sky smudged with streaks of gray, he had found what he was looking for. Clear tracks coming down from the eastern ridge to join the trail they had been following.

Wagon tracks! Even Merrie could see what they were.

"They put him in a wagon," she said, climbing off Sonnet. She knelt at his side.

"Good," he said, coming to his feet, his eyes following the neat lines as they curved away into the northwest. He seemed well satisfied with his find. "We can take it easy, now. Mount up."

"What do you mean, take it easy?"

"Think about it. Your father's not well enough to ride. They're taking care to conserve his strength, and their pace will be slow." His answer was really only partially true.

He was very relieved that the abductors had transferred Ash to a wagon. He'd had fears of them traveling by railroad train. That would have been better for Ash, but dangerous, too. If they had been discovered, they might have killed Ash instantly.

Liza and her friends were playing right into his hands, and he couldn't help but feel a sense of exhilaration. What was more, he had Merrie and they didn't!

They must have been riled to find her gone. He had a fleeting vision, then, of her bedroom in shambles. He had seen it on his quick visit back to the Spur.

He thanked his lucky stars she had come to him and not gone chasing off after the thugs with a posse of her own. He knew how impetuous she could be.

He avoided her brilliant gaze as he passed her to mount Cappoquin, his black stallion.

Merrie puzzled over his information. "Why do you suppose they're taking such trouble with him?"

Kyle pulled his horse's head around and set off. "You ask too many questions," he told her and settled into a canter.

"And I'm paying for their answers," she told him curtly.

"Don't have time. Got to catch up with some kidnappers first," he called back, effectively stopping her complaints.

He pushed hard, speaking little, never once looking back to see if she followed.

By the time the first evening star appeared, they had crossed into the flat, uncompromising plains that once had been home to thousands of buffalo and wandering Comanche.

No longer. Here were only ghosts, dust, and a treeless wilderness that gasped under the white heat of noon and moaned under flagellating winds. As on a great becalmed ocean, there was nothing here but lonely space, immeasurable and ambiguous. Even colors were mute, the sky and the land blended and unblemished by mark or identification. But Kyle Delancy seemed to know exactly where he was going.

Not once did he falter or change direction. He kept at a steady pace, his eyes fixed on some unknown place on the horizon.

There was no moon that night, yet Kyle showed no signs of stopping. By starlight, they followed the glistening river for mile after tedious mile. Merrie didn't dare complain, but watched his straight, wide-shouldered back with growing animosity.

She jumped almost out of her skin when he suddenly appeared at her side, grasping her arm with long, sure fingers. She realized she must have dozed off in the saddle. Her eyes wide, she stared at his shadowed face, harsh in the starlight, and heard him curse.

It was on the tip of her tongue to apologize for doing such a foolhardy thing, but the uncompromising granite of his expression made her push up her chin. She glared back at him.

"Does this mean we're stopping?" Her voice was challenging. She knew he had to stop at some time, even if only to rest the horses.

"Soon," he told her. "If you feel sleep again, call out. The last thing I need is to have you break your neck. Although it would certainly cut down your chatter."

He edged his horse forward again, and Merrie made a face at him.

"If the wind changes, you'll stay that way," his voice came floating back at her.

Merrie jumped. Exasperating man! How had he known?

THEIR CAMP THAT night was cheerless. Kyle was preoccupied.

"No fire," he said when she began collecting twigs and brush. "I don't want them to know we're behind them."

Merrie threw down the kindling. "You know where they are?" she said excitedly.

Kyle threw her a look that asked what kind of tracker she thought he was. "That's what you're paying me for, isn't it?"

Merrie hurried to his side. He was lifting the saddle off Cappoquin. Even after his recent drinking spree and their tiring day, he didn't show any signs of fatigue.

"How far ahead? How long until we catch up with them?" she asked, her eyes luminous, her eager face tilted up to his.

Kyle set his saddle aside and began rubbing Cappoquin down.

"Far enough." He nodded to Sonnet. "Better get started," he said, "or you won't get much sleep."

Merrie's temper flared. He had been obnoxious the whole day, and she'd had enough.

"Mr. Delancy, you will please answer me. I am, as you reminded me, the one who is paying for your services." She stepped closer to emphasize her determination.

It was a mistake. She was almost touching him. She could smell his scent. Even over the dust and sweat of the trail, Kyle had a definite masculine scent of his own. It triggered something very primal in Merrie.

It was one of the reasons she had had such a difficult time staying in her room after he'd made love to her, for she could smell him there. Now it came to her again. Faint, seductive, like silvery raindrops at night. She shuddered as it impacted her senses.

He wouldn't look at her, and continued grooming his horse. The animal's glossy hide quivered under each rhythmic stroke. Cappoquin stood very still, his ears pricked in bliss, his huge velvet eyes glazed.

"You seem to have no retention at all, darlin'. The name's Kyle."

"I know what your name is," she hissed.

He chuckled as she tried hard to deal with her frayed temper.

"Why don't you see to your horse and bed yourself down?"

Merrie plunked her fists onto her hips and tossed her head, sending her hat spilling onto her shoulders.

"Forget it. You can't just send me to bed like a child; I won't have it. I want answers, and you can keep your foul temper to yourself. This is a business arrangement. I will thank you to respect it as such and keep me informed at all times, and in a courteous manner."

He was silent awhile, leaning his head to rest briefly against the horse's flank as if he were suddenly tired. But then he turned to look at her. She was shocked at what she saw there. His eyes were hot, searing. She felt as if he were paring away her clothes, stripping her.

He let his eyes slip provocatively down her face, her neck. Her breasts seemed to swell, the nipples hardened to a tight ache as his eyes lingered there, only to flow once again down the length of her legs and sweep up again to hold her wide-eyed gaze.

He'd done this to her before. It was a prelude to his seduction of her, and she hated it, hated the terrifying loss of control it made her feel.

She backed away, one step and then another.

"The deal is, I give the orders and you jump. Now, Legs, do as you're told." He smiled then, but there was nothing nice about it. It was a nasty, knowing smile, one that did not reach his eyes. "Unless you want something . . . else from me?"

"The only thing I want from you is to find my father," she said, backing away another step.

"That's not what your eyes are saying, darlin'. Should I tell you what it is they're asking for?"

"You disgust me," she said. Blood surged into her face and neck, and the embarrassing stain made her all the more furious with him.

He changed then, like a sudden turnaround wind. All the petty games, the mock courtesy, even the short-tempered evasions he had flung at her all day—all vanished. In their place was a deadly, serious anger—hard, threatening, just barely restrained. "Then get the hell away from me, and stay away," he ground out.

Merrie's mouth dropped open with indignation. She sent him a filthy look, then quickly led her stallion to the other side of the camp and started rubbing him down, furiously muttering to herself all the while.

Kyle watched her go, her shoulders stiff with pique. Christ, but he'd better make her wear a duster or something. The way her backside and legs were displayed in those tight work pants, she was a danger to his every waking moment. Ah hell! Who was he kidding? He didn't have to see her to want her.

For several days, he had tried by drinking himself under the table at Dashers to put out the fire she had caused in his blood. Truth was, he had never burned as fiercely as he did for Merrie Sinclair.

He still couldn't quite believe his loss of control with her. It was unprecedented. He didn't participate in casual relationships. Not ever.

Not that there was anything casual about Meredith Amber Sinclair. She was incredibly sensual and innocent all at once. A potent combination, in his estimation of female allure.

He'd been so relieved when she showed up this morning. He supposed he thought she was coming to tell him he could shelve his conscience, that everything was fine. He felt like a bastard for wanting that, but he had no intention of marrying her, if he could avoid it . . . *as if she would even consent* . . .

And then she had barged in and bargained with him to take her along! Hell, he'd been fantasizing about carrying her off with him. Now, here she was, alone with him in the wild. She was like a blossom just come into flower. Her newly awakened senses beckoned, her famished eyes watching him, haunting his back all day.

She didn't know it. He knew he'd embarrassed her by pointing it out, but there was no mistaking the signs. He was experienced, and he instantly grasped the telltale attributes of erotic desire.

His only hope was to make the journey to Dodge City as quickly and with as few complications as possible. If he didn't think there was a strong possibility that he might have to use Merrie to advance his plan, he would never have agreed to bring her along. Even now, he cursed himself for considering it. It would take every inch of his self-control to keep away from her.

He calculated that with good weather and no complications they would reach Dodge City in a little over a week.

Not a great deal of time under normal circumstances, he thought grimly, but he wasn't so sure he could last that long without succumbing to the lure of Merrie Sinclair.

He wasn't sure at all.

TWENTY

ON THE THIRD day out, the heat was so intense that Kyle decided to stop for a few hours during the middle of the day. Apart from any other consideration, he wouldn't endanger the horses by exposing them when there was really no need. He was confident that they could make up the time during twilight and early evening.

The sun, a huge, blinding disc, seemed to consume the very colors from the sky. It was as if the vast expanses of the High Plains had been enclosed inside a white-hot cooking bowl. The land lay skeleton-bleak and flattened under the oppressive heat. Blistering air sank down like heavy sediment and sapped moisture from everything.

Under the canvas shelter that he had erected, for there was not a vestige of shade anywhere, Kyle dozed, his head rested against his saddle, his hat slanted over his eyes. Behind him, the two horses shifted now and then, their noses deep in their feed bags.

Merrie watched the rhythmic rise and fall of Kyle's chest and listened to the unvarying chomp of the horses. She couldn't sleep.

Unbearably hot, she felt as if her skin was too tight for her body. Even her lungs felt scorched. She had long ago doffed her waistcoat and now opened the shirt buttons at her neck and pulled off her heavy riding boots. She wriggled her toes appreciatively, but it did little to distract her.

Every cool, green river she had known, every delicious jug of water, every crystal raindrop seemed to etch itself upon her mind. Her throat grew tighter with every passing moment. It was sheer torment.

Worse still, early that morning they had passed one of the

narrow streams that fed into the Rio Cañado, as the old Mexicans called the broad river of the High Plains. If she took off now, she could reach the stream in very little time.

But Kyle had forbidden it when she had asked, saying that he wanted her rested. He intended to push on until late tonight.

What could it hurt him if he didn't know? she thought, casting a furtive look in his direction.

It was then she saw the snake.

A rattler. It had curled into the hollow made by his saddle, not two inches from his face.

Her scream caught in her dry throat. Her eyes locked on the creature, she felt for Kyle's gun, which lay between them, and forced herself to stand, very, very slowly.

The click of the trigger brought Kyle's eyes open, but Merrie's warning shout froze him instantly.

"Don't move, Kyle, don't move," she said urgently, the pitch of her voice high with nervous tension. Still, she managed to master her fear enough to keep her hands absolutely rock steady.

His brows rose in question, for he could see that she was looking beyond him, but he didn't move a muscle.

"There's a . . . a rattler next to your saddle. I'm going to blast it, okay?" Her voice trembled, but her hands remained steady.

She did not see the peculiar look on Kyle's face just then, for she didn't dare look away from her target.

"Hold it now, Legs," he said softly. The deep resonance filtered through her straining nerve ends like cool, soothing water. "Take a breath there and hold it. I'm going to roll and take the saddle with me. I'll count aloud—you fire on five. You got that?"

"No. It's too dangerous. Let me do it, Kyle. I know what I'm doing."

His voice remained perfectly controlled, smooth. "Do as I say. On the count of five, Legs. I'm counting on you . . ."

Merrie blinked. Devil's own, but the man was obdurate.

TEXAS KISS   171

Only Kyle Delancy would think to manage his own rescue and fool about at the same time.

But now was no time to argue with the devil. She heard him count, and then, as he shouted out "five," he catapulted to his left, hauling his beautiful Spanish saddle with him. The rattlesnake spiraled out of its coils, but Merrie's shot went clean through, right behind the head. The snake blew apart.

The gunshot reverberated all about her, and her heart clattered against her rib cage painfully. Her shoulder smarted from the recoil.

Dazed, she managed to pull her eyes away from the disintegrated remains of the snake, only to find Kyle's blue stare fixed on her. There was a look of pure disbelief on his face before he shuttered it. He rolled smoothly to his feet, brushed the dun-colored dust from his pants, and picked up his Stetson.

With a grin, he swept his hat over his knee with a flourish to rival the courtiers of old. "Much obliged, ma'am," he said. "That was fine shooting."

Merrie felt limp. He was too much. There was nothing trivial about a rattlesnake, but he was treating the incident as if it were a great joke.

She threw him a furious look and dropped his gun at her feet.

"I suppose you think you're welcome, but I can't quite manage that. It may be a shock to you, Delancy, but I don't need guidance. I'm quite capable of handling things my own way."

His congenial grin vanished. "No offense, but I had no way of knowing you could shoot so damn well. Also, I'm rather fond of my saddle and didn't want it damaged."

"Saddles can be purchased. Some things can't be."

"You're right," he said as if he didn't believe a word of it. "And you have my gratitude."

"It's time you realized you have to rely on your partner when you're traveling out in the wild like this. Women have minds, too, you know, and I know how to use mine."

Instead of mocking her, or flying into a temper at her

chiding, he appeared to consider what she was trying to tell him. Merrie was surprised.

"I agree. Next time I'll leave it up to you."

Merrie swung her hair up under her hat and sat down.

"Careful, Mr. Delancy, or I might begin to think you have streaks of civilization buried somewhere inside. That sounded dangerously like an apology," Merrie said, pulling on her boots. Hot it might be, but if there was one rattler around, there might be another. Not to mention scorpions.

"I wouldn't go that far," he told her.

She ignored him and did not assist in disposing of the snake but lay back against her own saddle and pretended to sleep.

He soon settled back down to sleep, and she waited until she heard his breathing even out. She was determined to slip away and have an invigorating swim, and blast Kyle Delancy if he didn't like it.

THE WALK BACK down the trail to the shallow stream was not nearly as difficult as she had thought it might be. The land sloped slightly down toward the stream, and although it was stifling, she took frequent sips from her water bottle, knowing that she would be able to fill it once she got there.

The stream cut across from east to west, and in places was no more than an inch or two deep. But she didn't care.

She stripped down to her chemise and pantaloons and waded in, gasping with delight and laughing at the joyous feel of the silver-green water sliding over her heated feet. She bent her knees and hit the water with both arms, sending glittering cascades of it high over her head.

Farther downstream, the sandy bottom fell away, in places quite sharply, to form eddying pools. Here the water was cooler, refreshing. She ducked her head under and swam along quite a way, kicking strongly, then rising up with a gush of water and a shower of silver.

After a while, she simply rested on her back, blinking at the dazzling sky and paddling her feet sporadically. It was blissful. She floated down on the gentle current, her backside scraping the streambed now and then, where the water was shallow. She knew that time was passing, and a reluctant voice inside her head warned her not to dally too long, but it was too wonderful a hiatus in endless weeks of travail. She simply didn't want to return to her dominating companion too quickly.

A few moments more wouldn't hurt.

Long glides underwater brought her back upstream to where she had left her clothes. With one last surge she surfaced, her golden hair streaming down her back, the water sluicing off her in glistening foils.

She saw Kyle immediately, of course. Who could miss him? She muttered a pox on her poor luck.

Briefly, his gun was pointed directly at her. He hesitated only another second, making sure there was no danger, and then holstered his gun, his movements like quicksilver. For comfort sake, he had hitched the gunbelt over Cappoquin's saddle horn.

He strode forward then, leading the horses into the stream, and stood holding their reins. The horses drank, necks stretched out over the water.

Kyle simply stared at her. His dark Stetson hid his eyes, but she could tell by the tension in his shoulders, and the tightness around his mouth, that he was pretty furious with her.

Oh well, she philosophized, it was bound to happen sooner or later on this journey. Kyle Delancy knew as much about flexibility as an iron rod.

She smiled brightly, determined to brazen it out. "Did you have a good sleep?"

His scowl deepened.

Suddenly, the very devil got into Merrie. She had just the way to cool off his temper.

She rose and waded to the water's edge. Her face as innocent as if God's angels took their cues from her, she came right up to him. Sonnet stood alongside, and she stroked down his flank as she smiled up at Kyle.

He watched her, the muscle in his jaw jumped a bit. He said nothing.

Suddenly Merrie stiffened, pointing behind him with her

mouth agape. As Kyle spun around to investigate, as she had known he would, she grabbed his booted feet and yanked with all her might. Kyle toppled over like a pillar.

The horses shied, wrenching their leads out of his hand and bounding through the water that shattered and frothed all about their hooves.

Kyle landed on his back, sending two beautiful arcs of water into the air, his protest scandalous, and very loud.

Merrie burst out laughing and jumped away. The look on his face was too delicious for words. She shrieked with merriment, falling back into water herself and splashing around.

Kyle recovered from his surprise and made a lunge at Merrie, catching her by the ankle. He pulled her over, ducked her under, then yanked her up by the arms.

Still choking with laughter, Merrie flailed her arms, sending spray after spray into his face.

She heard his deep laughter with surprise and delight. It was like glad music, splendidly male and brimming with joy. She realized she had never heard him laugh before, not really laugh.

They romped together, dashing each other with water for several minutes, until Kyle fell onto his back and lay there. He inflated his stomach and sent a stream of water up from his mouth as if he were a whale, and Merrie fell back, too, helpless with laughter.

"You've gone up a notch in my estimation, Mr. Delancy," she teased. "I thought you had no sense of humor at all."

"A whole notch? It doesn't take much to impress you, then does it?"

"Maybe not. I'm easy," she sighed, floating along on her back.

She was far too content to bandy words with him. But when she chanced to look over, she saw that he had risen and was standing there staring at her.

"On the contrary . . . ," he said, hushed now, his words tight. "Not easy at all."

He had lost his hat when he fell into the water, and now she could see his naked expression. His face was hard with wanting, his eyes smoked with heat. He could not hide the famished desire that was there.

Merrie recognized it. How could she not? She had lain awake at night tormented by that very look. It was how he had gazed at her that night at the Spur, in her bedroom, when she had risen from her bath.

Good Lord, but his eyes could scald!

She felt as if an ocean of blue had suddenly spilled its color into her, forever. She almost looked to see if any telltale signs were visible through her skin.

His mouth, more severely defined by his shadowed cheeks and chin, appeared lush, temptingly beautiful. His black hair, slicked back by the water, lay down to his shoulders in patent-leather shanks. Outlined in detailed perfection, the rangy length of his body seemed poised on the knife edge of a decision; was he about to snare her once again?

She forgot to breathe.

Every nerve in her body seemed to scream for his touch. She ached. Deep inside a tattoo erupted, a throbbing that made her dizzy with need.

It was all she could do to stop herself from rushing into his arms, flinging caution to the wind. She badly wanted to give in. To feel his body hard against her own, to have his mouth on hers, to feel wanted! Kyle made her feel that, she realized. She yearned to feel his passion again.

Her nipples contracted. Her breasts swelled, straining against the thin cotton of her bodice. She glanced quickly down again, embarrassed by her reaction. A gasp escaped her for she was as good as naked with her cotton underwear soaked through the way it was. The lacy ruffle at the neckline of her bodice hung down limply, exposing the tender pink of her nipples. Her pantaloons were entirely transparent, even her belly button was visible through the sheer material. Reflexively, she covered her dark triangle at the apex of her legs with one hand, her breasts with the other.

Her head jerked up. Kyle's blue gaze was riveted on her still, hot—stormy hot.

She felt the brush of heat. The fumes of it spun in her head.

And then an icy shiver ran down her spine. A thin tingling, a warning. He was the devil's own.

He had walked out once. He had taken what he wanted and left without a care.

He would do so again.

This time, there very well might be "consequences," to use his word.

But before she moved, he turned abruptly away, scooping his hat out of the shallows and gaining the shore.

"Fun's over. We're moving out."

Without turning back, he strode to where the horses stood cropping the short grasses and shrubby plants. For a moment he stood there gazing down tiredly and passed his hand back and forth over the back of his neck.

Still with his back to the water, he sat, removed his boots, emptied them, and shrugged out of his dripping shirt. When he rose, Merrie watched his muscles ripple as he sat his hat down on his head. He tilted it down across his brow.

She knew he was waiting for her to comply with his order to leave, but she couldn't move. She had no intention of testing him any further. No, that was not her purpose, but her unstable legs seemed incapable of obeying her.

His rigid spine and the adamant spread of his long legs warned her that he was seething with temper, his fuse close to the end. Still, he remained silent, his back to the stream, taut with strain—and whatever else he grappled with.

He mounted Cappoquin and trotted away without looking back. His naked shoulders, gleaming with wet droplets in the sunlight, were very broad. He rode tall in the saddle, with an effortless facility that exemplified his skill with horses.

And all Merrie could think about, as she watched him ride away, was how her hands itched to stroke the wet from his suntanned skin.

"Devil take it!" she moaned. "What has happened to me?"

TWENTY-ONE

MERRIE WOKE WITH the sun in her eyes. For a moment she didn't quite know where she was. Even after several days out in the wild, it took her a few minutes to orient her mind. Her back was sore, and her neck felt as if someone had twisted it like a rag doll's.

It was then she saw him. The gunslinger.

He was shaving, as he did every morning, but most times he was done by the time she woke up. She suddenly thought of her vision, the day she returned to the Spur with Ash. That day she had fantasized about watching him shave, she remembered, and she wondered if it had been a prophetic warning of sorts.

Kyle had made a ledge out of their flour box, and his shaving mirror was propped up in the crook of a tree. He wore only tight black pants and his boots. His hips were lean and narrow, especially in comparison to the width of his shoulders. His back was very strong, beautifully bronzed. Absolute perfection, she thought, except for the ugly brown scabs that marked where he had been shot.

Merrie watched the supple play of the muscles as he pulled the razor over his lathered cheeks. His forearms were muscular, too. She knew just what they felt like, for she had clung to them, gripping them with all her might, while he rode her to heaven on that one wild night.

Merrie squeezed her eyes shut. How could she be so depraved? It was impossible to put that vivid memory from her mind, especially when he displayed himself for her like this, she thought irritably.

Familiarity with their routine didn't seem to help either. For the past few days, she had been fighting a silent battle of wills with him. He seemed to delight in tempting her, bossing her around, regulating their very austere routine. While she, on the other hand, was not allowed to look at him sideways without him growling at her like a bear with a sore head.

He avoided talking to her. The nightly stops, the tedious ride into the north, even their cheerless meals were all endured in relative silence.

He allowed a fire in the morning. Shielded, it couldn't be seen from far away, he had told her. He would rise early, boil water for his blessed shave, then make an annoyingly competent breakfast of bacon, biscuits, and coffee for them both. He never asked her to do anything, but he never considered that she might have needs either.

After their contretemps at the stream, Kyle had not allowed her any time to herself. They had passed into dangerous territory, he had told her; outlaws and renegades roamed across these plains, and he wanted her where he could keep an eye out for her. Her daily toilet, abridged and restrictive, hardly allowed her time to splash her face and hands, let alone any opportunity to change into clean clothes or even wash her dirty ones.

She'd worn her dusty, grimy cotton shirt and work pants until she could endure them no more. Her hair was filthy, and her skin seemed to crawl on her back. Today she intended to bathe properly, or at least what constituted properly, seeing that she couldn't take off her underclothes. The river would have to substitute for a tub.

She knew he could see her out of the corner of his eye. She refused to let him see how agitated he made her.

"Morning," he said and wiped off the excess lather with a towel. "Coffee's ready. Better get going, we're moving out in five."

Merrie ignored him and took herself off to the river with a small bundle of her things. Let him wait, she thought, fuming. If he wanted to make an early start, he should have woken her earlier.

She took out her soap, towel, and a fresh shirt and saw to her needs. The water was chilly. She splashed her face, enjoying the refreshing tingle. But she hadn't even finished washing when Kyle rode up.

"You about done?" he asked, his voice deceptively mild.

"No, and I would appreciate some privacy," she told him.

She saw in a minute that he was not amused.

"Did I tell you we're leaving? You better know right now, I don't repeat myself, and I don't make exceptions. Now, I'm riding out. You had better follow me as soon as you can, or you'll be left behind."

Then he spurred his horse and rode back up the trail. Merrie stared after him. She thought he was fooling. He wouldn't really ride off and leave her, would he?

"Kyle," she called. She heard the tramp of hooves, but he didn't answer her.

She hurried out of the water and dried off her feet.

"Kyle," she called again. This time a little louder. Still no answer. By the time she had pulled on her boots and rushed back into camp, there was no sigh of him anywhere.

Their campsite was in a small scoop of land inside a ring of scraggly trees. Her bedroll lay upon the ground, her saddle and saddlebag next to it. Apart from Sonnet, the camp was entirely empty. All signs of their small fire had vanished; there was not even an indentation to mark where he had laid his bedroll.

"Devil's own," she fumed. "Kyle," she yelled now, panicked. She raced through the trees. The land lay flat around her, or seemingly so. There was not even a dust plume to show which direction he had taken. She whirled around, searching for any possible place he might be, but she didn't see him. "Kyle," she yelled. The sounds seemed to wither mockingly into the vast silence.

She felt absolutely bereft, terrified. She had not the slightest idea where she was. She felt like crying, very much aware of the hugeness surrounding her. "Kyle!" This time the terror in her voice was obvious.

There was nothing. No movement, no sound bar the hammering of her own heart. The day was torpid already, the horizon blurred against the endless scrub and sand.

Merrie's eyes burned under the relentless glare. She stared into the cavernous spaces, seeing the shimmer of mirages grow as the hot air began to rise.

With a cry, she saw his tall shape wobbling and wavering through the shimmer, then just as quickly the apparition vanished. Merrie whirled about, now this way now that, teased by the shape of horsemen vibrating on the edge of sight, only to disappear after a few minutes.

And then she really saw him. Her relief was so huge she almost fell to the ground. Because of a trick of the landscape, a small indentation lay just beyond the angle of her vision. Once he cleared the depression and rode up onto the flats, she could see him again. He was traveling at a steady pace. He didn't turn about.

Merrie used one of his expletives and raced back to get her things and take off after him. Anger spurred her. The taste of fear was still sharp in her mouth. She was fighting mad. How dare he scare her so!

She galloped like a desert fury, her hat thrown back behind her head, her golden hair streaming in the wind of her speed. She yelled out his name, screaming to make herself heard above the tattoo of her horse's hooves.

Kyle didn't even turn. He simply ignored her and kept his pace steady.

That angered Merrie even more. She knew he must be able to hear her by now. She was only a yard or two behind him and closing. Without thinking, she pulled her stallion up alongside his, jerking on the reins to slow her heaving mount, and punched Kyle as hard as she could.

"Devil!" she yelled at him, "You degenerate devil!" She was hitting him as hard as she could. "How could you?"

Kyle was too stunned for a moment to react. She was like a wind dervish, untamed and furious, her fists slamming into him again and again.

He would have laughed at her unprecedented loss of control,

TEXAS KISS 181

but right at the moment, she was getting a number of good swipes at him, and they hurt. Besides, he knew he would really hurt her feelings if he were to ridicule her attempt to maim him. He realized that she was nearly hysterical. The tension of the past couple of days had finally caught up with her. She had kept quite a tight control on her emotions, perhaps too tight.

Her tempter was ferocious—as impassioned as her lovemaking had been, a tempting voice buzzed in his ear, making him scowl.

But she was spooking the horses now, and he didn't want her hurt through her imprudence. In a trice, he dismounted and catching her mount as well, brought the two nervous beasts to a complete standstill.

Then, with a quick flick of his wrists, he managed to capture Merrie's flailing arms. With a heave, he brought her screaming and scratching into his arms. They tumbled to the ground. Kyle quickly brought her underneath him, his long legs locking hers in a fierce hold, her arms pinned beneath her.

She screamed at him again. "Don't touch me, you devil-hell, don't you dare touch me!"

Still she bucked recklessly, panting, her breasts buffeting against his chest. Kyle felt their supple fullness, the charged enticement of her lissome young body, and the craving for her exploded in his blood ten times more potently than ever before.

Her tousled hair was about her face, a haze of golden mist. All he could smell was her. All he could feel was her, writhing beneath him, slender and seductive. He wanted her so badly he felt scorched with the need of it. He hated the lack of control almost as much as he was puzzled by it. He prided himself on his self-discipline.

What in hell did she have that made her so appealing? Certainly it wasn't her retiring nature, for she was uncommonly independent and forthright. Far too much so for a woman. And as for her looks, well, he had enjoyed the company of far more beautiful women. Although she had an exceptional figure, he had known others equally lovely, except for her goddamn legs.

Those extraordinary legs he could feel in excruciating detail right now. She was trying her utmost to kick him.

And all he could think about was that one blissful night! Those legs.

With the last shred of sanity, Kyle knew that if he didn't release her immediately, he would not be able to stop himself from taking her. The realization brought ice-cold reason down on him.

But the cold gun barrel that settled at the base of his neck brought an instant and more deadly chill to his blood!

Shrill laughter, coarse and not altogether sane, pierced his consciousness. At that same moment that he felt the gun behind his ear, he felt a heavy boot on his back, and his guns were whipped out of their holsters.

"Don't think the lady cares for you, mister," said a whiskey scrape of a voice. "Leastways that's what it sounds like to me. Why don't you get up?"

Kyle complied, going into a crouch, his arms extended forward.

There were three of them.

It was testament to his obsession with Merrie that he had not heard them coming up at all. He cursed himself.

Two of the men were still mounted; the one who took his guns stood just behind him. They all had their guns trained on Kyle. But their attention was directed at Merrie. Her legs were splayed, and she was tousled and rosy from her intimate tussle with Kyle. He watched as realization of their predicament blossomed on her lovely face. Naked fear sprang full-blown into her eyes. Kyle felt a surge of hot fury unlike anything he had ever known before.

He went deadly still; his eyes fixed on his adversaries, he took their measure.

The one giving orders from his horse was an ill-kempt man with beacon-bright ginger hair. His eyes seemed to wander listlessly, ceaselessly, and his unsettling laugh spilled out of his ugly mouth in short bursts of sound.

The second man was fat, silent. From a distance, his piggy eyes scooped Merrie up, as if he wanted to devour her. The man behind him was big also, but there was no fat on him at all. He was all muscles, thick-necked and brawny. His boyish face was pleasant, if a little vacuous. He stuck Kyle's guns into his own belt with one beefy hand and grinned with greedy anticipation from Merrie to Kyle and back again, as if he didn't know which one he wanted to take on first.

"Yeah, we heard you from way back," baby face said, jerking his thumb in the direction of the open prairie.

"Why don't you take the man's place, Cody, and oblige the little lady? Littlewood and me will stake out ol' loverboy here, for some target practice. It always helps me get in the right mood," whiskey voice said. He laughed with gusto, ending on a shrill note. His fat companion, however, suddenly called out his objection.

"No. He always gets to go first," complained the man he'd called Littlewood.

"Shut your mouth, Littlewood, or it'll be your tongue that I stake out, and not loverboy."

"Tell him, Nutter," Cody said.

The fat man started complaining again, but Nutter whipped his ginger head about and cut him off sharply. "Clam it," he told his companion.

Cody moved then. He unfastened his gunbelt and his pants, dropping them both in his hurry to get to Merrie. Kyle's guns fell down with a clatter. Cody leered at Merrie, advancing on her with a shambling walk.

But Merrie was not the defenseless female they all thought she was. She knew how to use the long, strong legs she had been blessed with. There was power in those legs. Power and agility. Added to these was her outrage; it fueled her concentration.

Vaguely she heard Littlewood's complaints and Nutter's crazed giggle, as they moved in on Kyle. But her focus was on the advancing Cody. She waited until he was directly over her, the brutal smirk on his face telling her unequivocally what he intended.

With lightning strike, she brought her legs together, knees to her chest, then rammed them into his groin with all her might. The big man toppled almost on top of her, his raw scream reverberating into the still, blue morning. Merrie rolled away just in time to avoid being pinned under him.

She sprang up. She whirled, diving for the guns Cody had dropped, and snatched up the nearest one, her fingers trembling uncontrollably.

The fat man had just begun dismounting. Nutter was still in his saddle; she squeezed off a wild shot. It caught Littlewood in the flank. He yelled.

In the same instant that Merrie moved into action, Kyle did, too. He also moved like lightning, grabbing Cody's discarded guns and firing off three rounds in one smooth, quicksilver movement. He shot the gun right out of Nutter's hand, catching him clean through the wrist. His second shot was centered on the fat man's right hand. Both men howled in pain and surprise, dropping their weapons and cursing loudly.

Littlewood fell with a loud thud onto the ground and lay screaming from shock, his two wounds bleeding profusely, his one foot still caught in the stirrup.

The third shot was aimed at Cody's groin, but at the last moment Kyle moved the barrel a fraction to the left and fired off a shot high on his naked thigh. Cody screamed again, his horror clearly apparent on his babyish face. The next shot, fired just a second after the last, was aimed at Nutter again and took him in the elbow. He had been reaching for his rifle. His screech hung for agonized moments in the tense air.

"Anyone else?" Kyle hissed and then described an arc with his gun, first resting it on one target and then the next in turn. None of the three marauders made any further move.

Merrie straightened out of her crouch. Never in her life had she seen anything as fast or as lethally accurate as Kyle Delancy's gun work. She was stunned by it.

He was standing absolutely motionless, his legs braced far apart, bent at the knees, arms extended, his rock-steady hands clasped together about the butt end of Cody's six-shooter. His eyes were mere slits in his head. At the line of his jaw, a small muscle ticked, steadily, rhythmically. His scrutiny of the marauders didn't waver for an instant. He didn't care for Nutter's twitching fingers reaching down into his boot. He rightly assessed the man as the most dangerous of the three.

"I wouldn't advise it," Kyle said. His freezing voice was enough to stop any further movement from the man.

Very slowly, Kyle straightened and moved to where Cody had dropped his matched pair of Smith and Wesson six-shooters. He ducked and with one hand scooped them up.

"Merrie," he said with a jerk of his head, "relieve the *gentlemen* of whatever weapons they have left, horses too. Then get going."

"W-what about you?"

"I'll be along. I have something I want to explain to the boys."

Merrie nodded. Her legs were trembling; they didn't quite feel like her own, but she managed to walk across to where Nutter and the fat man lay nursing their wounds. She lifted the rifle and the Colts still on the ground, avoiding the men's faces and working as quickly as she could, given that she shook like a leaf. She untied the supply sack on the first man's horse, along with his canteen of water, and dropped them within Nutter's reach.

"Uh-uh," Kyle's harsh voice interrupted her. "Pick those up and get going."

Merrie turned, her face even whiter than before. "You can't leave then out here with nothing—"

"I said, get the hell out of here, and I mean it, dammit."

"Kyle, you—"

"Now!" he told her, his voice quiet, deathly quiet.

Merrie's shaking increased. She sucked in her breath. She had never sensed such violence in a man, never.

Kyle lifted his eyes to her for an instant. "Head out toward that ridge behind you. I'll catch up soon."

She quickly looked away and, gathering up the reins of the other horses, mounted Sonnet and cantered off in a cloud of dust.

KYLE DIDN'T COME quite as soon as he had said he would. At least to Merrie it seemed like hours before she finally saw his outline against the horizon behind her.

She had been in a state of terror ever since leaving him. Terror that he would get himself killed, terror at the nameless violence she had seen on his face. In fact, she had been listening for gunshots, because she was convinced he would kill the marauders, but to her relief she hadn't heard any.

He didn't speak when he rode up. His features were hidden behind a circle, the shadow cast by his hat under the midday sun. She couldn't see his expression. She didn't care if he was angry with her, she was horrified by what had happened, absolutely sickened by his sense of vengeance.

"How long do you think they can survive without food, wounded like that?"

Kyle looked at her, but he didn't answer her. He reached for the leading reins of the other horses, took them out of her hands, and tied them to his pommel. He rode on.

"It would have been kinder to kill them," she cried, spurring her horse after his.

He stopped then, turned, and waited for her to come alongside him.

"Sonsabitches were going to rape you," he bit out, his voice a mere whisper of sound.

"Do you think I don't know that?" she yelled back.

"No, I don't think you really do. Not really. You don't know what rape is, lady, or we wouldn't be having this ridiculous conversation."

"Oh, and what was it you were doing before they arrived? Was it so different?"

He stared at her. She couldn't quite see his eyes, but she felt the anger, the scathing fury of that glance, as well as if she had been scored by it.

He wasn't going to answer, she could tell.

At last he moved off; a dark, brooding mantle of concern seemed to cloak him.

"We've lost too much time," he told her without turning around, "or have you forgotten about your father?"

TWENTY-TWO

BY NIGHTFALL THE winds had picked up, and it became suddenly cold. Merrie was numb from both the chill wind and fatigue. Kyle had not spoken a word to her, pushing forward at quite a clip to make up for lost time.

They stopped long after the slender first-quarter moon had risen, and made camp. After a brief, unsatisfactory supper, Merrie curled herself in every available blanket and tried to sleep. But sleep just wouldn't come. The horror of the day, Kyle's ice-cold vengeance, and his obvious disapproval of her made her more miserable than she had ever felt in her whole life. She was dismayed that she found it necessary even to consider his approval. Why, in God's name, when she despised the man, should she feel so?

If she had not needed his help with finding Ash, she would have ridden away and never looked back.

But then there was this morning, just before those marauders had attacked.

This morning he had stirred up all those extraordinary feelings all over again . . .

One moment more and she would have succumbed. Just thinking about him, the solid feel of his magnificent body covering her own, made her feel weak with desire. Oh yes, she recognized what she felt as desire. He was, at the very least, an excellent teacher. Until he had touched her, she had not known about desire.

What troubled her even more was that she had been engaged to Matt for a year, and he had never once made her feel the smallest pinprick of desire. Why?

Granted, Kyle Delancy was uncommonly handsome; his tall, lanky frame and the way in which he moved were exciting.

Only a fool would pretend that his dark and dangerous looks meant nothing.

But Matt was handsome, too. He was tall and distinguished. An established gentleman rancher, he had excellent prospects and stood in good stead in the community.

Kyle was a wanderer. She knew next to nothing about him, nothing about his background, his roots. He was not quite as rough as he pretended to be. She knew that he liked fine things. His saddle was hand tooled in very fine Spanish leather, as were his holster and boots. His clothes were plain but store-bought and of excellent quality. Added to this, his speech was more refined than that generally used by drifters and gunfighters, except when he cursed, that is.

Of course, it was also true that Matt had never kissed her in the breath-stealing manner that Kyle did. Nor had he ever been anything less than a proper gentleman. But it was equally true that Merrie had never felt more cherished than when Kyle held her in his strong embrace. He made her feel special.

And then, with a sinking heart, she recalled the disturbing picture of Liza with Kyle in the house on East Street. How ecstatic her stepmother had been in the throes of pleasure. Kyle knew how to pleasure women, that was certain, and any woman would do. She wasn't special to him. It was a cruel illusion.

Out on the prairie, a coyote howled at the moon. The sound was lonely, infinitely mournful. Somehow it echoed exactly what she was feeling inside. That brought tears to her eyes, tears that she refused to give in to. It would be a cold day in Hell before she would admit to tears for such a heartless man.

"KEEP QUIET AND stay inside the brush," Kyle told her, crouching low. He swung noiselessly off his horse and dropped to his belly. His movements were efficient, unhurried. Thankfully the autumn winds had not yet stripped the feathery green from the sagebrush and aromatic mesquite that screened them. He went forward a yard or so and then stopped, parting the brush carefully so that he could gauge the threat.

The sun was low on the horizon, and dust tempered the

lowering clouds an angry crimson. A line of men moved out on the wide, dreary plains. A band of warriors rode there. Cloaked in the sanguine twilight, they seemed more a part of the dusk than real men. And yet Merrie had no doubt that they were very real.

They were Comanche.

Fierce, independent, they displayed their enmity ostentatiously in their war trappings, which even from this far distance, were clearly visible. There were six of them, mounted on dappled brown-and-white ponies. The warriors picked their way across the brushland, following the trail that Merrie and Kyle had taken that day. It was not a coincidence, that much Merrie knew.

She felt ice cold with fear. She fought to stop herself from moaning with it. "Let's make a run for it," she whispered, unable to contain herself any longer.

Kyle, though, didn't answer but watched the encroaching band without undue concern. His face was thoughtful, rather than worried. After a long, tortuous time, he rose and came to crouch beside her. His face was shadowed by his widebrimmed hat as he leaned over his knee, his elbow casually resting just inches from her frightened face.

She saw a white flash as he put a twig between his strong teeth and chomped on it. "You can relax, Legs. They're not after our scalps."

"H-how do you know?"

"They would never show themselves openly like this."

Merrie craned her head to peer around his crouching body. She was not convinced. The band of Comanche were getting closer. She could hear the stony rumor of the ponies' hooves, the occasional horsy snort whirring on the cold wind.

"Mount up, Legs, and trust me," Kyle said and slid into Cappoquin's saddle.

"Why would I do that?" Merrie muttered to herself, but she did as he told her and followed him out into the open prairie.

Very soon she could make out the painted features of the lead warrior. At some invisible signal, they all came to a halt, twenty yards in front of Merrie and Kyle. They sat in silence, stone-faced and alert.

"Kyle, for pity sake," Merrie whispered in shock.

Dangling from the leader's belt was a brilliant patch of ginger hair. Merrie thought she was going to throw up. She felt the surge of sickness in her throat.

"Keep quiet," Kyle told her, his voice low, controlled, his words leashing her in. "Calm. Count backwards if it will help, but keep steady."

He raised his palm in greeting and eased his horse forward. Separating from the band, the leader also advanced. The two men assessed each other through the gathering gloom. Merrie thought she would collapse in a heap on the ground from the tension.

It was unbearable, this masculine sensing ritual, this silent fencing. She didn't understand it. In panic she had simply gone along with Kyle's hazardous inclination. He always seemed indifferent to danger. But it went against her instinct, her true nature. She was angry with herself for allowing him to jeopardize her so, for she was convinced that she would die. Die . . . and by the savage hands of this terrible warrior who sported his grotesque trophies upon his belt.

Kyle somehow sensed her urge to run. He glanced at her over his shoulder. Sharp, intense, his eyes locked with hers for a moment only. He said nothing, but his look was plain. She sat stone still upon Sonnet, her own gaze riveted on Kyle's wide and sheltering back as he turned to face the Comanche.

Kyle's confidence was apparent in his stance. He sat tall in the saddle, vigilant. His rich voice, mellow as a bubbling brook, showed neither distrust nor overt friendliness.

"Greetings," Kyle said.

"To you, greetings," the Indian leader said.

Kyle glanced at the flamboyant sky and nodded his head.

"If you're hunting, you best get about it. The rains will come before morning."

A small light of amusement flared in the warrior's dark eyes.

"I do not hunt game, as you well know." His English was flawless. There was no inflection at all.

"You hunt men," Kyle stated. "Is the tally full, or are there others yet to hunt?"

There was a pregnant moment before the man spoke again. "The tally's full now," the warrior said.

"Then all is well," Kyle said.

"Not all. The coup must be shared. That is why we are here."

"I'm honored, but I don't think it's deserved. He was a natural born loser," he said, indicating the freshly scalped topknot in the warrior's belt.

The man chuckled. The sound was unpleasant, like gravel ground underfoot.

"But wily. He had evaded us for long and bitter months. I was about to leave the hunt yet again, when we heard *the loser* yelping. Because you made him yelp, you have saved me much, Man with the Sky Eyes."

"Then I am glad to have obliged."

"You are not curious about what he had done? You take my word that he did me an injury?"

Kyle nodded. "The injury he did you rests on your shoulders and is there for eyes to see that can."

It was true. The pain of great sorrow enshrouded the warrior. Dark and terrible were the secrets of his heart. Merrie felt suddenly ashamed of her trivial limitation, her fears.

"I am curious, Man with the Sky Eyes, why you left him alive."

"He tried to rape my woman," Kyle said, indicating a white-faced Merrie. "But he didn't succeed."

The warrior nodded sagely, then untied the grisly trophy and handed it to Kyle. He waited then, his dark gaze resting briefly on Merrie sitting upon Sonnet.

There was a silent exchange just then, and Kyle appeared to understand it. Dismounting, he unhurriedly hung the Indian's coup on his pommel, settling Cappoquin's shifting with the merest breath of a word. He came toward Merrie in the same relaxed manner. He could have been strolling through the hubbub of a country fair, so facile was his demeanor. But his eyes glittered a warning as he took the reins from her nerveless fingers. He lifted her off Sonnet's back and set her down. His brief but thorough look encompassed myriad emotions, but the message was clear. *Trust me. Do not move or speak,* it said.

He went to take up the leading reins of the other three horses, too, and with a swift flick of his hands unhooked them from Cappoquin's pommel.

Merrie couldn't have moved if her life depended upon it. Her fear was glutinous, suffocating. She watched mutely as Kyle led the palomino and the other three horses to the warrior.

The warrior seemed momentarily surprised, but he nodded gravely and took up the reins.

"We are bonded, Man of the Sky Eyes. So speaks Straight Arrow."

Kyle tipped up his head and said something then, but his voice was low and Merrie couldn't hear him.

The Comanche warrior seemed to absorb it. He murmured a reply and then, saluting, turned and rode off, the cavalcade of horses trotted obediently in his wake. His silent band followed.

As if released from a stagnating bewitchment, Merrie cried out in dismay and stumbled forward, her arms extended toward the Comanche. "No . . . you can't."

Kyle caught her. "It's done." His voice was edged with iron. She whirled on him, wild now, fiercely pulling away from him as if his touch were an obscenity. She would have run after the retreating Indians if he had not caught her back, wrestling her to the ground.

She fought him like a mad thing, scratching and kicking, sobbing out her anger, pent-up fear, and grief all at once. But exhaustion and the sum of all her distress quickly sapped her ferocious attack. She went still, but for her head slamming from side to side in negation of what had occurred, of what he had done to her. For he had stolen from her, yet again.

"He's mine . . . ," she cried achingly. "You don't understand, I raised him from a colt . . . He's mine. You can't give him away . . . Please, he's mine, my own . . . Sonnet!"

TEXAS KISS 195

He held her as she collapsed against him, softly sobbing out all her wounded heart onto his broad chest. His mouth swept over her quivering lips, warmly, easily, unhurriedly.

"I'm sorry, darlin'," he whispered as he brushed his tongue over her chilled lips, into her mouth, delving in long, smooth strokes, as if anything too abrupt would spark her wildness once again. He broke his kiss, raising his dark head to stare down at her tear stained face. "There was nothing else I could do," he told her, his voice deep, low with feelings she had never witnessed in him before.

Certainly there was no regret. No, Kyle Delancy was not concerned with fruitless regrets. Once he made his decision, he stuck to it.

He kissed her again, with enchanting gentleness, his strong fingers moving through her hair, coaxing and calming. His touch drifted to her neck. She felt the enticement of his knowing fingers working down her neck, her collarbone, and then slip inside her shirt to cup her breast and hold his hand over her beating heart.

He did not raise his mouth from hers for long, long minutes, and when he did, it was only to bring her closer, cradled against his hard body. He bent her head into his shoulder, his breath unsteady, and rubbed his cheek into the silken mass of golden hair.

"Jesus Christ, but I want you, Merrie," he said hoarsely.

Merrie stiffened. She was bruised, her self-esteem trampled. He had misused her in more ways than one, and she was angry, hurt. There was no way that she would allow him to touch her again, for she knew, as surely as the night followed the day, that Kyle Delancy was not the staying kind.

For a moment, sheer unreasoning rage filled her. She was furious that he would hold her as if he cherished her and not tell her that he cared for her. Oh yes, he wanted her. Wanted! But he didn't love her.

"What you want is a woman, any woman," she said coldly. She turned her face away from him, gazing unseeing into the failing light. She made herself lie there still and cold. She knew she didn't have the strength to resist him.

She need not have been concerned. Kyle sprang to his feet as if he had been stung with a whip. He didn't look at her, but walked away, leading his horse back to the screen of sagebrush and began to set up camp.

TWENTY-THREE

KYLE WAITED. His sensitive ears picked up the telltale sniffles Merrie was trying so hard to conceal. He ached to go to her, but he dared not. He burned too fiercely for her. He had only to scent her presence to feel himself ignite. He also knew that she was furious with him over Sonnet. She would never allow herself to be comforted, nor did he want to test her any further.

No, he didn't want any deeper involvement with Merrie Sinclair. What he really wanted was to escape her. To get as far the hell away as he could. He wanted to remove himself from the constant torment of those legs.

Those legs she had used as weapons.

Christ, but he had never been more thrilled than when she had rammed them into Cody!

Trust Merrie Sinclair to be competent at defending herself. He realized that he expected nothing less of her, even though he knew that the threat of rape was enough to paralyze a woman.

Kaiten had been unable to defend herself, and she had died . . .

But then, Kaiten had been a child, not a woman. She had died a child, trying desperately to rid her body of her already dead child.

As if cold water were splashing on his face, Kyle gave a start. He wasn't a man to dwell upon the past. His memories of Kaiten were never voluntary. Long ago, he had trained himself never to think about her, their impoverished life.

His dreams—now, his dreams were different. He had no control over those. In times of stress, he dreamed about Kaiten. Occasionally, when he drank too much, it would also happen. It was one of the reasons he rarely allowed himself to drink heavily; he hated losing control.

But now here it was; he was consciously comparing Kaiten to Merrie. Strangely enough, instead of it making him feel wretched, his memories were muted; it was as if a veil had been drawn between him and the past. In place of the expected pain, he felt a pensive remembrance, and something else.

He was aware of a vibrant and unidentifiable expectation. A *something* that waited just around the corner . . . waited for him! It niggled deep inside, refusing to be denied. Even though he frowned at it, it would not leave him alone.

For some time now, he admitted, he'd felt an optimism, a gladness. Could it have something to do with the aggravating Miss Sinclair?

True, she managed to provoke his temper as well as his lust at the drop of a hat, but she was never foolish.

Naive, perhaps, but not stupid. Of course she didn't know what she was saying when she accused him of trying to rape her. How could she? The truth of it was that he seemed to lose his control when he held her.

He glanced over to where she lay wrapped deep inside her bedroll. Only her golden hair peeped out at the top. She was curled up around her knees against the chill night. He could see the occasional shudder running through her lissome body. There was a moment then, when he hovered on the edge, wanting to warm her, comfort her, and knowing she would deny him.

Her accusation, that he was no better than the thugs who had accosted them, riled him. The difference between him and those animals was absolutely beyond her comprehension. What is more, he never wanted her to find out about that difference.

All his adult life he had examined those differences, especially the implications of rape. He knew the perilous blood that washed through his veins; he was Katherine Reed's son, after all. Denying her name did not eradicate that terrible truth.

His fear of that blood had forced him to exercise critical control over his lust. If anything, he preferred a little bodily discomfort to indulging in promiscuity. Family history aside, he was particular; he readily admitted it.

And as for the palomino, well, he'd had no choice. There had been nothing else to barter for what he wanted. The leader had specifically eyed Sonnet. He was not fool enough to insult a Comanche, renegade or no. The horse, after all, could be replaced.

He heard another slight hitch in Merrie's breathing, but it finally gave way to the regular rhythm of sleep. He waited a good long while, though, to be certain, and then rose and saddled Cappoquin.

Over the past week, he had grown familiar enough with Merrie to know that she rarely woke once she fell asleep. He would have to trust to that, because he needed to make sure that the Comanche would leave his quarry alone.

Notwithstanding his generous bribe of the horses, he knew the Indians respected little that had anything to do with white men. They had their own ways, their own honor. Few white men respected their ways, Kyle knew. Still, they had ridden out of their way to present him with his share of their coup.

Kyle understood loss. It was a common denominator and passed clear across cultural barriers. He had recognized it at once in the Comanche chief and felt that the man had seen it in him. It was the link he was relying on now. Nevertheless, he was a cautious man, never leaving anything to chance. So he rode out of their cheerless camp, hoping that Merrie wouldn't wake while he was gone.

He headed east under the thin moon. Several hours later he found what he was looking for.

His quarry.

Liza Sinclair and her friends.

It wasn't difficult to spot them; their bright camp fire was like a beacon in the night.

He knew where to look, knew exactly what route they were taking, where they were going. After all, they were in the jaws of his trap!

Since he had picked up their trail out of Hollow Creek, he had checked on them once or twice. But he did not want Merrie to see them. She would make a beeline for her father, or insist that they go in and rescue him immediately. Kyle was not about to jeopardize his careful plans by allowing her to do so.

The time for lengthy explanations was not now. Once they reached Dodge City, it would be safe to reveal his plans without Miss Sinclair going off like a half-cocked gun.

He left Cappoquin down the trail a way and crept forward on his belly to get a closer look.

Liza liked her comforts, Kyle noticed, no matter that she was on the run. Or perhaps she was so sure of herself, of her own invincibility, that she believed no one would be sent after them.

A tent had been raised alongside the wagon transporting Ash. Kyle could see one man lying against the back wheel of the wagon, a rifle across his knees. He was guarding the rear, apparently. It could have been Matt Cheston. There was no sign of Ash, and Kyle assumed that he was inside the covered wagon.

Liza sat before a small camp fire, wearing a thick sheepskin coat, and with a red plaid rug tucked around her legs against the chill night air. There was a man sitting next to her, and they were laughing together, sharing a lavish meal. It was spread out on the ground between them, on a folded checkered cloth. Their plates were piled high, and they drank from metal tankards, readily replenished at the barrel in front of the wagon.

Liza's companion was positioned just outside the light of the fire, his shadowed face almost entirely invisible. Kyle could only see the general shape of him, not any features. He was broad-chested, and his thick neck and brawny arms attested to a powerful individual.

Another man was stationed on a slight hill several yards away. The lookout. Not much good at his job, obviously, as he was staring directly at Kyle. But the lookout didn't see him, hidden in the general darkness, and Kyle was careful not to be caught silhouetted against the night sky.

Obviously Liza and her friends hadn't encountered any difficulties so far. Certainly they had not seen any Comanche; they were far too relaxed.

Naturally, that did not mean that the Comanche hadn't

spotted them. Kyle made a survey of the area immediately surrounding the camp; he found nothing. Perhaps the horses had been sufficient incentive, after all. Or perhaps, as was more likely, the Indians had other, more urgent, business of their own, like outrunning the Army, who would be after them soon enough for straying off the hellish reservations.

After reconnoitering the area thoroughly, Kyle set off back for his own camp to snatch a few hours of sleep. Perhaps the only good thing that had come out of the miserable day was that the rain seemed to have held off.

IT WAS HIGH noon by the time they reached the town of Beaver. There were few people about. A mangy dog lifted his head momentarily as they passed, but he was too despondent even to give them more than a cursory bark. A shutter banged noisily. From the saloon came the faint tinkle of glass.

Kyle hitched his horse in front of Sadie's Boarding House, which boasted on its blatantly misspelled sign that it was "The best meel n' bed yu ever did c."

Merrie hoped Sadie's cooking was better than her spelling, but she doubted that. The place was a shambles of peeling paint and broken shutters. Old refuse littered the weeds that grew man-high in the yard, and there were several panes of glass missing from the windows that looked out front.

Yet, the thought of sleeping in a real bed and eating a hot meal was enough to banish Merrie's dismal thoughts. She couldn't help smiling broadly at Kyle as she eased her tired legs over the saddle horn and dismounted. It had been hell to ride with him with his arm around her. Sheer hell. They had both of them been snarling at each other in short-tempered spurts all morning long.

There were several flea-bitten old men sitting on the porch in front of Sadie's. They all leaned forward in unison, joints grumbling, and gawked unabashedly at the two.

Kyle stopped and looked up at them.

"Afternoon," he said, hitching his saddlebag over his shoulder and pushing the battered front door open.

The old-timers just mashed their toothless gums together in what seemed like dumbfounded silence.

Maybe not too many folks passed by this way, Kyle thought irritably.

The inside of Sadie's was not much better than the outside. Dingy and gray with dust and neglect, the yellow, splotched wallpaper and dull brown wood surfaces made for a mournful atmosphere. A warped desk stood in the corner, and on it was a tarnished silver bell and a dog-eared book; the yellowed pages, stiff with age, were blank. There was no pen to be seen.

Obviously no one had stayed at Sadie's for a long, long time, or if they had, they had not bothered to register. Along one wall were a row of pegs for keys, along the other a rickety stair led upstairs. Behind the desk was a doorway, which opened when Kyle hit the bell on the desk.

A woman appeared, her surly painted mouth pursed thoughtfully for a moment as she contemplated them.

Merrie found herself staring right back. The woman was huge. Her pale arms were as thick as young tree trunks, and her bosom was absolutely enormous, her gaudy dress unable to contain even half of it. The citrus-colored satin was draped low and decorated in strategic spots with shiny bunches of false grapes and ivy. She wore another bunch of grapes and violets in her brazen yellow hair. Most astonishing of all, there was a small purple patch painted on one puffy cheek, in the shape of a wriggling fish.

Merrie had never seen anyone quite like her.

"What you want?" the woman asked, her belligerent eyes on Kyle.

"Two rooms, two meals, two baths," Kyle said.

The woman's chins jiggled a little. She looked quickly from him to Merrie and back.

"What you mean, mister? Two . . . ?"

Kyle held up one finger and then another. "Like so," he said.

The woman shook her head. She looked speculatively at Merrie a moment longer.

"Can't do."

TEXAS KISS

Kyle pushed his hat up a bit. "Why not?"

The woman's eyes slid back and forth between them again. "You twisted, mister? I ain't got no room for you. Now, if you want the little miss here to stay awhile . . ."

Kyle glared at her.

She glared back.

Merrie began to protest, but Kyle put up his hand. He had just spent the most frustrating, temper-shredding days of his adult life—out under a relentless sun, tortured by Merrie's lush backside jostling against his groin, tormenting him interminably. There had been moments when he had come close to flinging her to the ground and burying himself in her sweet body for about a year. He did not need any further provocation. He was at the end of his patience.

"You see those things behind you?" he asked the woman, his voice ice, his eyes blazing. "They're keys. I count about six of them hanging there. Six keys, six rooms. See what I mean?"

It was then Merrie realized that the group of old-timers had crowded in behind them and were standing there enjoying the show, their scrawny necks turning from one speaker to another in turn.

In the ensuing silence, Kyle seemed to grow and grow. He leaned his considerable height down to within an inch of the fat woman's face and placed both fists on the desk.

"What's your name?"

The woman's mouth opened and closed a few times, then turned down at the edges.

"It's all the same to me, but it would be nice to have a name," Kyle said.

"Why?"

"Because otherwise your gravestone's going to read 'Here lies blank,' just like this book." He pointed to the register without taking his deadly eyes from her quivering face.

"Sadieeee! I need you, Sadie! Come here," the woman yelled, her red mouth opening like a maw. "Sadie—"

The door behind her opened, and a short little man came in, a squawking chicken in one hand.

"Wha—?" he said, his bothered look turning to curiosity as he stared up at Kyle and Merrie. "What's doing for you?" He spoke with a strange accent that seemed to sing out the words, adding syllables and emphasis where none existed.

Kyle straightened up, slowly. He seemed to unfurl, attaining his full height with menacing intent.

"Two rooms, two meals, two baths," he said, the edge to each of his words razor-sharp.

The chicken went berserk just then, clucking its head off in a flurry of speckled feathers. The little man danced around, clutching it by the neck and trying to keep out of reach of its sharp beak.

Merrie chuckled; she couldn't help it. The whole thing was so absurd. She pushed her way in front of Kyle and smiled at the little man.

"Sir, we need food. We're tired, hungry, dirty, and we need you to fix that. Especially the hungry part."

It was the magic word. The man positively beamed.

"Eh, *mangiare, bene, bene.* Maked foods for watering mouth, *signorina.* This is promising you."

"Excellent," Merrie said, grinning at Kyle for a moment. His scowl deepened. "Show us to our rooms."

"Not can do it. Rooms busy," Sadie said mournfully. He jerked his free thumb in the huge woman's direction. "Swishtail Sally is keepa de rooms."

Kyle jerked his head from Merrie to Sadie.

"That's it . . . ," he said softly. He leaned over the desk and grabbed the man's shirt front.

"Leave him alone," Merrie and Swishtail Sally said in unison.

"Leave this to me," Merrie said and pushed him away. Kyle threw her a dirty look, but to her surprise and relief, he cleaved a way through the crowd of onlookers and slammed out the front door.

Merrie found him rubbing Cappoquin down a few moments later. Her face was flushed red, and she couldn't quite look him in the eye.

"So?" he asked eventually. He was clearly unhappy. That little muscle on his jaw was ticking once again. That usually indicated his displeasure.

"It's complicated," she said.

Kyle threw his hands into the air. "I don't believe this. *How* is it complicated?"

"They have only one room available. The others are taken."

Kyle was incredulous. "By whom? There's hardly a soul here."

"I think . . . That is . . . Swishtail Sally is a . . . a . . ."

"Whore—yes, that much I realized. But?"

"Well, she uses the other room for her girls . . ."

Kyle nodded. He looked up thoughtfully.

Merrie shook her head. "I'm not sharing."

"I'll take the barn, if they've got one, that is."

His comments, as he headed for the barn out back, would have been less than acceptable in polite circles, but were certainly not of much consequence in Beaver. They definitely didn't phase the old-timers on the porch, who seemed to relish each word of the conversation.

Cackling and rubbing their bony hands together with glee, they admired again the resolve and aptitude of Swishtail Sally! Her capacity for improvisation, and a quick buck, never ceased to amaze them. Her record was nothing short of miraculous. Not a single stranger had ever passed through Beaver without feeling the sting from Swishtail Sally. And up to now, Swishtail had been handsomely rewarded for her temerity, and in their turn, so had they.

Well, what was a madman to do if all of her whores were either pregnant or missing? The old-timers agreed, Swishtail would have been a fool to miss the opportunity of employing the services of "the pretty," even if her gunslinging companion did look a bit dangerous.

They hurried (as much as they were able) inside to get their riding orders. There was not much time between now and sunset, and they would have to hustle (as much as they were able) as never before to bring the customers the news about

Swishtail's new whore—"the pretty" with the golden hair and long, long legs.

"THAT'S ABOUT THE best pot roast I've ever tasted," Merrie said, looking hopefully at Sadie.

Sadie beamed. He was a genius with food. He was immaculately dressed in old-fashioned tails, his white shirt starched and snowy, his elegant mustaches pointed and waxed. He was as out of place here in these shabby surroundings, as was his superb cooking, much to Merrie's delight.

He had concocted a juicy pot roast flavored with whiskey, gravy-rich and succulent. He had served this with gingery carrots and puffy corn dumplings speckled with fresh chopped parsley. Merrie had managed two servings to Kyle's one. She pushed her plate forward for another.

Sadie shook his head sorrowfully. He thrived on the kind of acclaim this green-eyed lovely was giving his cooking. So few really appreciated his efforts, other than Swishtail, naturally—although there was nothing to say that Swishtail wouldn't consume just about anything that was put in the cooking pot.

"But especial, there isa de pie of apple, cavorting themself in cream." He bowed extravagantly and pointed to himself. "Eh, I bringing," he told them and whirled away, his tails dancing. He returned a few moments later with their desserts. The plates were soup bowls and helpings were enormous.

Kyle shook his head.

"We're setting off early tomorrow," he said, "so you'd better get some sleep."

"After I've finished this," Merrie said, her eyes lighting up at the sight of the glorious flaky pastry and chunks of golden fruit, all drowned in a wonderful yellow cream. "How do you make this, Mr. Sadie?" she asked, ignoring Kyle's frown.

Sadie quickly slipped into a chair beside her, his eyes adoring, and launched into a recital of his recipe.

Kyle scraped back his chair.

Merrie eagerly reached for his portion. "If you're not having this, would you mind . . . ?"

She tucked into his bowl as well as her own, making yummy sounds low in her throat.

From his lofty height, Kyle threw her another disgusted look.

Ignoring him, Merrie gave her avid attention to the cook's explanation of how he soaked the apples in brandy and cinnamon before cooking them. She knew very well it was infuriating Kyle, but she was determined that, here at least, he wasn't going to order her comings and goings.

She only looked up when he finally walked away, watching his long, easy strides, hearing the airy jingle of his spurs. Wherever he was, she thought irritably, whatever he did, he exuded a control, a dominance over his surroundings. He'd almost reached the outer hall when she heard his voice float back to her.

"Don't forget to bolt your door, Merrie," he called.

She had an almost violent urge to spite his petty authority, and for a moment she was sorely tempted to leave her bedroom door wide open.

TWENTY-FOUR

MERRIE SCREAMED WHEN the door hit the back wall, wrenching her out of a deep, pleasant sleep. She sat up, clutching the sheet to her chin, trying to come to grips with the fact that several men stood in the doorway gawking stupidly at her. Lamplight from the hall played upon their lecherous faces.

For a moment she wondered if her need to spite Kyle had indeed won over her need for security. Hadn't she bolted the door? And then she saw that someone had actually made a hole in the wall and pulled the bolt open.

The men ogled her, snorting and guffawing drunkenly. They were an unkempt bunch, shaggy-haired and unshaven. From across the room she could smell their unwashed bodies.

Merrie watched incredulously as one of them came inside. She hastily lit the lamp as the others crowded in behind the first man, grinning and swiping their filthy hats off their equally dirty heads.

"Sadie said you was beautiful," the first man said. He had a huge belly that flapped over his belt. His coarse shirt looked as if it had shrunk some and were in danger of splitting open any minute. The box he held out to her jingled. "We know you ain't house rates, so we took up a collection."

"Get out, you filthy hog-swilling creeps. Get out," she screamed at them. "Get out!"

They stopped dead in their tracks, their eager faces reduced to confounded astonishment.

"But, see, missy, we got twenty-three dollars here. Twenty-three . . . count 'em." The potbelly held out the box and shook it again.

Merrie yelled, jumping up on the bed, her sheet clutched against her, her golden, newly washed hair floating in thick, gleaming coils to her waist. She was thankful that she had decided to sleep in her cotton camisole and pantaloons, or otherwise she would have been entirely naked under her sheet. Still, it was mortifying to be seen so.

She was outraged, fairly bristling with fury. She knew that to them twenty-three dollars represented a tidy sum, but to her it was the very last insult she was willing to endure.

"You swill pot, I said get out, and I mean *now*!"

It was then Kyle came scudding around the corner. He had heard her scream and raced in from the yard. He came to a dead stop right behind the little bunch of confused men, a gun in each hand. It took him exactly three seconds to assess that Merrie was not in any real danger. He wanted to laugh out loud at the absurdity of the situation, but he didn't think she would appreciate it—not right now, in any case. Instead he swung his guns back into their holsters and rested his lean frame against the doorjamb, arms crossed, with his hat tilted over his eyes.

"The lady said out, Swill Pot," he said mildly.

The men jumped. They hadn't heard him arrive. Now they looked nervously from his shaded eyes to his gun and shuffled out of the room sideways past him, tipping their hats and mumbling their apologies.

Swill Pot remained behind. His nasty looks sharpened as he surreptitiously glanced from Merrie to the gunslinger, as if assessing his chances.

"I wouldn't," Kyle said softly.

The man grimaced. He was obviously well soused already, and it made him both witless and belligerent. "I already paid Swishtail for a go-around with your woman, mister," he told Kyle sulkily.

"Then take it up with Swishtail. I don't share what's mine," Kyle told him.

"Then why you sleeping in the barn?"

"You'll never know, Swill Pot, will you?" he said.

"Name's not Swill Pot," he grumbled, and at that moment Merrie cried out as the man suddenly swiped at Kyle with a hidden knife. Kyle reacted, instantly, explosively. He whipped out his gun and fired in less than the time it took to blink.

Swill Pot screamed as the bullet passed through his booted foot, and he fell to the ground, writhing. His precious cashbox dropped open, and all the silver coins spilled out, rolling and jingling about the floor.

The group of drunks came creeping back up the stairs, and Sadie appeared with Swishtail Sally at his side.

"Get this trash out of here," Kyle gritted out. He was dispassionate now, all amusement gone.

"You shot me . . . ," Swill Pot moaned over and over.

"Damn lucky I didn't kill you. Come near her again and I will. That goes for all you others."

Swishtail Sally made a nervous rumbling sound in her throat when Kyle's eyes suddenly slid over her. "You, too," he said.

"Sadie—" moaned Swishtail, but the little man erupted into a wild string of words in his own language and bustled her away as quickly as he could.

Merrie stared at Kyle, her green eyes wide with alarm. She was still staring at him that way when the men finally dragged Swill Pot out, cautiously removing their twenty-three silver coins from the floor as they left.

Kyle kicked the door closed after them. He did not take his blue-fire eyes from Merrie. His face was dark with wanting.

Merrie knew that look. Her knees felt weak. Suddenly breathing was not easy. A flaming vice seemed to squeeze her heart.

"You don't share what's yours?" she said, repeating his words. Her voice was mere breath, husky, sexy.

He shook his head very slowly.

She felt suddenly self-conscious. Her cheeks flushed hot with color. His admission played havoc with her equilibrium. "I didn't know I was yours," she whispered.

Oh, how she wished she were, she realized.

"I can't seem to let you alone, darlin'," he murmured. "And it's not for want of trying, believe me."

"Perhaps if we didn't spend so much time together," she

suggested, almost painfully. He was so obviously dismayed that he did want her.

Kyle gave her a wry smile and rubbed the back of his neck. "Trouble is, I don't have to be with you to see you. I just close my eyes and I can feel you, taste you . . ."

From across the room, he watched the blushing crests of her nipples harden beneath her thin cotton camisole, in reaction to his words.

It was the last straw, so to speak. Two day's riding with her in his goddamn lap had been torture enough. He had called a halt at noon because he simply couldn't stand it anymore.

But now . . .

He felt the heat of her body and knew his battle was well and truly lost. He could sense her excitement, her compelling hunger mingling with her fear.

Oh yes, she was afraid of giving herself to him, and he couldn't blame her. She didn't have any inhibitions when she gave herself—no defenses. At least none that he couldn't conquer. Their lovemaking had been potent—explosively hot. He knew he had never experienced anything like Merrie before.

"I'm staying the night," he told her, unbuckling his gunbelt and hooking it over the bedpost.

She still stood on the bed, looking silently down on him. He saw her shake her head.

"I'm staying," he said huskily, with a finality that made something hot inside her burst, splashing her with erotic flames.

He took her hand and slowly, very slowly pulled her down into his lap as he sat on the edge of the bed. Wordlessly, he ran a finger down the softness of her cheek, her neck, his gaze brilliant with passion. The breath caught in her throat as he traced over the swell of her breasts and then back up, to slide provocatively over her mouth, dipping inside, running smoothly over the sensitive insides and out over her lips again. His touch was light, mesmerizing, so incredibly intoxicating.

The lamp beside the bed was still lit. It cast a soft yellow circle onto her beautiful, troubled face.

"I can't help it, Merrie" he said at length. "Neither of us can. I must make love to you now, tonight." He brought his lips to hers, his touch unbearably tender.

And Merrie kissed him back. How could she resist? She could not. A tide of pure longing engulfed her, the need to be loved. Could he truly love her? Would he?

She refused to listen to the little voice on the edge of her mind telling her that she was a fool, twice a fool at that. Instead, she heard the song of her heart. Nor was there time for protracted thought, for the fevered, glorious passion of Kyle's kiss eradicated all else. His quick fingers rid them both of their clothes, and in no time at all she was lying naked in his embrace.

His tongue slid inside her mouth, weaving an erotic dance with hers while he spread her legs wide. He slid his naked length down her body, and at each breast he stopped and kissed the hard tip slowly, softly. Then he slid down farther and ran his tongue across the flat satin of her stomach.

His strong hands held her wide and open all the while. Not that she could have moved away from his embrace; she couldn't. She was enthralled, dizzy with pleasure. His mouth glazed the inside of her thighs, first one side and then the other. The sensations collided, raced along the nerve endings in tortuous spasms.

By the time she realized where his caresses were heading, it was too late. She felt his mouth move over her tender, pulsing center and shot up off the bed in shock.

"No . . . Kyle . . . ," she moaned, struggling to pull his head away.

"Just relax, darlin'. I won't hurt you," he said.

She could feel his warm breath on her intimately.

He stroked, calming her fevered flesh with his supple fingers, then with his lips he set all to flame once again.

He invaded, tasted, plunged into her relentlessly.

She gasped, fell onto the mattress, her back arched, straining against the wondrous pressure, mounting, mounting until she couldn't believe she would survive such pleasure.

She screamed as the sun exploded between her outflung legs and she felt the molten rivers spread out to every nerve in her body, even as he slid up and kissed her mouth.

I can taste myself, she thought wildly as he penetrated her warmth all in one, frantic movement.

He was kneeling in a moment. Hard and throbbing. He felt her climax still about him, small ripples of pleasure making her gasp and squirm. His forehead rested against hers as he fought for composure. She was so tight around him that he dared not breathe.

He shuddered as if with pain, pulsing inside her for long, rapturous moments. Then he raised himself on his strong arms and began flexing his rock-hard hips, grinding his pelvis against the satin smoothness of her belly. He grasped her thighs, bringing her up to meet his urgent thrusts, and then held her still as he savored the flood of pleasure that threatened to overwhelm him. Again and again, he enjoyed the incredible cycle, but each time the pace quickened a trifle, the force of his measured strokes increased.

Her golden beauty responded as he had known she would. She held frantically onto his arms, then smoothed her spider-like fingers over his back and buttocks while she waited for him to resume his gliding movements. She drew her fingers deeply into the valley between, enticing him, peeling the sensations like onion skins from his tortured nerve endings. She arched up into his embrace as he stroked, pulling him deep, bringing her incredible legs high about his flanks and goading him on.

It couldn't last—not as long as he might have wished. She was too wild, his need too raging hot after the past tormenting days and nights.

He climaxed with a groan of pleasure, violent spasms wracking through him for long, long minutes before he collapsed onto her.

He rolled to the side as soon as he was able and brought her close, resting his chin on the top of her head and bringing her hand to his hot mouth. Very gently, he kissed her open palm, turned her hand, and brushed his sensual lips over the back in salute.

It was enough for Merrie. There was no need for words. She would give this remarkable man everything he wanted, everything he demanded of her. Everything she wanted from him, she would take. He was, she thought with a secret smile, such a generous giver. Soon, she was convinced, he would tell her he loved her. She was sated, content; she fell asleep secure in his embrace.

He woke her in the night, assertively easing her onto her side and entering her from behind. He took her leisurely, his fingers pleasuring her breasts, the long, creamy sweep of her body, and tangling in the glossy curls between her thighs. He felt her swell up into his hands, her body convulsing as she cried out his name, climaxing endlessly. He was not long in following her, and they fell asleep again nestled close, Kyle's hand jealously draped over the lushness of her thighs.

MERRIE WOKE TO find Kyle sitting next to her on the bed, fully dressed. Grimy shadows announced the start of a new day. Merrie could see that he wore his sheepskin-lined coat. His dark hat, with its silver egg-shaped conchas about the band, was pulled down low over his eyes. Nevertheless, she knew he was watching her. Kitten-warm and content, she smiled up at him.

He didn't smile back. His expression was inscrutable. He rubbed his chin a moment, and Merrie saw that he had shaved. The scent of his shaving soap, like clean fern-strewn forests, swept over her, causing her belly to contract with desire. He was so handsome, so commanding and in control of his life, and she felt utterly helpless against his magnetism.

He did not touch her, yet the intensity of his gaze was intimate and thoroughly tactile. How long, she wondered, had he been sitting there like that?

A flash of gold winked in his hand before his quick fingers pocketed whatever it was.

"When we get to Dodge City, I'll marry you," he said softly.

Merrie felt the words, so gently delivered, cut through her beating heart. Pain overwhelmed her. Pain and humiliation. He would marry her . . . how magnanimous of him.

No declaration of affection, let alone respect. No question of *asking*. No thought about what she might want!

She gritted her teeth and exerted all of her faculties. There was no way, by tone or deed, that she would ever give Kyle Delancy the opportunity of seeing how much he had hurt her.

"In your dreams, mister."

She was delighted to see him start at her disdain. Whatever he had expected, it surely hadn't been that.

He rose quickly and went to the door. "I'm not arguing about it, Merrie. You won't have a choice."

"As you have so eloquently informed me, I *always* have a choice."

"Not this time you won't."

Merrie came up on one elbow and scowled at him. "You going to force me to say my vows? I'd like to see you try."

"I won't have to. Your father will, after I tell him I've compromised you and you're pregnant."

Merrie was shocked. She hadn't thought he could shock her any further. She had been wrong. She sat right up, the sheet falling to her waist, her nipples contracting with the cold.

"You wouldn't dare," she said hoarsely.

Kyle just cocked an eyebrow at her. His blue gaze swept over her naked breasts and then back up to her eyes.

Her nipples hardened into sharp points. They were sensitive, for he had paid good attention to her breasts the night before, and they seemed to react now as if his fingers played there, still. She hated his ability to stir such feelings in her, even from a distance.

"I'll see you downstairs. Don't be too long," he said from halfway through the door.

"Wait, Kyle, come back," Merrie called out urgently. "Why are we going to Dodge City?"

"To get married," he said impatiently.

"Oh!" she screamed in frustration. "Stop it. We're supposed to be after my father's abductors."

"We would be after them already, but we're waiting on you," he answered sardonically. "You better get going. God knows, with your appetite, we'll be lucky to head out by noon."

"Kyle, you come back and discuss—"

He didn't wait. He slammed the door shut behind him. She heard his booted feet stomp down the stairs.

TWENTY-FIVE

※

DODGE CITY WAS a rollicking town even after its heyday had passed. When the quarantine line finally restricted the drovers from bringing their cattle to the railhead, the town had been irrevocably changed. No longer did cowpokes thunder down Front Street, lariats swirling, to fall head and shoulders into troughs of gut-rotting whiskey. The stockpens that had once housed thousands upon thousands of Texas longhorns were derelict. Lawlessness, and the anarchy of the gun, were things of the past.

Nevertheless, it was a noisy town. It still boasted more than thirty-five saloons, seven dance halls, and the fabulous Theater Comique. Hotels and boarding houses abounded, as did the range and availability of goods. From smooth French brandy to that favorite of the cowmen, Texas Lightning—just about anything was available in Dodge.

A sign posted at the city limits warned visitors that carrying firearms was prohibited, by order of the sheriff, William Barkley Masterson.

Merrie noticed that Kyle took no heed of the sign. They blithely passed the sheriff's office, where other folks were lined up waiting to turn in weapons or retrieve them. It seemed there was a convention or celebration of some kind in town. At the far end of the street, a busy deputy directed people emerging from a stagecoach. The deputy spotted Kyle and flagged him down.

Merrie, riding the hack that they had purchased in Beaver, looked sharply at the silent man beside her. Kyle's guns were clearly visible, and he made no attempt to turn them in. Neither did he seem unduly perturbed about it, as the deputy came up to them.

"Oh, it's you, Mr. Delancy," the man said, tipping his hat in Merrie's direction. "We expected you back days ago."

"Is Bat around, Rolly?" asked Kyle, leaning his bent elbow on the saddle horn.

"He's up at Carlyle's, Mr. Delancy." Here he allowed his eyes to flicker inquisitively over Merrie sitting absolutely still atop her horse, her wide green eyes sparkling with attention. "Mrs. Graham needed him to manage a rowdy visitor."

"Anyone I know?"

The man shook his head and laughed. "Nah, some foreign dandy on his first visit to the Wild, Wild West."

Kyle gave a curt nod and kneed his horse onward. Merrie followed, feeling the deputy's eyes on her back.

They came to a halt in front of the hotel the deputy had mentioned—the Carlyle. Obviously a very fancy establishment, it had an entrance ornately garlanded with banners welcoming visitors from all over to the Ford County Fair.

The lobby was embellished with gold-fringed curtains, heavy walnut paneling, and polished brass. Merrie thought it looked rather out of place and gaudy, more apropos of New York or Boston, both of which she had visited with Ash when he'd been courting Liza.

A number of people greeted Kyle. The desk clerk rubbed his hands delightedly as he watched them approach.

Kyle, on the other hand, was about as congenial as a cornered bear. He growled at the little man behind the desk, and when the poor fellow explained that the room next door to Kyle's was not vacant for his young lady companion, Kyle frowned the clerk into retreat.

"Make it vacant, George," he said. Without looking at Merrie, he picked up both his and her saddlebags. There was no time for Merrie to explain that her room did not have to be next door to Kyle Delancy's—in fact she preferred it otherwise—for just then a very swarthy young man approached them.

He reached out his hand for the bags. Kyle handed them over silently, watching the grave young man with a significance that Merrie didn't understand. For an instant they stood inert, each

TEXAS KISS

clasping the saddlebags, neither giving over to the other. Merrie was convinced that more than those bags had been exchanged, but what exactly, she did not know.

The young man disappeared up the stairs with the bags. Kyle rubbed his chin and turned to Merrie. "You can wait in my room until yours is ready," he informed her.

Merrie wanted to slap him in the worst way, but the lobby was full of people. Exasperated, she followed him up the stairs, determined to have it out with him, once and for all.

Since Beaver, he had hardly spoken to her. She had ranted and raved at him. She had tried speaking softly, positively cordially, in her attempt to get him to see reason. He had refused to engage her in any way, merely telling her that he did not change his mind once it was made up, and that she'd better get used to the idea of marrying him.

When she changed tack, accusing him of bungling the job of rescuing her father, he looked at her a long, contemplative while. Then he'd jerked his eyes away from her, the small muscle in his jaw jumping furiously.

"You'll just have to trust me, won't you? I know what I'm doing," he had said.

Their journey had been unpleasant and tedious. It had rained for the past four days, only stopping this morning, an hour or so before they reached Dodge City.

Kyle's accommodation at the Carlyle turned out to be a large, comfortable room off a small vestibule. Here was none of the gilded pretentiousness of the rest of Carlyle's. The tones were subtle, the furnishings sparse but good quality. Highly polished cherrywood, reddish in tone, was balanced against the soft moss-green of the fine fabrics. There was a sitting alcove on one side, an airy bedroom on the other. The room was more than just sleeping accommodations in a hotel. This was Kyle's home, Merrie realized.

He stood before the large bay window that fronted the room. "There is a tub through the far door there. If you'd like to make use of it, go ahead."

Merrie sent him a dark look. "I don't want a bath. What I want is an explanation."

Kyle threw the saddlebags on the floor and stretched his back. "You need instructions on how to clean off trail dirt?" he said sarcastically.

"Kyle! What are we doing here? Is my father here? What about Liza and her fancy man?" Merrie felt the hysterical note slip into her voice, but she couldn't help it. He had been beastly to her the past few days. He thrived on taking her to the outer limits of bliss and then tossing her carelessly aside. It was intolerable.

"You mean you now believe I'm not her fancy man?"

"Kyle!" Merrie cried, exasperated.

Kyle must have sensed how close to the edge she was. He sighed and eased into a large wingback chair, propping one foot atop his knee and absently twitching the rowel of his spur. It jangled like soft laughter.

"Sit down, Legs. It's time we had a little talk."

Merrie came in and sat as he instructed.

So it was back to Legs, was it? That seemed to indicate a lighter tone. He called her Legs when he wanted to tease, to play with her, not when he was deadly serious. Then, it was Merrie, or even, on occasion, Miss Sinclair.

What, then, had brought him out of his somber mood? She suddenly realized that the swarthy young man from the lobby was standing behind her.

Kyle looked at him.

"Farro, this is Miss Sinclair. Merrie, Farro. He works for me. Reassure the lady, Farro, that her father's here in Dodge, none the worse for his captivity."

Merrie jerked out of her seat.

In a ghost of a voice, she accused, "How do you know that? How could you possibly know when we've just arrived?"

"Farro confirmed it." Kyle's voice was dead calm.

No, no, no. Merrie screamed wordlessly inside, deep in her heart. Betrayed! He had betrayed her. She had been with him every minute since they arrived in Dodge City—Farro had yet to open his mouth.

If Kyle knew Ash was here, *then he was responsible for bringing him here.*

She felt stone-heavy, as if the upper part of her body were sinking down to her boots. Her ears roared.

Her accusing eyes flew from Kyle to the dark young man and back again. How had she judged so poorly?

Kyle had abducted her father . . . Her frantic eyes searched the room, as she thought to find a gloating Liza standing there, and was surprised that she was not. Oh no, she had fallen for him—the devil-hell. He had tricked her. She had believed he would rescue Ash. He had betrayed her.

She felt the wild explosion of unreasoned terror rip through her, robbing her of breath, bringing down a torrent of black, thick unconsciousness. She pivoted on one foot, trying to grab hold of the chair, knowing she was fainting, but she missed and saw the ground rushing up toward her.

Twenty-six

"Merrie, darlin'." She heard his voice calling her through layers of unconsciousness. His warm hands soothed her forehead. She felt the brush of his wonderful mouth over her lips, her temple. The tremor of emotion in his voice was music to her soul. Surely he cared for her? She snuggled her cheek against his palm.

Oh, how I love him. The thought came to her whole and shockingly keen, cutting into her semi-bemused state. Wrenching her awake.

Her eyes flew open. They fixed on Kyle. There was no hint of tenderness in his face, nothing but a cautious, shuttered look that slapped against her heart, making it sting.

"Christ, you scared me," he said.

He sounded disgruntled, as if she had deliberately fainted, for no other reason than to irk him.

"I didn't mean to. I never fainted before," she heard herself say. She hated that she felt she had to excuse herself to him. "You scared me. You still do."

That earned her another cryptic look. "No, I'm not holding Ash prisoner. I wish you'd trust me, Legs. It would make things so much easier."

"On whom?"

"You're right."

Well, that was an admission, Merrie thought, as she struggled to sit up. She was in Kyle's big bed, lying atop the silvery gray-and-green quilt with a dark traveling rug thrown over her legs. Her boots had been pulled off, and her waistcoat and shirt were open at the throat. She glanced behind Kyle and saw Farro standing there, his pitch-black eyes and the rich tone of his skin announcing his Mediterranean heritage, Spanish perhaps, or Italian. Young as he was—he couldn't have been more than sixteen—he was self-assured, his polished exterior a stark foil against Kyle's lanky ruggedness.

Farro held out a small glass to her and nodded, his serious, unsmiling face as devoid of emotion as the very glass he held. His concern, however, seemed apparent in his words.

"Drink, Miss Sinclair. You need the sugar."

It seemed more than the mere offering of a drink.

She took it from him and sipped very tentatively. Warm honeyed liquor slipped easily down her throat. She wondered fancifully if it were poisoned.

Kyle seemed to read her mind. He winced. "I want you to trust me."

Oh, how she wanted to. But did she dare? "How can I? You don't tell me what's going on. How do you know Ash is here . . . ? Why didn't you tell me sooner . . . ?" Merrie felt the hysteria rising once again.

Kyle indicated to Farro that he should leave them. The young man took himself out and closed the door.

Panic fueled Merrie's already unsteady equilibrium. She felt her temper rise. "You're treating me like an imbecile who can't understand anything at all. But I hired you. You're being paid—don't shake your head at me, Kyle Delancy—paid to tell me wh—"

"I don't work for you; I never did."

Merrie felt as if her heart would fall apart.

"For Liza?" she accused.

"Ash hired me." He sounded tired.

Merrie was dumbfounded. She started to say something but changed her mind and instead asked him, "When?"

"Several months ago, while he was in New York. I'm a friend of Strafford's," he added at her puzzled look. "They called me to meet with your father. He had a problem. I know how to solve these kind of problems. It's my business." He shrugged almost apologetically. But when she said nothing he continued:

"Extortion. Someone's after the Sinclair gold. Ash didn't

know who, not in the beginning, anyway. Before he could do anything about it, he got ill. Now we know—Liza's behind it."

"I don't believe it." Merrie gasped. "Doesn't Ash give her everything she wants?"

"There's no telling what greed does to people."

Merrie thought for a moment. All the misery, the bewildered, lonely years because of Liza, erupted in her memory. It was, in a way, so strange to find that she had been right in condemning Liza as an uncharitable, spiteful woman. She simply hadn't realized the extent of her stepmother's avarice.

"I want her in jail. We need to rescue Ash immediately. You said you could do it, so do it . . . now!"

He shook his head. "Too dangerous." His eyes darkened to midnight blue with some startling emotion she could not fathom. "I've set a trap for Liza and her friends, and I'm not springing it until I'm good and ready."

Merrie's face was positively white. Kyle sat down next to her, but she shied away, moving back against the headboard, revulsion evident in her clear green eyes.

Kyle didn't move. "I won't hurt you, darlin'" he told her, quietly, confidently. "If you can believe any one thing, believe that."

"Why should I believe anything you say? I hired you to find my father, but all the time you deceived me. You were already hired."

His intense blue gaze cascaded over her, into her. She knew she hurt him with her doubts. Still, she waited for his answer.

"Have I ever lied to you?"

"Have you always told me the truth, all the truth?"

"No," he said sharply. "You don't get it yet. I allowed you to think you were hiring me, because that was the only way I could keep you near me and safe."

"Why? What do you mean? Safe from what? From whom?"

"Trust me. I'll tell you everything, if you'll just give me time."

"Tell me," she insisted.

Kyle shook his head. "Liza is a dangerous woman, Merrie.

Immoral. She uses her beauty to manipulate her lovers into doing as she tells them. If she told them to kill you, you would be killed."

"What are you trying to tell me?" she whispered. Dread was in her heart. Everything was confused, muddled, and she felt ill again. Her fear was luminous.

"I'm not her lover, for Christ sake."

"Then who is?"

He looked at her reluctantly. "Matt Cheston," he said, repugnance evident in his voice. "Your fiancé is her lover. Or one of them."

"I don't believe you." She had not thought he could shock her any further. She had been wrong.

And then, the picture of Liza writhing on the bed in the house on End Lane flashed before her eyes. She saw the rippling muscles, the taut buttocks of the man, his hips pumping, his head thrown back for a moment in climax . . . She saw . . . she saw . . . Oh, dear God, yes. His hair had not been black like Kyle's, it had been russet brown, shadowed by the dimness of the room.

It had been Matt.

She recalled quite clearly Liza's annoyance with Matt that day on the porch when she had found him kissing Merrie. Countless little incidents seemed to add credence to the notion.

Shame and humiliation flowered in her cheeks, in her soul.

Kyle reached out for her hand, but she withdrew it hastily beneath the coverlet.

"Don't," he said so very softly. "He's not worthy of you, believe me." He stood. "If it's any consolation, Liza is no more faithful to him than he was to you."

"I-I broke our engagement. After we . . . after Ash's welcome home party." She glanced at him with a flush of embarrassment. "I couldn't—wouldn't. I broke it off. He laughed at me." She sounded so dejected, so lost.

Kyle felt a surge of sheer joy. He had reached the door, but he turned now, grinning teasingly. "It wouldn't have mattered

TEXAS KISS 229

if you hadn't. You're going to marry me. As you know, I don't share."

She shook her head, sadly, slowly.

He came back to her quickly, taking her into his arms.

"Oh, yes, you are." He was determined.

His mouth brushed hers, stealing soft kisses, tender, soothing kisses. He knew she would not be able to bear being overwhelmed right now, so he kept his touch gentle, undemanding.

She didn't protest, didn't reject him. She felt the healing warmth, the strength he seemed able to impart with each langorous sweep of his tongue.

Sensing her capitulation, he pulled her up tighter into his embrace. His fingers gripped her upper arms; his chest brushed her voluptuous breasts.

He rubbed himself against the fullness, lifting her, dipping his head so that he could nuzzle her through her cotton shirt. Her head fell back, exposing the white column of her throat.

The gesture was an erotic invitation, even though she perhaps was not aware of it. Kyle groaned softly, and followed the delicate line of her jaw with his questing tongue. His fingers were busy with the buttons of her shirt when the door flew open.

He scowled as a tall, flame-haired woman came into the room. For one horrible moment, Merrie thought it was Liza, but this woman was much taller than Liza; in fact, she was even taller than Merrie. She was very beautiful. Her slanted eyes were dark and sensual, heavily lashed and absolutely ice-cold. Her mouth was wide, red with rouge, and yet quite lovely, the bow perfectly formed and accented by the cosmetic. She was dressed most fashionably, too, her bustle exquisitely draped about a posy of teal-and-gold-silk roses. Diamonds glittered in her ears, upon her fingers, and around her neck. For an evening at the opera, the brocade and blue-white diamonds were perfect, but for an afternoon in Dodge City, they were nothing short of ludicrous.

Farro put his not-so-cool face inside the door. "I'm sorry," he said and shrugged. "She wouldn't take no for an answer."

"George said you'd brought a *female* with you," the beautiful woman said, "but I had to see for myself. I rather thought you had more taste than that, Kyle, my sweet."

Merrie stiffened.

"Do come right in, Laura, and make yourself at home," Kyle said sarcastically.

"I am home, sweetie, or had you forgotten? Carlyle's is mine." The redhead walked to the bed and rudely looked Merrie up and down, wrinkling her nose in distaste.

"Thanks for reminding me. I wouldn't have known. Seeing that you've invited yourself in, let me introduce you to my fiancée, Miss Meredith Sinclair. Merrie, meet Laura Graham, proprietor of the Carlyle."

Laura's delighted trill cut Merrie to the quick.

"You must be obscenely wealthy," she gasped, wiping the make-believe tears from her eyes. "There is certainly not much else to recommend you."

"You're speaking to me?" Merrie asked, proud of the fact that her voice managed to convey an assurance that she didn't at all feel. "It's hard to tell. Your eyes don't focus that well."

Laura's back straightened a yard or so, but Kyle's expletive cut any retort she was about to make.

"Bloody hell, but I should have known it." Kyle was annoyed at Laura's intrusion, but quietly furious that she would so blatantly try to bait Merrie.

For several years now Laura had been after him. She did not want to marry him, so she said, simply become his mistress. Kyle had no interest in her at all. Laura's persistence had become problematic lately; in fact, she was becoming an embarrassment. He had stopped being polite about putting her off.

Now he intended to put a stop to her intrusiveness once and for all. Not in front of Merrie, however, but he would do it, and do it soon.

"Take care, Laura. The lady knows how to defend herself, pretty darn well."

Laura's elegant head swished in his direction. "Oh, I don't need protecting, sweetie, but maybe she does."

"You threatening my fiancée, Laura?"

"Your fiancée," she scoffed. "Really, Kyle, is she that far pregnant already?"

"I certainly hope so," he heard himself say, and then further surprised himself by silently amending that if she wasn't, he would do his damn best to make sure that she was, as quickly as possible.

The thought of her carrying his child produced a sudden, blazing exhilaration in him. Given his history, he shocked himself.

He glanced across the room at the disheveled urchin in his bed. She was still covered in trail dust, tatty and begrimed in her mud-splattered, sun-bleached clothes, and yet quite able to hold herself as proudly as if she were a duchess at a ball. He was damn proud of her.

If Laura Graham was shocked by his response, it was momentary, and she quickly recovered. She had no intention of giving up the fight just now, possibly never.

She was obsessed with Kyle Delancy. His dangerous looks excited her. She fantasized about him. Quite frankly, she was acutely incensed that he did not find her irresistible—everyone else did. The more he pushed her away, the more determined she became. No two-bit cowgirl was going to have him if she couldn't.

Her face took on a smug, complacent look as she leaned over Merrie. "Both you and the brat can be taken care of, like that," she said, snapping her fingers under Merrie's chin.

"That's enough," Kyle said his voice taking on a frosted tone that brooked no argument. He thrust himself between Laura and Merrie. "Farro, show Mrs. Graham out, now."

Fury sparked Laura's temper to recklessness. "How dare you speak to me like a servant. I'll thank you to remember that this is my hotel. If anyone is going to leave it's going to be her. I want her out of here!"

"You're being childish, Laura. Stupid, too, or have you

forgotten that I own a good chunk of the Carlyle?" Kyle's brow lifted in Farro's direction, and the young man took Laura by the arm with a muted apology and led her to the door.

She shrugged him off angrily and whirled about. The door slammed behind her with such violence that two small prints fell off the wall with a crash. The glass shattered on the hard polished wood.

Farro went off to obtain the necessary implements to clean up the mess, leaving the two of them alone in the awkward silence.

"Laura's a bit hot under the collar right now. I can only apologize for her," said Kyle, rubbing the back of his neck.

"She's your mistress?"

"No, she's not." He was emphatic. "She's an old business partner, I inherited after her husband died and she gets a bit proprietary now and then. I would have spoken to her earlier, but I had more important things to deal with first—you fainted."

Merrie's heart lurched. *More important* . . .

"You work with her?" Merrie asked.

Kyle shook his head. "I helped finance her operation some years ago when she needed cash to renovate the place. It's an investment only."

"I should have known," Merrie said. Hope stirred potently in her blood. *She was important to him.* She had always thought that she'd been simply an available body, but now . . . Surely she must mean something to him?

She smiled at him, her green eyes sparkling with wit. "She should have spent some of the money to hire a decorator. All those gold-and-pink cherubs, the amber mirrors!" She shuddered dramatically.

Kyle looked at her incredulously for a moment and then burst out laughing.

"You're bloody incredible, Legs. She's just mauled you with her spite, and all you can complain about is her taste in curtains."

TWENTY-SEVEN

THEY DINED TOGETHER in front of the open window in his bedroom. A sweet prairie night ruffled the moss-and-cream pinstriped damask curtains. After living outdoors for almost two weeks, both Merrie and Kyle were reluctant to abandon simplicity for the convention of a dining room.

It was late October and uncommonly fine. The moon had set already, but the stars were scattered in ostentatious drifts about the velvet sky.

Farro had brought up a tray of roasted quails, a medley of autumn vegetables, a huge covered crock of fragrant herb stuffing, and fat green beans laced with butter. There were two bottles of Sassafras wine and cognac for Kyle.

Merrie, always a hearty eater, found that fainting hadn't upset her appetite at all. She ate with gusto, and watching her, Kyle chuckled silently to himself. He wondered where she kept it all, for she was slender as a willow wand. He finished his meal, pushed back his chair, his long legs sprawled out in front of him, and lingered over his cognac. It was his own special supply. His adoptive father, Etienne DeLace had imported it for years. His widow, Mariette, still ran the family business and kept Kyle supplied.

The autumnal liquor spun in the snifter, cascading sluggishly down the bulbous sides. Kyle brought the glass to his nose, inhaled blissfully, and took a mouthful. It settled like silk on his palate, the fumes and taste mingling in an aromatic celebration of the senses.

A contentment, rarely felt in his life, seemed to flower inside him. It surprised him; he wasn't the stay-at-home type. But he enjoyed the relaxed camaraderie he and Merrie appeared to be sharing this evening. He was especially charmed that she'd chosen to remain barefoot. Somehow, that exemplified a casual acceptance of him on a fundamental level. He really liked that.

She looked right at home among the familiar surroundings of his things, too. Looking across and seeing her there in his room, at his table, just felt so right.

She had bathed and changed into clean clothes. Her sun-gold hair, gleaming clean, had been twisted into a quick knot at the base of her neck and seemed determined to wriggle free. Already there were several long strands that had come loose and lay curling about her lovely face.

Her cheeks glowed with health, and the gold tone of her skin from her recent sojourn outdoors made her green eyes seem even more vivid, her hair that much brighter.

"That was delicious," she said and pushed her plate back almost regretfully. "Your friend might not be hospitable, but she has no shortcomings when it comes to food."

"Don't say I'm not discerning."

"She is also very beautiful, but not as beautiful as Liza," Merrie said. It was an implied accusation and revealing. She felt her cheeks burn with discomfort.

All her insecurities came rushing back. There were too many unknowns about Kyle Delancy. She desperately wanted to trust him; she really did. But she was too vulnerable to his charm, too exposed in her young life to disappointment.

Although she was now convinced that it had been Matt, and not Kyle, she had seen that day with Liza, it did little to secure her belief in fidelity. If anything, it reinforced the opposite.

She had lost Ash to Liza for many years, until he realized what was happening between them. Oh, he had tried very hard to make it up to her. And he had, in thousands of ways. Yet it was always there between them, causing strain and heartache.

Matt, too, had been stolen away, and while she was not hypocritical enough to mourn his faithfulness, she was aware of a fundamental wrong that had been done to her.

And what of Kyle? Was he lured by Liza, or perhaps the Sinclair gold? Laura had accused Kyle of wanting her for her wealth. Was she right? Merrie felt torn between wanting to believe in him and being fearful of disaster. The problem was, she was afraid it was too late for her to guard her tender heart. Much too late.

Kyle watched her through his lashes. He seemed to divine her feelings. "No one's more beautiful than Liza. But I'm not involved with her, if that's what you're hinting at, and I'm not telling you again."

"Then *why* won't you go after her? What are we doing here? I want my father set free. It isn't safe for him; he's ill." She felt the bright spots of color on her cheeks flame again.

"He's much stronger than you think. He's here and he's quite safe. I've told you that. They're holding him at an old farmhouse just outside the town. My men are there, watching around the clock. Liza won't hurt him, she needs him."

"How do you know?" Merrie said sharply. "How do you know what Liza will do?"

"Your faith in me is overwhelming," he said sarcastically and took a long swallow. He sighed. "I guess I want you to trust me without explanations, but you're too damn suspicious, Legs. You don't trust anyone. I think it comes from being self-reliant."

"You disapprove?"

She was defensive about her independence, he knew, and for good reason. Not many men liked the idea of an independent, free-thinking woman. He wasn't all that sure that he liked the idea. Still, there was something amazingly comforting in knowing, truly knowing, that he could rely on Merrie in a difficult situation. He had never considered it possible that a female might be one hundred percent dependable when the going got rough.

"On the contrary," he heard himself say. What in hell was happening to him? In the past few hours he had contradicted all the fundamental tenets of a lifetime. He swore softly and poured a second tot into the snifter, watching the thin stream of amber tumble in splendid indolence into the crystal.

Merrie sensed that he was about to break and tell her what she wanted to know. She waited on the edge of her seat, eyes shining, heart pounding in anticipation. She was not wrong, and yet she could not have been more astonished at what Kyle revealed to her.

"What I'm going to tell you will seem . . . well, a bit strange. But hear me out, okay?"

Merrie nodded slowly.

"You've got to do better than that. You've got to try very hard to understand the whole story, and not jump to conclusions. Okay?"

"I'll try," she said.

"It's like this . . . Matt Cheston is not Liza's only lover. There is a second man involved, and he's running this extortion thing. We don't know who he is. I came to Hollow Creek to try and find out, but he's too smart and stayed hidden."

"A-a second man . . . ," Merrie said, thinking of the night she had hidden in the arbor. Liza had been arguing with a man. "I-I saw him, I think," she said aloud.

When Kyle frowned, she explained about her adventure the night of the party.

"Sounds like our man. But we still don't know who he is. He's been very clever—covering his tracks. But he's the brain behind this thing—no doubt about it."

"I don't understand. What about Matt?"

"He's their patsy. They needed Cheston in case Ash died and left you to inherit. Cheston marries you, they control Cheston—simple."

"But then Ash didn't die right away."

"Right. And the gold stayed hidden. Liza couldn't find a trace of it. Not for want of trying, mind you. She had scouts out investigating every association Ash ever had. So, we decided to help her find the gold. That way, we'd smoke out our mystery man. We know he won't trust anyone when it comes time to collect the gold. He'll be there, in person.

"We arranged it so that when they came to collect, we'd get them. The plan was simple. We had to lure them out.

TEXAS KISS

"I sent a letter, under the name of Jessop Farraway, Ash's attorney, knowing Liza would discover it. The letter explained that Ash could sign over custody of the gold to his daughter Meredith, but only in person, and only in the presence of Jessop Farraway—here in Dodge City. It was important that they bring Ash here safely, and they have."

Merrie gazed at him, stupefied.

"You *arranged* for Ash to be abducted?"

Kyle shrugged. "We had to make them believe the gold's been here all the time."

Merrie was incredulous. "You . . . you made me think you were tracking them," she cried, hot with anger. "And all the time . . . Devil be damned, but you're the lowest . . . How could you do that to me?"

As she was about to swing by him, he grabbed and jerked her into his arms.

"Ash and I agreed. You weren't to be involved unless absolutely necessary."

"You'll never get me to believe it. I've been sick with worry, sick with fearing for his life these past few weeks. Ash wouldn't put me through this hell," she cried, fighting him now, distraught and disillusioned.

He held her tightly, his arms wrapped around her, securing her struggling body to his.

"I'm sorry, darlin'," he whispered. His mouth covered hers briefly, lifted, stroked, and soothed, and lifted again until she quieted. "I never would have agreed if I thought it would hurt you like this."

He managed to supplicate her without any difficulty, she thought.

All the fight went out of her. Why did she constantly give in to him, why?

"Look at me, Merrie. I want you to believe me."

An ocean of feeling was in his voice. She heard not only the words but the need behind them.

"I believe you," she told him, her voice softer than the night wind that teased the curtains.

He kissed her passionately, feeding her spent fury with his own desire, torching the already brilliant emotion and transforming it into sexual need.

There was never a question that he wouldn't triumph. He could play her any way he wanted. She despaired, even as she reveled in the glory of his kiss.

And when he felt her respond, fully, sweetly, his kiss went wild. His mouth plundered her. All-consuming and volatile, his need was upon him. He felt compelled to give in to the wildness, to just simply let go.

A swelling heaviness invaded Merrie's limbs. Her bones seemed to dwindle away, dissolve into her flesh. She craved him, in her soul, in her body. There was nothing but that fulsome, ardent longing to be filled by him, to bend and loosen the boundary that limited her. She wanted to be part of him. She wanted him profoundly.

Somehow he managed to unbutton her shirt and pull her work pants down over her hips while still standing in the middle of the room. He made no effort to get to the bed. He tugged her pants off one leg, hearing the material tear as he wrenched it down over her foot. He was aware of her fingers at his buckle, and then his were there also, helping to unfasten the buttons of his pants, his waistcoat and shirt. It took but a second to free himself and raise her high over his slightly bent legs.

Merrie cried out as he lifted her onto his pulsing erection. He gripped her hips and brought her legs to lock around his waist.

"Easy, darlin'," he breathed, and raised his mouth to take her lips as he lowered her, sliding deeply inside, hot and powerful. She felt herself stretch and stretch some more; he seemed impossibly huge. A searing bliss gushed though every delirious fiber of her body. Tiny circles of pleasure rippled out from the scorching center of her being, spiraling outward and upward. The world spun chaotically out of control, and it was difficult to accept that she was a mere earthbound mortal.

He sensed her need for him to pause a moment before resuming his steady pistonlike movements. His legs, strong as steel, were braced to support both the weight of her body and the impetus of his relentless action. But he was too fired himself to prolong their amorous play. A few forceful strokes brought him to volatile release.

He arched into her convulsively, as the rush of ecstasy trumpeted through his body. Nor did he release her immediately. After a gasping hiatus, before even his breathing returned to something resembling normalcy, he lowered her onto his bed, falling down beside her, holding her fast to his chest.

Eventually, shaking his head in disbelief, he turned to gaze into her eyes. "You do it to me every time. I think I can manage you, govern my cravings, then I touch you and wham! I go crazy."

Merrie laughed. He sounded so aggrieved, she couldn't help it. His words made her heart soar. He might not love her yet, but at least she made him crave her. And if he needed to keep her close . . . well, then anything was possible.

"Woman, you're driving me out of my mind," he said, even more disgruntled than before. "I confide my troubles, and you laugh at me."

Merrie laughed again. This time she burst with it. Tears streamed down her face, and she gasped with mirth.

Kyle watched her, altogether unamused.

Merrie shook with laughter; she rolled from side to side, aching with it.

She saw him rise, kicking off his boots, remove his shirt, and strip off his tight denim pants. He turned purposefully to the bed and began removing the remainder of her clothes, until she lay there naked and open to his white-hot scrutiny. She saw the humor in his blue eyes, the wicked lights behind them, and stopped laughing.

"I'm pleased I amuse you, Legs, 'cause now you're going to amuse me," he told her, husky-voiced.

She shook her head, too relaxed and weak from laughing to move.

"Oh, yes you are, and it takes more to amuse me than it does you, a hell of a lot more," he said as he began caressing her luxurious breasts.

Very soon Merrie was moaning with pleasure, her laughter put aside.

TWENTY-EIGHT

BAT MASTERSON WAS a good-looking man. Given to wearing expensive duds like an Eastern dandy, he had a reputation as a hard-drinking, gambling man of uncertain temperament. The law was any way he wanted it to be, some said, and certainly subject to change, depending on circumstances, and the time of day. But he had curbed the anarchy that had plagued Dodge City in its early years, tamed the rowdy cow town, while managing somehow to leave its spirit intact. And to his credit, Bat Masterson never turned his back on his friends.

Certainly Kyle had never had occasion to mistrust him, but maybe it was that Bat liked Kyle Delancy. He admired his independence, even his arrogance to a certain degree, because Kyle never used it coercively. But he enjoyed the man's company at the card tables. In a pinch, he had even been known to stick a temporary marshal's badge on Kyle, although both understood that Kyle preferred working for himself. And why not? It had made him a good deal of money.

They sat over breakfast in Kyle's room. Bat grinned at Kyle, his second cup of coffee, this one laced with whiskey, raised to his mouth. He sipped and set it down. "I wouldn't have believed it, but last night, I happened to see Laura's face down at Long Branch," he said referring to his brother's saloon.

"Laura's been more than her usual . . . ah . . . difficult self," Kyle admitted coolly.

Bat was amused at his friend's understating of the facts. What he did not find funny was Laura's unhealthy attempts to snare Kyle Delancy over the past few years when the man so obviously was not interested.

Last night at the Long Branch, Laura had looked madder than a wet hen. That was the reason Bat was still listening to

Kyle's request. "And that's why you want me to set Rolly watching after your lady? Being that you and Farro are too busy setting up this deal down on Front Street?"

Kyle shifted a moment, and Bat had the distinct impression that his friend was embarrassed. He was intrigued. Nothing and no one could ever have provoked such emotions in the Kyle Delancy he knew. But then, it was obvious the man was head-over-heels in love and not quite himself. Bat Masterson couldn't wait to meet the young miss who had wrought such changes in his freedom-loving friend.

"Not exactly," Kyle said. "It's a little complicated."

"How so?"

"Dammit," he muttered and silently told himself that there was no way around this one. Aloud he said, "Merrie's skittish. She may run, and I want her kept here until Reverend Bright can marry us. It's only for a few days."

Bat laughed out loud. "A 'little complicated'?" he spluttered. "I'd say that's complicated, all right. But hell, Delancy, with all the females in Ford County and beyond drooling to get you leg-shackled, can you tell me why you chose one that doesn't want you?"

Kyle watched him out of glittering blue eyes and smiled. "It's none of your goddamn business, Masterson." A smoky vagueness drifted over his face just then, and he added, "And she does. Want me, that is."

Bat trawled in his laughter like so many wriggling fish, but he was clearly enthralled by this new side of Kyle Delancy. Not for anything would he miss the opportunity to goad him.

"You say for a few days? Like how many days?"

"A week at most. Mrs. Bright isn't quite sure when her husband's getting back."

"Well, I don't rightly know. Pat Meadows is going on an errand for me—leaves today. I'm kinda shorthanded right now."

"I only need Rolly. Farro can relieve him."

"Why don't you just use your innate charm, then, and *ask* her to stay put until Reverend Bright arrives back in town?"

Kyle glared at the sheriff. "Because even if she said yes, I wouldn't trust her. She's a bit headstrong, likes to have things her own way."

"And you don't, I suppose," said a light voice from the doorway. Merrie stood out in the vestibule. She'd spent the last few hours before daybreak in her own room. For the sake of propriety and her good name, Kyle had insisted.

He came toward her at once. His eyes traveled the familiar territory of her leggy body, as if reassuring himself that she was real. She looked very young, and golden from her hours in the sun. She was wearing a thin cotton blouse, as green as her eyes, and her tan work pants. Her hair was tied up with shiny ribbons, a thoroughly female touch that negated the masculine attire. She was also barefoot.

"Actually, I only want you," he told her softly, much to the fascination of Bat Masterson.

Even though Kyle had made passionate love to her until the early hours of the morning, even though he should have been replete, he felt again the persistent call to possess her. Holding her was the only curb against deprivation.

Merrie felt the brush of his hushed words against her cheek, as if he had stroked his warm and clever fingers over her sensitive skin. She blushed, as he'd known she would. He smiled down at her as he took her hand and led her into the room.

"Come and meet Sheriff Bat Masterson, Merrie," he said and made the introductions.

Bat grinned as he shook Merrie's hand. "So you're Ash Sinclair's girl. It's a real pleasure, ma'am, a real pleasure."

"Sheriff," Merrie said, as if she weren't wearing faded masculine clothing and no shoes, and as if calling on gentlemen in their hotel rooms early in the morning were commonplace.

She wasn't surprised he knew her father. Ash had been doing business in Dodge City since its very early days and was a friend of the founder and owner of the general store, Robert Wright.

"Please don't let me interrupt your breakfast," she murmured politely, indicating that he should sit.

"I'm sure you're hungry. Join us. The Carlyle prides itself on its popovers." Kyle said. He chuckled at the look she threw him, but she wasn't able to drag her eyes away from the generous basket of piping hot pastries. Sitting next to it was a chubby glass dish of strawberry preserves.

Bat pulled another chair up to the table and waited to seat her. "I believe congratulations are in order," he said, sitting down opposite her. Kyle glowered at him.

"For what reason?" Merrie said, although she knew exactly why, having overheard a bit of their conversation.

"On your upcoming marriage. I must say, Miss Sinclair, I'm impressed. Yessir, nothing short of marvelous. Never thought to see the old bachelor leg-shackled."

Merrie swallowed a mouthful of buttery pastry, licked a drop of crimson jelly from her bottom lip, and smiled sweetly at the man. "I hope you won't be too disappointed, then, Sheriff Masterson, when I tell you we're not getting married."

There was a clear invitation in her eyes as she smiled at him. Merrie had never played the coquette in her life, but she was unable to prevent herself from doing so this once. She abhorred the masculine proclivity that assumed every female put on the earth was determined to "leg-shackle" the very first potential man she met. The entire attitude infuriated her.

Kyle, however entertained by her quick wit, was not able to overlook the searing, unreasoning jealousy he felt. When it came to flirting, he found he had no sense of humor at all.

"The subject of our wedding is not open to discussion," he informed them both, his voice sullen. He turned toward Bat. "Why don't you repeat your earlier news for Miss Sinclair's benefit, Masterson? I'm sure she'll find it engrossing."

No longer puzzled by his friend's capitulation, Bat Masterson gave a belly laugh. Merrie Sinclair was an absolutely perfect mate for his friend. They were one dymanic couple. The sensual charge between them was tangible. It was in every look that passed between them, every gesture, every possessive word.

"Why, certainly, Delancy," he said and grinned, "if you think it might keep her in town awhile," he added wickedly and bent his head in Merrie's direction. "There's this fair come to town; you may have noticed. Ford County Fair is a most edifying and popular event hereabouts."

"Get to the point, Masterson," Kyle said impatiently. Farro had just come in, and Kyle wanted to get going. There was no way he was leaving Merrie, however, until he had a commitment from Masterson that he would see to her safety.

"Well, as I was saying, it draws all kinds of folk. Some good, some bad. One of the ways we keep the town from being tore up is by having everyone register their weapons at my office."

"I saw the sign as we entered," Merrie said, sitting straight up, the crumbling pastry in her hand forgotten for a moment. "You have an interesting name on your list of registered guns?"

Bat's eyebrows rode up his forehead. "She's sharp," he said to Kyle. "You got it, Miss Sinclair. Matt Cheston. Come to get supplies from Wright's General Store, among other things. His traveling companion's name was even more interesting, though." He glanced quickly from Merrie to Kyle and back. "Miss Meredith Sinclair, was the name given."

"But . . . ?"

"You can see now why I found meeting you so interesting. You don't look anything like the lady who rode in with Cheston."

"Let me guess," Merrie said darkly, "a stunning redhead, right?"

When Bat nodded, she rose in agitation.

"Why is she using my name? What have you planned here?" She glared accusingly at Kyle.

He placed his hands, palms open, on the table and pushed his chair back. "See what I mean?" he asked Bat. "Trust isn't one of her strong points."

"Don't fool with me, Kyle," she warned him.

"Darlin', believe me, that's the last thing I would do," he assured her.

"Kyle I—"

"Calm down, Legs. Let me explain. You're Ash's heir. Liza thinks the Sinclair gold is in the Corona Bank vault. If Ash, under duress, presents her to the attorneys and witnesses as Meredith Sinclair, *then she will become you. In the terms of the will, that means the gold becomes hers.*"

Merrie's face was blanched with shock. "But I never heard of this bank vault, this Corona Bank. For the last year, I've been looking after all Ash's business. Surely I would have come across it."

"No. It doesn't exist. I made it up. You remember I told you about the letter that I sent?"

"The one you used to trap Liza?"

He nodded. "Farraway and Hargraves agreed to assist us. Their help is crucial; we had to make Liza believe they'd been holding the Sinclair gold all along."

"Liza knows they're Ash's lawyers. She would never expect a trick from them, right?" Merrie said.

"Exactly. But they've never met her, and the best she knows, they've never seen you, either—at least since you grew up. Any day now, she'll bring Ash to town, not as his wife, but as his *daughter, Meredith*. We'll be waiting."

"So you see, Miss Sinclair, there's no point in rushing in prematurely and putting your daddy in danger," Masterson said. "According to the fake letter Kyle sent, your daddy must personally present his heir in front of witnesses." Bat set his coffee cup down.

"That's clever," Merrie admitted after absorbing everything for a moment. Her smile was sunshine bright. She leaned forward eagerly. "What can I do to help?"

TWENTY-NINE

"WHAT DO YOU mean, nothing?" Merrie asked, her voice laced with affront. "I'm not used to sitting back, letting the world pass me by, Kyle, and I'm not starting now."

Bat's plump cheeks jiggled suspiciously, and he pushed back his chair and rose. "Think that's my cue, Delancy," he chortled. "Yessir, think I better be moving along."

"What about Rolly?" asked Kyle, rising with his friend.

"Oh, I'm convinced. You could sure use the help. He'll be around before you can say fire!"

"Much appreciated," Kyle said, shaking the other man's outstretched hand.

Bat winked at Kyle, then bowed his head in Merrie's direction. "A real pleasure, ma'am. Morning, Farro," he said as he took his hat from the young man and left.

"I didn't mean to send him scuttling away," Merrie said, twisting her napkin absently.

"Relax. He doesn't do anything he doesn't want to, Legs." He smiled slightly at the rosiness in her cheeks. "Now, how about coming over here and giving your husband-to-be a good-morning kiss?"

"I'm not marrying you, you stubborn man."

"Then what'd you come here for? This morning, I mean," he clarified. He sauntered back and sat down as if he didn't have a dozen things to do, didn't have a bevy of men to instruct for the day, didn't have Farro waiting there, watching them with serious, forlorn eyes.

He was bemused at his growing obsession with Merrie. Even more, he was astounded by his lack of resentment at the upcoming nuptials. Merrie's resistance he didn't for a moment consider to be anything more than nerves. After all, her father's marriages had both ended in despair, one through negligence, the other, well, with Liza . . . Who could blame her for being hesitant?

"For my boots."

He nodded in Farro's direction. The man was standing there like a doorpost, his eyes fixed on some invisible spot, holding her scuffed and battered riding boots in one hand. They had been polished and cleaned up as much as possible, but they were a sorry sight.

She mumbled her thanks and took them from him.

"Actually, that's not a bad idea," she heard Kyle say, as if she'd momentarily left the room and missed a pertinent part of their conversation. "Why don't you visit Wright Brothers and get yourself some new boots and a dress. You never can tell, you may just jump up one morning and feel like you want to get married!"

He ducked as her boot came flying perilously close to his head. He was still in high spirits when he left some fifteen minutes later with Rolly securely ensconced and Merrie boiling mad.

THE DAYS PASSED very slowly, with Farro relieving Rolly at lunchtime each day. It wasn't as if they restricted Merrie in any way, but on the other hand, she was not allowed near the livery stables or the railroad. When the stage came belting through and stopped in a cloud of dust outside the Carlyle, Rolly actually placed himself before the door, legs spread wide, arms akimbo, and wouldn't let her out until they heard the whoop and holler of the drivers steering their team out of town again.

There was a great deal of hustle and bustle around the town, plenty to see and do. On one particular afternoon, Rolly showed her the solicitor's office of Farraway and Hargraves on Front Street. It was a narrow place, sandwiched between A. B. Lent, Bridlemaker, and the barbershop. A glimpse through the small windows revealed the dim interior, suitably furnished in musty browns and well-buffed oak, it exuded the well-to-do ambience of respectability.

TEXAS KISS

At Wright Brothers, she purchased a few items to supplement her wardrobe, seriously damaged by weather and, to her embarrassment, Kyle's impatient ardor. There were a stack of well-thumbed Penny Horriblies that she had never read, and after much deliberation, she greedily piled five of them into her basket.

She also bought a jar of wondrous lemon-colored cream, that pledged to "fade the most stubborn of unsightly freckles and help regain lost youth." The half dozen freckles that sprinkled her nose were the absolute bane of her life. Back at the Spur she had pots and bottles of ointments and potions—none of which had ever worked. That didn't stop her accumulating new ones.

Actually, Wright Brothers was a wonderful store, ten times bigger than Linnett's. The variety and range of items was staggering. One could purchase anything from mocha and java coffee to bushel baskets, kerosene jugs to tilting water basins, chased gold watches to stoneware water coolers. The list was endless.

Still annoyed with Kyle's authoritarian ways, she refused to buy either a dress or boots. But when she returned to the hotel late in the day, both she and Rolly were laden down with parcels, bags, and boxes.

Kyle still wasn't back, nor was there any sign of Farro. Merrie sent Rolly down for a supper tray and took a long, leisurely bath dosed with a good capful of silky bath oil, one of her numerous purchases. Very soon she was comfortably in bed, avidly reading a Penny Horrible and eating fat lemon-curd tarts, making crumbs and licking the sticky filling from her fingers.

The book was rollicking fun and totally absorbing, so that when the ruckus began outside her bedroom door, she jumped nearly out of her skin.

"Get out of my way, or I'll shoot you," she heard a woman shriek. It was Laura Graham, arguing with Farro. She could hear him equivocating, patiently, gently.

"You cannot go in. Miss Sinclair is resting. Please, Mrs. Graham, wait and speak to Mr. Delancy about it."

"You get out of my way, you little ferret. You have until the count of three. I've been waiting all day to get to that hussy, and if you make me, I'll shoot you out of the way."

"Give me your gun," Farro said.

Merrie's temper ignited. She quickly pushed the tray aside, hitched her bothersome new nightgown in bunches around her knees, and went to open the door. Farro would not be permitted to "sacrifice" his life on her behalf. She had no time at all for such lunacy.

Wrenching the door open, she fairly bristled with anger as she faced the elegant and overdressed proprietress of the Carlyle.

"'The hussy,'" she announced, "is all ears. What is it exactly you cannot wait to tell me? Something succulent, I hope. You have a way of boring me to tears, you're so predictable."

Farro took one shocked look at Merrie standing in the doorway of her room, clad from head to toe in some sort of shroudlike garment (actually it was Merrie's hopelessly unsuitable choice for a nightgown), and gawked. Then, taking advantage of the diversion, he snatched the gun out of Laura's hand and raced off. He had to try and find his employer before the two women killed each other.

Laura was stunned, not as much by the blond girl's words as by the thing she was wearing, or rather . . . what seemed to be wearing her.

It looked like a tent, a very shapeless tent. There were simply yards and yards of dreadful grayish-white flannel that fell from a smocked yoke. Two-inch stripes of pale blue satin flowed between panels of gray and purple velvet bows and ruffles. If that was not ugly enough, there was a train that fell from an elaborate matching panel across the shoulders, also large enough to shelter a small reception.

Merrie's experience with apparel was limited to the purchasing of her work clothes. Even though she enjoyed shopping as much as any other female, she really didn't have a clue what was suitable and what wasn't.

"Where in God's heaven did he find you?" Laura said in

disbelief. "I think you're wearing the curtains from the Theater Comique."

Merrie stuck her nose into the air. "That's it? You came to talk about *decorating*. God knows you need to talk to someone."

Laura's brows drew together. "What I have to say to you, Miss Snoots, is leave my man alone. He's mine. I want him, and I'll have him when you're gone. The how and when of that is entirely up to you. You can go now in one piece, or you can go later in several pieces. What's it to be?"

Merrie almost felt sorry for Laura Graham. Her obvious desperation was utterly pathetic. "Your threats are inconsequential. Mrs. Graham, you're a rank amateur next to my stepmother. I've had more than nine years to polish my retaliatory skills, and I'm good at it."

"You are flesh and blood like all the rest of us, Miss Snoots, even if you are a rich one."

"I'm also younger flesh and blood," Merrie said, guessing at the woman's vanity, "and stronger than you."

Laura's fury exploded in a stream of vicious spite. At the same time as she was calling Merrie every foul name she could think of, she also swiped up the heavy brass door stop at her feet. It was a cylindrical piece of metal, flat on one side, with scrolled end pieces.

Laura moved on Merrie, her hand raised high, ready to strike. She grabbed handfuls of the voluminous nightgown and yanked. Merrie, clumsy in the bulky flannel, could not move quickly enough to evade the crazed woman. She rolled aside as the brass came crashing down, just missing her shoulder and smashing her forearm.

She screamed with pain. But she was now more hopelessly tangled in her nightshift than ever, and she brought her head about in time to see Laura raise the brass once again. Sheer terror knifed through her. She knew she was going to die.

A shot rang out. Laura swung toward the sound.

"Don't move or I'll shoot you next." The words were clipped, decisive, ice-cold.

Kyle! Thank God, Merrie cried silently, shifting about to see his lanky frame outlined against the doorway. His face was a mask of rage, his eyes deadly, his smoking gun pointed directly at Laura.

"Not a hair, Laura, do not move a hair."

He came swiftly into the room, snatched the brass from her upraised hand, twisted her arm behind her back and holstered his gun, all in one move. His blazing eyes lit on Merrie lying confined by her nightdress in a great, untidy heap.

"You alright?" he said, icy, brusk.

She managed to nod, but in all honestly she felt quite sick.

His gaze lingered but a moment longer. "Get Bat," he told Farro above Laura's vitriolic shrieking. He jerked her arm higher up her back. "Shut up, or I'll really hurt you," he told her.

She kicked violently at his shin, but one more jerk on her arm brought compliance. The caustic stream from her mouth dried up instantly.

Kyle dragged her to a chair, shoved her down, and fastened her hands behind the backrest with his bandanna.

He turned then to Merrie, who had managed to get off the floor only to find the world swaying precariously from side to side. Her arm throbbed violently. She was more than ready to allow Kyle to carry her next door to his room. His scent, the warmth of his solid chest, brought a sudden rush of tears to her eyes.

"Don't cry, darlin'. Please," he whispered, unaffected compassion evident in his plea.

"I'm sorry," she said, wiping the wetness away with her hand. "I don't know why—"

He set her down on his bed and stroked the wayward strands of gold from her high forehead, studying her face, sliding his fingers over her damp cheeks. He squeezed his eyes tight for a second, as if trying to regain his composure, and leaned forward to kiss her eyes. "No, I'm the one who is sorry. You'll never know how much."

She couldn't stand to see him torture himself. "Kyle, I baited her. It's partly my fault she attacked me."

"Christ sake, Merrie, don't ever say that to me again. You are not to blame for Laura's lunatic behavior, only Laura is. Where did she hurt you?"

He was furious and determined, Merrie saw, and there was no point in fussing about it. Anyway, she hurt too much to pretend otherwise. She lifted her battered arm for him to inspect. Kyle's sure fingers gently inspected the nasty gash.

"You're going to have a bruise as big as Texas, darlin'," he said after a while, "but no bones broken, thank God. You'd better get a wedding dress that has long sleeves."

Merrie frowned at him.

"I won't need a wedding dress. I'm not getting married."

He didn't answer her for a moment, but cupped her cheek and bent his lips to brush over her eyes. "I want you to rest while I sort out this mess with Bat," he told her. "But when I come back, you can do me a favor, all right?"

She shook her head. "What kind of favor?"

"So trusting, Legs, aren't you?"

Behind his teasing smile, Merrie heard the merest echo of a hunger so raw, so deeply buried, that it was shocking.

Her head jerked, as if some invisible noose had yanked on her neck, as if some distant scent had found its way through the walls of the past and floated into the present, carrying with it memories too harsh, to brutal to face the light of day.

Something warm flooded her heart just then, a quick pulse of longing to soothe the hurts from Kyle Delancy's life. That he should reveal his silent wounds to her even for a second touched her more profoundly than love words or gestures.

"I do trust you," she told him. Her words were hushed, suffused with all the passion she felt for him.

He seemed to absorb that her answer went beyond mere words. The haunting shadow vanished, and his intense eyes found her own. Unspoken dreams seemed to glimmer there, promises for the future.

What he was about to say Merrie never knew, for sounds

outside the door distracted him. He smiled and kissed her lips, and then his glance fell on the tent she was wearing. His eyebrows rode up, and he gave his head a little shake, before getting up to answer the knock at the door.

Merrie felt like screaming. She was so certain that he had been about to tell her he loved her.

"Kyle." Her voice sounded urgent, tight with hope.

He turned toward her sharply.

But it was too late. His mind was on Bat waiting outside, she could see.

"You asked me for a favor?"

He nodded, deadpan, and pointed to her nightgown.

"Get rid of that, will you, Legs? You might find you're a widow as soon as a bride. The sight of that could kill even the strongest husband."

"You won't have to worry, then," she told him, "because you won't be my husband."

THIRTY

~≋~

"And do you, Meredith Amber Sinclair, take this man, Kyle Delancy, to be your lawfully wedded husband, from this day forth and forevermore?" the pastor said, bending his head in anticipation of Merrie's response. He had heard that the bride was a trifle reluctant.

There was silence in the Carlyle's ornate reception room. Merrie felt Kyle's fingers tighten. He had laced hands with her, his long, rough fingers stroking incessantly throughout the brief ceremony.

She glanced at him. He was entirely composed. Not a single emotion crossed his handsome face.

But she could feel, through the strong grip of his fingers, the very pulse of his heartbeat. It was chaotic, intense. As if she had been stung, she felt the longing in him—the *want*. Somehow she knew he wanted her, just as she finally admitted she needed to be wanted by this man, and this man alone.

"I do," she said, and heard the collective sighs from behind them. Bat Masterson and Farro had come to stand witness for them.

"In that case, I pronounce you man and wife," said Reverend Bright. "Congratulations."

Cheers erupted in the lovely room that today had been transformed into a wedding chapel. Rich velvet curtains, thick wool carpets, all in tones of ruby and sapphire, had been softened by yards of shell-pink tissue and ribbons draped over a cornice behind the pastor. A small white mat for the bride and groom lay on the floor, flanked by two tall vases full of late-blooming wildflowers and feathery-soft grasses.

Kyle did not wait to be told to "kiss the bride;" he tugged Merrie into his arms and kissed her with such enthusiasm that her makeshift veil, a beautiful Spanish shawl that Farro had dug up from someplace, tumbled off her head.

Bat Masterson bent to pick it up and handed it to her, his sharp eyes dancing with good cheer at her very pink cheeks.

"As best man, I claim a kiss from the bride," he told Kyle and elbowed his way between them.

Kyle's magnanimous grin curled about the edges after a few brief seconds, and he pulled Merrie away from the well-groomed sheriff, steering her toward Farro.

Farro shook Kyle's hand with great solemnity and brought Merrie's hand to his lips in a brief salute. His young face remained as grave as ever, but he had chosen a bright scarlet boutonniere for his lapel as a sign of celebration.

Ever since they had arrived in Dodge, Farro had worked diligently to find wedding apparel for Merrie; obviously he took no more notice of her stubborn refusal than Kyle seemed to. But in the end, she had to admit, she was thrilled that he had managed to find her such a magnificent gown. There was a Spanish flavor to the full-skirted taffeta. The sleeves were high and ruffled about her white shoulders, and the waist dipped into a vee, showing off the slender length of her supple body. The taffeta was the softest rose color, with tiny pale gold buds appliquéd over traceries of embroidered leaves. The skirt was deeply scalloped to show the gold-and-magneta flowered petticoats underneath.

Somewhere or another Farro had found a gifted seamstress, for the dress fitted Merrie as if it had been made for her. Except for the waist, which was a big tight, the dress was perfect. Her shimmering hair was swept up into a chignon and held there with two silver combs.

Kyle thought she looked more beautiful than ever before. There was a certain . . . Well, he couldn't quite put his finger on it, but there was something about her that made his insides quicken with sudden heat. He needed to hold her; he needed to surround her with his protecting love.

Merrie Sinclair-Delancy, he reminded himself, was essential

to his life. He felt a tiny thrill of fear rocket through him. It was dangerous to want someone like that, he knew.

The pastor was shaking his hand, gabbing on about his good fortune and years of happiness ahead. The choice of words jarred Kyle out of his reverie.

There were those, he knew, who would be only too quick to point out that his good fortune amounted to a considerable mountain of gold. Merrie was a very rich lady. His client, he thought with a cold dash of unease, might have strong objections to this marriage. Yes, Ash Sinclair might have strenuous objections.

Kyle had been so intent on getting Merrie to agree to his proposal that he hadn't considered the full implications before. Now that he thought about it, he knew he wouldn't allow it to make any difference. When he made up his mind, he made up his mind.

Sure, his first impulse had been his sense of responsibility. He had compromised Merrie. He had stolen her virginity. But what he had taken had enriched him beyond gold. He didn't know how or even when he had fallen in love with her, but he had.

He couldn't think of living his life without her. He wouldn't. It was that simple.

It was that complicated.

Whatever they had to deal with—Ash, the gossip mongers—they would do it. So long as Merrie believed in him, he did not care much about anyone else. If he had to take her away from her wealthy family to establish his credibility to her, then that is what he would do.

She smiled at him from across the room. Farro had just handed her a glass of champagne. She was radiant. He had heard it said of brides before, but he had not known what it meant. Now he did. He tipped his glass to her; she mimicked him.

Suddenly he wanted the room cleared. He wanted her alone. He wanted to tell her that he loved her.

He didn't get his wish. Just the opposite.

The doors to the small reception room burst open just then. About two dozen of Dodge City's finest citizens filed in. All Kyle's old friends had come, many of the hotel staff, and even a few of the homesteaders he had helped with difficulties over the past few years. Kyle was stunned.

His startled eyes found Bat Masterson and Farro grinning back at him like cats who had stolen the farmer's cream.

"We just couldn't resist. You getting hitched and no one knowing! Doggone! If you'll all pardon my language, ladies, but we couldn't let it happen. Could we, Farro?"

"And we have another surprise, Mr. Delancy," Farro said, and he went over to a side door and opened it. There stood Mariette DeLace. Kyle's adoptive mother.

He went forward eagerly to embrace her. Somehow his voice had disappeared.

Mariette's pudgy arms went about his neck as he bent down, and he felt the wetness on her cheek as she laid her face against his.

"So proud, my son, so proud of you," she said. "They didn't want me in until the vows were safely said. Some nonsense about the bride being unsure."

"I can't believe you're here, Mariette," he managed at last, holding her at arm's length and staring at her. To him, she was as lovely as ever—an elegant, neat, little woman with a flare all of her own.

"Nor can I. Mr. Masterson wired me urgently on Monday, and I hardly had time to pack before catching the train."

"You've been traveling for days. You must be tired out."

"Not at all. That kind Mr. Meadows was very solicitous of me. The journey was most pleasant."

Kyle was astounded. "Pat Meadows?" He'd known Meadows for the past three years, and he'd never encountered a solicitous moment in his company yet. Not only that, but the man looked like a clerk or a bookkeeper, rather than one of the sharpest shooters in the county. He was slight, stoop-shouldered, and the very antithesis of what one expected a lawman to look like.

"Yes, I believe the gentleman's first name is Pat."

Kyle was incredulous. "Pat Meadows escorted you from New Orleans?" he stated, as if he didn't quite believe his own ears.

"Couldn't let the lady travel by herself, now, could I?" Masterson said with a self-satisfied look. "So, I sent the best man I had to escort her."

"But how—"

"Farro. He told me you were going to marry Ash's daughter. I didn't believe it either. That night at Long Branch, I saw Laura's face. Then I knew."

Mariette looked puzzled. "Laura? That is odd. I thought Mr. Meadows said your bride's name was Meredith."

"Uh . . . it is," said Kyle with a short laugh. He had no intention of explaining Laura's compulsive behavior to Mariette. It would upset her. "Let me introduce you, Mariette."

Merrie was busy talking to George Masterson, Bat's brother. She lifted her startling green eyes to Kyle as he came forward with the elderly lady dressed in satin and lace that exactly matched her silvery hair. She was extraordinarily elegant and walked as if she were ten feet tall, when in fact she was barely five. But from her small slippered feet to the egret feather stuck into the diminutive hat on her head, the lady epitomized the word "stylish."

It was obvious that the woman and Kyle shared a very special relationship. The way they stood together, the incredible softness in Kyle's blue eyes—these things alone told Merrie that much. But the emotion in Kyle's voice confirmed it.

"Mariette, I want you to meet my wife, Meredith Sinclair-Delancy. Merrie, this is my mother, Mariette DeLace."

Merrie smiled as the little woman rose up to take her hand and kiss her on both cheeks, tears streaming down her face. "So wonderful. I'm spilling over like a fountain, I'm afraid, but I couldn't be happier, so I won't apologize."

Merrie detected the slightest accent.

"Nor would I ask it, Mrs. DeLace," said Merrie. She was

almost in a state of stupor herself, with all the surprises of the day—her own acquiescence not the least of these. But now she was meeting Kyle's mother, and there was more mystery here, for their names, while similar, were not the same.

"Mariette, please. You and I will have plenty of time to talk, to get to know one another," she said. "But for now I wish you to know what pleasure you give me, for I can see how good you are for Kyle."

"I wouldn't put too much faith in appearances. She's inconvenienced me more than anyone twice her size," said Kyle.

"This is excellent. Too smooth a sail and you would fall asleep at the helm," Mariette said.

Bat Masterson chuckled. "Let me tell you what he means by 'inconvenience,'" he said, taking the old woman's arm. "Let's go over there and sit down."

"Don't you listen to what he says, Mariette," Merrie called. "He's in league with Kyle."

Mariette gave a knowing laugh. "They think they can fool us, don't they? But we can talk later, Merrie, *n'est-ce pas?*"

Kyle relinquished his hold on Mariette's arm and took Merrie's instead. He spun her about. "Have I told you that you look beautiful?"

Merrie laughed. "So do you," she said. And he did. He was breathtakingly handsome, especially today.

His dark frock coat and trousers were severe but fitted his lanky frame perfectly. Exactly the color of his eyes, his embroidered silk waistcoat sparkled with brilliant gold buttons. There was something very debonair about the way Kyle wore his clothes. He always managed to make the most simple outfit look exceptional.

Merrie glanced down at her lovely gown. "But if I do, it's thanks to Farro. I wonder where he found this dress. Certainly not at Wright Brothers."

"How do you know? You never looked there. Rolly told me."

"No, I didn't."

"Because you had no intention of marrying me, right?"

Merrie flushed. "No."

Kyle brought her closer. He ran his finger under her chin and bent his legs a little so that he could look into her eyes.

"What changed your mind?"

"You. The night Laura attacked me. I just knew I couldn't be whole without you. I felt you couldn't be without me, either."

Kyle felt his heart expand. "Let's go upstairs," he whispered in her ear. "I have to tell you something."

Now it was Merrie whose heart suddenly leapt about in her chest.

"Do you think we can?"

"There are no rules, Legs, remember?"

"But all these people, your friends."

"They'll all understand."

"Your mother?"

"We can spend time with Mariette tomorrow, and the day after that."

They slipped out the side door and into the lobby. George waved and hurried over to wish them joy and years of happiness. Several guests overheard him and also wished them well. They added one or two rather suggestive bits of advice for Kyle that made Merrie blush. Before his door, Kyle stopped and lifted her.

"We might have started off on the wrong foot, but we're going to do things right from now on, darlin'," he said, his voice husky with desire.

Merrie looked up at him. She leaned forward and kissed his mouth. "I wouldn't have had it any other way."

Kyle laughed and carried her over the garlanded threshold and into their new life.

THIRTY-ONE

They left the window open. Even though it was fresh outside, the evening air was pleasant. The breeze cooled their heated bodies, brought prickles along their naked limbs, which were entangled between the linen sheets.

Merrie lay against Kyle's broad chest, and he stroked his long fingers down her spine, around the curve of her beautiful bottom. Then he went lower, between her legs, sliding his fingers into the slick warmth there. She felt the shivers begin inside.

How could it be? She was replete, sated after this tempestuous lovemaking. And yet he had only to touch her to arouse her again.

"You're greedy, my little darlin', and I love it that you are," he said.

"How can you tell?" she asked.

Kyle chuckled. For an answer he slid his fingers up her spine and down into the secret wetness again. Then he rolled her onto her stomach and brought her hips up off the bed; her shoulders remained flush against the sheet. Gently he pushed her knees wide apart and, kneeling behind, invaded her softness with a steady surge of his hips.

Merrie gasped. The position afforded him incredible depth. Pleasure screamed through her like shooting stars. She felt almost faint with it. He pulled her hips toward him, and she arched. Then he began thrusting in and out, deeply, deeply, his gliding movements fervent, rhythmic.

He leaned over her. She felt him rub against her back, his lips, cool and delicious, began nibbling along her spine, sending shivers streaking through her. She felt his hands drift over her breasts, cupping the fullness, clasping their rounded weight with erotic fever. The crests tightened. His fingers plucked at them, stimulated the hardened coral tips to almost unbearable sensitivity. The breath left her in shuddering bursts.

But then, his fingers slipped down—down over the smooth tautness of her belly. He spanned her hip to hip with one sweep of his hand, his fingers tracing over her, teasing the curls, sliding into crimson folds slick with passion.

He tugged gently on her, setting up a rhythmic vibration that sent tremors racing through her body. Sharp, vivid, the sensations caused a tempest. She quivered, reared back against him. Rapture!

It seemed to Merrie that she was filled to her soul with his flesh, with his love. They were one, inseparable, an entity molded together by their ardor, like precious metals melting together in the fury of the furnace.

Turning slightly, she saw his dark body covering her own pale length. She caught a glimpse of his large hand, moving sinuously, drawing out her pleasure. It was almost too erotic, too intense.

She felt him quicken his pace. The friction sent her spinning further into a delirious whirl where all things vanished and there was only feeling. She heard the rush of his breath in her ear. The thunder of his heartbeat echoed her own. She bucked, pushing forward into his hand, her hips rocking, frantic now, reaching, reaching for the magic.

She climaxed fiercely, her cry abandoned, wild.

She fell forward, but Kyle caught her up, held her to him so that she felt the hair on his body rub against her smooth skin. He held her tight, kissing her nape, soothing the fluttering of her breasts with soft sweeping strokes. Murmuring huskily, he told her how she fired his blood.

He kept her flush against him for a few minutes, but then he began slowly again. His movements were expert: flexing his hips, thrusting gently, then harder and harder until she was once again caught up in the ecstasy. This time when she exploded, she took him with her, rapturous and replete.

Kyle fell back against the mountain of pillows, one hand still wrapped in the golden bounty of her hair. His joy in her seemed endless. It no longer surprised him. Somehow, somewhere, he must have done something to deserve her. It was a mystery. He sure as hell didn't know what it could have been, but he wasn't going to question it either.

After a few moments, he gave a playful tug and Merrie rolled over and snuggled against his side.

"You're beautiful," he told her. He ran his hand over her hair, pushing it away from her face and kissing her lips.

Merrie smiled at him, sleepy and content as a kitten.

"Do you think you could eat something? I asked Farro to see that dinner was sent up for us later, but if you're hungry, I could get you something now."

Merrie shook her head. "I only want to sleep. I'm suddenly tired out. I don't know why."

"All the excitement. Also, since we got here, you've become lazy. You're used to working long hours, not sitting about in hotel rooms."

Merrie hitched the sheet up over her breasts and worried her bottom lip. "Speaking of work, I hope you realize that I can't leave the Spur until Ash is strong and well."

"I hadn't really thought about it. Once we free Ash, we'll have plenty of time to discuss it."

Merrie's green eyes narrowed with worry. Kyle chuckled and tilted her chin up. "Come on, Legs, relax. I don't have any objections to moving my business to Hollow Creek. So if that's what you're worried about, don't."

Kyle, I— Oh," Merrie stammered. She wanted desperately to hear from him that he loved her before she confessed to him. But she was bursting with love for him. His generosity, his gentleness overwhelmed her. Instead of blurting out the words, she scrambled onto her knees and threw her arms about him, hugging him tightly and kissing his face all over.

"Darlin', I love you, too," he said and chuckled as she planted feverish kisses on his nose and eyelids, ears and chin. Finally he grabbed her to his naked chest and brought her squirming under him.

"I never thought you would say it," she breathed happily. "I didn't think it was something gunslingers admitted."

"Stay around, Legs, and you'll hear a number of other admissions that might interest you," he told her and brought her laughing mouth to his.

BRIGHT AND EARLY the next morning, Merrie woke and found the world reeling. It was as if she had drunk a bottle of wine, or so she imagined.

One eye opened and quickly shut when the room tilted over. In panic, she clutched the bedclothes on either side of her. A moment later, she sprang out of bed and rushed to the fancy bathing chamber that opened off Kyle's bedroom. She was violently sick. Fortunately, she found the basin in the nick of time.

Strangely enough, as soon as she was done, she felt much better, although a little shaky. She stood up. Her legs wobbled. Looking up, she found Kyle staring at her. He was stark naked, one raised arm propped against the doorjamb, a thoughtful hand stroking his stubbly chin.

"You all right?" he asked. His voice was still husky with sleep, and his eyes looked drowsy and sexy.

"I don't know."

"You going to be sick again?"

"I don't think so."

"Come back to bed, then. I'll get you a glass of water. Maybe you drank too much champagne yesterday."

"I didn't have more than a glass, and I hardly ate dinner. I didn't feel like it, if you remember?"

Kyle tucked her in and went over to the remains of their supper tray to get a clean glass. Merrie watched his lanky progress across the floor. He had a beautiful body. He was lean and muscled, and his very long legs and meager movements gave him a stealthy, prowling kind of look. His glossy black hair swept across his shoulders as he moved. The sculpted grace of his back, the smooth marble of his buttocks, exemplified male strength. There was nothing self-conscious about him. He was absolutely comfortable with his nudity.

He came to her, his blue eyes reflective, and sat beside her on the bed. "Sip it," he told her, putting the glass in her hand.

She did. The water felt good slipping down her throat.

"Legs," Kyle said, taking the glass from her, "is it possible you're pregnant?"

Merrie looked up, startled for a moment, and did a quick count. Eventually she nodded her head—one slow nod, full of wonder, full of dazed hope. "It's possible," she said dubiously, for she almost couldn't believe that such a miracle could happen to her.

"You haven't had your time since before the night of Ash's homecoming, right?"

Merrie nodded, flustered. He was so casual. Even after the intimacy they had shared, she found herself a little shocked. Yet there was no doubt that he had opened the world for her, peeled back the confining covers with his forthright passion. She felt her heart expand.

Kyle brought her into his embrace. "Darlin', I think we got married just in time," he told her.

"Do you . . . really think it could be?"

Kyle smiled into her eyes, his face as full of wonder as was hers. "I sure as hell hope so, Legs. I couldn't think of a better wedding gift." He tried for a nonchalant manner, but she heard the crack in his voice.

He smoothed the hair back from her forehead and planted small, sweet kisses on her eyelids, the tip of her nose. Suddenly, a thought struck him, and he groaned in mock dismay. "I just hope Ford County's stocked well enough to keep you fed, now that you'll be eating for two."

Merrie frowned at her new husband, but that only made him laugh even harder.

"I knew marrying you was a mistake," she sighed.

Kyle let one dark brow rise. "Come, prove it, darlin'" he told her and enveloped her in his steely embrace.

THIRTY-TWO

THEY WERE SHARING a wedding breakfast with Mariette in their room when the ruckus began. Pounding footsteps echoed up the stairs. Kyle shot out of his chair. With lightning speed, he had his guns strapped around his narrow hips. He whipped the door open in time to see Bat Masterson and Farro running toward him.

"They're on their way," Bat gasped out. His chest was heaving. Obviously, they had run all the way from Front Street to the Carlyle.

"How many?" Kyle asked. He didn't need to ask which "they" Bat was referring to. He knew.

After months of planning, the day had finally arrived. Merrie could see the excitement on his face. She felt icy cold. Unable to move or speak for a moment, she simply sat there, watching. She felt Mariette DeLace touching her hand reassuringly, but she could not tear her eyes away from Kyle.

Farro leaned against the doorjamb, winded. His great, serious eyes seemed darker than night, and as shiny as wet stones.

"Three."

"Including Sinclair?"

Merrie tensed.

Bat nodded.

"He looks fit enough," Masterson added. "Riding unaided. They haven't harmed him; they need him to look healthy."

Kyle's fists curled. "Liza's boy show his face yet?"

"Nope. Meadows says he wearing the bandanna over his face, but it's him, all right, our mystery man. It's definitely not Cheston or the wagon man."

"No sign of them?" Kyle asked sharply.

"Seems Liza left 'em behind."

Kyle glanced from Bat to Farro and back.

"Alive?" he asked.

"Meadows is not certain. He thinks he saw movement inside their hidey-hole after the others had left. He didn't hang about to make certain because he wanted to keep an eye on Sinclair until Rolly takes over for him," Bat said.

"Is Ash . . . You sure Ash is all right?" Merrie asked anxiously.

Kyle swung about at the sound of her voice. She was white. Her eyes wide. There was an edgy look about her face. The strain was too much for her. He didn't like to see her like this.

"He's just fine," chorused Bat and Farro together.

Kyle saw Merrie tense up even more. He glanced meaningfully at the men. "I'll be along in a minute," he said. "You go on ahead and get the men into position. You know the drill by now."

He drew Merrie up into his arms. "It's nearly over, darlin'" he said quietly. "Just hang on a little while and trust me. Ash will be here before the day is out."

"What's going on, my son?" Mariette asked, rising from her chair.

"It's a long story, Mariette, but we're about to rescue my new father-in-law from his miscreant wife."

"Kyle," Mariette said, shocked. "how can you speak of Merrie's stepmother in such a disrespectful way?"

Merrie choked. Kyle chuckled.

"I think Merrie takes exception to my kindly description of her stepmother," Kyle explained.

Mariette pursed her lips. She disliked it when people spoke ill of others. She doubted such a well-mannered girl as Merrie would countenance such slander.

"What a thing to say," she said, staring from one to the other.

"Merrie can tell you all about it, but I have to go. I don't want Liza to catch sight of me before I'm good and ready."

Merrie, though, had ideas of her own. She grasped his arm,

imploringly. "Kyle, I want to be there. *I must be there.* Please, I want to see Ash for myself," she said.

"We've been through this, Merrie. I can't afford to be distracted. There's too much at stake here—your safety not the least."

"But I wo—"

"Legs, you'll have to trust me in this. I don't have time to argue."

It was the very worst thing to say to her right then. Her emotions were frayed to the limit.

"He's *my father*. I do things my own way." Even as she spoke, she was dismayed that the new and tender bud of their marriage could so easily wither. Couldn't he see how his stubborn authority hurt their chances for happiness? But no! He was aggravating and self-centered, and he could not see beyond his pride!

"Not now, Merrie," he said and reached for her, his tone conciliatory. Warm fingers wrapped sinuously around the top of her arm.

She wrenched away. "No. I won't be ordered around. It's time you remembered that I'm an adult." His overbearing authority, his inflexible determination that things would be done his way and no other, riled her.

"An adult?" he queried, just as she was about to storm out the door. The ice behind his mocking tone brought her to a halt.

Merrie swung around. Green lightning clashed with blue. They glared at each other in furious, edgy silence. They were completely oblivious to the fact that Mariette was still in the room with them. Only they existed, their passion and anger a spinning belt of flame encircling them. Theirs were two strongly independent wills vying for power in the distinct belief that each of them was right.

Kyle took a deep breath. "I'm warning you . . . Listen to me."

Merrie tossed up her chin. "Warn all you like," she told him defiantly.

He gave an exasperated grunt. "This has been a long time in

the making. I won't allow you to jeopardize my plan, *wife*. So, sulk, whine—do anything you like, but don't interfere."

Merrie jerked at the insults. "Sulk?" Merrie screamed. "You devil-he—"

Kyle grabbed her flaying fists. With a flick of his wrist, he had her locked against his chest, his large hand anchored in her golden hair. He tugged and bent her head farther back. He glared down at her outraged face. Her rose-soft lips quivered with temper.

Kyle squeezed his eyes shut for a moment.

When he opened them, he met green fury from beneath her half-shuttered eyes.

Damn his beautiful bride, he thought fiercely. Time was against him. He knew she was reacting out of fright, the nerve-shredding tension of the last few weeks, but he simply didn't have the time to soothe her. Somehow he had to stop her from doing anything willfully foolish.

"Put aside your selfish, spoiled-little-girl tantrum, Merrie, and think of our baby."

She flinched and jerked away from him as much as she was able; he held her fast. She shook her head in mute denial that she would ever endanger their child.

Kyle took advantage and quickly bent his mouth to hers. His kiss was brief but fierce. "Just stay put," he rasped against her burning lips.

In another instant, he was gone.

Flushing, Merrie turned to find her new mother-in-law's eyes appraising her. Oh, God, what she must think of me? Merrie moaned silently.

But Mariette DeLace was delighted with her new daughter-in-law. Never had she seen her handsome son so alive; his passion-filled eyes reflected the deep emotion of his heart. Kyle's icy control over his emotions had always troubled her. She felt it was unhealthy to repress hurts and anger to the extent he did. Now, however, he seemed to have found his soul mate, and Mariette felt contentment for the very first time in a long, long while.

TEXAS KISS

She smiled warmly at Merrie. "You have magic, you two. And much more in common than I first realized."

"We both have tempers, you mean?" Merrie asked with a tiny smile of embarrassment.

Mariette gave a very Gallic shrug. "That was a lovers' tiff, *n'est-ce pas*? I was thinking more of your unhappy family lives."

"He has never spoken about his family."

"Nor will he. His mother was cruel beyond belief. I do not break confidences when I tell you this, for I believe it is your right to know."

Merrie glanced at the door longingly.

Slowly, reluctantly, she came and sat in the chair next to Mariette.

"Tell me," she said simply.

Mariette nodded. "His mother prostituted one child and tried to do the same to Kyle. He ran away, taking his sister with him. She was already quite ill when they managed to escape into the slums of New Orleans. Kyle was only nine years old and responsible for both Kaiten and himself."

Merrie's horror was clear. Immediately she recalled Kyle's anguished cries the night he lay in a fever from his gunshot wounds. She had wondered who Kaiten was. "His sister?" she whispered.

"She died in childbirth. She was only twelve."

Merrie was horrified. She felt a sick surge in her belly. "Oh," she gasped. She couldn't imagine such things happening to children.

"Kyle was near death himself by that time. There had been little food, and what they had went to Kaiten. But it was really his grief that was killing him."

"But you saved him, you took him in," whispered Merrie.

Fiddling with her lacy handkerchief, Mariette took a deep breath. "No, he saved us."

Merrie looked sharply at the older woman. Mariette smiled softly. "My husband and I had lost our own son. Finding Kyle was like a miracle to us."

They were silent awhile as each dealt with the monstrous brutality of Kyle's early life. It was not easy.

"No wonder he adores you," Merrie said eventually. "You do not have a selfish bone in your body."

"Oh, yes, I do. I'm selfish enough to want the best for Kyle, and I do believe he has found this in you."

Merrie winced. "You can see how happy I make him," she said tiredly.

"You certainly provoke him, *chére*," Mariette said and laughed. "But come, tell me about your stepmother, Merrie. She must have done something dreadful to warrant such . . . such dislike from you."

"She's . . . It's difficult to know just where to start with Liza. We never got along. I suppose you could say that I intuitively knew that we wouldn't. Neither of us made it easy; we just tolerated each other. But greed told in the end. She wasn't content with what Ash gave her; she wanted the Sinclair gold."

"The Sinclair gold?" Mariette asked, her eyes wide. "Tell me about that."

Merrie launched into an explanation that concluded with Kyle's plan to trap Liza and her fancy friend.

"They may even have reached Front Street by now," she ended, gazing wistfully out the window.

"Kyle did not want you near the place, Merrie. You must listen to my son in this matter," said Mariette adamantly. "He has years of experience with wrongdoers."

"I'm sure he has," mumbled Merrie, unconvinced. She got up and went to the large bay window that faced onto the street.

Down below, people bustled along the wood sidewalks, carts and horses crisscrossed the main thoroughfare, churning up brown dust and a cacophony of sounds.

Just then, Merrie caught sight of Laura Graham. At least, it certainly looked like Laura from behind. She was surprised. The woman approached a Mexican man slouched against the railing. The two had a brief exchange. The hackles on Merrie's neck stood up.

What was Laura up to? she wondered. According to Kyle, Bat Masterson had Laura under lock and key until she agreed to sell up and leave town. Either that, or Kyle would insist on pressing charges against her for assaulting Merrie. Perhaps Laura had decided and was leaving town?

The two in the street had finished their conversation and moved off. Merrie watched Laura vanish around the corner and promptly forgot about her. She had other things on her mind.

Like how to get away from her gentle mother-in-law and find her way to Front Street.

Merrie was determined to lend her help and make certain Ash was safe—no matter what her authoritarian husband wished. It wasn't that she wanted to provoke his anger; she simply wasn't the type to sit back and let others sort out her problems for her. Surely, once his temper calmed, Kyle would understand that.

There was, however, no point in hurting Mariette's feelings or causing her worry. Merrie hid a little yawn behind her hand. Without seeming to do so, she glanced at the bed and then at her mother-in-law. Thankfully Mariette DeLace was a sensitive woman. After Merrie's third seemingly innocent yawn, she rose.

"Why don't I go along to my own room and let you rest awhile?" she said.

"That's most considerate of you, Mariette," said Merrie. "I am a little tired. I guess the excitement . . ."

"Think nothing of it, dear Merrie. I shall see you at luncheon, *non*?"

Merrie nodded, then saw her out. She waited a good long while before she hurriedly took out her riding pants and shirt.

Not ten minutes later, she rushed down the Carlyle's broad steps and headed toward Front Street. She had only gone a few yards when she remembered Kyle's words about being seen out on the street. It wouldn't do for her to be caught out in broad daylight where Liza could spot her; that would give the game away. She thought about it for a moment and ducked off the main way.

Unfortunately, she was unfamiliar with the town and soon managed to get herself lost. Devil have it! she thought irritably. She really had no idea where she was.

While she stood there floundering, unsure of exactly what to do, the door behind her opened, and a woman came out with a shopping basket on her arm. She had a small child in tow, and the little boy peeped at Merrie around his mother's skirts. The woman threw her a few hostile looks, while she locked her door and pocketed the key.

"Ah, excuse me, but I seem to be lost. Which direction is Front Street?" Merrie asked quickly.

"Be off with ye," the woman said, her tone suspicious. "Don't hold with no beggars. And don't ye be hanging around when my Bert comes in, ye hear?"

Merrie gasped at the woman's rudeness.

"Be off, I say," the woman repeated, and clutching the boy's hand, she hurried away.

There was nothing Merrie could do but risk the main roads. But, to her dismay, when she reached the packed dirt thoroughfare, she was no better off than before. Absolutely nothing was familiar.

Gritting her teeth, she took careful note of where she was, then began systematically working her way in one direction. She hoped it was the right direction. Logic told her that she would eventually get to the far side of the town.

After what seemed like hours, she finally came to familiar territory. Her relief was immense. There before her was Front Street. And there, along the very next side street, three horses were tied to the railing. Two of the horses she knew at once. The gelding was Liza's; the other was also a Spur horse. The third she wasn't sure about.

Her heart began to hammer. Her mouth was dry. Her stepmother was here. That meant Ash was here, too! They must be inside the office of Farraway and Hargraves.

Now, how did she get a look inside the office without being seen? She was crouched down next to a rickety old cart, peering across the narrow gap between the houses, when she first felt a thrill of fear. There was a footstep in the alleyway behind her.

She swiveled on her heel, but it was too late. She felt the whisper of air about her ear just before the blow to her head sent her into a pitch-black abyss.

THIRTY-THREE

IT WAS A Mexican hat she saw when her eyes jerked open. Misty unconsciousness slipped away, wrenching her into terrible reality.

She was trussed up and gagged! The suffocating cloth had been brutally tied about her mouth, stretching, rasping against the tender corners. There was a coppery taste of blood in her mouth, and fear knifed through her soul.

At the same moment, she comprehended that the cart she was in, a wagon that had lost its canvas coverings, was being driven at breakneck speed over rutted ground. She was tossed furiously from side to side. Her head banged hard against the wood seat, her shoulder hit the floor, then she was lifted and flung down again by the impetus of the wild ride. Jarring pain shot through her. She thought she would throw up, and she fought her panic and the surge of bile, gritting her teeth against the tight gag in her mouth.

The cart careened through a choking cloud of orange-brown dust. Flashes of sky sprinted overhead; a tree, a rocky wall, and then Merrie's eyes glimpsed again the Mexican hat. The man wearing it was hunched down over the driver's seat, leaning forward, whipping his mounts furiously. His sombrero had fallen back, exposing his dark curly hair. There was something familiar about both his head and the large woven hat.

The sombrero was flamboyant, the band colorful and broad. Yes, she had it! The man Laura Graham had been speaking to outside the Carlyle—they were one and the same, she would swear it.

But the head was that of Matt Cheston! Surely not. Could she have banged her head so badly that she was seeing things now?

She turned her aching head a fraction and closed her eyes against the blinding pain.

But when she opened them again, she was certain it was Matt.

He was abducting her! Why? How had it happened?

Front Street! She had spotted Liza's horse . . .

She remembered the feel of someone coming up behind her . . . the black pain descending . . .

Matt Cheston must have snatched her from the street. Why? Did that mean that something had gone wrong with the plan? Had Liza somehow managed to escape Kyle's net? Was Ash alive?

She felt ill.

The thought of facing Matt horrified her. He had used her, betrayed her. He had pretended to court her while all the time he had been in love with her stepmother.

Merrie did not pretend that she was brokenhearted over Matt's deception. She was not a hypocrite. Right from the start, the feelings she'd had for Kyle were altogether different from anything she had ever felt for Matt Cheston. No, she did not pretend heartbreak. But he had injured her pride, he had injured her family. He had used her and Ash for cold, heartless gain. That she could not ever forgive him.

But her shock was compounded when she saw the repeater rifle. It was jammed in between the seat and Matt's leg. Very few people owned them in Hollow Creek, that much she knew. She recalled, with ice-cold horror, that Kyle had been shot with a repeater rifle. Could it be mere coincidence? She doubted that. Matt had tried to kill Kyle, she was sure.

Had they known about Kyle, even then? Were all his plans ruined?

Merrie felt a shiver of fear slide down her back. Hot tears streamed out of her eyes. Now was not the time to feel sorry for herself. But she couldn't help it, she did. She was bruised—her heart, too. She curled up as best she could, drawing her knees in to her chest. Her feet had been bound, too. The rope burned and chafed her skin.

The wild ride went on. Never in all her life had she felt so alone, so horribly frightened.

What would Kyle do when he returned to Carlyle's and found her gone? He would be furious with her. Furious. The small muscle along his jawline would tick. Oh, how she longed to soothe her fingers over his hard jaw, kiss the tension away.

"Kyle," she cried. "Please . . . find me."

But how could he find her?

She peered over the back slats of the wagon, but her hope died. A thick funnel of choking dust followed them, and that was all.

The rough track behind them was empty. Nor did she see any sign of habitation—no homestead, barn, or pen, no railroad or false-fronted building to hint at a town. They raced like thunder through billowing prairie land that stretched around them like a great inland sea of wild grasses. Huge and solemn, its desolation was overwhelming, isolating.

Where were they going? There was nothing out here, nothing.

Just as Merrie began to wonder how long the horses could maintain the pace, they came to a sudden stop.

Merrie tensed. Prickles of fear played along her spine. What now? What would he want from her?

It didn't take too long to find out.

Matt bounded down from the high driver's seat and sprang onto the flatbed of the wagon. Without ceremony, he hauled her up. Grasping her roughly by the arm, he jerked her along with him off the wagon.

"Surprised?" he drawled. "You sure don't look it."

No sooner had her feet touched the ground, than she was hoisted up over his shoulder, too shocked and frightened to do anything but hang there like a limp sack.

She gasped as his shoulder bit, none too gently, into her stomach, and her heart fled to her toes. She was terrified that such rough treatment, the jarring ride and panic, might harm the new and fragile life she believed was growing inside her. It was up to her, she realized with a quaking heart, to keep as calm as possible.

It was not easy to do. From her upside-down position, Merrie felt the world catapulting around her. They seemed to have come to an old farm. Scattered about, she spied bits of fencing, the rusted remains of a pitchfork, several cans, and a leaky, wood water trough.

Matt checked their surroundings, his six-shooter ready in his hand. From her awkward perspective, Merrie saw that he was making for a shack built into the slope of a hill. It was no more than a lean-to and apparently deserted, except for the stink of grime and the scurrying creatures that vanished into the rotted walls and sod ceiling when Matt kicked open the door.

"For such a skinny girl, you sure weigh a ton," he grumbled as he threw her down onto the packed earth floor.

Merrie was winded for a moment. She lay on her back, eyes squeezed tight as she struggled to right her breathing. A second later she opened her eyes, flashing furiously at him. Then, taking careful aim, she suddenly kicked with her bound legs, a fast springlike motion that connected with his shins.

He jumped, swearing loudly as her booted feet, even bound as they were, hammered his legs.

He was not slow to react.

He leaned over and slapped her face.

The blow sent stars spinning through her head, and she regretted her impulsiveness, especially just after vowing to remain calm and reasonable. She lay inert, her head turned away from him, so he could not see the rage in her eyes.

"You always were a spitfire, weren't you, honey? Spoiled, wanting your own way in everything, right? Well, you just ran out of luck, honey, you sure did, 'cause we're gonna play it my way this time."

Lifting his poncho, he took off his belt—a battered leather strap with a tin buckle. Merrie shrank. He was going to beat her! Her eyes widened in horror as he leaned down over her, wrenching her onto her stomach. Merrie's heart labored in her chest.

No! She could not help the muffled groan of terror from behind the gag. But the dreaded beating never came. Matt had other ideas, at least for now, she realized, heartily relieved. He passed the strap between her bound feet, tying it tight, then looped it between the ropes about her wrists, which were tied behind her back. The effect was unbelievably uncomfortable. Her legs were jerked up behind her, and straining against the bonds only helped to truss her up even more. She felt like a Christmas goose.

Matt tipped her over onto her side and stood, dusting his hands together with a satisfied slap.

"There now, that should hold you awhile. Got to ride back and check that your boyfriend is nowhere in sight. Don't want him finding you until I'm good and ready. And, honey, you better hope that he wants you back bad enough to do a fair exchange, or I'll just be forced to kill you."

Merrie watched as he strode out of the hut, his sombrero bouncing jauntily around his neck.

What did he mean? A fair exchange? For what? The gold?

Did it matter? Kyle would trade with him for her, she was certain. Ash would give them the gold.

She should feel relieved that she knew, more or less, what Matt wanted with her. She was a bargaining chip, and at the least, he would have to make contact with her husband in order to gain what he wanted. Kyle would know that she still lived and who had taken her.

So why did she feel this unease?

Icy thrills of fear slid up and down her spine, crawled into her brain, grating against her expectations.

She did not know why. With a shiver of distaste, she watched furtive scurrying movements in the shadowy recesses of the hut, and felt a deep and immutable terror build inside her. By the time Matt came slamming his way back into the hut, she was nearly fainting with panic.

"DON'T," SHE SAID as Matt came toward her with the gag. She had sworn not to beg, not to display any weakness in front of him, but she was loath to have that dreadful rag shoved back into her mouth.

He had taken the gag out to allow her to eat. Now, however, their sorry meal of dried salt beef and sourdough biscuits (made by him and almost inedible) was done.

"There is no one about to hear me, even if I do scream," she told him.

He grunted, and his eyes scoured her for a moment. With a nod he threw the gag down on the floor. "You better be sure to show proper appreciation, honey. Don't make me sorry, or you'll be sorrier, get it?"

Merrie nodded and lowered her lashes to mask her fury. Appreciation indeed! If he so much as touched her, she knew she would kill him, or at least try her damndest to.

The hut was gloomy. There was no lamp. The place was filthy, littered with piles of debris that rotted in the damp. Merrie saw a broken shoe, a chipped crock, and a stack of unraveling sacks. They were the kind of hessian sacks used for transporting wool to market. There were numerous household items that suggested a homesteading past.

Dusk fell. Through the dirty little window, the very last of the daylight traced feebly over the remains of the hearth—now a forlorn pile of scarred and broken bricks.

Merrie watched the shadows creeping in from the walls, glad in a way that she couldn't see the nasty look on Matt's face. There was no vestige there of the man she had once known. She wondered how he could ever have hidden this ugly side of himself from her. Just looking at him now made her feel ill.

What she had once considered his pleasant face had somehow altered; his mask had slipped, revealing only his greed and malice. His gentlemanly manner had vanished. In its place was crude, violent language and shifty, erratic behavior.

Silence grew between them, and Merrie felt as if she would burst with the strain. Her pulse was heavy in her throat. Surely the thunder of it was loud enough for him also to hear it?

Sitting hobbled to an iron rung that had once hung above the chimney corner, she watched his eyes swivel toward her. She

TEXAS KISS   285

did not need to see him clearly to know that he was appraising her. The knowledge terrified her.

She hoped that she looked as dreadful as she felt. Still, a warning thrill of fear slid down her back as his brooding glances tended to linger over her.

Merrie realized the direction of his thoughts and knew she must distract him, and quickly, too.

"I need to go outside," she said softly, holding her fingers over her mouth.

"You just went an hour ago," he snapped.

"It's . . . well . . . I'm going to throw up. My, ah, condition has that effect," she said.

"Your condi—" Matt seemed to take her meaning. He stopped then and gave a scornful laugh. "Hah! How the mighty Miss Meredith Sinclair has fallen," he shouted, throwing his head back and hooting with amusement. He slapped his knee. "If that don't beat all. I could hardly get a peck, but you spread your legs mighty wide for the gunslinger, didn't you, Miss High and Mighty Sinclair?"

He let her out and she was duly sick. It did not take much these days. When she was done, he grabbed the neck of her shirt and shoved her back inside.

"I had no idea you despised me that much, Matt. Why did you ever court me if you felt that way about me?" she asked as he retied her rope.

Matt laughed again. This time, though, his voice was laced with bitterness. "Because Liza wanted it," he said.

"Why?" Merrie queried, not really expecting him to answer.

To her surprise, he did, although he seemed to be speaking to himself rather than her. He wearily rubbed his forehead with his hand.

"In case we couldn't *persuade* your old man that it was better for his health to tell us where the gold was hid. I was going to marry you and get the gold that way. I did everything that bitch wanted me to do, and then she went and snuck out on me." He rose and hit the table with his fist. Again and again he pounded the table, making the remains of their supper dance.

"Bitch! I did everything she wanted me to do . . . everything. And she repaid me by running off with that scum!"

He swung around, glaring at Merrie through the murk. "Well, you just see who get's the last laugh here. I'll make them sorry they ever tried to cheat Matthew B. Cheston."

Merrie shrugged. "That is like the pot calling the kettle black. After all, you cheated on me; you cheated on my father, too, or had you forgotten that?"

"And what about you? Miss Prim and Proper? You're as much a slut as your stepmother. Or are you going to tell me that the bastard you're carrying got there in some miraculous way?"

"My child is not a bastard. Kyle and I were married yesterday. If I were you, Matt, I would seriously consider the consequences of harming either of us. Kyle Delancy tends to have a short fuse when it comes to my safety. He shot one man through the foot for daring to impinge upon my good name," she said, thinking of their contretemps at Sadie's. "Another unfortunate was staked out in Indian territory and left to a roving band of Comanche."

Matt snorted contemptuously. "You think I'm scared of that two-bit gunslinger? Huh! I shot him easily enough last time, and I'll shoot him again. This time, though, he'll die."

Her earlier suspicions had been correct. She was appalled at his callous indifference. "Don't be too sure. He will be expecting you this time. You did say you wanted to bargain with him, right?"

Matt sent her a crafty look. "He's going to give me Liza in exchange for you."

Merrie felt a quick surge of joy. So, Kyle had her! His plan had succeeded. Liza and her boyfriend were Kyle's prisoners. That meant Ash was free—thank God.

The look on Matt's face told her that he was scheming. Probably he thought to trick Kyle by shooting him once the exchange had been made. Merrie didn't consider that a probability. Her husband was too smart and too fast for Matt Cheston. Still, she wasn't so certain about her own safety. Matt was not rational. Perhaps, she thought, she could unnerve him enough to keep him away from her.

"You forget, he's a tracker. A good one, at that."

"Shut up," he snarled.

"Liza won't cooperate," she said softly.

"What?" he shouted. "What in hell d'you mean?"

"Her boyfriend. She won't want to leave without him. She obviously prefers him to you."

Matt jumped up and laughed. The sound sent screams jarring down Merrie's back, for it was unbalanced, colder than gravestones.

"Think I'm dumb? I'm leaving that mongrel sheriff with your gunslinger's friend, Masterson. He can rot in jail or go to the hangman, more like. I'm only sorry I'm not there to see him swing, damn his stinking hide."

Merrie's eyes widened. "What mongrel sheriff?" she queried.

"Tom Hagan." He spat the name as if it were a curse, and perhaps to him it was. "Meanest bastard to walk the earth. Shoot a man in his sleep. Would have, too, if I hadn't wised up and got out of there before he done it. Old Jerome, he weren't so lucky. They got him."

"H-how? I mean, he was going to kill you, shoot you?" Merrie asked.

"You deaf? I just said so, didn't I? Got suspicious when your stepmother refused me. I'm not dumb. I know the signs. I suspected it before we left Hollow Creek, but the damned bitch fooled me. But once we reached open country, I could see. Hagan was running the show, not Liza.

"She just did like he said, all sweet as you please," he added in a mockingly girlish voice. "Well, let me tell you, she's gonna do just exactly what I say when I get my hands on her."

"*If* you get your hands on her, you mean," Merrie said, still bent on trying to persuade him to let her go and escape himself. It was a mistake. The man went berserk.

He slapped her across her face, furious and out of control.

Merrie reeled, crying out in pain. Matt heard it and straightened.

"I'm gonna have her back, or someone's going to die," he snarled. "And when I've got her back, I'll teach her to mind me."

Merrie gasped. She had not seen the rage, the burning fury, in Matt before this moment. His bloodshot eyes seemed to see things that were not there; they twitched uncontrollably. His ashen face was flecked with sweat even though the room was quite cold; in fact, Merrie was shivering from it. Matt was a man obsessed. Liza was his obsession. There was no doubt about that.

He ranted on, stamping about the hut in his fury. Every now and then he aimed a kick at Merrie. His booted foot caught her knee once, her upper leg another time. She screamed with shock and pain. His next kick went wide, and she managed to scramble out of his way.

"Bitch, whore," he shouted, seeming to confuse Merrie with Liza for a moment. He lunged at her.

"I'll teach y—" he yelled, as Merrie, terrified that he would kill her, jackknifed her body. Matt tripped over her legs and fell, his head slamming against one of the bricks from the old chimney corner. He lay there, insensible.

Merrie gazed down in horror.

She scrambled up as best she could, leaning over his prone body. Hysteria rose in her chest, choking her. Black spots swirled frantically in her head. Her mouth was as dry as sawdust.

But then she heard the faint stirring of Matt's breath and shrank back from him as far as she could.

She squeezed her eyes shut against the sudden helpless flood of tears that burned behind her lids. Oh, Kyle, she thought bleakly, please find me before this maniac comes completely unhinged.

THIRTY-FOUR

"Farraway and Hargraves, Attorneys at Law," the sign said. Kyle glanced swiftly down the street and back to the shingle that swung to and fro in the light breeze. Everything looked perfectly normal, he thought with satisfaction.

He turned the brass doorknob and went inside. A staid and somber atmosphere greeted him; old furniture, the scent of leather-bound books, the inkwells, even the silver coffeepot were imbued with a quality of restraint and value.

Both lawyers, ever faithful to Ash Sinclair, had enthusiastically espoused Kyle's plan. Jessop Farraway had even volunteered to help; he remained behind. All the rest of the staff had been sent off home; Kyle had arranged for his own men and Bat's to take their place.

Farro, dressed in the typical high-necked suit of a law clerk, stood behind the front desk of polished oak. A stoop-shouldered secretary sat at the desk, his hands shuffling through the morning mail. On closer inspection, Kyle could see that, minus his deputy's badge and guns, Pat Meadows made a perfect secretary.

"All ready?" Kyle asked, closing the door.

Bat Masterson popped his head out from behind a curtained alcove. He grinned like a wolf. "You bet," he said.

"Everyone knows their part," Kyle said, leaning one hip against the edge of the desk. "Don't anyone move till Farro says, 'This is the first signature record.' That's the signal. We move the minute he finishes speaking, because he will be able to see that everyone is exactly where we want them. Everyone clear on that? Good."

He turned to Bat. "Rolly's ready. I just made certain he was in place." Rolly was stationed on the outskirts of town.

There was nothing further to do but wait.

The clock on the wall moved with painful lethargy. The clunk of the slowly moving hands was reminiscent of the unheard hooves of the horses riding into town.

The sound was mesmerizing.

Kyle's mind drifted . . . He saw his beautiful new wife blossoming, growing round with his child . . .

The thought of becoming a father stirred something fundamental inside him. He felt a surge of pure fear, and clenched and unclenched his hands to free the tension that wrapped them in invisible bonds. But even as his gut clenched, he knew a rush of joy. It was tempting to yield to the joy, very tempting.

Christ, but he had never known so much happiness was possible. How had he deserved it?

He didn't want to question the why of it. He was beguiled, seduced by a golden-haired beauty with the longest legs . . .

He shook his head at the wonder and felt a quickening in his blood at the memory of those incredible legs wrapped securely about his flanks.

She was passion. She was his. He could not get enough of his shimmering seductress.

And now that passion had created a child.

The wonder!

He thought of his child growing inside her, tiny, defenseless, their own small miracle.

He vowed he would not fail Merrie. He would not fail his child. If there was any benefit to be derived from the ordeal of his own terrible beginning, it was the knowledge that he would never allow a child of his to suffer the way he had.

Never—not while he lived.

He dismissed Merrie's show of temper that morning as nerves. His mind was awash with gentle thoughts.

The doorbell jingled.

Betty Meadows and her little daughter came into the office. She smiled shyly at the men and nodded.

"Rolly waved his hat," she told them.

The signal!

"Places everyone," Kyle called. "This is it," he said and slipped behind the green curtain with Bat.

Betty left with a large, white, legal-looking envelope in her hand.

Soon after, the doorbell jingled again.

Through a chink in the curtain Kyle saw Liza come in, Ash Sinclair right behind her, supported by a large, heavy-chested man. Kyle nudged Bat.

The man kept his hat on, but there was no mistaking him any longer. It was Tom Hagan! The Hollow Creek sheriff sauntered in holding Ash Sinclair firmly by the arm. His insolent expression pleased Kyle because it meant that their ruse had worked. Hagan was not in the least suspicious.

Hagan kept his hand on Ash's arm.

To anyone who didn't know better, the gesture might have seemed solicitous, nothing more. But Kyle guessed that Hagan had a pistol pressed into Ash's side to ensure his cooperation.

"Good day to you, ma'am," Kyle heard Meadows say. "Can I be of assistance?"

"I have an appointment with Mr. Farraway. I'm Meredith Sinclair, and this is my father."

Meadows rose attentively, and a perfectly servile smile touched his thin lips.

"Mr. Sinclair . . . why, I hardly recognized you, sir. What a pleasure to see you after all these years." He bowed deferentially and turned back to the woman. "And Miss Sinclair, we have expected you these past several days," he told her, waving a hand in the air.

Farro moved quickly to bring two chairs forward, one for the lady and the other for Ash Sinclair.

"Yes, well, we were slightly, ah, delayed," Liza said, helping to seat Ash. Hagan stood directly behind.

Meadows hovered over Ash. "May I say, Mr. Sinclair, how thankful we are to see you recovered."

Ash Sinclair gave a small nod.

"There, Father, rest," Liza murmured, patting his arm. "My

father, as you know, is not well. He cannot converse very well, so please direct your questions to me."

Meadows made a great fuss over that announcement, shaking his head sadly and clucking out platitudes. Farro, meanwhile, went to make Mr. Farraway aware that his clients had arrived.

"We'll conduct all our business out here so your father may be comfortable," Meadows told them. He went to the door then, locked it, and rotated the sign to indicate that the office was closed.

A quick look of panic flashed over Liza's face, and she glanced quickly at Hagan, who was frowning fiercely.

"What's that in aid of?" Hagan demanded.

Meadows managed to look as scared as a rabbit. He gazed up at the huge man over the edges of his horn-rimmed glasses. "So we won't be disturbed," he explained.

"Oh, let's get on with it," snapped Liza. "I mean, where is Mr. Farraway? I want to get done."

"Here I am, charming lady. Welcome, welcome, my dear Mr. Sinclair," Jessop Farraway said. His severe dark suit with tails gave him an important air. His impeccable white shirt had a starched, stand-up collar, and there was a shiny, black satin stock about his neck. He swept into the room, gravely welcomed Ash Sinclair, and congratulated him on his recovery. "And you, Miss Sinclair, we meet at last. So delighted, delighted."

With a flourish of his tails, he sat, while Farro and Meadows flanked him like trained guards.

"Now, to work," he said, snapping his fingers in the air. Meadows produced a heavy folder, bound with a dark ribbon and marked with the name "SINCLAIR" in bold capital letters across the front. In his other hand, he held a narrow strongbox made of shiny steel, fastened with a large silver lock.

These items he placed, with ceremony, before Farraway.

Farro assisted Meadows as they began laying out papers, while Farraway explained that for the transaction they would require three sworn witnesses.

TEXAS KISS   293

Liza nodded impatiently. "So I understand. Is there a problem?"

"No, no, dear lady. There is nothing to concern yourself with at all. Everything is perfectly in order," Farraway told her, his face wrinkled with worry lines.

"Then . . . ?" Liza prompted.

Farraway coughed delicately. "Well, dear Miss Sinclair, your pardon, but I must ask how Mr. Sinclair can sign authorization? He seems, if you will excuse me, unable. Unless you, my good man," he said, looking up at Hagan for the first time, "could assist?"

Liza nodded rapidly. "Jack's here to help."

"Your name is Jack?" asked Faraway.

Hagan nodded.

"Come around here then, my good fellow," he said, indicating Ash's left side.

Hagan wanted to protest. The position would incumber his shooting hand.

His eyes scooted around the office. He hesitated.

"Get along, *Jack*," Liza snapped impatiently. Her eyes flashed at the wall clock, and Hagan seemed to take her meaning then, for he came out from behind Sinclair, to where the lawyer indicated.

Farro shuffled through the papers until he pulled one from the pile and handed it to Farraway.

"*This is the first signature record, sir,*" he said.

At that moment, several things happened. Farraway dropped into a crouch. Meadows swept his gun up from under the desk. He pointed it directly at Hagan. Hagan stood gaping, his firing hand caught in a vice-like grip by a not-so-debilitated Ash Sinclair.

Liza screamed as Farro whipped his gun out and held it at her head. But not before the green curtain was swept aside and both Kyle and Bat rushed out, guns raised, triggers cocked.

Kyle grabbed Liza, while Bat stuck the muzzle of his gun into Hagan's neck.

"Well, well," Kyle mocked, "if it isn't 'Miss Sinclair.'

Strange, but I thought she was fair-haired and beautiful. My mistake." He dangled the cynical implication in her face, knowing just how vain she was.

"You," Liza hissed. Her fantastic eyes fairly ignited with fury. "I told you to get rid of him," she screamed at Hagan. "I told you he was dangerous."

"Shut up, bitch," Hagan yelled. "Don't say nothing and they ain't got nothing on us."

"Oh, I somehow doubt that, Hagan," Bat said. "Fact is, I can pretty well charge you with breaking every law ever made, from abduction to murder, not to mention dishonoring the office of town sheriff."

"Don't forget horse thieving, extortion, conspiracy, and adultery," Ash said, letting go of Hagan's wrist.

Hagan swore and tried to lunge at Ash, but Bat tapped him smartly behind his ear, and the man crumpled.

"Oh, I intend to forget none of it, sir," Masterson said, without missing a stroke.

"I never stole any horses, nor did I kill anyone," Liza shrieked, struggling in Kyle's grip.

"No, a paragon of virtue," Kyle said.

Ash turned tired eyes on his vicious wife. He got slowly to his feet. His ordeal had worn him down, yet he was still an imposing man. His great dignity, the sweep of silvery hair on his head, accorded him an aura of distinction.

Liza hissed and spat, throwing obscenities at him; cruel words poured from her mouth. She condemned him for his generosity, for his restraint. Everything he stood for, she ridiculed.

"You're flabby, weak. You sicken me, old man," she scoffed. "You and that puny daughter with her boy's clothes."

Kyle shoved her arm high up behind her back. "Your watch your mouth," he hissed in her ear.

"Let her have her say, Delancy," Ash Sinclair said, wearily. "Neither Merrie nor I ever hurt you, Elizabeth. We gave you a home to do with what you wanted. A family, ready and willing to accept you. We never denied you anything."

"Huh! You gave her everything, you gave me nothing. Nothing! She swayed you in every decision you ever made. You're weak, feeble. Even your bloody manhood is feeble. You think I married you because I wanted that! I wanted your gold, you decrepit old man. Right from day one, I wanted your gold!"

Ash didn't flinch. He heard her out in silence. His scorn silenced her at last. "If there was a charge I could levy against you for what you've done to my family, especially to my daughter, who never wanted anything more than a mother, I would have them throw that at you also. As it is, for her sake, I intend to write to the governor asking that you get the maximum punishment the law allows. I want you to think of that as you travel to prison, Elizabeth. I want you to think long and hard."

"You stupid, stupid bastard. You think with my face and brains I'm going to sit in jail?"

Ash smiled. It was a cold smile, a terribly cold smile. It stopped Liza's tirade. "You're so smart, Elizabeth? I don't think so. You see, the gold you wanted so badly was at the ranch, in front of your eyes, all along."

Liza straightened up. Tense and furious, she glared at Ash. "What do you mean? I tore the Spur apart. I searched every corner of that whole rotten place."

Ash shook his head. "The Zeus clock. The one you hate so much. The nuggets are kept in the false base. They have always been there. Right in front of your clever eyes."

Liza screamed. She screamed out her foul abuse, until Kyle clamped his hand over her mouth.

"That's enough of that, I think," he said.

Ash nodded and sat heavily in his chair.

"Take them away, Bat," Kyle said, jerking Liza toward Meadows. Meadows came about the desk and twisted her arm up behind her back. His gun was flat up against her ribs.

Farro hurried to the door, unlocked it, and opened it with a flourish.

"March," Meadows ordered Liza. Masterson maneuvered a

groggy Hagan through the door. Farraway left with them, to tell his family all about his adventure. He proudly carried out Liza's parasol and Hagan's confiscated gunbelt, and a store of tales to tell for many winter evenings to come.

"Well, Delancy," Ash Sinclair sighed, "I guess we pulled it off."

"I guess we did at that, sir. How about a toast? Farro, if you would?"

"Seeing that Gillian is not here, I think I might," Ash said.

"I won't tell," Kyle assured him with a smile.

"You'd better not. She's a feisty lady, that one. Takes no prisoners, no prisoners, at all."

Kyle grinned. It seemed Ash wasn't beyond noticing a comely lass, no matter how ill he had been. He took the cognac Farro handed him and raised his glass. "To your health, gentlemen, and the successful completion of a difficult assignment."

"My thanks to you," Ash said, raising his glass as well. "Especially to you, Delancy, on an impressive operation. Everything went exactly as planned, eh, Delancy?"

Kyle shrugged. "Not exactly, sir," he said and refilled his glass.

"Oh, something amiss, then? Something I should know about?"

Kyle nodded. "Um, not what I'd call amiss," he said vaguely. He glanced at Farro.

The younger man seemed to take the hint. He excused himself and scooted out the front door, closing it behind him.

Kyle offered Sinclair another drink. The man nodded, handing him the glass.

"Excellent stuff," he said.

"You like it?"

Ash nodded. "Don't think I've tasted anything so fine. Better make it a small one, all the same."

Kyle poured the gold-brown liquid. "My father imported the stuff from a small monastery in France. When he died, they allowed me to continue the business. Actually, my mother runs

TEXAS KISS

it, for the most part. Farro, the young man you just met, works with her. If you like, I can get you some."

"I like," Ash said. "But we'll just have to think up a good ruse, so Gillian won't find out about it. Can't see the harm in it myself, but she's adamant about it. Says I won't recover if I drink. I think that's sheer hogwash, myself."

"I'm sure we can get around Gillian," Kyle assured him.

"So, now, Delancy, what is it you want to tell me?"

"It's like this," Kyle began. To his amazement, he felt embarrassed. How in hell did you tell someone he had just become your father-in-law? Not easily, a little voice teased.

"Dammit, you'd better know . . . I married Merrie yesterday. I love her. One hell of a lot, I might add, and she loves me. Although, she put up a fuss for a while, I admit. There was no choice, actually, as it turns out," he muttered on, hoping that if he just kept talking long enough, Sinclair would come around to his way of thinking. "Not that it would have made any difference. I'd made up my mind, but—"

"Kyle, Kyle," they heard a voice crying out, accompanied to the sound of running feet. A moment later Farro burst in through the door, "Mr. Delancy," he cried urgently.

Kyle froze. The hair on his neck stood up. He straightened up from the desk. He knew something was wrong, and that it had to do with Merrie. He just knew. He turned ice-cold eyes on the panting young man.

"What happened to her?" he asked in a deadly voice.

"She's gone."

"Speak to me, Farro," he demanded.

The young man's black eyes were wide, fearful. He was clearly distraught. "Mariette left her to rest in your room. Something made her uneasy, and when she went in to check, Merrie was gone."

"The time? The time, Farro?"

"A few minutes ago. It doesn't mean anything, though, because Mariette left her directly after they'd finished breakfast. That was hours ago."

"And that's it? No one saw anything else? George, anyone, see her go?"

Farro shook his head.

"But they found Laura going into your room with this," he said, handing Kyle a folded piece of paper. "Seems she's giving Cheston a helping hand. I had Rolly detain her."

Kyle scanned the note, his jaw twitching frantically as he did.

Ash Sinclair rose unsteadily to his feet.

"The bastard's got her—Matt Cheston," Kyle growled. "He wants an exchange. Liza for Merrie."

"Let me read it," Sinclair said, reaching out for the note.

"Farro, take Mr. Sinclair to Carlyle's. I'm going to get Bat and the boys, and I'll meet you back there. Cheston wants us to put out a signal if we agree to the exchange, but we're going to fix him. He'll soon learn that people like us just don't care for people like him," Kyle said grimly.

Ash Sinclair put out his hand and grasped Kyle's arm. "You go get my daughter back, son. I'm gearing up to be a grandfather, and you better see that you don't let me down."

Kyle's blue eyes widened in surprise. How had the old man known?

"Well, you said there wasn't any choice in the matter," Sinclair said, answering Kyle's unasked question. "Well, didn't you? I assume you meant that she was pregnant by the time you got to the altar?"

Kyle nodded. "But you better understand, sir, it would have made no difference to me. You see, I realized that I didn't want to face life without her."

"Then don't, and you'll get no argument from me."

"I don't intend to, believe me," Kyle said, and he strode purposefully out onto Front Street.

THIRTY-FIVE

STIFF AND SORE, Merrie eased her bound hands a little. They burned from a lack of circulation. She could feel her fingers swelling out. The cords had cut deeply, and she was frightened. Every part of her ached. She was bruised and exhausted, for she had only managed to doze now and then, fearing Matt would suddenly decide to exact retribution from her.

He didn't. He awoke groaning a few minutes after he had fallen, morose and silent. Without looking in her direction, he stumbled out of the hut, grabbing his gunbelt and his poncho as he went. She hadn't seen him since.

Now her greatest fear was the rising nausea that assailed her in the mornings. If Matt didn't come in soon, she was going to be sick right inside the hut.

When at last the door opened, and a rosy wedge of morning light spilled into the hut, she had only enough time to warn him of impending disaster.

Thankfully, he didn't hesitate. He yanked her up, cursing roundly, and fairly threw her out the door. She fell forward, helpless to stop herself, but he yanked her up onto her knees. Some modicum of shame must have plagued him then, for while she bent double racked by dry heaves, he bent down behind her and cut through the ropes around her hands.

Merrie screamed. The pain of it was terrible. Suddenly loosened from their bonds, her hands and arms felt as if they were on fire. Gasping, crying incoherently, she tried to bring her arms around to her sides. Agony!

Matt stood gaping at her, but he made no move to help her.

"I won't tie your hands again," he grunted shamefacedly. "Come in when you're done," he added and went back inside the hut.

He didn't leave her out for long—at least to Merrie it seemed an awfully brief amount of time. As soon as she returned to the hut, Matt tied a rope to her hobbled feet and tethered it to the iron rung. His face was sour, his hands rough as he fastened the knots.

"I'm going to ride down the trail and see if your boyfriend . . . ah, excuse me, your husband," and here he gave a mocking bow, "has made any move yet," he told her.

Merrie said nothing.

The sombrero flopped about his face, but she still saw the baleful gleam in his expression. "You better start praying he has Liza ready to exchange, or it's gonna go bad for you."

It was hard to recall the man who had gallantly courted her for over a year. Matt Cheston, she thought, had definitely been consumed by madness.

As soon as he was gone, Merrie began working on the ropes. Her desperate fingers tugged at the knots until they were raw. If things didn't go Matt's way, she knew he would hurt her worse than last night. She couldn't risk injury to her baby; she simply couldn't.

But there was no way to loosen the ropes that tied her; Matt had been too thorough. At last, disgusted and frustrated, she slumped against the wall, trying to keep her spirits from flagging by conjuring images of Kyle . . . smiling at her, whispering love words . . .

Oh, Kyle. Please God, let him find me.

The hut became warm; time passed. She became drowsy.

She slept deeply, passing from one dream to another in which she was pursued by shadowy demons who threatened her, and the bundle she carried at her breast. She woke with a sob of defeat, as the door of the hut banged open.

Matt Cheston glowered at her a moment, then came in. Merrie was instantly alert. Tense. She watched him with unblinking eyes.

She could tell from his sullen expression that he was not happy. He sat scowling into the gathering gloom. As the moments became hours, and the hours passed into darkness, he continued to stare at nothing—unspeaking, his mood morose.

Merrie was terrified. She was not certain if he was aware of her being there, nor did she want to bring attention to herself. On the other hand, she had to know what was going on. Had he ventured back to Dodge City? Had he seen Kyle, spoken with him?

Not knowing was driving her crazy.

It was on the very tip of her tongue to ask him, when he suddenly spoke out of the darkness. But it wasn't to her he was speaking—it was to himself. He sounded strange, almost bewildered; it was as if he couldn't quite comprehend what had gone wrong with his lovely plan.

"Guess I'll just have to break her out of jail," he said finally.

"Who?" Merrie asked softly. Although she knew, she wanted to get him talking. "What happened? Did you see Kyle?"

"No marker. I waited and . . . What's the bastard planning?" Matt seemed to become aware of Merrie again.

He rose and came over to where she scrambled up into a sitting position.

"Delancy's up to something," he said fiercely, shaking her by the shoulders. "You sure he'd want to trade for you?"

"Yes," she gasped. "What happened? What marker?"

"I wrote him a note. Told him if he wanted to see you alive, he had to tie a red cloth to the tree at the fork northwest of Dodge. That way I'd know he agreed to trade Liza for you. There was no red marker."

"Maybe he didn't get your note?"

Matt started. Clearly that possibility had never occurred to him. He'd given the letter to the proprietor of the Carlyle. The woman liked money and hated Delancy, it seemed. The bitch had promised him that she would give the letter to Delancy. Could she have double-crossed him? Sure she could; she was a woman, wasn't she?

"Shit!" he hissed and flung Merrie away.

He slumped back down against the wall, reverting to his brooding while Merrie's heart beat a tattoo in her chest.

"Why don't you write another, Matt?" Merrie suggested out of the darkness. "You could sneak into town and leave it at the Carlyle yourself. That way you would be sure he gets the note."

Matt jumped up and took a step toward her. He wagged a finger at her, his stance belligerent, his body constricted with tension. "Very clever, honey, and no doubt every goddamn lawman in Dodge will be hidden along the road just waiting to pick me off. No."

"You could take me with you. They wouldn't shoot, not if I was with you," she said, desperate to try any means of getting as close to Kyle as she could.

"Shut up," he snarled. "I'm trying to think." He swung a fist at her, but she ducked deftly, and his swing went wide. Enraged, he swung with his left hand, but his movement was arrested in midair. He pivoted around facing the door, his head cocked to the side. Listening.

Merrie jumped to her feet. It was unmistakable. There was someone outside. Several someones, by the sound of things. Matt reacted quickly. He grabbed her, shielding himself with her and pulling his gun from its holster.

"Delancy," he yelled, his voice high and cracked with alarm. "That you, Delancy?"

There was no reply.

"Masterson? You there?" he yelled again. Still, there was no reply. They could hear the soft tread of booted feet. Matt gave a short giggle. It sounded mad, chilling. He bent down and brought a wicked knife out of his boot, his gun still pointed to the dark door.

Merrie's eyes were used to the darkness inside the hut, and she saw him raise the knife. He twisted toward her, knife held out in front of him. She screamed—terrified, helpless to stop the ghastly sounds erupting from her throat.

Matt yanked her against him and cut through the tether. He was panting, feral in his excitement. "Hear that, Delancy," he screamed gleefully. "I'll slice her up good, y'hear?"

No answer came. The night outside was still.

Matt giggled again.

Merrie stood absolutely rigid.

Matt inched forward a step, pushing her in front of him.

"Now, you listen to me," he yelled. "We're leaving. Your little wife and me. We're heading out, and you're gonna make a nice clear path for us. You hear me, Delancy? I want two saddled horses out front of this do—"

He never finished his sentence. The door to the hut slammed back with such force it came off its rusted hinges. Several men rushed into the hut. At the exact same moment, another man came catapulting though the crumbling sod roof, almost on top of them.

Merrie found herself yanked down onto the floor. A hard body covered her, pressing her down flat. She heard the simultaneous bursts of gunfire from all directions and screamed her terror into the dirt floor.

And then there was silence. Dark, almost painful silence. The stench of gunpowder filled her nostrils.

Dimly she felt the man on top of her roll to his feet and scoop her up. She knew him. The beloved scent, uniquely his, his touch, ever gentle, even in this fierce embrace, marked him as her own. Kyle Delancy. Her husband.

"Darlin'," he whispered, his voice choking with emotion. "Tell me you're all right, please . . ."

She sobbed in relief, rubbing her face against his hard chest, burrowing against him as if she couldn't get close enough. Nor could she find the words to assure him that she was fine; she could only nod her head. "Oh, Kyle, Kyle," she sobbed, over and over.

"Bring me that goddamn lantern," he rasped at someone, cradling her close. "It's all right, darlin', hush, now, hush."

"He hated me. I thought he was going to kill me," she whispered.

Kyle clutched her to his chest. "He's dead," he said grimly. "He'll never hurt you again, I promise," he told her, stroking the dark bruises along her cheek. "You're safe now, safe."

He inspected her under the lamp's yellow flame. He felt her ribs, her arms, her legs, swearing when he saw the rope burns.

He growled fiercely as he unwound the ropes from her ankles with as much care as he could. He winced as she cried out.

"She all right, Delancy?" one man called out. Merrie thought she recognized Bat's voice. She could see the shadowy shapes of men behind Kyle's broad shoulders.

Her husband swept her up against himself, taking her lips in a fierce, breath-stealing kiss before answering. "She's better than all right, aren't you, Legs?" he said, but his voice remained grim. "Still I think the doc should take a look. Think you could manage to ride into town?" he asked her.

She nodded. Nothing was going to keep her in this dreadful place a second longer than necessary.

Very soon she was snug in Kyle's lap, Cappoquin carrying them back to Dodge City at a nice steady trot. Moonlight flooded the rutted track in magical silver-blue. Midnight shadows feathered their way, and the crisp air was scented with autumnal smoke.

Around them rode the sheriff, his men, and several of Kyle's people, too. Most were young men, full of reckless enthusiasm and exuberance for life. They joked and commented upon their victory, bragging about their own part in bringing it to a successful end. Their vitality was contagious.

Merrie found her battered spirit reviving. Warmly wrapped in a thick wool blanket, her head resting against Kyle's heart, she felt secure, safe, and above all, cherished. She was wanted by this extraordinary man; the wonder of it filled her with joy as boundless and full as the burgeoning moonlight that fell all around them.

As they rode, Kyle told her that Ash was fine, none the worse for his ordeal at Liza's hands. Liza and her boyfriend, Tom Hagan, were being sent to Austin to stand trial for abduction, adultery, and murder. He didn't expect them to see the light of day ever again.

"Whatever her crime, she's still better off safely in prison. I think Matt was quite insane in the end. If he'd broken Liza out of jail, I'm not sure she wouldn't have suffered a worse fate," Merrie said with a shudder.

"I'm tempted to break her out of jail myself and deal with her. She started this thing, after all, and she put you in danger."

"But I'm fine, now, Kyle. Really I am."

"Sure," he said, his face taut with worry. "You're all bruises and cuts. I'd like to bring that bastard back to life so I can deal with him again, too."

"As I said, I don't think he was quite sane. At times I think he thought I was Liza. Her betrayal unhinged him."

"He hit a woman. Bad enough. But he hit my woman! Don't you go defending him," he told her, his voice chill.

Merrie smiled at the hot look in his face. "I'm not defending him," she assured him. "In a way I earned these myself," she told him, touching her bruised cheeks.

"The hell you did," Kyle swore.

Merrie put her fingers on his mouth to stop him.

"I kept throwing up. I didn't want him to hurt the baby. Above all, I couldn't have stood it if he had defiled me. Not that he tried," she added hastily as he stiffened furiously, "but I wasn't about to chance it."

She felt Kyle shudder. His jaw was set. He nuzzled against the top of her head, squeezing her hard against his chest. *"Dieu vous garde,"* he whispered.

Merrie smiled. "What did you say?"

"It's one of Mariette's little sayings. God keep you, and He did."

"I'm sure God did his part," she told him with a little laugh, "but I did mine. You have no idea how nausea dampens a man's ardor."

Kyle squeezed her again. Suddenly she heard a deep laugh grumbling in his chest. It burst out of him in a shout. "Legs, you're an original. No wonder I love you. You are a courageous lady, and without doubt the fastest imagination in the West."

"Actually, there is a serious consequence to all that throwing up," she told him, her green eyes dark with passion.

Kyle's eyes jerked to hers.

"And that is?"

"I'm starving. I could eat a chuck wagon."

Kyle laughed again. Gladness sounded deeply in the melodious notes of his mirth.

"Ah, Legs," he chortled, "and perhaps you could work up an appetite for things other than food—when you're done at the table. I'm pretty starved myself."

EPILOGUE

※

"Honestly!" Sonna said, exasperated. With a plunk, the sweet peas she was shelling dropped into the tin basin on her lap. She glanced at the parade of men out in front of the veranda.

Kyle paced down the front path, while Ash and Buck Peterson trod back and forth along the length of the veranda. A group of cowboys sat along the fence posts, worrying thin hickory sticks between their teeth, or whittling bits of wood.

Every now and then, one or other of them would glance up at the corner window. It was opened against the summer heat; pastel-green curtains peeped through. At intervals, Merrie's laboring cries could be heard, low and keen, and every man there would freeze.

"Give me a light," Ash Sinclair growled at his foreman. He clenched a fat cigar between bared teeth.

"Boss, you're not supposed to light it. Miss Bishop said."

"Give me a light," insisted Ash. He was remarkably well these days. His bright green eyes, so like his daughter's, sparkled with energy and zest. He had put back some of his old weight, his arms and legs had filled out again, his chest was broader. He could not ride for as long as he used to, and his working days were shorter by several hours, but he was happier now than he had been in many a long year.

Another sharp cry made his head wrench about.

"Give me a goddamn light," he repeated, sticking his cigar almost into Peterson's face.

Sonna's eyes flew heavenward, but she knew better than to open her mouth.

"I can't take much more of this," Kyle thundered as yet another cry came through the window. "I'm going up."

"You can't," admonished Sonna. "You're filthy, and Miss Bishop already kicked you out of there."

Kyle swiped his hands down his grimy work pants. He had been hurrying to finish the roof on their almost completed new house, when Spiker came to call him.

Kyle hadn't bothered to change. He had barely made it off the roof without killing himself, then he'd raced up the valley, almost riding Cappoquin into the ground in his hurry to get back to the Spur. When he finally burst into Merrie's bedroom, he had run into an impediment by the name of Gillian Bishop.

Cool, calm, and perfectly Gillian.

She had assured him that everything was under control, except for himself, and that he was unwanted and unwashed. He could, she counseled him, join the gathering throng outside the window. She would call him when his child was safely delivered.

Kyle had protested. He argued that Merrie needed him, but Gillian was adamant. All he was doing, apart from trailing filth into the room, was upsetting Merrie.

For the first time in his adult life, he was at a loss as to what to do. He wouldn't jeopardize Merrie in any way. He was frantic. He knew all the things that could go wrong. He kept whispering that it was different, that Merrie was not Kaiten. She is older, in excellent health, he assured himself. It did little to restore his faith.

Now he glared up at the window. "Bloody sergeant major! She's not going to stop me," Kyle growled, making up his mind. "Sonna, get me a clean pair of pants."

"But—"

"No buts. If you can't find one of mine in the laundry, get me one from Ash's room."

Sonna shook her head and set her bowl aside. "You're asking for it," she warned.

Kyle took off to the rear of the house. There was a spigot out back over the water trough. A tin can of lye sat by it. Many of the hands used it to clean up when visiting the main house.

Kyle pulled off his sweaty shirt and ducked his head under

the spray of water. In no time at all, he was refreshed and clean. After donning a clean pair of pants he stormed up the stairs to the top story of the house and jerked open the door, ready to do battle with Gillian Bishop.

To his surprise, she merely motioned him forward.

"You're just in time," she announced cheerfully. "I need you to stand behind her. She's almost ready to push."

Kyle's long legs brought him quickly to Merrie's side. He felt a surge of fear as he stooped over her. She was arched against the headboard, her sweat-slicked face contorted in agony. He smoothed the damp hair from her forehead.

"Merrie, darlin'," he whispered.

Merrie's eyes remained tightly shut.

Kyle's anxious gaze flitted to Gillian who was bustling about folding snowy-white cloths and sheets and piling them on a nearby table.

"She's busy. She can't answer you right now," the stately Englishwoman said.

"What the hell do you mean?"

Gillian's harsh frown cut across the room.

But Kyle was not intimidated. Far from it. "I repeat, what the *hell* do you mean, she can't speak?"

"She's concentrating on not pushing," she told Kyle in exasperation. "It's not easy," she added as he began to object.

Kyle's mouth hardened into a thin line. Merrie was groaning. He looked frantically from his heaving, twisting wife to the calm Englishwoman. The latter was stooped over his wife, examining her progress.

"She's supposed to goddamn push!" he bit out. "Even I know that much."

Gillian's head came up sharply. "Are you implying that I don't know my business?"

"Hell no. I'm *telling you*, you—"

"Kyle," Merrie wailed, her green eyes opening wide. She bent her heard forward, straining, her mouth squeezed over a cry.

"Darlin'," he said, immediately contrite, "tell me what I can do. Please, my sweet darlin'."

"You . . . can . . . swear you won't do this . . . to me . . . again," Merrie panted.

Gillian sniffed. "Fat chance of that," she told Kyle, swatting him out of the way and bracing her hands on either side of Merrie's hips.

At that moment, Merrie gave a piercing cry.

Kyle pulled the nurse's hands off his wife's heaving abdomen.

"You're hurting her," he thundered.

Merrie cried out again.

"Get behind her and push her forward, you stupid man," Gillian said, her voice firm. "Your baby's coming now."

"Now?" Kyle repeated, parrot-fashion.

Gillian didn't reply, because at this point Merrie began straining forward with all her might. Kyle, propping Merrie up from behind, lent his weight and soft words of encouragement, until with a breathless sigh, he saw the dark head of his baby emerging from Merrie's body.

Not two minutes later, the sweetest sounds he'd ever heard in his life rent the air: the lusty crying of his tiny daughter protesting her extremely rapid entry into the world.

He was stunned. Stunned and incredulous. As Gillian cut the cord and cleaned the baby's face, all he could do was grin until his face hurt. "She sure is a fast shooter," he said, pride evident in his voice. He clasped his wondrous wife with trembling hands.

"A perfect little girl," cried Gillian, "and so much hair . . ."

The baby was small but beautifully formed. She had long, long legs, and a full cap of glossy black hair. Kyle and Merrie thought she was the most beautiful child they had ever seen.

Gillian wrapped the baby and put her into Kyle's arms. "Hold her while I clean Merrie up."

"Hello, baby," he crooned to the little girl, whose dark, unfocused eyes were almost the exact color of his own.

Gillian was efficient and soon had Merrie sitting propped up against a mound of snowy pillows. She was pale and clearly exhausted, but she reached out for her baby eagerly.

With infinite care, Kyle brought her to Merrie and eased her into his wife's arms.

"Oh, she's exquisite, Kyle," said Merrie, gazing down into her daughter's face.

The tiny rosebud mouth yawned wide, and the baby's eyes fluttered closed. Both parents laughed.

"And real interested in the proceedings," Kyle quipped. His eyes shone with love as he looked at his daughter and his wife.

"You look as if you could do with a nap, too, Legs," he told her. She didn't argue when he took the baby from her. She was exhausted. Her labor hadn't been that long, but it had been fierce.

A sharp call from below alerted them that the crowd outside was waiting expectantly.

"Hey, what happening up there?" they heard Ash Sinclair shout.

Gillian piped up. "Plenty."

Kyle went to the window and held the baby up for everyone to see. "It's a girl," he told them in a glad voice. A great cheer erupted outside. Ash was slapped on the back. The cowboys threw their hats into the sky and plucked them back as they spun down, calling out their glee and congratulating one another as if *they* had done something infinitely clever.

"Idiots," Kyle said with a grin.

He looked down. The baby snuggled against his chest, warm and tiny in her soft blanket, her lashes shiny wisps of black against her shell-like cheek. She seemed altogether uninterested in the ruckus downstairs. She slept on undisturbed.

Merrie was almost asleep when Kyle knelt beside her and kissed her tenderly. Then he brushed his lips over his daughter's forehead. "Say good night to your mother, little Legs," he whispered.

Merrie's green eyes flickered. "You better name her, Kyle. I won't have her being called that," she told him in a surprisingly argumentative tone.

Kyle grinned. "I think we should call her Kaiten Miranda Delancy. What do you think about that?"

"Kaiten," Merrie sighed, slipping down on the pillows. "I like that . . ."

"I think she would have liked it, too," he said.

"Kaiten it is, then," Merrie sighed.

"I'll take Kaiten to meet her grandfather, shall I?" Gillian said. "That way you can tuck your wife in?"

Gillian left them then, and Kyle slipped his arms around Merrie, drawing her to his chest and rubbing his chin into the thick silk of her hair, "I have something for you, Legs. It's not grand, or even costly, but it comes with a legacy," he told her gravely.

She watched him draw away and take from his pocket a slender golden chain with a locket attached. For a moment, he held her mother's locket up to the light. Then, his piercing blue gaze warm upon her, he fastened the locket around her neck.

He had kept it all this long time, she thought, her heart full to overflowing. Somehow this locket had become an emblem, a golden link to the very first day she met Kyle Delancy. He had changed her life forever. "Thank you, for making me feel so cherished, so wanted . . . ," she whispered.

Kyle held her to his heart. He felt his smile reach all the way into his soul. "That you are, darlin'" he said, rubbing his chin against her hair. "You are definitely wanted."

Wildflower Romance

A breathtaking new line of spectacular novels set in the untamed frontier of the American West. Every month, Diamond Wildflower brings you new adventures where passionate men and women dare to embrace their boldest dreams. Finally, romances that capture the very spirit and passion of the wild frontier.

__MY DESPERADO by Lois Greiman
0-7865-0048-4/$4.99

__NIGHT TRAIN by Maryann O'Brien
0-7865-0058-1/$4.99

__WILD HEARTS by Linda Francis Lee
0-7865-0062-X/$4.99

__DRIFTER'S MOON by Lisa Hendrix
0-7865-0070-0/$4.99

__GOLDEN GLORY by Jean Wilson
0-7865-0074-3/$4.99

__SUMMER SURRENDER by Lynda Kay Carpenter
0-7865-0082-4/$4.99

__GENTLE THUNDER by Rebecca Craig
0-515-11586-X/$4.99

__RECKLESS HEARTS by Bonnie K. Winn
0-515-11609-2/$4.99

__TEXAS KISS by Alexandra Blackstone
0-515-11638-6/$5.50

__GAMBLER'S DESIRE by Maryann O'Brien
0-515-11658-0/$4.99 (July)

Payable in U.S. funds. No cash orders accepted. Postage & handling: $1.75 for one book, 75¢ for each additional. Maximum postage $5.50. Prices, postage and handling charges may change without notice. Visa, Amex, MasterCard call 1-800-788-6262, ext. 1, refer to ad # 406

Or, check above books   Bill my: ☐ Visa ☐ MasterCard ☐ Amex
and send this order form to: (expires)
The Berkley Publishing Group   Card#_____
390 Murray Hill Pkwy., Dept. B   ($15 minimum)
East Rutherford, NJ 07073   Signature_____
Please allow 6 weeks for delivery.   Or enclosed is my: ☐ check ☐ money order

Name_____   Book Total $_____

Address_____   Postage & Handling $_____

City_____   Applicable Sales Tax $_____
                                          (NY, NJ, PA, CA, GST Can.)
State/ZIP_____   Total Amount Due $_____

If you enjoyed this book, take advantage of this special offer. Subscribe now and...

Get a Historical

No Obligation

If you enjoy reading the very best in historical romantic fiction...romances that set back the hands of time to those bygone days with strong virile heros and passionate heroines ...then you'll want to subscribe to the True Value Historical Romance Home Subscription Service. Now that you have read one of the best historical romances around today, we're sure you'll want more of the same fiery passion, intimate romance and historical settings that set these books apart from all others.

Each month the editors of True Value select the four *very best* novels from America's leading publishers of romantic fiction. We have made arrangements for you to preview them in your home *Free* for 10 days. And with the first four books you receive, we'll send you a FREE book as our introductory gift. No Obligation!

FREE HOME DELIVERY

We will send you the four best and newest historical romances as soon as they are published to preview FREE for 10 days (in many cases you may even get them before they arrive in the book stores). If for any reason you decide not to keep them, just return them and owe nothing. But if you like them as much as we think you will, you'll pay just $4.00 each and save at *least* $.50 each off the cover price. (Your savings are *guaranteed* to be at least $2.00 each month.) There is NO postage and handling—or other hidden charges. There are no minimum number of books to buy and you may cancel at any time.

FREE
Romance
(a $4.50 value)

Send in the Coupon Below

To get your FREE historical romance and start saving, fill out the coupon below and mail it today. As soon as we receive it we'll send you your FREE Book along with your first month's selections.

Mail To: **True Value Home Subscription Services, Inc. P.O. Box 5235
120 Brighton Road, Clifton, New Jersey 07015-5235**

YES! I want to start previewing the very best historical romances being published today. Send me my FREE book along with the first month's selections. I understand that I may look them over FREE for 10 days. If I'm not absolutely delighted I may return them and owe nothing. Otherwise I will pay the low price of just $4.00 each: a total $16.00 (at *least* an $18.00 value) and save at least $2.00. Then each month I will receive four brand new novels to preview as soon as they are published for the same low price. I can always return a shipment and I may cancel this subscription at any time with no obligation to buy even a single book. In any event the FREE book is mine to keep regardless.

Name		
Street Address		Apt. No.
City	State	Zip Code
Telephone		
Signature		

(if under 18 parent or guardian must sign)

Terms and prices subject to change. Orders subject to acceptance by True Value Home Subscription Services, Inc.

11638-6

AWARD-WINNING NATIONAL BESTSELLING AUTHOR

JODI THOMAS

__ **TO TAME A TEXAN'S HEART** 0-7865-0059-x/$4.99
True McCormick needs a gunslinger to pose as Granite Westwind, a name True uses to publish her books of the Wild West. She finds her legend in a Galveston jailhouse—Seth Atherton. True is fooling everybody, until the bullets start to fly and True begins to fall in love with the hero she created....

__ **THE TEXAN AND THE LADY** 1-55773-970-6/$4.99
Jennie Munday left Iowa for Kansas to become a Harvey Girl—only to meet Austin McCormick, the abrasive Texas marshal on her train. When the train is held up, Jennie learns the law can be deadly... and filled with desire.

__ **CHERISH THE DREAM** 1-55773-881-5/$4.99
From childhood through nursing school, Katherine and Sarah were best friends. Now they set out to take all that life has to offer—and are swept up in the rugged, positively breathtaking world of two young pilots, men who take to the skies with a bold spirit. And who dare them to love.

__ **PRAIRIE SONG** 1-55773-657-x/$4.99
Maggie is Texas born and bred. When this beautiful Confederate widow inherits a sprawling house of scandalous secrets, she also is left with a newfound desire—for a Union Army soldier.

__ **NORTHERN STAR** 1-55773-396-1/$4.50
Hauntingly beautiful Perry McLain is desperate to escape the cruel, powerful Union Army captain who pursues her, seeking vengeance for her rebellion. Yet, her vow to save an ailing soldier plunges her deep into enemy territory...and into the torturous flames of desire.

Payable in U.S. funds. No cash orders accepted. Postage & handling: $1.75 for one book, 75¢ for each additional. Maximum postage $5.50. Prices, postage and handling charges may change without notice. Visa, Amex, MasterCard call 1-800-788-6262, ext. 1, refer to ad # 361

Or, check above books Bill my: ☐ Visa ☐ MasterCard ☐ Amex	
and send this order form to:	(expires)
The Berkley Publishing Group Card#_____	
390 Murray Hill Pkwy., Dept. B	($15 minimum)
East Rutherford, NJ 07073 Signature_____	
Please allow 6 weeks for delivery. Or enclosed is my: ☐ check ☐ money order	
Name_____	Book Total $_____
Address_____	Postage & Handling $_____
City_____	Applicable Sales Tax $_____ (NY, NJ, PA, CA, GST Can.)
State/ZIP_____	Total Amount Due $_____